HIGH
JOVE HO

We at Jove Books are thrilled by the enthusiastic critical
acclaim that the Homespun Romances are receiving. We
would like to thank you, the readers and fans of this wonderful series, for making it the success that it is. It is our
pleasure to bring you the highest quality of romance writing in these breathtaking tales of love and family in the
heartland of America.

And now, sit back and enjoy this delightful new Homespun Romance . . .

SNOWFLAKE WISHES
by Lydia Browne

Praise for Lydia Browne's Homespun *Honeysuckle Song*:

Titles by Lydia Browne

WEDDING BELLS
HEART STRINGS
PASSING FANCY
SUMMER LIGHTNING
HONEYSUCKLE SONG
AUTUMN FIRES
SPRING DREAMS
SNOWFLAKE WISHES

Snowflake Wishes

Lydia Browne

JOVE BOOKS, NEW YORK

SNOWFLAKE WISHES

A Jove Book / published by arrangement with
the author

PRINTING HISTORY
Jove edition / November 1997

The Putnam Berkley World Wide Web site address is
http://www.berkley.com

ISBN: 0-515-12181-9

A JOVE BOOK®
Jove Books are published by The Berkley Publishing Group,
a member of Penguin Putnam Inc.,
200 Madison Avenue, New York, New York 10016.
JOVE and the "J" design are trademarks
belonging to Jove Publications, Inc.

PRINTED IN THE UNITED STATES OF AMERICA

10 9 8 7 6 5 4 3 2 1

1

*H*AL *S*INCLAIR LAY asleep in his lumpy rented bed, the stinks and smells of a thousand boardinghouse meals breathing out from the mattress, and dreamed.

New York City danced like a painted lady under the smeary glare of gas lamps, people everywhere experiencing every emotion, usually at the top of their voices. The roar of the city echoed like the sound of any other great natural force, the wind or the sea. You could never be alone there, but why would you want to be?

He dreamed that he walked through the city, from north of Central Park down to the very tip of Manhattan Island. He walked the dirty streets of the Bowery, waving to toughs and urchins. He walked the wide boulevard of Fifth Avenue, lined with the block-long homes of the rich, and exchanged pleasantries with rich men and their diamond-studded wives.

Everyone nodded and smiled at him and everyone knew his name, from the immigrants fresh off the boats to the cigar-smoking bosses who ran the city on a solid platform of bribery and intimidation. Though they didn't all like him or the things he wrote, he knew he had their respect. He wrote good copy, sometimes commanding the city's ready sympathy to aid fifteen people in an airless tenement, sometimes displaying for her lighter pleasure the genteel adventures of the rich.

Hal woke up to a cool dawn sky, the pearly clouds hanging like another curtain outside his window. For an instant after his eyes opened, he didn't know where he was. The room was no help. It looked and smelled and felt like every boardinghouse room he'd lived in since leaving his mother's house nearly twenty years ago.

Then he remembered. No brisk city awaited him outside the door. He couldn't go out and be brought to nerve-jangled life by a jolt of New York City air, stronger than coffee.

Swinging his legs out of bed, he sat up with a self-pitying groan and sent a glance heavenward, somewhere on the other side of a stained plaster ceiling. There was no help to be found in that direction.

Hal stumbled toward the window, passing his hand over his whiskery face. Grasping hold of the window frame, he shoved with all his might. He'd failed to open the window last night, but now he was determined that either the window would open or his back would break. At last, with the screech of a dry frame rubbing against a swollen sash, the window opened.

The morning air blew over his bare chest, carrying a chilly touch of the autumn night within it. Outside, the hills beyond the town were turning slowly to gold, a forested fortune. Every now and again, a red maple would shoot up like a geysering flame against the background of gold, contrasting with the trees still stubbornly clinging to their summer attire until the last moment.

"That's a view," Hal admitted grudgingly.

The rest of it, however, left a great deal to be desired. His window, as his landlady had told him proudly, looked right out onto Main Street. Hal looked up and down it, hoping against hope that a town had grown up in the night. But it looked just the same as when he'd gotten off the train yesterday evening.

To his left, heading out of town, the marshal's office, the livery stable, a few frame buildings that were probably houses with picket fences and the railway depot. Directly across from the boardinghouse was a desolate sight—a boarded-up saloon. Hal sighed, another hope shot from under him.

To his right, a general store with a large sign informing passers-by, all of whom presumably already knew it, that this was the General Store. Next was a little storefront with the undertaker's parlor downstairs and the doctor's office upstairs. "They get you coming and going," Hal mused with a wry smile.

A barbershop squeezed in next to them, followed by a few more houses, some without picket fences. At the very end of the street were a church and a schoolhouse, both bare-board.

On the boardinghouse side, the street looked much the same. Toward the church, narrow frame houses seemed to huddle together as though guarding against a common enemy. Farther down the road, a milliner had set up hopeful shop next to the boardinghouse, with the bank directly across the street from the marshal's office. From his brief jaunt in the dark last night, Hal knew that the last frame building on this side before the train tracks was his personal little piece of real estate.

The worldwide headquarters, the hub of the wheel of world news, the sole holing of The *Brooklyn Herald*, the paper of which he, Hal Sinclair, was the editor-in-chief. He was also reporter, copy boy, delivery boy and, for all he knew, printer's devil.

Hal groaned again and gave serious thought to just going back to bed. Instead, he washed his face before shaving it. The soap bubbles in the bowl made him remember that if he'd only known who Bubbles Fitzwater was before going to see her act at the Alhambra, he would have given her wretched performance rave ratings. Instead, he'd written, quite truthfully, that the middle-aged woman had a voice that was a subtle mixture of foghorn and screech owl and that she danced with her veils like an aged ostrich with lumbago.

Regrettably, the _New York Daily Regard_ had recently been sold to a self-made millionaire. Bubbles Fitzwater was his long-standing _cherie d'amour_. Hal couldn't believe it when his editor and old elbow-bending buddy had told him. "Well, Mr. Clyde's no oil painting," Evans said. "And when Miss Fitzwater said she wanted to make her New York debut, he arranged it."

Hal had let loose with one of the more spectacular anatomical impossibilities. Evans had nodded. "I'm just sorry I wasn't here to warn you."

"You couldn't have known." Hal had shrugged, wondering how long it would be before another paper would take him on. The market was as tight as he'd ever seen it. Changing the subject to conceal his worry, Hal asked, "How was Louisa's birthday?"

"She couldn't believe it. You were right, Hal. Even married women like diamonds. And the night at the Waldorf really put the capper on the evening." Evans winked salaciously and returned to business.

"Con should have warned you about Mr. Clyde and his . . . ahem . . . friend."

Hal shrugged again, more elaborately. "He wants my beat. I wish him luck with it."

The editor leaned back, the cracked leather of his chair gaping to let little bits of stuffing float to the grimy wooden floor. "I might be able to save something from all this, if . . . you'll apologize to Miss Fitzwater."

"In print?"

"Not while I'm in charge. But you leave town for a while."

"I could use a rest."

Hal gave Miss Fitzwater full marks for taking his apology so gracefully. Though she wasn't any younger or more talented at close range, she did remind him of his third-grade teacher, the only woman who'd ever made him cry. But seeing Hal grovel wasn't enough for ol' Marcellus Clyde. He wanted his pound of flesh.

At first, it hadn't sounded as bad as it turned out to be. "Brooklyn?" Hal said, brightening when Evans first broke the news of his banishment. "That's not so bad. I can take the trolley car in, catch a show, see you and . . ." He ground to a stop because Evans was shaking his head, slowly, mournfully, reluctantly. Hal could still recall with the clarity of a daguerrotype the look on Evans's face when he broke the melancholy news.

There was another Brooklyn . . . way out West. Clyde had told him that this misbegotten desert would give Hal an opportunity to experience "real life." As though what he'd known in New York and on his travels was only a game of make-believe.

Shaved, dressed and in no mood to face breakfast, Hal Sinclair descended the stairs and opened the front door. Once again he looked up and down Main Street. Nothing had changed except that a black-and-tan spotted dog lay in a patch of sunlight in front of the milliner's.

"Welcome to Brooklyn, Missouri," Hal said. If he'd been a spitting man, he would have.

"What's he doing now?" Sissie Albright hissed from behind her best friend's back.

Rachel Pridgeon put her eye to the tiny gap she held open between the pale blue curtains of Sissie's Millinery Shoppe. "He's walking," she said. "Very slowly. And I think he's talking to himself."

"Talking to himself?" Sissie echoed. "Is he crazy?"

"You can't tell by looking," Rachel said. "He doesn't *look* crazy, but I suppose it's possible."

She stepped back when Mr. Sinclair seemed to be on the verge of turning his head in her direction. Sissie gave a nervous giggle. "Did he see you?"

"No. I don't think so."

"Oooh, he is just so handsome." Sissie rushed forward. She always moved in short, jerky runs like the mouse her late father had called her. She peered through the gap. "I've got a weakness for black hair."

"You've got a weakness for men, Sissie."

She giggled in response. "Oh, I know. They're just so . . . so mysterious. You can't hardly help being interested."

Rachel smiled behind her friend. To hear Sissie talk, one would think she was a hardened seductress with a hundred scalps dangling from her belt. In reality, she could hardly bring herself to speak about business to a feather merchant, fatherly men all of them, let alone a stranger from New York City.

"Mrs. Jergens says he's got blue eyes," Rachel said, fanning the fire.

"Oooh, blue eyes! I think it's the mustache that makes me go all weak at the knees. It's just like the villain's in that play we saw."

"No, it isn't. That was a big ugly thing with waxed tips; Mr. Sinclair's is just a line on his upper lip."

"But it makes him look . . . I don't know . . ." She giggled again. "Kind of wicked."

"Wicked or not, you're going to have to talk to him."

"Me?"

"You want to run an advertisement in the paper, don't you? How are you going to do that if you don't talk to him?"

"I couldn't! What if he twirled his mustache at me?"

"I told you. That's not the kind you twirl. Besides, if he's taking over the *Herald*, he'll be so glad to see an advertiser he'd be more likely to kiss you than scare you off."

"Rachel!" Sissie whisked the curtains together and turned a shocked glance on her friend.

"He'd do the same for Mr. Gladd or any other merchant in town. You must start thinking like a businesswoman, Sissie."

"If only you'd come into the business with me, Rachel. With your head for figures, we'd be a success in no time."

Once again, Rachel refused. "I'm happiest teaching the children. I don't want anything else."

"It's a sinful waste," Sissie said. She parted the curtains again to peer out. "He's almost out of sight."

"You might as well open the curtains then."

"I suppose so."

Rachel reached up to jerk the curtains apart when she stopped and applied her eye again to the gap. "It's Mrs. Dale . . . she's coming out of her house. . . . She's dressed up like Saturday night! She's staring at him . . . in another minute . . . ! Oops, there she goes! Slap into the McGoverns' fence."

"Is she all right?"

"Um, blushing, but otherwise unharmed."

"What's he doing?" Sissie asked in an eager whisper. "Is he crossing the street to help her?"

"I don't . . . no, he isn't. He tipped his hat though."

"That's something. But he can't be much of a gentleman."

"Of course not," Rachel said. "He's a newspaperman."

"Oh, I don't know," Sissie mused. "You didn't know Mr. Rudolph. He was as nice as the day is long. The whole town was sorry when he died."

Briskly, Rachel flung open the curtains she'd helped sew. She hid her thoughts, pondering idly the reason people say "the day is long" when it was the nights, sleepless, worry-laden nights, that stretched out to eternities incalculable. Rachel gave herself a little shake, a warning to get her thoughts under control. No point in worrying Sissie with her strange ideas. She said, "It must be nice to be so liked."

"Oh, everybody went to the funeral!" The milliner sighed thoughtfully. "I wouldn't mind going the way he did. The marshal found him with his head down on his desk, just as if he'd gone to sleep on the job." The irrepressible giggle broke out. "Fancy me lying there among the fake fruits and the feathers . . . Mr. Schur would have to say how I dropped in harness!"

Passing over this gruesome picture, Rachel said, "This Mr. Sinclair has some big shoes to fill, then."

"Oh, yes. Mr. Rudolph had big feet . . . oh, you mean, Mr. Sinclair will have to work hard to win us over? I think he will. We're not much on strangers here in Brooklyn."

"Everyone's been kind to Lyle and me, especially you, Sissie."

Sissie waved a hand in dismissal. "Fiddlesticks! As sweet as you are? Though that brother of yours . . . I swan! It's a good thing the marshal's taken such a shine to him! Otherwise, he'd be running wild with those Bannerman boys."

"Lyle's not the only one Mr. Hunnicut's taken a shine to, Sissie," Rachel said slyly.

"Pooh! I'm not interested in a man nearly forty that's never been married before. I don't want to break in my own husband." She giggled. "Let the marshal have Mrs. Dale. But I reckon she ought to put her spectacles on first! No point buying a pig in a poke!"

"Sissie, you are so bad!"

The two young ladies began to straighten the store prior to opening. Rachel helped, more for the sake of Sissie's company than because she had any real interest. They lifted sheets off the display cases and folded them neatly. Rachel whisked around with a dyed turkey-feather duster while Sissie counted out change. "Eight, nine, ten!"

She stacked the bills neatly in the old cigar box where she kept her cash. Here her artistic talents had demonstrated themselves when she'd wrapped the box in gold fabric with a big bow on the front. It was still a cigar box, but an elegant one. Then she tapped her fingers on the glass surface of the case.

"I've got ten dollars here that says you won't be the first woman to talk to Mr. Sinclair."

"Sissie, don't be silly. Besides, Mrs. Jergens talked to him when she rented him a room. And you know what she said!"

She'd said that her new tenant had a tongue that could skin a turtle. Sissie always heard the gossip first. Something about trying on hats just naturally made women inclined to talk.

"All right, the first *since* Mrs. Jergens. Besides, she doesn't count . . . that was business."

"And what am I supposed to talk to him about? The weather?"

"Why not? Ask him if it's the same in New York as here. Ask him any ol' question you want. He must know all about the latest scandals! Go on. I dare you."

Rachel looked out the window into the empty street. He

did have a wicked look, that Mr. Sinclair, and she'd had enough wickedness to last her a lifetime and then some. She shrugged and shook her head. "It's too silly to talk about."

"Look, ten dollars is ten dollars. You go down to his office and talk to him. If you stay five minutes, the money's yours."

"You don't have money to throw around like that."

"I'm not going to lose. You are. You'll lose your nerve before you even get over the threshold." Suddenly, her cheerful giggle rang out again. "I know I'd lose mine. He's so handsome!"

Above all else, Rachel wanted to fit in, to be accepted. She'd seen the young girls in her school daring and double-daring each other to perform foolish feats, like walking a fence or kissing a boy. The oldest ones were only a few years younger than she was. If she had really come from the background she had invented for herself, dares would have been a common game.

"All right," she said, with a resolute nod. "I'll go talk to Mr. Sinclair. You'll see. He's just an ordinary man—nothing to be afraid of."

"Five minutes, and the money's yours." Sissie touched the watch pinned to her shirtwaist. "I'll time you with this."

"You won't have to," Rachel said, putting her hand to the door latch. "I'll be there much more than five minutes."

"Wait! Wait!" Sissie scurried into the back room and came out with a cloth-draped plate. "Here. Take these cookies down as a how-de-do present."

Rachel said, "Why? I'll just ask him about advertising on your behalf."

"You need an excuse or everybody in town'll talk."

"Not if I explain. . . ."

"Oh, explanations aren't any good. Let 'em see this plate and you won't have to explain anything."

Rachel didn't understand the finer points of this reasoning. She asked cautiously, "Won't it look like I'm out to catch a man, though?"

"Well, certainly!" Sissie said, rolling her eyes at the naivete of the question. "Everybody understands *that* without being told, don't they? If you're single, you must be on the catch for a husband . . . any husband. Even somebody else's!"

Certainly the covered plate seemed to be a respectable alibi. The McGoverns, who sat on their porch every fine day, waved at her and threw some laughing words across the street. Rachel couldn't catch all of them . . . something about the way to a man's heart. Nonetheless, she felt heat blossom in her cheeks at the conclusions the couple obviously had drawn. "Darn Sissie anyhow," she muttered before giving a cheek-aching smile and a nod to the older couple.

The roller shade behind the glass insert of the door to the newspaper office still hung down. Rachel paused on the top step, wondering if Mr. Sinclair had continued on down the street. Maybe they'd only assumed he'd been going to the *Herald*'s office. She would try the door handle and if it didn't turn, she'd go back to Sissie, conscious of having made a good-faith effort.

The door opened all too easily. Awkwardly balancing the plate in one hand, Rachel stepped in. The office smelled dusty and she didn't have to look far to know why. Her skirt left a trail of clean floor behind her, while the desk in the middle of the room and the windowsills were blurred with undisturbed dust. A fat brown spider had spun herself a comfortable web across the back slats of the desk chair.

Rachel called out a tentative hello. A male voice answered, indistinctly. Using her free hand to keep her skirt up out of the dirt, she walked forward to put the plate on the desk. Hearing a step, she said brightly, "You've got your work cut out for you in cleaning up this place."

"You wouldn't know of anybody who'd like to help me?"

"You'd need an army." Smiling, Rachel turned. He leaned against the doorjamb that led to the back room where the presses must be stored. His coat and pants were marked with grayish dust. Her smile dimmed a little as his bold eyes dropped for a moment's survey of her figure.

"I'm Rachel Pridgeon," she said baldly.

"Are you? Is that Miss Pridgeon—I hope—or Mrs.?"

"I'm the schoolteacher."

"Oh, so it's Miss."

Rachel had dealt before with men who thought a single woman was interested only in flirtation, or worse. The best thing to do, she'd found, was to pretend that there was no meaning beyond the obvious in even the most outrageous comments. It could be thought of as a game, and sooner or later she always won.

Now she said, "Yes, it's Miss. They don't take to married schoolmarms in these parts. You must be Mr. Sinclair?"

"Call me Hal."

"What's it short for?"

"Nothing."

"Come now. Hal isn't short for 'Nothing.' They'd call you 'Not' or 'Thing' if that were the case." Treating men like unruly little boys worked well at deflating their desires also. She turned her bright, firm smile on Mr. Sinclair just as if he were a small boy refusing to give his full name on the first day of school.

His really remarkably blue eyes narrowed. "My given name is Hal, Miss Pridgeon. It was my father's name too."

Just how broad his shoulders were, Rachel saw when he stood up straight and walked toward her. He should have had rounded shoulders and a pasty complexion, legacies of time spent over a desk in an unhealthy city. Instead he had a breadth that went well with his height. His eyes were clear, especially as they flicked over her once again, more as if taking her measure rather than her measurements. Rachel studied him more carefully as well.

Each black brow had a kink in it, toward the nose on the left, toward the ear on the right. He had horizontal lines of concentration carved into his forehead and tiny lines radiated out from his dark-lashed eyes. Otherwise, his skin was smooth and tanned, the cheeks carefully shaven. The dimple in his chin might have been feminine on another face. As it was *his* face, his features worked to combine into a masculine ideal. Rachel doubted many women said no to him.

"Cookies?" he asked, reaching out to lift the cloth from the plate.

Rachel didn't flinch, even though his blunt-fingered hand came close to her chest. "That's right. Oatmeal and raisin."

"Did you make them?" He picked one up and looked from it to her, as if wondering which one he should bite. Sissie was right. His smile was wicked.

"No, my friend Sissie Albright made them. *Miss* Albright, if you're interested in knowing that."

"I'm a newspaperman, Miss Pridgeon. I'm interested in everything. And everybody." He bit the cookie, swallowing it in two bites like every man ever born. "Excellent," he said with a nod.

"I'll tell her you said so. Would you happen to know the time, Mr. Sinclair?"

"Sure." He dusted his fingertips together and reached into his trouser pocket. "Ten twenty-five. Are you in a hurry?"

"In Brooklyn? No. I just promised my friend I'd be back in five minutes. It was nice to meet you, Mr. Sinclair."

She put out her hand in the most natural, businesslike way imaginable. Not in the least surprised when Mr. Sinclair held on to it, she nonetheless felt a momentary pang of disappointment. Somewhere there had to be a man who didn't run true to type. Not that it mattered. Even if she happened to meet the most wonderful man in the world, a man ordained by heaven to be hers, she'd turn her back on him. She had lied a thousand times to be who she was today but her whole spirit revolted at the thought of lying to a man if she loved him.

"Miss Pridgeon," Mr. Sinclair was saying, his voice throbbing the slightest bit. "I wonder if you'd mind staying for just a few more minutes."

"Why?" she asked, a wealth of suspicion in her tone.

"I'm at a loss," he admitted, allowing her to regain her fingers. "I don't know a soul in Brooklyn and I need help."

"What with? I mean, with what?"

"Put yourself in my place, Miss Pridgeon. Here you are, fresh off the train, and somebody expects you to write a newspaper—an entire newspaper—about people you don't know, in a place you've never been before, and out of a dusty, spider-strewn office. And in walks a woman—a very lovely woman if I may say so—a woman who can help you."

Rachel couldn't help the twitch her lips gave. "Is this the way you talk to women in New York City? No wonder you're going to be living here. Getting laughed at that much has to be hard on a fellow."

He reared back, the lines in his forehead becoming more pronounced. Then he began to grin. The laughter changed him, drove away the hard light at the back of his eyes, and took at least five years from his face.

"All right," he said in a much more natural tone than he'd used so far. "I confess. I don't talk much to schoolteachers."

"We're like everyone else. What do you want, Mr. Sinclair? If I can help you, I will. And so would anyone else in Brooklyn, if you ask nicely."

"I honestly do need to know something about this town before I put out my first edition."

"As in . . . ?" she prompted.

Once again he smiled, a warmer smile but still with that hint of calculation that troubled her. "Anything you want to tell me," he said. "I only wish I had a clean chair. Maybe I should call on you . . . this evening?"

"That's impossible," she said firmly. "You will be busy this evening."

"I don't think I have any other plans."

"You will have." Saying no more, she walked toward the door. "Enjoy the cookies, Mr. Sinclair. Please take the plate back to Sissie when you're done. She's the owner of the millinery shop."

Rachel stepped onto the street, feeling more than a little satisfied with herself. She would bet genuine money that Mr. Hal Sinclair had rarely, if ever, had a woman walk out on him, his mouth left full of pretty speeches and nobody to hear him.

She came up even with Mr. Hudson, rattling his keys as he unlocked the bank's front door. "Good morning, Miss Pridgeon."

"Good morning, Mr. Hudson. How are Mrs. Hudson and the girls?"

"Very well, thank you. They're very excited about their piano lessons. You're starting tomorrow?"

"That's right." She began to tell him that she saw promise in both of his daughters when she realized he wasn't paying attention. Instead, he had tilted his head to look past her shoulder. Then a sly smile showed for an instant beneath his sandy bush of a mustache. "Have you an admirer, Miss Pridgeon? And him only come to town last night?"

With something akin to fear, Rachel turned her head to look around. Mr. Sinclair had come out onto the boardwalk and stood staring after her. Had he been there ever since she'd left, watching the sway and swing of her walk? Catching her eye, he waved and went back into the newspaper office. Even at that distance, she could tell he swaggered.

Rachel was no longer sure who had won their first encounter. So far, it seemed as though honors were evenly divided, although catching sight of the McGoverns, who had also witnessed Mr. Sinclair's actions, Rachel decided he'd had a little bit of an advantage. *He should enjoy this moment*, she thought. *We'll meet again tonight and things will be different.*

2

$\mathcal{S}$ISSIE HAD CUSTOMERS when Rachel burst into the store, the bell over the door ringing like a fire alarm. Rachel paused on the step, seeing the ladies look around with curiosity as they were interrupted in the middle of a sentence. It was Mrs. Schur, the pastor's wife, and her soon-to-be-married daughter. They smiled and greeted Rachel before turning again to their shopping.

Instantly dredging up a smile, Rachel strolled with elaborate casualness over to a counter to look at garters. Some found Sissie's open display of "delicacies" to be immoral, but Sissie even talked of putting a corset on a bust stand in the front window. She hadn't gone that far yet. With Sissie, however, one never knew.

By concentrating, hard, on the enormities Sissie might yet commit, and picturing the shocked faces of townsfolk, Rachel managed not to explode like an overpressurized locomotive while Sissie dealt politely yet firmly with Mrs. Schur's good-natured dithering.

"I don't know," she said for the eighth time. "I never had lace on my drawers when I got married."

"Oh, Mother! Don't be old-fashioned," Dorothy said, running her fingers over the fine white muslin.

"You'd find it difficult to find undergarments without lace these days, Mrs. Schur. Especially for a bride."

"I don't know. What will her father say?"

"Daddy won't know."

"He's sure to see them hanging on the line, Dorothy. 'Sides, I couldn't deceive your father. Maybe it's best I make your drawers myself. I've made enough for you all these years; one more pair won't matter none."

"But Mother . . . it's my wedding! I can't wear home-made to my wedding!"

Dorothy had the pink-and-white complexion and flaxen hair of a girl on a Ponds advertisement. With so much beauty, it was possible to overlook her phenomenal lack of intelligence. When Rachel had first taken over the school in the spring, Dorothy had been in her last weeks as a student. At that time, Rachel had yet to learn how to control her features and so, briefly, had been thought by her students to have a facial tic.

It had developed quite suddenly during oral examinations when she'd heard Dorothy describe an iris as "a kind of bird found in Africa," and go on to say that Beethoven was "a musical instrument as large as a piano." It was amazing how quickly Miss Rachel's twitching lips had cleared up once Dorothy Schur graduated. Graduate she did, for as her own father explained to the superintendent of schools, "The Lord never meant for jungles to grow in deserts, man."

Fortunately, the young man she was going to marry in the spring didn't much care for general knowledge. Rachel pictured long winter evenings spent in companionable silence, until Dorothy and Ed's children started coming. They'd find plenty to do then. Lyle certainly kept her on the watch.

If she hadn't thought that Sissie would pursue her up hill and down dale to hear the tale of her adventure, Rachel would have headed home to start doing laundry. How one little boy could go through so many pairs of socks . . . not to mention pants, shirts and underpants. While she thought about all the work that was waiting for her at home, Rachel's anger—never long-lived—faded. Instead, she sighed with resignation.

At last Mrs. Schur decided to take the drawers with the narrowest lace trimming, though at the last moment it seemed certain she'd change her mind and pick out the flannel ones. She only returned to the lace when it seemed certain Dorothy's pale blue eyes would overflow. Once Sissie laid the drawers of choice in a box, lined with tissue paper, however, Dorothy began to chatter about her dress, her flowers, her shoes . . . everything but the groom.

Rachel wondered if any thought of Ed Greely, the real, live Ed Greely who came home every night with dirty hands from the fields, who wanted dinner on the table, who would probably snore—though Rachel had no factual knowledge of this—entered into Dorothy's fluffy head. Or did Dorothy see her wedding as an end in itself, the "happy-ever-after," never mind the "morning-after?"

She said something to that effect to Sissie, after the mother and daughter left. "Rachel Pridgeon, that's the most cynical thing I ever heard of! No bride thinks about the morning after, or no woman would ever marry."

"And you call me cynical!"

"Oh, I have a reason to be that way. I'm a spinster forever and happy to be so but you . . . you're going to get married one day." She mimicked Rachel's stern shake of her head. "Go on. You've been setting the men of this town wild with your red hair ever since you got here. It's just a matter of time before one of 'em sweeps you off your feet."

"Who, for instance? Mr. Fredericks with his five children? It's all I can do to keep up with one child. Some sharp-talking traveling man who doesn't want ties? And what am I supposed to do with Lyle? Maybe Marshal Hunnicut would have me—if he wasn't making eyes at you!"

"Or maybe some smart city fella who just happens to run a newspaper?" Sissie giggled behind her hand.

With great emphasis, Rachel said, "Don't be ridiculous."

"Oh-ho!" Sissie reached up to draw down the blind in the front door and then she turned the knob to lock it.

"What are you doing?" Rachel asked.

"Making sure we're not interrupted. Now . . . tell me everything!"

"He liked your cookies."

"Never mind the cookies. What's he like?"

"Who?" Rachel asked teasingly.

Sissie let out a frustrated growl. "Talk!"

Relenting, Rachel said, "He's very good-looking and, yes, his eyes are blue. . . ." For a moment her voice caught. She coughed and added, "They're very blue. But he's awfully fresh."

"Fresh? Fresh how?"

"You know. He looks at you like he's wondering what you look like . . . underneath." More quickly, she said, "Honestly, talk about thinking you're God's gift to womankind! Can you believe he actually wanted to call on me? Tonight?"

"Already? What kind of perfume do you use, anyway?"

"Oh, it's not me, Sissie. He's the kind of man who'd try to make a pass at any woman in skirts, so long as she wasn't actually still in pigtails or knocking at death's door. When you talk business with him, you'd better do it from the other side of a brick wall."

"He doesn't sound like the kind who'd stay where you put him. So what else happened?"

"Nothing."

"Nothing? You went from giving him cookies to his asking to call without anything else in between? He *is* fresh."

Rachel had to tell, for she knew that Sissie would hear the whole thing from whoever the next person was to cross her threshold. She couldn't expect Sissie to keep her door locked indefinitely.

"Well . . ."

"Go on."

"He did come out of the office to watch me walk away."

She hurried to add, "I didn't know he was there. I certainly didn't know he was watching me."

"How far out did he go?"

"All the way out. He stood right on the boardwalk."

"Did anybody else notice him? The McGoverns?"

"And Mr. Hudson."

"Oh, dear." Sissie bit her lip. "I'm so sorry, Rachel. It was wrong of me to dare you to go. I hate to think what folks are going to say now."

"What can they say?" Rachel asked, rallying. "Maybe we're making a mountain from a molehill. It's not as if Mr. Sinclair admires me, or anything like it. He was just getting some of his own back." She explained.

Sissie said. "He couldn't have picked a better way to do it. Everybody in town will be gabbing about you now . . . and with the welcome party tonight! Mrs. Schur's on her way to invite him now. Let's hope she doesn't talk to anybody first."

"Let's hope she does," Rachel countered. "Maybe she'll call it off."

"She can't. She's got to be gracious toward everybody—Heaven save me from ever being foolish enough to marry a minister! No, the only thing to do is for both of you to go to this tonight and let everybody see that you're perfect strangers. Of course, you'll have to keep Mr. Sinclair from taking too great an interest in you."

"Don't worry. He's not interested. He's just exactly what you called him. Wicked."

"Wicked . . . how?"

Rachel said slowly, "My stepmother told me once that if I ever met a man whose eyes made me feel . . ."

"What? What did she tell you?"

The firelight had sent huge shadows careening up the side of the mesa while she tended the meat roasting over the fire. Her stepmother nursed her infant son and talked about the old days, when she'd been the toast of San Antonio for her singing and her dancing. "Then just as I knelt to pick up the coins on the stage, in came your father and I knew he was my destiny."

"How did you know, Madrastra?" She'd heard the story before, of course, from her father. The pretty Mexican woman had always smiled tenderly but had never put forward her side. Rachel had known why Lupe told her now without a word being spoken. She was growing up and several of the men had noticed it, even if her father had not yet seen it.

"I knew when I saw his eyes. He looked at me so steady, as though he would remember me forever. I cannot remember what he said to me but when he spoke, I felt I would run mad if he wished it. I tell you now, querida. If you ever meet a man whose eyes look like that, whose words make you feel like that, run away. Steal a horse, stop a train at gunpoint, fly from the cliffs if you must, but run." Even as she gave this strange advice, she was looking down into the face of her son and smiling.

Rachel blinked, coming back to the present and the eager face of her friend. It was a long way to travel, even in thought, from the moon-washed canyons of the Arizona desert to a millinery store full of dainties in a tiny Missouri town.

"Made you feel like . . . what?" Sissie demanded again.

Rachel didn't so much shrug as shake her shoulders, as though freeing herself from some entanglement. "All Mr. Sinclair made me feel was aggravated," she said.

"You don't look aggravated." Sissie peered at her friend, her pretty brown eyes squinched up comically. "You look all pink. I wonder what Mr. Sinclair thinks about you?"

"I don't care. He's the kind that gives city slickers a bad name."

"He sure is good-looking though. I like 'em tall and lean like that."

"'Such men are dangerous,'" Rachel quoted lightly.

"I tell you what, Rachel. I think we need a man like that around Brooklyn. Stir us all up, I shouldn't wonder. Maybe he'll trifle with my affections too."

"I wouldn't be at all surprised if he does. All I hope is that Mr. Sinclair goes back to wherever he came from, and soon."

*   *   *

Sissie had been quick with sympathy when she heard what Rachel was going to do with the rest of her free afternoon. But doing laundry had become one of Rachel's favorite tasks once she'd moved to Brooklyn. No more drawing water by hand, or crouching over the muddy stream if she chose to take the clothes to the water instead of the other way around. Though her back might still ache after a day spent scrubbing, the sheer delight of abundant water brought up by a firm thrust on a pump handle made up for the labor.

Then she could carry the basket outside to hang the clothes on her very own line, not draped over whatever scrawny bush survived the desert heat. The breeze was fresh and cool and never bore a burden of gritty yellow sand. True, the hot winds of Arizona did dry things quickly, but never cleanly. If she never smelled sagebrush and dust on herself again it would be much too soon.

For a moment, she enjoyed a sense of deep satisfaction. Then it made her laugh silently at herself. All she had done, all she'd set her will to accomplish, all the lies she'd told to become honest and to stay honest, and one would think it had all been merely for the pleasure of clean clothes rather than for a clean spirit.

Rachel put up her hand to tuck back a loosened strand of her hair and looked out over her domain. The backyard had two trees, one on either side against the fence. The clothesline ran between them, all gay with fluttering clothes. She'd planted flowers in the spring and seen them come up in the summer. Though the blossoms were long gone, Rachel could still look at the neat beds with pleasure. Though her house was small, three rooms downstairs and two upstairs crowded under the peaked roof, she cherished caring for it more than if it had been a palace.

Most schoolteachers roomed with families during the year but when she'd told the Brooklyn board that she'd be bringing her half brother, they arranged for her to take this house at their expense. Rachel didn't ask who'd lived there before her, though she'd found a torn tulle frill bright with spangles under one of the beds and a cache of empty whisky bottles in the shed. The board had painted the inside and left what furniture there was. Rachel's gratitude had only reinforced her hunch that Brooklyn was the right place for her and Lyle to live.

A scrambling, scratching noise at the very bottom of the yard made her look that way. A dark head, a dirty face, a knee with a hole in the trousers came up over the fence. Lyle caught sight of her as he pulled himself up. For a single instant, the surprised fear of a criminal at bay showed in his big green eyes. Then a mask of indifference dropped over his features and he slid down from the top of the fence.

He'd lost his shirt and the hole in the knee of his pants wasn't the only one. Nonetheless, he walked with a swagger that would have seemed excessive in the walk of a hardened pirate, let alone in that of a seven-year-old boy.

Rachel forebore asking where he'd been. She knew he'd only lie—not because he was afraid of her or any punishment, but because he didn't like anyone to know his business. Instead, she asked, "What would you like for supper?"

Lyle shrugged. "It doesn't matter. Do I gotta go to this stupid party tonight?"

"Yes. And it won't be stupid. You like Mrs. Schur."

"She's all right. But I don't like *him*. He prays too much."

"We pray."

"Not like that. You pray for me; I pray for you. He prays for nobody I ever heard of."

"He's a preacher. That's his job."

Lyle had a remarkable variety of shrugs. Sometimes he communicated more with a twitch of his shoulders than with a whole volume of words. Now he made it clear that Mr. Schur's poor choice of profession was no reason he should take an interest. "Fry me up some chicken tonight?" he asked, changing the subject.

"I don't have any chicken to fry."

The boy looked around shyly and then sidled over to his sister. "I know where I can get some. Nobody locks their henhouse doors around here."

"No, Lyle," she said firmly.

"Ten minutes . . . and nobody will know."

"I'll know, and so will you."

"You can trust me," he said with the laughing gleam in his green eyes that reminded her so much of her father's. "And I know I can trust you."

"It's wrong."

"What's so wrong? Somebody's got a whole flock of chickens and we don't have nary a one. That seems more wrong to me than just . . . borrowing one."

"Call it what it is, Lyle. It's stealing. We don't steal." She let out the exasperated breath she was holding, reminded herself yet again that two years of her training was nothing compared with five years of bad example. More brightly she said, "We'll have the rest of the rabbit pie I made yesterday and there's apples for dessert. Mrs. Schur's going to have cake tonight so we won't need anything else."

His lower lip stuck out sulkily. Then, brightening, he asked, "What kind of cake?"

"I don't know. But Mrs. Schur knows you're coming so it's bound to be something you like." She reached out to ruffle his dark brown hair. It had the red glints in it that came from their father, Lyle's green eyes like her own. The rest of his coloring—his smooth brown skin, his dark hair, lashes and brows—came from Lupe, his mother.

While they ate, Rachel read aloud from *The Adventures of Tom Sawyer*, the only book in the world that could hold Lyle's attention for even five minutes. Maybe Tom's behavior wasn't the best example for a boy like Lyle but he needed to learn that books were his friends.

"I sure don't see what call Tom had to come back and write that message to his aunt. Seems mighty foolhardy to me."

"He didn't like to think of her worrying about him." Rachel polished an apple to a high gloss and tossed it lightly to her brother.

He caught it on the fly without a moment's thought. With a chunk of it tucked in his cheek, he said, "That's foolish. Women are bound to worry no matter what a feller tells 'em."

"Well . . ." Rachel hesitated, not wanting to scare him away by forcing his confidence. On the other hand, this conversation had an ominous ring. "I think . . . I think we'd rather know. We'd rather have a cause for worry than have to worry about everything under the sun."

"I guess. Say! He didn't leave that note anyhow, did he?"

"No, he didn't."

"Smart." He crunched the core of the apple in half with a quick stroke of his white teeth. "Say, d'you know I can spit an apple seed six foot?"

"Six feet."

"Six feet. I can. Wanna see?"

"I'll take your word for it." She watched in surprised approval as he cleared his place. Casually, she asked, "What did you and Marshal Hunnicut do today?"

"I helped him polish up his brass tack for tonight. He's hoping Miss Sissie'll take a drive with him after the party." He glanced at her with a line of trouble in his brow. "Don't let on . . . naw, you'll stand fire."

"Thank you, Lyle. Ummm, I don't like to ask, but your shirt was new just last winter . . ."

Lyle's eyes widened as if he only just remembered that he had no shirt. For a fleeting instant, he looked to be only seven, as the hardened muscles around his mouth relaxed. "I know just where it is, Rachel. Won't take me but a minute to run for to fetch it."

"Thank you, Lyle. I'll wait for you and we'll walk over to the Schurs' house together."

"Yeah, all right. I'll hurry back and wash up 'fore we go." He wasn't two steps out the back door when he started to run, his bare feet thudding on the hard earth. Rachel hoped the lure of Mrs. Schur's cake would be stronger than his reluctance to hear Mr. Schur pray.

Rachel went up the stairs to the second floor, hearing only the squeak of the loose steps. Sitting on her simple bed, she tugged the pins one by one from her hair. Beyond her bedroom window, the sun had been lost behind clouds on the horizon. It would be dark soon. She paused as she raised her hairbrush, hoping to hear the slam of the front door.

It did not come, not when she put her hair up again, hoping always and forever for a method that would keep the soft, heavy stuff on her head instead of tumbling down her back. She heard only silence as she washed her face and neck, though she lifted her dripping face from the bowl twice believing she heard it.

Then she put on a clean shirtwaist over her gray poplin skirt. A last glance in the mirror to set her straw hat demurely on her head and she was ready to go. Yet she sat down on the worn coverlet of her bed to wait.

She heard a wagon pull at the Schurs' house and a gaggle of young women got down to go inside. She heard the slow clop of a heavy horse's hoof and the cheerful greetings that came from the people on the porch as they recognized the doctor. She heard a burst of music from the harmonium and wondered if there would be dancing. But no sound of Lyle returning to the little house.

The knock that rattled the window startled Rachel, on the prick for the kind of sounds Lyle would make. "Who is it?" she called, her voice floating out the open window.

She heard only the breeze for a long moment after she asked. The silence pricked at the vigilance that never slept. Quick as thought, she slid her hand under her pillow to touch the cool metal of the pistol she had hidden there. "Who is it?" she called again, her tone hardening.

She heard a whisper, with a giggle in the depths of it that made her smile as she recognized it. Then a fairly deep male voice said, "It's Marshal Hunnicut, Miss Pridgeon. Miss Albright and I have come to take you over to the Schurs' house."

Rachel could imagine them standing at her front door, the tall, loose-limbed marshal gazing down, entranced by the petite and pretty Sissie holding on to his arm with a shy mixture of pride and reserve. Sissie might swear his charms were lost on her, but Rachel guessed otherwise.

"I'm coming down," she called and returned the pistol to its hiding place.

When she opened the door, she fancied that she looked as though she'd never touched a gun in all her life. No doubt the marshal had heard of Egan Delmon's gang; most lawmen had. However, very few people in the world knew that the notorious outlaw had been a father, as well as a name to be feared. Her father, as a matter of fact.

3

THE MOMENT HAL Sinclair set eyes on Mrs. Schur, he knew she was the woman he'd been looking for. Slight, with hair so smooth and tight it looked like she'd borrowed it from a statue, she fluttered behind the refreshment table, neatening away a stray crumb here, straightening a napkin there. Every so often her pale eyes would search the small group who sat and stood in her front parlor, searching for her husband or her children.

Hal all but rubbed his hands together in glee. Get her alone, give her a little undivided attention and she'd spill over like a jar of dry beans. All the gossip would be his. All the truth about the nice, normal people who had come to this "social" to meet him, the new editor of their paper.

Smiling apologetically, he stepped out of a conversation going on around him about cider-making. He didn't even like apples but he supposed there might be a story in it. Hal had never been responsible for filling up the blank pages of a whole paper before. A reporter didn't have to think about those things.

Thinking about the people he'd met so far this evening, a banker, the town doctor, the undertaker, and their families, Hal thought that he'd be lucky to get out one issue a month. They all looked so simple and upright that it was absolutely dispiriting to a man who made his living nosing out corruption and public sins. Even the mayor failed him as a source for headlines. Hearing him talk about his duties as father, owner of the general store and public official, Hal soon realized that Mr. Gladd was too busy to be anything but honest. He'd begun to feel that gossip was his only recourse.

"I wanted to thank you again for giving this party, Mrs. Schur," he said, approaching her. "I feel very welcome in Brooklyn now, thanks to you."

"Oh, my. It was nothing, really. Everyone's so helpful. . . ." She looked up and down the crowded table, at all the good things the ladies of Brooklyn had made in their kitchens. With a tiny pat, she straightened the lace doily beneath a two-layer cake, half gone now. Hal took up an empty plate in his hand.

"Ah, but you baked this wonderful cake yourself, didn't you? May I beg another slice? I shouldn't, you know. I've eaten until I'll have to be rolled home like a beer barrel but . . ." He smiled at her as she cut a large wedge and pushed it onto his plate. Taking a bite, he rolled his eyes in an ecstasy that was perhaps exaggerated, but not faked.

"How do you get it this light?"

A little color, not unappealing, crept into cheeks that had obviously been scrubbed, morning and night, with home-made soap. "It's the beating," she confided, leaning forward over the table. "I don't tell everyone, though there's plenty would like to know, but you being a man and all . . ."

"Oh, I'm safe and silent, Mrs. Schur. I must say though, your cake is much tastier than what Mrs. Jer . . . maybe I shouldn't say anything . . ."

"Mrs. Jergens is a good woman," Mrs. Schur said piously. "What kind of cake did she have tonight?"

"I couldn't tell you, to be honest. It was white."

"Icing?"

"No, ma'am." He'd learned long ago the value of a boyish smile.

Mrs. Schur clicked her tongue chidingly. "Let me just cut you another little slice . . . I baked this cocoa cake here too."

Light her cake was without a doubt, but the slice she gave him was thick enough to strain his muscles. He set it down on the table and plied his fork while she, under the illusion that she was explaining why Mrs. Jergens gave the *impression* of being mean while really being a generous-hearted soul, gave Hal the full story on why there was no "Mr. Jergens."

The tale bordered on the scandalous. Hal knew he'd never print it, but he figured the more he knew about the townspeople, the better. Then he heard a bustle by the fringe-bobbled arched entrance to the parlor. Looking that way, while nodding and muttering a "most interesting," Hal saw a familiar red-haired girl walk in.

She was with some long-legged man in a dark suit. He hastily doffed his round-brimmed hat at the sight of all the ladies and revealed a head that gleamed in the lamplight. Hal didn't know why he suddenly found himself smiling.

He deflected Mrs. Schur from repeating herself and asked, "Who's that . . . who just came in?"

"Who?"

"That . . . man." He thought it safer to ask her about the man rather than the striking girl.

"Oh, that's Marshal Hunnicut. All the young girls are just wild about him."

"Are they now?"

"That's what my daughter Dorothy says. Not for herself, mind you, not when she's getting married in next to no time. But all the others . . . They make his life a misery. Always giggling around him, giving him looks in church . . . I don't know what their mothers are thinking of. My mother would've skinned me alive if I so much as spoke to a man without her standing by my side."

"These are terribly lax times, Mrs. Schur."

"That's just what Mr. Schur says."

"I couldn't help noticing that girl who came in with him. Is she one of the local nuisances?"

"Oh, no. That's Miss Pridgeon, our new schoolteacher. Pretty thing, isn't she? Never cared for red hair in the ordinary way, but she's pretty enough to stand up under it."

"It seemed to me, just for a moment, that I might have met her before," Hal said, not untruthfully.

"Really now?" Mrs. Schur leaned forward a mite. "In New York, do you think?"

"I can't say. . . ."

"You see, truth is we don't know much about her. She's from out West. My cousin is kind of in the way of being a minister himself and I happened to mention in a letter that we were in a state about finding us a schoolteacher who'd stay put. We've had a few that just couldn't stand the quiet. Another of 'em up and married almost as soon as she stepped off the train. So when my cousin McLean said he knew just the girl, we took her on his advice. Nice girl, all the children love her to death, though that brother of hers is a right hellion—"

"*Mother,*" said a peeved young lady, who came up to stand next to Hal. "Mother, look at you. You've got cake icing all down your front."

"Do I?" Mrs. Schur said, peering down at her lace tucker. She paddled at the frosting, smearing the chocolate butter cream. "This is my daughter, Dorothy," she said. "Dorothy, this is . . . I better get it with a damp cloth."

Hal looked with approval at Miss Dorothy Schur. He always had a soft spot for a blonde. The dumber, the better. Something in this one's flat, shiny eyes said she was as dumb as could be. She hadn't giggled yet, though Hal felt sure it was just a matter of time.

"Do you think you'll like Brooklyn, Mr. Sinclair?" she asked.

"I won't lie to you, Miss Schur. I had my doubts about coming here, but now that I met you, they're all gone." There it came, clear and sharp, the kind of laugh that charmed the first dozen times before the thirteenth repetition made you want to strangle the maker.

Hal drew the girl out, getting her to talk by listening to her with a mixture of flirtation and respect. It went right to Dorothy's head. No one listened to her much, except her fiancé and he didn't have much time right now, what with the harvest to get in. So she chattered happily and thoughtlessly as a parakeet to the handsome newcomer.

Rachel noticed that Hal Sinclair and Dorothy Schur had their heads together by the refreshment table. She wasn't alone in noticing, but it troubled her that she'd seen them so quickly. What business did she have searching a room for that irritating slicker the minute she walked into it?

Sissie had been stopped in the doorway by Mrs. McGovern, leaving Rachel and Marshal Hunnicut to come in together. Now the milliner came up to her friend and slipped her arm about her waist. "Do you see him?"

"Who?"

"Mr. Sinclair. Is he here yet?"

"No," Rachel said, determined no one else should know how foolish she was. "I haven't seen him yet."

"Ooh, there he is, there he is," Sissie said in an excited whisper, her feet shuffling on the shining wooden floor. "And making up to Dottie Schur already . . . not that she seems to mind."

The pastor's daughter giggled, the glittering sound breaking over the assembled guests. More than one head turned. More than one tongue clicked. Then the conversations resumed, a little more hurriedly, a little more hushed.

"He'll end by setting us all topsy-turvy," Sissie said. "Isn't it exciting?"

Marshal Hunnicut's voice was like himself, slow, precise and deep. He said, "I don't think Ed Greely'll think so. Look at his face."

The two young women turned to look at the farmer, who was sitting on a plush sofa looking, in his tight collar and thin necktie, as restless as a tied dog. A plate sat on his knee, an untouched slice of cake with the fork sticking straight up in it like a flag of conquest, while he looked at his bride-to-be. Hurt lines wrinkled his forehead and his broad shoulders slumped.

Sissie said, "Go over there and make a third in that conversation, Rachel."

"Me? Why me?"

"You've already met him. It won't look so odd if you do it. 'Sides, you can kind of edge Dorothy out of it and send her over to talk to Ed, like she should."

"What makes you think . . . ?"

"You were her teacher, weren't you? Dorothy'll listen to you her whole life 'cause she won't ever realize you can't still put her in the corner for doing wrong."

Rachel said, "What a prospect! I never realized when I started I'd be responsible for Dorothy Schur for the rest of my days. All right, I'm going. But I've changed my mind. I *do* intend to collect that ten dollars you owe me."

As she walked away, she heard the marshal ask, "What ten dollars?" and had the satisfaction of hearing Sissie hem and haw for an answer.

Rachel stood just out of nudging room behind Dorothy's elbow. From here, she could see Hal Sinclair's eyes very clearly. The heavy-seeming lids had fallen half over his eyes, leaving only a glitter of blue behind his absurdly thick lashes. She could see laughter in their depths, a merriment that did not show on his steady lips or sound in the seriousness of his tone as he answered one of Dorothy's foolish commonplaces.

Then his gaze shifted and he looked past the girl's shoulder and saw her. Then his lips did twitch and Rachel wondered if she looked so much the stern schoolmarm that the sight of her made him laugh.

"Dorothy," she said, stepping forward. "I haven't seen Ed tonight. Couldn't he come?"

The pretty blonde turned her head vaguely, searching the corners of the room. "He's here someplace, I guess. He doesn't much like parties."

"Why don't you find him for me? I haven't seen him . . ." No need to make up a reason for Dorothy.

Chances were good she'd never remember who had sent her to look for her own fiancé.

"There he is, behind Mrs. Dale," Dorothy said, pleased. "I guess he'd like to meet Mr. Sinclair."

Hal said, "I know I'd like it."

She gave him a dreaming smile, then drifted away, her small feet under her white skirt as aimless as clouds. Altering his tone to sly cynicism, Hal asked, "Come to save the little lamb from the wicked wolf?"

Rachel stood a little straighter. "Not a very dangerous wolf."

"Not a very intelligent lamb. Just the sort to walk into a den unawares. Now, you, on the other hand, Miss Pridgeon . . ."

"I've already been in the wolf's den, Mr. Sinclair, and escaped with a whole skin."

"I'd like to see proof of that boast one day." He had the slyest, wickedest smile, an odiously confident smile, that said he knew her better than she knew herself. If there was anything in the world more infuriating than that look from a near-total stranger, Rachel didn't know what it was. She'd started out with nothing but the best intention of being a good neighbor to a newcomer to their little town, to show some of the same warm hospitality she'd received here on her arrival. Now she was angry.

A good, clean anger, it made her stand a little more proudly and brought the fresh pink into her cheeks while brightening the sparkle in her eyes. Hal reflected that there was nothing more charming than an angry red-haired woman but he felt it would be taking his life in his hands to say so. He knew they'd gotten off on the wrong foot but it would be more amusing if he didn't apologize for a day or two.

She said, "You do know that the lamb is engaged?"

"Yes. Does it matter?"

The color in her cheeks intensified. "Of course it . . ." She seemed to realize her voice had risen. With a false smile that wouldn't have fooled a baby, she turned her head from side to side so that everyone in the room could see that she was having a pleasant conversation with Mr. Sinclair. It seemed to Hal that everyone in the room was interested. He wondered what would happen if he invited Miss Pridgeon to step outside into the cool evening air. Probably mass fainting spells and a call for someone to fetch a rope. Or Mr. Schur.

In a more moderate tone, she said, "Of course it matters. Dorothy and Ed are going to be very happy together, if nothing happens to spoil it."

"Like me?"

"Like a stupid quarrel over jealousy."

"It doesn't do a man any harm to be a little jealous, Miss Pridgeon. Sharpens their interest, makes them wonder if they've not been a little too cavalier in considering the young lady to be sewn up and in their vest pocket. Now, for instance, if your 'friend' happened to see how pretty you look right now, he might feel he has cause . . ."

"Do you ever stop flirting, Mr. Sinclair?"

"I haven't started flirting yet, Miss Pridgeon. At least, not with you."

"Telling me I'm . . . what you said . . . that isn't flirting in your book, I suppose."

"If that was flirting, the encyclopedia must be full of it." He wished he dared take her hand, but she might explode like a roman candle. Dropping his voice to an intimate whisper, he added, "Facts are facts, Miss Pridgeon, and it's a fact that you are looking exceptionally pretty."

"Besides," she said, ignoring this provocation with a toss of her head that loosened a red-gold curl to fall and bounce beside her small ear. "I haven't got a beau for you to make jealous so you can stop flirting with me, even if I believed you were doing it from unselfish motives. I only came over here to stop Dorothy from making a fool of herself and I won't stay to let you make a fool of me."

"Allow me to make it easier for you, Miss Pridgeon. I'll leave to get you a glass of this flat punch and while I'm gone you can drift into conversation with someone else."

She had wisps of hair falling into her eyes too. When he left, he heard her blow them off her forehead with an exasperated puff. Hal wondered if she were as peppery as this all the time, or if he just brought out the best in her.

He kept an eye on her. She fell into conversation fairly quickly with an older couple. Something about their eyes, their smiles, told him that they were teasing her. Though she obviously returned light answers, her cheeks retained the carnation pink that he'd called up.

Then that tall fellow she'd come in with appeared beside him at the punch bowl. "How do? I'm Benson Hunnicut."

"How do you do, Mr. Hunnicut," Hal sized the other man up. His handshake gave the indication of great strength without making an arm-wrestling match of it. Hunnicut had a good jaw too and the kind of straight eyes that seemed to command honesty. Hal had spent enough time down at the local precincts to know, even without Mrs. Schur's information, that he had just met a lawman. The honest ones all looked alike, just as the ones on the take all resembled one another.

Showing off, Hal asked, "Much crime around here?"

"Not much," the marshal allowed with a short, huffing laugh. "Little hen robbery now and then. Sometimes some of the farmhands get a mite rowdy, just when the spring gets into 'em. You know. Not much for the paper, I'm afraid."

"That's what most people tell me. The issues of the *Herald* might be a little brief."

"Nobody minds that. No news is good news, eh?" The marshal laughed.

Hal smiled. "You can't expect me to agree with you. If there's no news, I don't have a job. I'm sorry—is it Sheriff Hunnicut, by the way?"

"No, we're not far enough west for that. Some folks call me constable; others like marshal. I'm kind of partial to marshal."

"And a poet too."

But the marshal had reached past him for a cup and was ladling punch into it. He said, "We're all curious as to why Marcellus Clyde sent you out here. He hasn't seemed to care much about the *Herald* one way or t'other since Mr. Rudolph died."

"I met Mr. Clyde in New York and told him I was anxious for a change of scene." Hal had decided earlier to give this answer if anyone asked. He'd learned his lesson after spilling the facts about Clyde.

"Well, you sure got the change you were after, Mr. Sinclair. You a hunting man? Mighty good hunting around here. We got opossum, raccoon, now and then a fox . . ."

"I'm not much of a shot. Living in New York, you know."

"Sure. Well, you want some practice, just let me know." He filled a second cup and picked them both up, cradling them tenderly one in each hand. Hal suddenly remembered that he had been on an invented mission to get punch for Miss Pridgeon.

An easy matter to joggle a man's arm, accidentally. The pink punch splashed out, a good portion of it landing on the lawman's tan trousers. "I beg your pardon," Hal said, flashing out his handkerchief.

"Oh, that's okay. Mighta happened to anyone." Hunnicut brushed the liquid off his pants leg with the flat of his hand. "Don't think it'll even leave a mark."

"Your wife'll get it right out, I'm sure."

"She would, if I had one. Maybe Miss Albright'll oblige. There's nothing that gal can't do."

"Miss Albright? I haven't had the pleasure . . ." Maybe it wasn't Rachel Pridgeon the marshal wanted. Hal asked himself why he should care, then hastily reminded himself that news was news.

"She's a grand gal. You'll like her; everyone does. Don't know about a woman going into business for herself, though. Looks a mite strange to these old eyes."

"It's common enough. Some of the best places in New York are owned and run by women. I've even heard predictions that one of these days they'll be running the country."

"Heck, man, they do that already. Ask any married man—they know."

They shared a man-of-the-world laugh. As he turned away to carry that long-overdue cup of punch to Miss Pridgeon, Hal discovered that he was finding it surprisingly easy to talk to the citizens of Brooklyn. A refreshing change from the sharp verbal fencing that made life in the big city so spirited. He could stand living for a while in a place where no one seemed to understand sarcasm or put on a mask of cynicism to be fashionable. However, he had no intention of making it too permanent a change—he might lose his edge—but he could stand it for a while.

"Here you are, Miss Pridgeon."

At the sound of his voice, her eyes widened in shock. He knew it was because she hadn't expected to see him beside her again. "I'd forgotten I'd asked for it," she explained, not looking at him, but more as if the explanation were for the pleasant-faced older couple who stood with her.

Miss Pridgeon said, "Mrs. McGovern, Mr. McGovern, may I present Mr. Sinclair? The McGoverns live right across the street from the newspaper."

Some quality of warning in her tone informed Hal that she considered this important for him to know. He turned a charming smile on the couple. "Then we're neighbors."

"Neighbors?" the man said, his voice surprisingly light for a man of his years. His abundant hair had turned gray, not iron-gray, but a softer shade like the lost feathers from a pigeon's breast. "Maybe you didn't hear right. We're across the street from the paper, not the boardinghouse."

"To a newspaperman, Mr. McGovern, the newspaper *is* home."

Mrs. McGovern looked a few years younger than her husband. Her cheeks were crisscrossed by tiny lines, pulled into being between her smiling lips and her squinting eyes. She looked as if she enjoyed laughing. She said in a mock-scolding tone, "That's no way for a man to live. That was Mr. Rudolph's whole complaint. If he had a nice young lady to come home to every evening, he wouldn't have dropped dead in his office."

"Where would he have . . . ?" Hal began to ask, only to feel a sudden sharp pain grind into the top of his left foot. He glanced down to find the heel of a buttoned shoe laid firmly on the surface of his boot.

"Did you know Mr. Rudolph well?" Rachel asked the

older couple brightly, giving no indication by her voice that she was cheerfully inflicting pain on another human being. Hal slid his foot out from beneath hers, scraping the leather more deeply still.

"Tolerably well. We had him over to supper a time or two," Mrs. McGovern said.

"I've heard nothing but good about him. Sissie told me that he was a real fine man."

The McGoverns echoed that assessment. Hal asked, "As long as we're talking about old friends, Marshal Hunnicut gave me to understand that you might know Marcellus Clyde?"

"Oh, dear, is that the time?" Mr. McGovern asked, hauling his gold watch out of his vest pocket to compare it with the hand-painted one on the mantel. "We'd better speak to our hostess, Mercy. You know you said you wanted an early night tonight."

"That's right," Mrs. McGovern said, though her tone was doubtful. "So nice to have met you, Mr. Sinclair. We'll meet again, I'm sure."

"I'll look forward to it," Hal said with the slight bow that always went over well with any older woman.

When he straightened, after the McGoverns had gone, he found he had to bear the focus of a pair of very disgusted green eyes. "I can't make you out," Miss Pridgeon said. "One minute you're rude and conceited; the next you're being . . . I don't know . . ."

"Charming? Enthralling? Suave? Pick one."

"Whatever it is, you're still being conceited. Do you think everyone's going to like you even if they never know who you really are?"

"Now that's an interesting way to put it, Miss Pridgeon. Seems from what I've heard, nobody knows exactly who *you* are."

"Me? I haven't anything to hide."

"Then why doesn't Mrs. Schur know everything about you right down to your shoe size? Which by the way must be bigger than it looks. You've left quite a bruise on my foot."

"Good." She dropped her long lashes over her dazzling eyes as her full mouth tightened. He felt that she was ashamed of her quick retort, that she feared sinking, not in his estimation, but in her own. After a pause, she said, "Mrs. Schur can ask me whatever questions she likes. If she hasn't, it may be that she just doesn't find me very interesting."

"Impossible! There's not that much around here to keep a person's attention except the actions of his neighbors."

"You sound as if you know a lot about small towns," Miss Pridgeon said.

"It's been said that New York City is nothing but a lot of small towns with no space in between. Anyway, don't try to change the subject. I want to know about you. Maybe I'll feature you in the paper."

"Don't bother." She turned as if to go. Hal found a strange desire bubbling up within him. A desire to keep her there by some outrageous comment. He wanted to see that defensive light come up in the clear depths of her eyes. It gave them a glow like a sunlit stained-glass window.

"'Woman of Mystery Becomes Schoolteacher.' Hmmm, not a bad headline if I do say so myself."

Her gaze did fly to his face then, her eyes huge. Not with anger or spirit but with sharp alarm. Hal began to reach for her hand, wanting to take back what he'd said since it disturbed her so, even as his newspaperman's soul wondered. He was forestalled by a commotion on the porch. The front door flew open and a small, grubby boy, his pants in tatters, came hurtling in like a cannonball. "Rachel, Rachel?"

"I'm here." Miss Pridgeon knelt down as a path opened between her and the boy. She opened her arms and he ran to her. He stopped short just before she could gather him in. With a self-conscious attempt to achieve calm, he crossed his arms over his bare, goosefleshed chest and said, "I'm all right. But the cows are in the graveyard again."

This sounded mildly amusing to Hal. There might still be cows in Central Park, there to feed the rich men's children the same tuberculosis-loaded milk that the poorest child received, but New York hadn't quite reached the fashionable peak of grazing cattle on their ancestors. He wanted to make a dry comment to someone, only to notice that the room was suddenly less crowded. Men and women, younger and older, were hurrying out, leaving their plates and cups just where they were.

"Come on," Rachel said, rising and giving him an assessing glance. "You might as well come along. Who knows, you might actually be useful. Doubtful, but stranger things have happened."

4

THE BROOKLYN GRAVEYARD had more people buried
in it than Hal would have expected from the size of the
town. He realized this after barking his shins on what
seemed a hundred tombstones in the first five minutes. They
seemed to spring out of the ground at him, knocking into
him, tripping him and then disappearing.

"Stand still," he said, swearing. He supposed there was
some dire spiritual penalty awaiting a man who swore in a
cemetery, but he felt he could plead extenuating circumstances. Hearing voices, he plunged off in their general
direction only to come down headlong over another hand-
carved monument. "Blast!"

"Mr. Sinclair?"

He knew that laughing voice already, though usually
when Miss Pridgeon spoke to him she sounded about the
way he felt now. "Careful," he said. "I think this place is
haunted."

"I've never seen any ghosts in it."

"They don't need to materialize; they let their headstones do their dirty work." He heard her laugh and knew a ghost wouldn't stand a chance.

The only illumination came from the scattering of stars over their heads. A few people had apparently conjured lanterns out of the air, but they were down by the church. Hal wasn't used to being out at night, except in cabs. He said as much when Miss Pridgeon appeared beside him with the suddenness of an owl.

"Don't you people know it's not civilized to run around in the dark? I can't see my hand before my face."

"Close your eyes for a minute; they need a chance to get used to the dark."

When he opened them again, he could make out the oval of her face and even the dark pools of her eyes. Standing up, he said, "Maybe you'd better hold my hand."

"You're not *afraid* of the dark, are you?"

"Petrified. Besides, you don't know what I've been through. I need someone to protect me from the boggles."

"Boggles?"

"Didn't you have an Irish grandmother to tell you about the boggles, Miss Pridgeon?"

"No." Her tone was skeptical, though still with the hint of laughter in it.

"I did. And what Katherine Sinclair didn't know about the things that walk wasn't worth knowing. Once she told me a story about a graveyard very much like this . . . only older, of course, being as it was in the Old Country. It seems that—"

"Save such stories for Halloween and credulous children, Mr. Sinclair."

"You sound as if you don't believe in ghosts. They don't like that. Maybe I better hold *your* hand."

She pulled her wrap a little more tightly around her, tucking her hands under the soft stuff at her elbows. "There aren't any ghosts here. Just the loved ones of the people of Brooklyn. If they do haunt, it's only because they're interested in what's going on."

"I'll add a special edition of the paper just for them."

A deep moan, sounding as lost and lonely as any ghost could be, interrupted him as he began to develop this theme. He was not proud of the fact that he jumped about a foot. "What in the name of . . . ?"

Miss Pridgeon's laugh had something of the impetuous quality of a spring, bubbling up irresistibly from the depths. "Haven't you ever heard a cow at milking time before?"

"Sure, I kept a whole herd in my apartment."

"Come on. We'll work her around to the gate."

Hal followed her, while she waved her arms and said, "Tush, tush," to the shadowy bovine form he could glimpse against the whitewashed fence. When she told him to, he followed suit. He felt more than a little foolish, wondering what the boys in the press room would say if they could see him now. However, since a good half of the people in the cemetery were also waving their arms and making strange noises, he supposed he didn't stand out as much as he thought.

"Come on, Bessie," Rachel said. "Move on."

"Is that her name? It doesn't surprise me. Every Bessie I ever met was stubborn."

"I suppose you've known a lot of women by that name. Or just a lot of women . . . period?"

"Oh, one or two. You know how it is."

"No. Come on, cow, move along." Hal could hear that she'd moved toward the head of the animal. "Are you stuck?"

"Is she stuck?"

"No, she's just found something good to eat. I'll pull her by her headstall."

"Let me." Hal reached out toward the cow's head, guiding his hand by the faintly reflective white patches on her slowly chewing cheeks. He slipped his fingers under the leather strap that went over her ears and tugged. "Come on, Bessie. Come on, old girl. Don't keep Daddy waiting."

He heard Rachel laugh, a merry sound that set him smiling. "Did you talk to all your Bessies that way?"

"No, most of them I had to promise something to get them to move. A new hat, a box of chocolates . . ."

"Keep it up . . . she's moving!"

"A fur cape, a diamond bracelet, a Paris flat . . ."

The cow was practically at a jog-trot. As Hal bobbed along at her side, he kept chanting. "A debut at the theater, a smart landau with matching carriage horses . . ."

"Okay!" Rachel called. "I've got the gate open."

Scenting the other cows, Bessie trotted through the gate as sweetly as could be. Still laughing, Rachel swung the gate closed. Hal didn't know whether it was clever tactics on her part or just chance, but she stood on one side of the gate while he was on the other. He laid his hand over hers where it rested on the top rail.

"I may have known a Bessie or two, but there's never been a Rachel in my life before." Funny how he knew where her ear was, just the right height for a voice held to a whisper.

She slipped her hand free. "Then you've something to look forward to."

"Oh, I do. I look forward to getting to know you better." He'd liked the feel of her hand. Rougher, maybe, than the perfumed fingers of a society woman's, a hand used to doing its own work, it had been warm beneath his. Had it trembled the merest bit before she'd taken it away?

"Mr. Sinclair . . ." she began, and he could tell by the way she bit off the words that he'd brought the sparkle back into her eyes, even though he couldn't see them.

"Yes, Miss Pridgeon?"

She hesitated, and then said, "I've heard a rumor that you were sent here by Mr. Clyde himself. Is it true?"

"It's true. Do you know Mr. Clyde? Personally, I mean."

"No. I've only lived here for a little more than a year. Mr. Clyde's been gone for a long time . . . fifteen years maybe. He was born here, before there was even a town."

"Marcellus Clyde was born *here?*"

"That's what folks say."

"I didn't know that." An idea for a story began to bubble in Hal's head. Maybe if he did a flattering write-up of Clyde . . . interviews with the oldest inhabitants . . . a few hundred words of flattering copy . . . and sent it to

New York . . . His pride slammed the door on that notion. He wouldn't lick Clyde's boots to escape from a situation that *not* licking his boots had put him in. Maybe it wasn't sensible, but he'd get back to New York on his own somehow.

He said impatiently, "Never mind Clyde. What about you, Miss Rachel Pridgeon? What do you want?" This time he reached over the fence to take her hand.

She tugged free and said sharply, "Stop that! I don't like to be manhandled."

"It wouldn't hurt you to be just a little friendlier."

"You don't need *me* to be friendly. You have a knack for making friends. Say . . . Dorothy Schur?"

"She's a nice girl, but strictly an infant so far as I'm concerned. I'm sure she'll make her fiancé, what's-his-name, a first-rate wife. Besides, there's a big difference between a girl like that and one like you. I could really talk to you."

"Talk? You mean flirt. I think, given half a chance, you'd be bad for my reputation, Mr. Sinclair."

"Reputation?" he echoed, laughing. "With you on one side of the fence and me on the other? Who could see the harm in that?"

"But we're alone. And towns tend to be straitlaced about their schoolteachers and men. I'll go in."

Hal hadn't jumped a fence in years, not since an incident in his cub reporter days when he'd needed to leave a bull-infested pasture more quickly than he'd gone in. It was amazing to find the old skill hadn't deserted him. He landed on his feet on the other side and caught up to Miss Pridgeon in a stride or two.

Maybe she tossed her head when he appeared beside her. At any rate, she gave a cry of vexed alarm. "Oh, shoot." Stand still a minute. My hair's coming down."

"It is?"

"Yes. Put out your hand."

"My hand?"

"To hold the pins," she snapped.

"Oh!" He held out his cupped hands and felt the cool

slide of metal hairpins as her fingers delicately touched his palm. Hal let his imagination play with the image of Rachel Pridgeon, her beautiful red hair falling in waves over her shoulders and breasts, framing a square-jawed face softened into beauty by the heat of passion. . . .

"Almost done," she grunted between clenched teeth. She took the last several pins from his hands.

"Does that happen a lot?"

"Too often. My hair's heavy and though I use big pins to hold it, it always slips down. By the end of a busy school day I look like I've been dragged backward through a bush, more often than not. I've thought about having it cut. . . ."

"Don't do that!" He coughed. "I mean, a woman's crowning glory and all that . . ."

"I guess. But it's an awful nuisance. Men have no idea."

"That's so true, about a lot of things. For instance, I wouldn't know how to teach school, or trim a hat or sew."

"Those things are easy to learn. I wouldn't know how to do any of the things you do, like write a newspaper story, or run a press. Or even flirt outlandishly."

"I could teach you how to run a press."

Once again, she laughed. "You wouldn't, by any chance, be looking for someone to help you get out the paper?"

It was a new experience for Hal to be seen through so fast. Usually it took people a while. "Something like that," he admitted. "Of course, what I'd really like to have is a sturdy boy, about say seven or eight years old. Bright, though, he has to be bright. A quick-learning lad. I thought, as schoolteacher, you might be able to recommend . . . Say! What about that nice-looking kid who told you about the cows. Who's he?"

They'd reached the porch of the Schurs' house. The lamplight spilled out of the windows, showing him her skeptical eyes and the strand of hair, missed in her tidying, that fell onto her collarbone. He wanted to twine the strand around his finger, to learn if it was as smooth and silky as it looked.

Rachel said, "You must know he's my half brother. Most

of the people you met tonight made sure to mention that, I know."

"Yes. But sometimes asking the same question of different people leads to some interesting answers."

"That's a little unfair, isn't it?"

"No more than when you do it to your pupils."

"That's not the same! I have to find out what they know."

"So do I."

"You're impossible," she said, then looked past him as her attention was caught by something beyond him. Hal felt a bit nettled that Rachel didn't have her entire attention fixed on him alone. He looked in the same direction and saw a woman walking along, her hand groping the fence for guidance exactly as if she were blind.

"I'd better go help her."

"Who is it?"

"Mrs. Dale. She's a widow and the McGoverns' neighbor."

"Is she . . . blind?"

"She might as well be. She refuses to wear her glasses. Vanity, you know."

Before Rachel could step down, a man appeared out of the darkness beside the woman. He tipped his hat. Hal watched Mrs. Dale start when the man spoke to her.

Hal asked with a chuckle, "Does she talk to lightposts?"

"She would, if there were any. I think it's silly, but she seems to think that men won't look at her if she wears glasses."

"She may be right. Is she pretty?"

"Many think so," she answered, her voice tight. Then she said, with less restraint, "When I have to wear glasses, I'll wear them. Better that than to spoil your sight."

"*When* you wear them? Is it ordained that you will?"

"Probably. You've seen old-maid schoolteachers before. Crabby, gray-haired, with spectacles perched on the end of their noses after years of reading in the wrong light."

"Sounds like a dreadful future."

"On the contrary, I'm making it my life's goal."

Hal stepped up to share the stair she was on. The

lamplight showed him the sudden alarm in her eyes, close to his. Hal didn't touch her, not even a steadying hand at her waist.

"I've seen emeralds in golden settings," he said, keeping his voice low and even. "I've seen arboreal forests with the sunlight shifting down through the treetops and the deep green wave of the storm-tossed ocean rushing onto the shore. But never in all my life have I seen eyes with the green of all three together and lit by the light of a pure soul."

Her eyes were dazed as she blinked up at him, her smile gone away to nothing but a curving mouth fallen a little open. Her hands were clasped at her breast. Hal wondered if her lips could possibly be as sweet as they looked.

Rachel knew the only thing in the world that kept her from being kissed by Hal Sinclair was the creak as the gate at the bottom of the walk opened. He drew back and the drumming in her ears subsided. As he turned to face the people coming toward the house, she noticed that his smile seemed forced for the first time that night.

Somehow she gathered together the remnants of her wits in order to greet Mrs. Dale and the mayor. He guided the widow up the stairs, looking harrassed by the responsibility. Mrs. Dale peered around her to see who was speaking.

Rachel asked, "Have you met Mayor Gladd, Mr. Sinclair?"

"Of course we've met, little lady," Mr. Gladd said, beaming. "I've been hoping the paper would start up again. Need to know the news in my business. A flood somewhere or a drought can have quite an effect, don't you know."

"Yes, sir. You can rely on the *Herald*. The New York office has promised to put Brooklyn on the telegraph service and to arrange for me to receive the 'ready-print insides.' The front and back pages will be reserved for local news and advertisements. I'll hope to see your name there."

"That's fine, fine! I can get stock prices; it's the news that makes those prices that I need to see."

Mrs. Dale turned to Rachel. "It's so exciting to hear men talk business!" She had a high, fluttering voice so that her every word seemed to drift down from heaven on a feather.

"Yes. I think I'll go in. It's starting to get a little too cold."

Though Hal seemed to be listening to Mr. Gladd talk about the market, he turned his head to say, "I don't find it . . . cold, Miss Pridgeon."

"I do. And getting colder."

"I'll come with you," Mrs. Dale said. She started off with a confident step, came within an inch of crashing into the doorjamb, but corrected her steps at the last instant to go inside.

Rachel saw Sissie Albright sitting by herself on Mrs. Schur's prized fainting couch, ordered that spring in plush green velvet from Montgomery Wards. She hurried to sit beside her, feeling as though she'd reached a haven. "If you see Hal Sinclair come through that door," she whispered sharply, "start to talk to me like I'm telling you the most fascinating things in the world."

"Whatever for?"

"I don't want to talk to him again tonight."

"Your cheeks are red as roses, Rachel. What has been happening? Did he . . . make an advance?"

"No. Well, not exactly. I mean . . . he's outrageous. That's all. He's just outrageous."

Sissie leaned forward, her brown eyes snapping with excitement. "Outrageous? Everyone else is saying how pleasant he seems."

Rachel realized she was all but panting with indignation. She stopped herself, took a deep breath and let it out in a silent gust. Looking at her friend, she saw that Sissie didn't have to pretend to be enthralled. "Yes, he is pleasant. It's just the way he says things."

"Like what?"

"Nothing. I mean to say that sometimes he says something ordinary but the tone of his voice, something in the look in his eye . . . I can't explain it very well but it's very rude."

"I think he's fresh, but I like it. Oh, he's coming in now." She giggled.

"Keep talking, Sissie, and no matter what, don't leave me."

"Oh, it's all right," the other girl said, glancing with elaborate casualness toward the door. "He's gone to help Mrs. Dale with the refreshments. Golly, he is nice looking. I do like a man with a full head of hair."

As the man and woman passed the end of the fainting cough, Rachel heard Hal say, "That's a very interesting brooch you have on. Was it a gift?" Mrs. Dale began to talk of her late husband. Rachel realized he was hard at work.

Though she continued to speak to Sissie, she feared that her answers probably didn't make much sense. Not that it mattered; Sissie made up her own conclusions twice as fast as she could be given them. Rachel agreed with Sissie's repeated statement that Hal Sinclair was attractive. She also agreed that he seemed very clever too, and could make any woman laugh.

On her own, Rachel decided that he might make a good friend, once convinced that she didn't like or approve of his outlandish flirting. She'd continue to be calm, rational and unemotional. If he became too familiar, she'd put a stop to it at once, firmly but politely. Eventually, he'd understand that he didn't need to play the courtier where she was concerned, that friendship didn't require a steady stream of compliments or a display of insincere romance. It wouldn't be long before Hal could forget she was a woman and he a man; they'd be friends.

Glancing casually over her shoulder, Rachel saw that Hal was all but surrounded by ladies of the town. Some were laughing, others were looking up at him with slightly shocked eyes. He chucked Mrs. Schur under the chin and had Mrs. Jergens blushing like a schoolgirl. His voice rose above the chaos. "I'm sure there are no nicer women in the world than right here in Brooklyn. And none more charming."

Sissie also half turned around, sighed and said, "I wish all men knew how to talk like that."

At that moment, Rachel declared an iron-clad resolution: Never believe a word Hal Sinclair says.

5

$\mathcal{W}$HEN MARSHAL HUNNICUT asked if he could see her home, Sissie agreed, reluctantly. She had already refused to go on a drive with him, though she'd heard that he'd spent half the day polishing horse brasses. Some sixth sense told her that the marshal's recent shyness toward her combined with his noticeable attentions to her comfort meant that the moment she'd been dreading was quickly approaching.

On the one hand, she wanted to get the moment over with as quickly and painlessly as possible. On the other hand, there was something to be said for delaying the inevitable as long as humanly possible.

Sissie lived above her store in a tiny apartment that she treasured for its solitude. One of six children, she'd never had a bed all to herself before. Afraid that the peace of mind she found there would be spoiled by an emotional scene, she paused on the small porch of her establishment to take a deep breath of the cool evening air. A drift of chimney smoke lay like a hazy aura above the main street.

"It's starting to get nippy in the evenings," Benson said.

"Won't be long before the snow flies. I can't wait. I love snow." Sissie caught herself. Maybe it was not wise to speak of love just then. "Of course, I like this time of year real well. Everything's so crisp and clean-like."

"Sissie . . ."

"Not that I'm not real fond of spring and summer . . ."

"Sissie . . ." He cupped her elbow in his palm. She could feel the warmth of his hand. Quickly, she moved away. He said her name again, with more than a little confusion and reproach. Suddenly, with a flush of cowardice, she couldn't bear the thought of hearing that confusion turn to pain.

"Well, good night, Marshal. I've got to get up early tomorrow so I'll—"

"Not just yet. Please?"

For the first time in her life, Sissie understood the full meaning of "feet like lead." They felt that cold and heavy as she turned back toward Benson, a tall shadow on her porch. "Only for a moment, then."

"Sissie, I've got a little money put by and one thing about the law, it's steady work. You wouldn't ever want for anything that you needed and by and by we could manage the things you want as well."

"Benson . . ." She'd never used his Christian name before. She wished she could summon up enough pride to call him Marshal now, coldly and formally. Maybe that would stop him.

His voice deepened, husky with the need to get it right. "I'm older than you, of course . . . I guess it must be by fifteen years. Do you remember the first time we met? I bet you don't."

"Yes, I do. You'd just arrested my father."

"Drunk and disorderly," he said. "I didn't know any better than to pick him up then. I'd only been here a couple of weeks. I saw you in the back of the wagon when your mama came to get him. You were just a little bit of a thing, all tangled black hair and big eyes. I remember thinking you'd be pretty if you were cleaned up and . . ." He laughed softly. "You sure did."

Sissie remembered that day. The sun had been blazing hot, dazzling her eyes that had wanted to see everything in the town that she'd hardly ever stepped foot in. She remembered thinking that the new marshal was a giant, the tallest man she'd ever seen. She had wondered if he ate little girls for breakfast and had kept a wary eye on him just in case. She hadn't known then that he had a heart just as soft as butter.

Benson took her hand in his, rubbing his thumb nervously over the back of it. Sissie let it stay in his grasp, not resisting, the only consolation she could give him. Serious again, he said, "Sissie, do you think . . ." His voice broke a little and he cleared his throat. Then, slowly, as though he weighed each word as he spoke it, he said, "I want to marry you more than I've ever wanted anything in my life. Will you be my wife?"

She tried to withdraw her hand. His fingers tightened for an instant, then he released her. "Oh," he said. The sound hung between them, then silence rushed in like a tide to separate them. She felt as though she were standing over his body, as though she had killed him without a word of explanation.

Sissie put her hand to her cheek when the first tear dripped onto her blouse. She hadn't even known she was crying. Then she heard a breath catch like a sob, only it wasn't hers.

"Oh, please," she said, reaching out to the shadow that was Benson Hunnicut. "Please don't. I . . . it's not you. I don't want to marry anyone, ever. I just couldn't."

"I know I'm not what a girl dreams of for a husband. . . ."

"But you are, Benson. There's a dozen girls in this town who sigh over you. I can give you their names. Any one of them would be thrilled—"

"I don't want them. I want you." He caught her hand again, but it wasn't enough. He seized her by the waist with both hands, pulling her close, bridging the cold distance. "I can't help it. I love you."

For one instant, Sissie stood still under his kiss, fighting down the wildness that wanted to break free. She hadn't known until then how much she'd wanted him to kiss her, to have his strong hands holding her hard against him. But if she lost her head now, if she gave him back even one of the fervent kisses he pressed to her lips, then she'd be a fool forever.

She wouldn't have believed it would take so much strength to push him away. Turning her back on him, she wrapped her arms around herself, wanting to hold on to his warmth for just one more second while she refused him finally and for always.

This time he listened while she told him that she would not marry him. Quickly, her voice breaking with her heart, Sissie reassured him that there wasn't anyone else.

"Then there's still hope for me? I mean, if there's no one else you care for like that?"

"No, Benson. I'm not going to marry anyone. Not you. Not anyone. Not ever."

"But—"

"Please." She wished that she could be angry with him. All she could bring herself to say was, "I'm tired."

His footsteps dragged away. Sissie counted them with her heartbeats. He stopped. At his first word, she could tell that his eyes were as full of tears as her own. "You've made sure we're both going to be lonely for the rest of our days, Sissie. I'm near forty years old. I've never found any woman but you I want to marry. I don't think I ever will now."

"No, Benson!" She turned and ran down the steps between them. "No, you must find someone. Really, there's many girls . . . Barbara Lane, Annie Strecklow . . . Or Mrs. Dale—she's a widow and perfectly charming; you know she is. Any one of them would be so proud and pleased to have you for their husband."

"Let's not talk about it. I've said all I mean to." He started away.

She called to him as he reached the path. The light was

stronger there and she could see the defeated slope of his shoulders. The sight seemed to catch her heart and twist it. The pain was just that real. "Benson, please don't let this . . . I still want . . . I need your friendship."

"You'll always have that, Sissie," he said without turning. "And the rest will be waiting for you, when you need that too."

He walked on.

Sissie slumped against the porch post, all the strength running out of her like water from a broken jug. If only she could believe that he meant it. If she lost his friendship because of this, she'd never forgive either of them.

Rachel finally captured Lyle before she started for home. She'd had to all but dig a tiger pit to do it, but she secured her brother's escort. "I was counting on you to go with me tonight," she said, trying to allow no more than a hint of reproach in her tone. "You promised you would."

"I met some fellers," he said, giving a sudden wriggle like a not-quite dead fish.

Rachel only tightened her grip. How many women had heard that excuse from the man in their life? "I met some fellers who wanted: One—to run me for governor. Two—to go to the saloon for a couple of rounds. Three—to rob a train." Her father had been notoriously famous for excuse number three. But they all meant that some woman waited while her man did more "important " things than whatever she'd asked him to do.

"A gentleman would do what a lady asked him first, Lyle. And if he couldn't make it, he should apologize to her."

"Sorry," he muttered.

"You will notice that I haven't asked you whether you put the cows in the cemetery. I think it would be very nice of you to admit it without my asking."

"No, honest. I didn't have nothing to do with it."

"'I didn't have *anything* to do with it.'"

"Golly, I know *you* didn't. 'Cause the fellers . . ." He shut his mouth so tight that white dots stood out on either side.

"You tell the 'fellers' that if they were trying to disrupt Mrs. Schur's party, they didn't. We all had a very nice time, even if we did have to chase cows in our good clothes."

"I heard Mr. Hudson done stepped in a cow pie," Lyle said, giggling at the perfect humor of it.

"I know Ed Greely did."

"Shoot, that don't matter. He's a farmer—he's always stepping in something! But Mr. Hudson's so fancy. The only thing as would've been better would've been that damn-fool Dorothy stepping in it. Can that gal holler!"

Rachel gave the thin arm she held a shake. "Speak respectfully of Dorothy Schur, Lyle. She's older than you are, a lady, and soon to be married. She deserves your respect."

"She's still a couple ears short of a corn crib."

"What's that?"

"Nuthin'."

"That's what I thought. Don't let Mr. Greely catch you talking that way about her. He's already promised to give you a hiding if he catches you around his orchard again."

"What's he want with all them apples? He's got acres of 'em. Ain't likely he'd miss just one or two or six."

"He gives us plenty. The one you had at supper came from his trees."

"They just taste better if'n they're stolen."

Rachel resolved not to read *The Adventures of Huckleberry Finn* to Lyle. They already had far too much in common philosophically, not to mention the fact that both of their fathers came to a bad end. She reached out to brush Lyle's hair off his forehead, though she kept her grip on his arm despite the tender feelings in her heart. She missed her father—the laughing, loving man who had seemed bigger than any problem a beloved daughter could bring to him—and could only imagine that Lyle missed him even more.

She'd always known about her father's "profession." It had been an accepted part of her life. Even his occasional longer absence in jails—until the gang could break him out again—had been understandable. Some men toured the country selling wholesale goods, ribbons, liquor and the like; some men went to jail.

Rachel understood now that this easy acceptance had been the biggest reason her stepmother had wanted her son raised away from the influence of the Delmon Gang. Law and order should not be so easily ignored or so easily forgotten.

Maybe it was too late for Lyle, she thought later, listening to him slosh water around in the bathtub she'd dragged into the kitchen. Certainly not even the kindly authority of Marshal Hunnicut had succeeded in entirely erasing Lyle's reckless and even lawless ways. Some nights, she'd lay awake for hours, worrying about his future, only to go on in the morning with her resolve strengthened. She'd save him yet for a respectable, decent life.

Lyle came out ten minutes after he'd gone into the water, rubbing his head with a towel and looking consciously virtuous as he clutched another towel around his skinny waist. Rachel held him still while she performed an inspection.

"Lyle," she said with a resigned sigh. "There's enough soil behind your ears to fill a wheelbarrow. And look at your nails."

He inspected the black half-moons with an expression of amazement. "I did clean 'em," he said. "Guess it's stained right in to the skin. Blackberry juice does that. I found a whole bush of 'em that ain't been picked over yet. If you want, I can show you—"

"Don't change the subject. Use the nail brush on your fingers. You might take it to your elbows and knees while you're at it. When are you going to learn that it's quicker to do it right the first time?"

He shrugged, patiently resigned to submitting to her foolish notions about cleanliness and godliness. Rachel passed over most of the other black marks on his skin as bruises resulting from his heedless methods of travel. He'd also all but ripped the nail of his big toe off, not to mention sundry scrapes on his knees.

She sent him back to the kitchen with a swat on his

towel-swathed rear. He'd no sooner reached the doorway when someone knocked furiously on the front door.

Rachel said, "Who could that be this time of night?"

"I'm guessing it's Miss Sissie."

"Sissie? Never at this hour . . ."

"I bet she's come to tell you she's thrown over the marshal. Golly, and I thought Dorothy was chuckleheaded."

"Did the marshal tell *you* he was going to propose?" Rachel asked, so taken up by wonder that she neglected to chide him for disrespect.

"He didn't have to tell me, just like I don't gotta be told she turned him down."

Rachel gazed in puzzled wonder at her young brother before the renewed knocking at the door called her away. "Who is it?" she called.

"It's me. Sissie."

When Rachel opened the door, her friend stumbled in, her blue woolen cloak clutched about her as though the night were blowing a frigid storm rather than a mildly cool breeze. Rachel put her arm about her friend's waist and guided her to a chair in the kitchen, ignoring Lyle's protests of invaded privacy.

"What's wrong? Here, sit near the stove," she said, feeling the shivers wrack Sissie's slender frame. "Let me make you some tea."

"Yes. Yes, please." Sissie pushed the hair off her forehead. She gazed about her for an instant, as though unsure of her surroundings. Then she caught her breath on a painful sigh, tugged a handkerchief from her pocket and began to cry into it with bitter sobs.

Rachel glanced over her shoulder at Lyle. He hadn't yet resubmerged himself into the tub but had been amusing himself by floating bits of kindling on the surface. "Get along to bed, Lyle. Now, Lyle!"

"But my bath . . . ?" he asked with a sideways glance.

"You should have thought of that sooner. Go on. Miss Albright's upset."

Lyle grinned all over his wry little face at the thought of skipping his bath. Her next words wiped the smile off, as

though she'd passed the chalkboard rag over a drawing.
"You can finish it in the morning."

"But it'll be cold!"

"Get along, Lyle." Rachel gave him a warning glance and
he shuffled out. She wished she could be sure he'd not
stopped to listen at the door. Lyle tended to know things that
others would rather keep a secret. She'd never actually
caught him eavesdropping, but how else would a young boy
know so much of what went on in the private hearts of
Brooklyn's people?

Rachel fished in her pocket for a clean handkerchief and
gave it, without a word, to Sissie. She poked up the fire in
one of the burner compartments of the stove and set the
kettle on over the open-work ring. Mrs. Schur had sent her
home with half a cocoa cake. Rachel cut two slices, leaving
enough behind to appease Lyle during his inevitable two
A.M. raid on the kitchen.

While the tea steeped, Rachel laid out everything on the
table. She had only plain napkins and plates, no "best" china
or fine linen, but everything here was hers, bought and paid
for. She could be satisfied that at least her good fortune had
been no one else's ill fortune. No one had a gun stuck in his
face for *these* dishes.

"Come and eat, dear; you'll feel better."

Sissie raised her head from her hands, her pretty eyes
swollen and red. "What am I going to do?"

"Eat cake. Drink tea. Tell me what is the matter."

"It's Benson. Oh, I didn't know it would feel like this!"

"What would?"

"Turning him down." She sniffed, turning her handkerchief in her hands to find a dry spot. "He asked me to marry
him. Oh, I *wish* I could!"

Rachel pushed a mug of hot tea along the scarred surface
of the old milk-painted table. "Here. Drink it up."

The other girl clutched the earthenware, leaning over it as
if it were a campfire. "What am I going to do?" she asked
again.

"When did he propose?"

"You don't sound the least bit surprised," Sissie exclaimed, her head snapping up.

"Lyle suggested that it might be the problem."

"Did Benson tell *him*?"

"I don't think so. But you know what Lyle's like. It's as if he had a telegraph wire connected to everyone in town."

"No, you're right. Benson wouldn't say anything to a little boy."

"Of course," Rachel said, pursuing her own thoughts for a moment, "they did spend most of today together. If the marshal seemed unusual, it wouldn't take much for Lyle to guess." She caught her friend's questioning look and added, apologetically, "Everyone in town knows Benson Hunnicut's wild about you. I hadn't been here two whole days before I heard the entire story from Mrs. Schur."

"Well, they'll have lots more to talk about tomorrow. There's no way to keep it a secret, not when he won't be coming around any . . . any . . ."

Quickly, Rachel pushed the plate into Sissie's hand. "Eat that," she ordered. "You can't eat Mrs. Schur's cake and cry. It's against all nature. Besides, salt wouldn't taste good on it at all."

Though Sissie didn't smile at her wit, at least she didn't drop any tears into the cake. After two bites, however, she put it on the table. "My stomach hurts."

"I guess that's understandable."

"And he was so sweet about it!" Sissie suddenly exclaimed. "He couldn't have been any more sincere. He said . . ."

"Don't tell me," Rachel said, not unkindly. "He meant whatever he said for your ears only."

"Yes." Sissie's sigh was nearly a moan of pain. This time, not even the swirl of dark chocolate icing on top of the cake could prevent an overflow of tears. Rachel felt ashamed of herself for even attempting such a distraction. She turned her head, unable to watch her friend's abject misery.

After a moment of listening in unbearable silence, she rose to her feet. "I'll get you another handkerchief."

As she passed down the narrow hall to the stairs, she saw

a light cross the window in the front. She froze, thinking of the gun all the way upstairs. Dashing noiselessly forward, she flattened herself against the wall. She listened hard for the sound of voices. The soft knock at the window beside her made her heart spring like a frightened doe.

"Miss Rachel?"

She glanced down to see the marshal's face, weirdly lit from below by the lantern he carried. Feeling more than a little embarrassed—how much of her strange behavior had he seen?—she knelt down to work the window catch, wondering if she'd ever get over her fears of being found.

He watched the window go up and then whispered, "Is Miss Sissie with you, ma'am?"

"Yes, Marshal, she is," Rachel answered, pitching her voice to a whisper.

"Thank goodness. I went back over there and found she'd gone. I reckon . . . I reckon she's telling you all about it?" Rachel nodded dumbly. Even in the softness of the lantern light, she seemed to see new lines carved in his rugged face. She was amazed again by how much sorrow could be compressed into half an hour.

Marshal Hunnicut said, communicating his desperation despite his forced whisper, "If only you'd find out *why*, ma'am! She wouldn't even tell me *why*, only that she wouldn't." He closed his eyes and swayed like a big tree in a strong wind.

Though Rachel felt deeply sorry for the lover, she had to say, "I can't force her confidence, Marshal. And I couldn't tell you even if she told me herself."

"I'm not asking for you to tell me the reason," he said. "But you've got a good head on your shoulders, Miss Rachel. All I'm asking is for you to tell me whether or not it's a sound reason. Just come to me and say yes or no. I'll understand. If it's sound, then I'll try to forget about the whole thing. But if it's not . . . Oh, God, why won't she have me?" His voice had begun to rise.

Though Rachel felt sure Sissie wouldn't hear anything over her own unhappiness, her house was not very solidly built. She put her hand over the marshal's where it gripped the sill and said, "Hush! I'll tell you what you want to know, as soon as I can. I'll tell you yes or no."

"Thank you," he said, his hand turning under hers. It felt hot and dry. "I know you're her friend. And mine."

"You'd better go, Marshal."

"Is she in the kitchen?" he asked, turning his eyes that way. Rachel felt as if the man's whole soul strained toward Sissie, the way a compass needle fights to find the north. "Maybe if I talk to her again . . ."

"She's too upset," Rachel said. "You'd better go."

"What? She's upset?" His eyes lit with hope and his voice raced with eagerness. "You mean she regrets it? Maybe I ought to ask her again?"

She dragged her hand free and reached for the window sash. "I wouldn't tonight, if I were you. She's in no shape to listen and she'd only turn you down again. I guess you've heard enough of that for one evening."

"Yes, ma'am." He looked as forlorn as a puppy in a snowstorm as she brought the window down. Rachel felt prickly with guilt at having to shut him out. He should realize, however, that he'd do himself no good at all by forcing the issue tonight. Sissie would just refuse to listen to a word.

Rachel checked on Lyle when she went upstairs after the handkerchief. He slept with his arms thrown carelessly above his head, shadows deep beneath his eyes. She stood and watched him for a moment in the light of the single candle that she'd picked up off the hall table. With his lids closed over his quick-flashing eyes and his smart mouth relaxed, he looked like the little boy he was, his innocence returned for a few hours. She wondered what he dreamed of.

When she returned to the kitchen, she found Sissie drying her face on a dish towel. "I'm better now," she said, answering Rachel's query. "I . . . I'm sorry to be such a fool!"

"Are you a fool?" Rachel asked, filling her cup.

"It's foolish to weep over a man, isn't it? I always swore no man would ever make me cry and here I am, leaking like a gutter, over Benson Hunnicut of all people!"

Rachel could remember hearing her stepmother saying, "Love is watered with tears." However, she didn't think now was the right time to quote her. She said instead, "I wonder why the marshal decided to ask you tonight?"

"Who can guess? Maybe because the season for crime is over and he can relax for a while."

"I didn't realize crime went in cycles." In Arizona, she reflected, the only time her father's gang wasn't busy was during the brief rainy season. For the rest of the year, as long as trains and stagecoaches ran regular routes, they kept busy.

"There's always less for him to do in the wintertime." Sissie shook herself all over as though trying to be rid of a spiderweb. "What does it matter? I don't care what he does or when. Oh, why do men have to complicate everything with love?"

"It's funny. I don't think of men as the more romantic of the sexes."

"Oh, but they are!" She sniffed twice and blew her nose on the first hankie. "They are. Only a man would try to turn friendship into something else. Did I ever give him any hint I was looking for more? No. Did I ever flirt with him? No."

"Well, now . . ."

"I *didn't*. Not really."

Thinking of Hal Sinclair's incessant flirting, Rachel relented. "No, I don't suppose you did. Not really."

"No, I should say not. Did I ever give Benson Hunnicut the slightest encouragement to propose to me? No. Definitely no. Yet he decides out of the blue that he's in love with me and wants to marry me. He said . . . he said . . . such beautiful things."

Rachel handed Sissie the second handkerchief she'd brought down. Sissie's own handkerchief, a damp rag on the table, she spread over the stove handle to dry. She had a feeling Sissie was going to be needing it.

With this flood of tears had subsided, Rachel pushed the teacup, refilled, into her friend's hands. She asked, "Do you want to tell me why you can't marry him? He is some few years older than you. . . ."

"It isn't that. What would I do with a man *my* age? Besides, I've known 'em all since school and there isn't a one of 'em I'd give the time of day to."

"Did you tell me about all the nice young men in town and how I should find one for myself?"

A tiny smile slipped onto Sissie's lips. "You ought to know that a body gives different advice to her friends than she takes for herself. Besides, you *haven't* known them all forever. There's always a chance one of them will take your fancy and you won't hear a word against him from me!"

"Thank you; I'll remember that. But about the marshal . . ."

The smile trembled and died away. "Do you know what he reminded me of, this evening? Of the first time we'd met. Do you know how I first met the marshal?" She didn't wait for Rachel to shake her head. "He'd just arrested my father."

"Your father?" Rachel tried to remember ever hearing of a rogue named Albright. Of course, Sissie could have changed her last name, just as Rachel had exchanged Delmon for Pridgeon.

In a small, shamed voice, Sissie said, "He was the town drunk."

"Oh, my dear . . ." Rachel said sadly. She was glad to realize, however, that gossip in Brooklyn had its limits. Though she'd heard all about Sissie's relationship with the marshal, complete with attendant guesses about the probable date on which the pretty young milliner would finally give in, no one had ever said a word about her father's habits.

Sissie tossed her head, pride hardening her features. "Our marshal before Benson never used to bother to arrest him. It didn't taken Benson long to realize that there was no point in putting him in jail until he sobered up because as soon as he was free he'd be right back in the saloon. I don't know how my mother stood it."

"And you won't marry Benson because he arrested your father?"

"No, not because . . . I had a brother and sister, too. Will started drinking too, when he was just a kid. He fell off his horse into about two inches of water and drowned. He was seventeen. That sobered Father up for all of about a week. Nancy took off 'round then. Last we heard, she was working in a dance hall somewhere out West and we've never heard from her since, but I don't imagine she's become a nun in the meantime, do you?"

"And your mother?" Rachel asked after a moment.

The angry flame that had dried Sissie's tears went out. "I don't know how she stood it. She just went on working and slaving. When Father died . . . has it been four years already? When he died, she just wound down like a . . . like a clockwork toy. I tried to make things easier for her; we moved into town and I started working but she just laid down and died. I tried . . . I tried. . . ."

Rachel couldn't stand it any longer. She came around the table and knelt beside her friend. Reaching up, she put her arms around Sissie's waist. It felt just as if she'd put her arms around the wooden Indian in front of the General Store. "Don't think about it now. Don't think about any of it. Do you want to sleep here tonight?"

Sissie nodded, as if her head had grown too heavy for her neck. Rachel stood up, helping Sissie to her feet. "It'll be all right," she said soothingly, talking the same optimistic nothings that she'd used when Lyle hurt himself as a toddler. "You'll sleep and things will look so much brighter in the morning."

Rachel loaned Sissie her second nightdress and helped her into it. The smaller girl seemed to be dazed, her eyes blank. "There now," Rachel said, helping her under the covers. "I'll fill up the hot-water bottle and be right back."

Sissie turned her head on the pillow, her hair flowing over the white case in smooth, dark ripples. "I can't marry him, knowing I could give in to it at any time, can I? What kind of wife would I make, when the thirst might come on me at any time?"

"Just sleep now, Sissie. I'll leave the candle right here in the hall."

When she brought up the hot-water bottle, Sissie's eyes had closed. Though Rachel did not believe she was asleep, her breathing still catching and hurrying, she didn't say anything.

Rachel usually sat up late. She liked to read while the world went dreaming by, enjoying the sensation that hers was the only light burning for miles. Also, though she rarely admitted it even to herself, to sleep meant to be defenseless. Anyone could sneak up on a sleeping person.

Tonight, however, Rachel did not enjoy being the only one awake. It felt lonely, even though both the beds upstairs were full. She couldn't concentrate on *Uncle Tom's Cabin*, even though she'd come to the most exciting part—Eliza's escape. She'd never had the opportunity to read it through before let alone have enough understanding of it to make up questions for her students. Yet it was said to be the district school inspector's favorite book. He was fond of buttonholing students in order to ask searching questions about Topsy, Little Eva and Simon Legree. If he wasn't satisfied with the answers, he could send in a ruthless report on the quality of teaching in Brooklyn.

Suddenly eager for a breath of air, Rachel wrapped herself in Sissie's cloak and stepped onto the tiny front porch. Overhead, breaking clouds, only just lighter than the surrounding night, hastened away with vast, silent speed. The rustling trees by the churchyard seemed to only intensify the silence. Rachel had no idea what time it was but if she walked out into the street she could see the depot clock. Having excellent sight, sometimes she could manage to distinguish the position of the black hands against the white face.

The whole length of the street, from the church to the depot, was lightless, except for one square window. A window where the curtains must have parted just enough to let this one streak of light escape. Rachel had spent only five minutes this evening with Mrs. Jergens, but she'd learned in less time than that the fact that her star boarder had been given the best room in the boardinghouse. Hal Sinclair must be a night-lover too.

6

$\mathcal{R}$ACHEL AWOKE TO the echo of a sound heard in her dreams. She sat up, wincing in pain at the crick in her neck from sleeping with the crown of her head wedged into the corner of the too-short sofa in the parlor. She blinked down at herself, her best dress sadly crushed, her stocking feet peeping from beneath the crumpled hem.

She pressed the heels of her hands lightly against her closed eyes, remembering. Last night, she'd gone up to her room only to find Sissie sprawled at an angle across the bed. It had seemed simpler at the time to stretch out, so to speak, on the sofa. The knitted comforter that she'd pulled over herself lay on the floor. Was that why she'd dreamed of leaping over ice floes—because she'd been chilled? Or was it a remnant of *Uncle Tom's Cabin*?

Feeling about two thousand years old, Rachel stood up only to crumple a moment later because her left leg was still asleep. She grimaced as pins and needles tormented her.

Around her, the house sat silently, waiting for the daylight to grow stronger before it awakened. Lyle and Sissie must still be sleeping. She'd make up some flapjack batter to feed them—it was cheap and filling. She even had some blackberry jam from August, the very first she'd ever made. It had actually turned out to be edible, surprising her, for it had looked to be so difficult when Mrs. McLean had made orange marmalade.

After the batter was made and the griddle left to heat, Rachel sat down at the table and drew forward a blank sheet of paper. She had not written the McLeans in some months, leaving her feeling wretchedly ungrateful. Everything she had, everything she'd become, she owed in large part to the quiet missionaries in California. When she'd run away from Arizona, five-year-old Lyle in tow, it would have been so easy to go astray. The McLeans had saved her from dire fates, completed the education begun by a stolen encyclopedia and arranged for her to find a new life under a new name.

She had just begun to write to them about Lyle when she heard a door slam upstairs and the rattle of hasty feet on the stairs. Standing, she sent to the doorway between the kitchen and the hall to whisper loudly, "Lyle, don't wake . . ."

Sissie stood in the hall, still in her petticoats, her hair spiky and her eyes rolling. "I just woke up and I . . . I found this. . . ."

As if it were a dead rat, she held Rachel's pistol in cringing fingertips. Sissie's teeth chattered as she forced out another few words. "It was under your pillow. I put my hand under and I . . . touched it. . . ."

Afraid it would go off if it hit the floor, Rachel walked up and calmly relieved her friend of the black gun. She checked the safety with an automatic flick of her eyes. Ashamed of how comfortable the slightly oily metal felt in her hands, Rachel hid the weapon behind her back. The sight of it seemed to both fascinate and repel Sissie.

"It's all right," she said, somewhat lamely. "I keep it for protection."

"Pro-protection?"

"A woman alone . . ." Rachel said, letting her voice trail off, not wanting to give some complicated explanation.

"Can you shoot it?" Some of the color crept back into Sissie's too-pale cheeks.

"It wouldn't be much good if I couldn't."

"No. Can you teach me?"

"You?"

Sissie nodded. "I've been thinking about it."

"But you . . . you seemed so frightened of it."

"Of course I'm frightened. I hate loud noises and besides, it's not something you *expect* to find in your bed when you first wake up." She paused. "Well, obviously you do, but I don't!"

"I'm sorry you were startled," Rachel said. "I didn't even think about this last night or I would have taken it with me. I'll put it away."

"I'm very serious about learning to shoot a gun," Sissie said, following her own thoughts. "I agree with you about a woman living alone without . . ." She drew a deep breath. "Not that a husband's much help from what I hear. Most times a woman has to kick him out of bed if she hears a strange noise. Now, if I had a gun . . ."

"You can't just shoot out of the window every time you heard a cat yowl. You'd wake the neighbors." Keeping the gun behind her, Rachel asked, "Do you want flapjacks for breakfast?"

"You don't have to feed me," Sissie protested. "It's bad enough I stole your bed." She grew earnest. "I want to thank you, Rachel. I needed to talk to someone and I like you. You don't try to convince anyone of what they should do 'for their own good.' How I hate that phrase!"

Rachel just said, "Help yourself to the flapjacks."

She put the gun in the top drawer of her bureau and glanced at herself in the cracked mirror. *"Teaching her to shoot might make folks ask how you got to be so handy with a shooting iron. I don't think you dare risk it, but how to keep Sissie from talking?"* Even as she turned away, she felt an inner certainty that she'd shortly be showing the town milliner how to blaze away at tin cans.

Lyle's bed was not only empty, but cold. Rachel had noticed not only that both pieces of cake were missing this morning but also that the pyramid of apples she'd carefully constructed had become seriously lopsided. Rachel knew the signs. Lyle had taken at least half a dozen apples, supply enough to sustain him for the entire day. She supposed it was a good sign that he'd taken these apples instead of stealing them from a neighbor. If only she didn't feel that she had somehow failed him by letting him run so wild.

Sissie, who showed a remarkable talent for changing the subject whenever they came too close to talking about Benson Hunnicut, got dressed after the flapjacks and went to work. The two young ladies had put their heads together over breakfast and created a story about a long-cherished plan for Sissie to spend the night at Rachel's the night of the welcome party.

Let those of little imagination decide that a long night of giggling chatter had brought up dark circles beneath Sissie's usually dazzling eyes. There were not many people without imagination in Brooklyn. Whatever was unknown about the marshal's heartache would be invented, and the bare facts would be dressed in wonderful, invisible cloth.

Rachel had never respected her friend more than when she adjusted her borrowed hat to a more becoming angle and set off for her little store. It was as though she watched a frail ship set off, steering straight for a stormy horizon.

In a way, Rachel could be glad that Lyle had chosen today to try one of his disappearing acts. Once the stove cooled, she'd have to embark on emptying out the clinkers and ashes, one of the messiest and most tiresome jobs a housewife had to face. She tied up her hair in an old rag and put on her most frequently darned dress before going downstairs again.

She dragged out on to the back porch two old chairs that Mrs. Dale had given her when her new furniture had come. A few minutes with a borrowed saw had evened out the legs. Now Rachel thought she'd paint them while she waited for the stove to cool.

She indulged herself with a tuneless whistle as she

slapped on white paint. Trying to get the paint on the turned legs, she sprinkled her face with a carelessly flaring brush, giving herself a spattering of white freckles. Once she dropped the loaded brush, leaving a wet splotch on her apron. But the sun beat down warmly while she worked and a fresh breeze carried away all smell of paint.

However, she felt the sting of her deplorable appearance when a pair of highly polished brown boots came around the corner of the back porch. She raised her gaze over neatly ironed trousers, a well-fitted coat over a crisp white shirt, feeling more and more grubby with every passing second. However, when she looked full into Hal Sinclair's face, her spine stiffening, what she saw there changed her pique into warm sympathy. With his bloodshot eyes and the mouth that repeated licking of his lips did nothing to moisten, Rachel realized that compared with Hal, she was in perfect condition.

"What happened to you?" she asked, never wondering whether she had the right to ask.

"Your town marshal," he said, his voice rough. "Do you have any coffee . . . any *quiet* coffee?"

"The boardinghouse too noisy for you?" He nodded, groaned and seemed almost ready to clutch at his head, which must have been giving every signal of toppling. He forced his hand down, though he stood there blinking like a daylight-struck owl. She took pity on him. "I'm sorry; I only have tea."

"Tea will be fine . . . fine."

He sank heavily into one of the kitchen chairs while she drained off some hot water from the stove reservoir. Then she poked more wood into the stove and set the kettle on. "It'll only be a minute or two," she said, wiping her hands.

"Thanks. You may be saving my life."

"How did you get into this condition?"

He was pressing his hand against his forehead as if testing his temperature. He peered at her from under the strong-looking fingers. "I'd only been back in my room for about ten minutes last night when your marshal knocked on my door. The first words he said were, 'Did you bring any drinking liquor here from New York?' "

"Oh," Rachel said, with understanding.

"At first, I thought he was asking for legal reasons. I noticed that your saloon is closed and had assumed that the town is dry."

"All but dry. A few folks still prefer Grandma's squeezings when they can get them."

"Well, your marshal wanted something a tad more professional. As it happened, I had a bottle of . . . ahem . . . Grandpa's favorite along with me."

"Whisky?"

"Straight off the boat from the land of peat and clear-running burns . . . sometimes including the poet."

" 'Wee timorous beastie'?" she hazarded.

He nodded and groaned, squeezing his eyes shut. "Don't let me do that again. Anyway, we polished off the bottle at about two o'clock in the morning. Then he wended his way home and I collapsed onto the early medieval torture device Mrs. Jergens claims is my bed."

"I would have thought you'd still be in it. What are you doing here, Mr. Sinclair?"

The kettle whistled with a piercing shriek. Hal shuddered, moaned and laid his hand on the table, crossing his arms over the back of his skull. Moving as quickly as a leaping doe, Rachel snatched the kettle off the stove, using a corner of her apron to protect her fingers. She poured the boiling water into the teapot, whose glaze was crazed though the pot didn't leak. With a glance at the suffering man, she added another teaspoon of tea to the pot. Hot, sweet and strong ought to make him feel better.

He opened one eye as she put the mug beside him. "Bless you," he murmured.

Rachel sipped at her cup and watched in amazement over the rim as he gulped down the scalding-hot liquid. "Doesn't that hurt?" she asked.

The tea seemed to have revived him. Some color had returned to his face. "There isn't much leisure in my life. If I don't drink and eat as soon as I get served, it never fails that I have to leave my meal to go cover a story. Most newspapermen can drink very hot drinks; usually they can drink other people under the table as well."

"Not you?"

"Your marshal must have a cast-iron stomach. . . . I beg your pardon."

"I live with a seven-year-old boy, Mr. Sinclair," she declared with a proud toss of her head. "I'm familiar with much worse things than stomachs. And please stop calling him 'my marshal.' He isn't mine."

"I know that. After you've stayed drinking with a man for four-and-a-half hours, there's little you don't know about him."

"He told you about . . ." She remembered in time that Mr. Sinclair could charm information out of a dead coyote and clamped her lips together before Sissie's name could escape.

"The reason I'm here is your . . . Marshal Hunnicut made me swear on my mother's grave that I'd come here first thing in the morning and find out Miss Sissie's reason for turning him down."

"I can't . . . You promised him that last night? And you're here this morning?"

"Yes," he said, sitting there looking as pale as a newly risen ghost. "I wish you would tell me so I can go back to bed."

"You kept your promise?"

"Naturally. Always keep a promise to a man who carries a gun, Miss Pridgeon. That's advice that I heard once from a man who ought to know. I offer it to you free of charge, which is something less than I paid for it."

Looking at him wonderingly, she refilled his cup and put forward a hesitant offer of a pancake. His shudder and the instant return of a tinge of pea-green in his complexion made her withdraw the suggestion.

She supposed no man could look cocksure after a night's drinking with a heartbroken marshal. Certainly a lot of Mr. Sinclair's brashness had evaporated. He hadn't even tried to flirt with her. Rachel found herself liking him more than she would have dreamed possible yesterday.

"I wish I could help Marshal Hunnicut," Rachel said. "But I can't betray Sissie's confidence. I can't tell him the reason she won't marry him. That's something he'll have to find out for himself."

"He wants to know if it's a good reason."

"How can I tell? It sounds reasonable to me, but it might not seem that way to him."

"Just between you and me," Hal said, leaning forward, a lock of black hair falling onto his brow, "no reason, short of Miss Sissie's taking the veil, would satisfy the marshal. I've seen many men decided on a course of matrimony, but never one as determined to commit that mistake as your . . . I beg your pardon . . . as Miss Sissie's marshal. I was glad I'd only brought the one bottle along. I hate to see a man cry and he was on the verge of crying when he left."

Though his tone remained light, there was no sparkle in his deep blue eyes. Rachel wondered how far Hal Sinclair's sympathy went. His concern certainly *seemed* real.

She said, "I'm sorry for the marshal. It must be very hard being in love like that. I hope . . ."

"You hope?" His smile seemed dry, as though he wanted to smile at her expense. "Let me guess. You hope one day some man will feel that strongly about you."

"Well, that would be nice," she admitted, "but that wasn't what I was going to say. I was going to say that I hope I never get it that bad for someone. A man could trample your heart into the dirt so easily if you gave it over to him like that."

"Do you think Marshal Hunnicut might have his trampled by Miss Sissie?"

The paint 'freckles' on her nose had begun to dry. They tightened and she put up her hand to rub them. His eyes moved with her hand. He smiled at her, not as he'd smiled at her yesterday, not as if he were planning how to charm her, just another woman among thousands. He smiled at her as though she charmed *him*. "I'm sorry to interrupt what you were doing. If it's any consolation, I think your tea saved my life."

"You do look better." She peered more closely. "Did you shave?"

Quickly, he ran his fingertips over his mustache. "Don't scare me like that! I was so dull-witted this morning I could have shaved it off and not noticed."

"I like it," she said after a moment's consideration. "I'm not much for mustaches as a rule . . . especially the big, fluffy, soup-strainer kind. But I like yours."

"Thank you. I don't like soup-strainers either. They tickle. Or so I've been told."

"Yes, they do," she said. When he raised one eyebrow in a silent question, she retorted, "My father had one!"

"What was he like?"

"My father?" She thought of all the lies she'd practiced, the stories she'd told inquiring minds. Instead of choosing to tell about her fictional father's fruitless search for gold in the Superstition Mountains, she said, "I think he tried to be a good father. He liked to have a good time and as long as things went his way, he *was* a good father. When things went wrong, he was apt to walk away. My older brother worshiped him."

"Did you?"

"For a long time I did. But people change, don't they?"

He sighed as if at a memory. "They do."

If someone had foretold to her yesterday that she would spend a good hour just talking with Hal Sinclair after only knowing him—and not liking him—for twenty-four hours, she would have laughed in their face. Yet, when she glanced at the clock with the dented face, an hour had passed. Her teapot was empty and his color had come back.

"Are you sure you wouldn't like a pancake? It won't take but a minute."

He looked past her, with a look in his eye that told her he was gauging his condition. "I think . . . I think I could eat . . ."

"Well, if you change your mind, I'll just have to think it's my cooking that's put you off."

"Tell me something," he said, as she busied herself wiping off the griddle. "Why isn't school in session? It is Thursday, isn't it?"

"That's right. But I'm not teaching because there aren't any students to speak of." Seeing his puzzled look, she added, "Most of my students belong to farming families. If I held school at this time of year, most of them would have to stay home to help their fathers with the harvest. In a week, though, the last crops will be picked and on their way to the silos or market. Then we can have school for nearly all the winter—unless the snows get too deep. Then through spring until planting."

"So for the next two weeks, you're fancy-free?"

"Not exactly. I have a lot of work to do on this house before winter sets in. I also give piano lessons—Holy cats! Is that the time? I'm supposed to be at the Hudsons' in next to no time to start the twins' lessons!"

He stood up when she did. "Go get changed," he said. "And don't forget to wash the paint off your nose."

She was washed and dressed in nothing flat, tearing at ties and yanking her stockings on anyhow. Still sticking pins in her hair under her hat, she trotted down the stairs. A smell of cooking struck her. Late as she was, she couldn't resist turning into the kitchen.

Hal sat at the table, calmly eating flapjacks and turning over the pages of Harriet Beecher Stowe. "You cooked?" she said in wonder.

"Of course. I'm a bachelor, you know, and I get tired of eating out." A quick frown drew his brows together as he looked at her. He stood up, pulling his handkerchief from his hip pocket. "You've still got paint on your nose."

Rachel took the large cloth and gave her nose a rub. He raised his hand, his forefinger extended. "Not there. Right . . . here, let me."

He put the tips of his fingers under her chin to steady it. With the forefinger of his other hand, he scratched gently at the bridge of her nose. They stood so close together that she could feel the stir of her hair where his breath touched it. He gave off a fragrance of sandalwood soap and a definite odor of ink. Strange to say, she liked it. She liked it a lot.

"There!" he said. "That does it."

He didn't take his hand away. He pressed up gently with his fingers, tipping her head slightly back. His gaze swept over her face and fixed on her eyes. "I meant what I said last night. About your eyes," he said, unsmilingly.

"I . . . like blue eyes," she said vaguely.

His mouth twisted suddenly, his gaze growing more intense in an instant. She knew without question that he'd kiss her. Rachel tossed her head and stepped back. "I've got to go," she said.

"I'll clean up before I leave."

"Thank you." Then she fled. As she trotted through her house, she felt that she hadn't really fooled Hal at all. It might look as if she were running to keep her appointment, but they both knew she was running away from him and herself. Because that was what frightened Rachel most of all. Not that he'd nearly kissed her, but that she'd wanted him to.

7

THE FIRST EDITION of the newly staffed *Brooklyn Herald* came out that Saturday afternoon. It was brief, only one sheet, printed front and back. Hal peeled the first complete copy off the plate and looked at it with pride. He'd done it. He'd done it all. He'd written it, he'd locked the letters into the form—upside down and backward—and he himself had turned the crank to make the press ink itself with the roller and then lift the paper against the type.

He put on his hat, leaving an inky thumbprint on the brim, and hung a sign on the door declaring his intention of returning shortly. The lively breeze that blew down the middle of Main Street made him clutch the still-damp paper more tightly, even before he did up the buttons on his coat.

Hal looked both ways up and down the street. Who to show the paper to? Benson Hunnicut still looked as morose as a streetcar conductor with flat feet. He wouldn't be able to work up any enthusiasm for someone else's job well done. Mrs. Jergens? Though she seemed to think of him as something of an ornament to her boardinghouse, Hal felt she'd simply say 'How nice,' and get on with the important job of polishing a floor or her cooking. Sissie Albright might show the proper enthusiasm but would she really understand his accomplishment? Hal thought not.

Maybe he should just fold his precious paper up and mail it East. Evans would understand, though the fact that there only was a single sheet with no advertising would make him groan sympathetically. There wouldn't be any fresh news for Evans—Hal didn't even know if the news would be fresh to Brooklyn as most of the information on the sheet had come over the telegraph. Hal couldn't be certain that the stationmaster hadn't already broadcast all the best stuff to his cronies.

Then, at the far end of the street, he spotted a woman crossing, one hand holding her hat down. The perfect clarity of the October afternoon meant he could see every detail, as though he looked through a magnifying glass at one of those perfect miniatures the Dutch Masters liked to paint. The sunlight picked out the glinting red under Rachel's straw hat while the breeze plucked at the bright blue shawl pinned across her breast. Hal watched her go into the schoolhouse.

He hurried up the street, trying hard not to picture her reaction to his work. Those kinds of mental plays never turned out. The other person never said the things that would let you be as clever as when you had the chance to plan it all out in advance. All the same, he went on imagining what Rachel would say and what he would answer.

When he reached the schoolhouse, he could hear her voice as she went around the inside, opening windows and singing. Her voice wasn't of professional quality—it faded to a ghost on most of the high notes—but it was the song of a contented woman. Then he realized she sang "*La Sepultura Solitaria*" or "The Lonesome Grave," a Spanish dirge, predicting the bad end achieved by girls who allow their affections to latch on to the wrong kind of man. He'd often heard it when out in New Mexico and points west. But she sang it with such happiness underlying the mournfulness that it might have been a wedding march. Hal began to wonder what she had to be so happy about.

He entered, walking through a dismal anteroom where a row of hooks awaited children's coats. The schoolroom itself was a large, rectangular room with narrow windows on both sides. From front to back ran four rows of benches and desks, with an aisle down the middle. A chalkboard, a large globe and an empty flagpole stood on a slightly raised dais, with a teacher's desk taking up most of the space. Hal didn't see Rachel but he could hear her.

"Hello?"

The song cut off in mid-verse, just at the moment when the young woman realized her lover has been unfaithful. Rachel's red hair appeared above one of the students' desks in the front row, the curls ablaze in an errant shaft of sunlight. "Oh! Hello. Watch where you step, please."

Hal walked down the aisle toward her. A large bucket sat beside her where she kneeled on the rough pine boards of the floor. She held a scrubbing brush in one hand and all around her the floor shone shiny-wet. Putting back the loose hair from her forehead with the back of her empty hand, she said, "I wish there was something easier to use for floors. You can scrub bare wood 'til you're blue and it's still not right."

"Why don't you varnish the floor? I don't mean you personally. . . ."

"I expect it would come to that, actually. But I can't afford to buy the varnish and the school board isn't likely to vote money for something like that. You should have been here for the ruckus they kicked up over buying that." She hitched her thumb over her shoulder at the globe. "Do you know, not one of my students believed the earth was round when I got here?"

"Sounds possible. What did the other teachers teach?"

"I don't know. They might have told the children the earth was round but they couldn't get them to believe it."

"And now they know?"

"Now they know," she said, smiling.

"Tell me, Miss Pridgeon," Hal began, leaning his hip on

the foremost desk, "is it valuable to know that the earth is round? I mean, if you think about it. I can't remember a time when I needed to know that."

The best entertainment Brooklyn had to offer, in his humble opinion, was watching Rachel Pridgeon get huffy. Emotion brightened her already notable complexion, made her eyes go wide so that he could look right down into the green, and made her say her thoughts aloud despite her attempts at meekness.

"Of course you need to know things like that! Where would we be if everyone thought the world was flat? There'd be no advances made at all and we'd all be wandering around believing that a giant rattler eats the sun every night!"

"Isn't that what . . . which Indian tribe is it . . . some tribe in the Southwest believes that, don't they?"

"I don't know. Did you want something, Mr. Sinclair, or did you just come here to get my dander up?"

"No, I had a purpose." With a flourish, he shook out the sheet of newsprint.

"You finished it?" She dropped the scrub brush and stood up. With great care, she wiped every drop of water off her hands with her apron before reaching out for the newspaper.

"It's a little short," he said. "My 'patent inserts' haven't arrived yet."

"Patent inserts?" she asked, not reading the paper yet, just admiring it like a jewel.

"Sometimes we call 'em 'ready-prints.' We'll be getting ours from St. Louis. They'll do the international stories and most of the political stuff. Sometimes they'll add something of public interest like . . . I don't know . . . the biggest pumpkin ever grown or a horse that can count. I'll put the inside pages between the sheets I print and there you have it! A six-page newspaper every week!"

"That saves you a lot of time." She hadn't really been listening. Her eyes were focused on the page before her. She had started to read.

Hal saw that she'd tucked up her skirts before she'd cleaned the floor. She had slender ankles encased in cloth high-button boots and the smooth white skin of her calves was revealed. He felt heat rise in his face, while his collar suddenly seemed too tight. Then he dragged his thoughts away from her ankles and studied her face as she read.

Her head had the inquisitive tilt of a red squirrel's, like the ones that used to play in the spindly oaks that lined his street in New York. Thinking of her like that cooled the sudden revival of his attraction to her. It had made him uncomfortable, as if his whole skin had begun to itch, and he was glad it faded. In the last few days, he'd felt a friendship grow between himself and the schoolteacher. He realized that he would miss it, if it disappeared or was transformed, even into something warmer.

She glanced at him. "It's good," she said, smiling. "I like what you wrote about yourself."

Hal rubbed his hands together and shook his head modestly. "Well, I thought that *I* might be the big news around town this week. So a few facts might make people more comfortable with my presence here."

"Did you really interview Prince Edward?"

"Yes, when he made a visit to New York. I was just a kid but I got the story. Had to track him into a Turkish bath, believe it or not."

She had a delightful laugh. It didn't remind Hal of silvery bells or gurgling brooks. Unforced and natural, Rachel's laugh gave him a good opinion of himself whenever he heard it, making him believe for a moment that he was as witty as he hoped.

Rachel whistled, low and soft. "*And* Jim Corbett? He was the World's Heavyweight Champion, wasn't he?"

"Yes. How did you know that? It's not the kind of thing women usually know."

"Oh." She hesitated, a little more color washing onto her cheeks. "I knew someone . . . my father, in fact . . . who'd seen him fight once and could still remember every detail years later."

"A great fighter. But I've also spoken to presidents and robber barons and society ladies."

"Which story are you proudest of?" she asked, her eyes still skimming over the newsprint.

"I didn't mention that one."

As he had intended, she lowered the paper again to fix him with that emerald gaze. "Are you going to tell me?"

Hal hesitated. Would she think he was boasting? She'd been impressed by the famous people he'd written about, but it was a light astonishment that expressed itself in a whistle, not awestruck demands to hear every detail.

He said, "There was this tenement, see, and—"

"Tenement?"

"A big apartment building that's divided into lots and lots of little rooms. The rooms are cheap and the landlords don't bother themselves over how many dozens of folks sleep in 'em. I've seen families of fourteen crowded into rooms smaller than your kitchen, morning, noon and night. No windows, no light, and if somebody gets cholera, it can wipe out the whole crowd and nobody the wiser."

She had closed her eyes, wincing at his description. "Like the debtor's prison in Dickens," she murmured.

"Look," he said, and paused. He reached out to drop his hands lightly over her forearms. Her sleeves were pushed up and the skin there was smoother and softer than silk. Hal shook her slightly, his grasp tightening. "It's nothing you need to know about—that kind of ugliness. It doesn't have to touch you."

"Should I only worry about the things that happen here?" Her eyes open, she stood still, letting him hold her. Then she moved back, her hands slightly up as though to signal surrender.

"No, of course not. But there's nothing you can do. I did my best . . . the story I wrote broke up a group of landlords who were grouping together to fix prices so nobody could find a place to live without paying through the nose. But even I know that I couldn't help everybody. What can you do?"

"Nothing, I suppose."

"Then why make yourself unhappy about things a thousand miles away?"

She lifted her shoulders in a quick shrug. "You're right. After all, there's poverty here too. Some of my students come from the hardest of hardscrabble farms. Some of them can't come in the winter because their shoes won't keep out the snow and they have no coats."

"I haven't been here long, but it seems to me what's needed in Brooklyn is some business other than farming. For instance, I was surprised to see the saloon . . ."

"They closed it before I came."

"But it would make some money."

"From where?" She folded the paper carefully and put it on her desk. Her thoughts seemed far away, yet when she spoke it was on the same subject. "The money would come from the pockets of the farmers. That's taking it away from their wives and children. It would hardly help the town's prosperity."

"I suppose you're right." Hal nudged the bucket with the tip of his toe. "Are you getting ready for your students?"

"Yes," she said. She seemed glad of the chance to talk about her work. "Mrs. Garrett's the last one to have her fields picked. Everyone will go out and give her a hand this week—Monday and Tuesday. Then next Wednesday the children come back."

"I'll be here to write about it, if that's all right with you. I can publish a list of all the children's names."

"Oh, they'd love it!" she exclaimed, her eyes sparkling.

"You can tell me what the subjects for the year are going to be, and any little facts you know about the school. . . ."

"You ought to talk to the school board. I don't know anything but what they've told me."

"Yes, I'll interview them too." But he planned to give the town worthies very little space. This might be a chance to get to know more about the lovely Miss Pridgeon.

Rachel asked, "Mr. Schur will ask for volunteers to help Mrs. Garrett get her crop in, but everyone is already planning to go. Are you?"

"I wouldn't know what to do. I've never harvested anything before. Why does Mrs. Garrett get extra help?"

"Oh, anyone who needs help has only to ask for it and

he'll have all he can handle. But Mrs. Garrett is different . . . you'll see, if you go."

"Well, if you're going to be there, you know I won't be far away."

He couldn't miss the expression of distaste that crossed Rachel's lovely features at this gallantry. She wrinkled her nose and pinched her lips together tightly. He couldn't help chuckling at the charming freakishness.

"I wish you wouldn't say things like that!" she said the words seeming to break through a dam of politeness.

"Why not? Most women—"

"Yes, I know. Most women would be charmed. But every time you say something so false . . ."

"False?"

"Insincere."

"I'm perfectly sincere."

"No, you just say it because you think that's what I want to hear. But every time you talk like that all I can think about are all the other women you must have practiced on and then . . . and then . . ."

Hal crossed the floor to her, his reporter's instincts sharpening. She stood on the dais, a few inches off the floor, which put their eyes on the same level. "And then . . . what, Rachel? Jealousy?"

"I don't know you well enough to be jealous," she said, keeping her head up, not flinching from his gaze.

"How long do you have to know someone to be . . . friends?"

"I'd like to be your friend," she said. Her hands had gone behind her for support on the desk top.

"And I'd like to be yours." He felt that in one more instant she'd be offering to shake hands. Hal didn't want that. Her smooth, rose-colored lips, untainted by rouge, soft and heart-shaped, had been haunting him since they'd chased cows in the graveyard.

He brushed his fingers over the smooth swell of her cheeks, feeling her stiffen. She licked her lips and said, "Um . . ."

"Shhh." He tilted her head slightly and kissed the pale

freckle on the bridge of her nose. Rachel relaxed, her sigh of relief whispering between them.

Then Hal kissed her mouth.

It was easy to avoid Hal on Sunday. Rachel melded with the female flock that huddled together to discuss everything from child-rearing to cooking. Most of the women only came into town on Sunday, their one day of rest. Even then, most had been up even earlier than usual to get their families' breakfasts, baths and clean clothes.

Lyle, too, had been dunked and scrubbed, rendering him fit for human company for once. He was already inside the church, being spoken to at length by Mr. Schur on the subject of digging for buried treasure in Mrs. Schur's daffodil beds.

Rachel's heart ached for Sissie, also clinging to the crowd. She was doing her level best to seem as usual, chattering like a magpie, her fluttering hands like two butterflies chasing each other in the sunshine. Yet instead of being alive with good cheer, she seemed desperate. Several friends asked Rachel whether Sissie was feeling entirely all right. Loyally, Rachel said that she was and went to take her friend's arm as they entered the church.

Sissie's fingers gripped her arm with unhappy strength. "Have you seen him?"

"Who?"

"Benson."

"No, I don't think he's here yet."

Hal sat up in front, apparently a willing captive of Dorothy Schur. Ed Greely sat on the end of the pew, his very back indicating a deep peevishness.

Rachel wondered if Hal had kissed Dorothy yet. She'd been trying to convince herself for a little less than twenty-four hours that Hal kissed every girl he met and that therefore his kissing *her* yesterday meant nothing. She almost would have persuaded herself when she would picture his face again when he had at last lifted his head. She could swear that his eyes had been misty. He had not spoken, just turned on his heel and walked out of the school, leaving her breathless. It had been a long time before that floor had gotten scrubbed!

A loud wheezing at the front of the church indicated that Mrs. Schur was pumping up the harmonium. With a quick glance at the notice board hung on the pulpit, Rachel looked up the opening hymn. She nudged Sissie and pointed to the title. "Be of Good Cheer for Thy Redeemer Returneth."

Sissie leaned against Rachel for an instant, silently acknowledging their friendship. Then, as the first notes puffed into the air, she opened her mouth to sing with her neighbors. But a whisper of voices at the rear of the church interrupted the hymn-singing. Heads turned to look down the aisle. Sissie and Rachel looked too.

"Oh, mercy!" Rachel said. Sissie was speechless.

The marshal had come in late, a fair widow on his arm. Mrs. Dale, still without spectacles, nodded blindly to her assembled acquaintances and, by mistake, the empty pulpit. But it was not the unaccustomed pairing that made the people of Brooklyn stare and whisper.

With natural courtesy, Marshal Hunnicut had taken off his hat when he'd entered the church. But instead of the tanned skin of his bald head, he had a luxuriant crop of boot-polish black hair. A little too long, and not quite straight, the inky hanks fell into his eyes and brushed his ears.

Compelled without knowing why to look at Hal, Rachel saw him sink down in his seat, holding his hymnal over his face. Dorothy Schur said something to him. Rachel saw him shake his head without revealing himself.

"Do you think . . . ?" Sissie whispered, with a glance at the people around her. More softly, she added, "That's not for me?"

Rachel said, "Somebody should do something. We should sing or something."

Around them, faces were reddening fast with the effort of keeping laughter bottled up and corked. The undercurrent of voices expressing wonderment had begun to change into titters and giggles. Someone several pews back couldn't hold it in, and a shout of laughter went up, hurriedly transformed into an explosive cough. In another moment, the whole congregation would be laughing at the marshal.

Rachel suddenly stood up, as if propelled. She cast a warning glance around at her neighbors and began to sing the opening hymn all by herself. After the first phrase, Sissie stood up too and then, of all people, Lyle. Before they'd reached the chorus, everyone was singing. If a few people couldn't keep from laughing, the joyful noise drowned them out.

When they'd all sat down again, the marshal had seated himself somewhere. As Mr. Schur mounted the several wooden steps up to his pulpit, Sissie said, "Thank you. I hate to see him humiliated, even if . . ."

Rachel tried hard to keep from looking at Hal, doing her best to fix her attention on the pastor's important spiritual message. Yet she could not keep her gaze from drifting that way.

He sat, comfortably, one arm along the back of the pew, coincidentally, perhaps, the side where Dorothy sat. As though he felt her gaze, he glanced casually over his shoulder and met her look head-on. He applauded her silently. Several women also turned around to look back, saw him looking at Rachel and raised their eyebrows or smiled indulgently.

Rachel snapped to a ramrod straightness and stared straight at Mr. Schur. But she heard little of the sermon.

Monday was not so easy. For one thing, she had not slept well. Her sleeping mind seemed determined to force her to relive that moment by her desk.

Lyle leaped around, content for once to stay by her side as she packed her picnic for the afternoon meal. Mrs. Hudson had paid her enough for the twins' first piano lesson so that there was fried chicken in the basket. They'd be riding to the Garrett farm with Ed Greely, Dorothy and her parents.

Somehow, Rachel didn't feel the least twinge of surprise when she saw Hal Sinclair in the back of the hay-filled wagon. "Hey, there, Hal," Lyle said as he scrambled over the tailboard.

"Lyle!" Rachel rebuked him with her sharp tone. "That's no way to speak to an adult!"

Hal said, "Oh, we're old friends. Right, Lyle?"

"Sure. He's been learning me how to run a printing press. It's . . ." He seemed to realize he showed an unmanly amount of excitement and so let his sentence die. His shoulders, one strap of his overalls falling free, moved in a sinuous shrug, indicating his boredom. Next thing, he clambered up onto the buckboard, inserting himself between Ed and Dorothy to comment on Ed's handling of the reins. Rachel didn't know if Ed's lack of response came from indulgence or from heartbreak.

Rachel turned her rebuking eyes toward Hal, lolling among the hay as much at ease as any farm boy. There'd been plenty of running commentary yesterday on his unseemly attentions to Dorothy. Rachel had already tried to warn him off once, with no effect. Now, however, that they were friends . . . she tried again to block the memory of his kiss. A blush heated her face, deepening when he smiled.

"You're looking—"

"Never mind that!" she said quickly. "Save your compliments for those who like them."

"All right. I will. Mrs. Schur!" he said, standing up to help the older woman into the back of the wagon, a courtesy he'd not extended to Rachel. "How lovely you're looking today! I've never seen a more becoming hat."

"Oh, do you like it? I didn't know . . . Mr. Schur thought it might be too giddy for a pastor's wife. . . ."

"Not at all!" Hal said heartily, shrinking back to avoid being hit in the eye by a spray of silk delphinium. "A pretty hat only makes a lady more charming."

Mr. Schur set their picnic basket in the back of the wagon. "What did you pack, Lucy? An anvil?"

A faint color came into Mrs. Schur's cheeks. "You always say that . . . every year."

"One thing is certain," Hal said. "That basket will be light as a hot-air balloon when we come back. No cooking of Mrs. Schur's ever went wasted."

Ed Greely turned his head to glance into the wagon. "Everybody here?"

His fiancée said, "Not Miss Albright or the marshal."

Lyle let out an audible groan. "Lovebirds," he said.

"Lyle!"

Mr. Schur said, "Don't reproach a child for speaking truthfully, Miss Pridgeon. It's not much of a secret in town that Marshal Hunnicut is fond of Miss Albright."

"Oh, wouldn't it be wonderful to have another wedding so soon after Dorothy's?" Mrs. Schur turned to Rachel. "You'll make such a lovely bridesmaid, dear."

Her daughter said, "I hope they won't want to get married too soon after me, or nobody will remember my wedding at all!"

Rachel tried very hard not to exchange a glance with Hal. When she couldn't bear it anymore, she did look out of the corner of her eye at him, only to find him rapt in contemplation of the checks on his trousers.

Lyle nodded down the street. "Here they come. Sissie's way out in front and who's that with . . . oh, Mrs. Dale."

"Oh, dear, you don't think they've quarreled," Mrs. Schur said, her tender heart instantly bruising for Sissie.

The pastor nodded sternly. "Maybe it would be as well if I dropped a word in the marshal's ear. A man needs to make a choice and stick with it."

Rachel and Hal spoke together. "I wouldn't . . ."

Now they looked at each other. Rachel had never known such complete communication with merely a look before. She'd given speaking looks to Lyle, often enough, but this was her first time experiencing an equal exchange. Their thoughts seemed to leap the intervening space and silence to reach instant agreement.

What they could hear in their innermost hearts was a sincere "Oh, mercy! What a day this is going to be!"

8

"*WELL*," RACHEL SAID brightly after the silence had lasted for an uncomfortable amount of time. "We certainly have a nice day for it!"

Murmurs of agreement answered her. They'd already left town and were journeying up the dirt road that led east. The tall trees on either side of the road dappled them with intermittent sunshine, while the sun did its best to warm them. The leaves were crimson now, and gold, with hardly any green left except for an infrequent pine keeping the memory of summer year-round.

Mrs. Dale put her face up to allow the moving sun and shadow to pass over it. She said with a contented sigh, "I do hope these clouds don't mean rain."

As they all considered the unsullied blue of the sky without a cloud to be seen, another silence fell. It was left for Hal to say without a tremor, "We'll just have to hope for the best."

"Are you an optimist, Mr. Sinclair?" Mrs. Dale asked, looking at Sissie with eager expectation.

Hal said, "On a day like today, it would be a crime to be anything else."

Rachel shifted uneasily on the bed of hay. Though it cushioned them against the shocks of the road, it did prickle. "I should have thought to bring a blanket," she said.

"I'd ask you to share ours, but there really isn't room," Mrs. Dale said complacently, linking her arm through the marshal's to keep him from giving Rachel his place.

"Thank you anyway, Mrs. Dale. Maybe next year I'll remember to put on a third petticoat."

Mrs. Dale caught her breath, shocked. Leaning close to Hal, her whisper audible to everyone else, she said, "My dear Miss Pridgeon, you mustn't say such things in front of men . . . they're liable to get the wrong idea about you."

Mr. Schur said, with a chuckle, "The Lord doesn't mind how many petticoats a woman wears, Mrs. Dale. It's the modesty of her soul that matters."

"Far be it for me to contradict you," Mrs. Dale said with a simper, "but when I was a girl—not so long ago—we were ashamed to step outside without at least three petticoats on."

"I remember that," Mrs. Schur said. "Awfully warm in the summertime . . . especially when one of them was flannel. You young girls don't know how fortunate you are. Crinolines too!"

"My mother wore those, I remember," Marshal Hunnicut said, his first contribution to the ride.

"Lands, how difficult they were to manage!" Mrs. Schur said, looking back across the years. "If a girl wasn't careful, it would swing up just like a bell!"

"I remember how graceful you looked the first time I saw you," her husband said. "Like a flower walking."

A rose color shaded Mrs. Schur's dry cheeks. "Why, Joshua!"

He put his arm around his wife and leaned over to whisper something in her ear under her bonnet. She cast an embarrassed glance around and said, "Joshua . . ."

Rachel, sitting closest to them, turned her head away to watch the scenery. In reality, however, she looked out of the corner of her eye at her friends and neighbors. There was something about riding higgledy-piggledy in the back of a hay-filled wagon that brought youth back. It made her feel young too. Strange how Ed and Dorothy sitting so properly up front, with Lyle between them, seemed a pair of respectable householders taking their rowdy youngsters for a ride. Strange that the youngest of them should seem to be so much the oldest.

To look at Sissie sulking one would think she was no older than Lyle. Not that the marshal was any more adult! Playing up to one woman to make another jealous was about as juvenile a trick as could be played. Mrs. Dale behaved like a spoiled child when she allowed the marshal's attentions. The pastor and his wife cuddled together like a pair of adolescents. As for Hal . . .

No. Try as she might, she couldn't think of him as other than a grown man. Even with a strand of hay between his teeth and his hands behind his head, he looked like a man who knew his own mind. He'd get whatever he wanted.

Rachel closed her eyes. The memory she'd fought slipped into her mind the moment she dropped her defenses. His hands had been warm against her face, the mild roughness of his palms from operating the press adding a prickle of excitement. The sharp rich smell of the ink clung to his clothes.

He'd kissed her nose, gently, as though she were a child on the way to bed. Rachel had wanted to speak then, to remind him of the liberties he was taking. Looking at her with his head tilted to one side, a fond smile bending his lips, he'd quieted her with a "shh."

Then he kissed her, full on the mouth, as no man had ever done, though some had tried. It had been a shock, not because a man kissed her, but because it was Hal. Hal's mouth touching hers, his hand slipping into her hair to hold her still, Hal's arm around her waist, lifting her up to meet him.

She'd looked other men in the eye when they'd tried to

steal a kiss by the stream or over a cooking fire. A haughty expression and a threat to tell her father or her elder brother and they'd slink off like a spurned coyote. Only Digger Cosgrove had persisted and he'd walked bowlegged for a week after. No, a mere stolen kiss wasn't enough to make her scuttle from Hal.

She'd kissed him back.

She'd slid her arms under his coat to feel the warmth of his body singe her skin. She was the one who'd pressed up against him, shamelessly enjoyed the hardness of his body against hers. She had been the one to sigh and to whisper his name when he'd scattered kisses over both sides of her neck and her ears. Gooseflesh formed even now on her arms as she seemed to feel again the way his mustache had tickled.

Deep shame filled her heart again as she recalled how quickly he'd left her. She dared not look at him for fear she'd see that he'd been thinking of it too. Or worse, that it had meant as little to him as she suspected.

"Here we are," Ed said over his shoulder.

Easily the most prosperous farm in the county, Garrett's sat on a low slope which was echoed in the cat-slide porch roof that came down almost to the ground. White pillars supported the porch roof, but couldn't be more than six feet tall, making the house from a distance look like a doll's. For the rest, three eyebrow windows peered over the porch while a meandering vine dotted the whole front with the last pink roses of the year.

A drive, lined with slim-trunked trees tipped with gold, encircled the house. Ed drove his team up to the front and got down to give Dorothy a hand. Lyle had already jumped down and run off. In the rear, the marshal swung Mrs. Dale down and then helped Mrs. Schur while her husband steadied her from the back.

Rachel didn't like the thought of being alone with Hal even for a moment. Sissie had already begun moving toward the rear of the wagon, her face expressionless as she prepared to suffer an indifferent touch from the man she loved.

Hal cleared his throat. Rachel flicked her eyes left to look at him. He put out his hand. "May I help you?"

"No, thanks." Quickly, she grasped the iron rail that framed the bench seat. She pulled herself up, one foot finding the wagon frame. Swinging her foot onto the seat, she stepped up, leaving him gawking behind her. With a polite smile thrown to Ed Greely, she took gratefully the hand he offered her with automatic politeness.

"Thank you for driving, Ed. I never felt one bump."

"I'm pleased to hear it, ma'am." When she would have walked on to join Dorothy and Sissie who stood chatting with the Schurs, Ed poked her elbow with a wavering forefinger.

"Miss Pridgeon, could I . . . reckon you'd know."

"Know what, Ed?"

"Dorothy sure looks up to you, ma'am. Maybe you could drop a word to her?"

A twinge in her conscience warned Rachel that she knew perfectly well what Ed wanted her to talk to Dorothy about. Sissie had cautioned her that sooner or later Rachel would find herself dragged into the relationship of her former student. She looked into the young man's troubled, truculent eyes and said, "Ed . . . it's not really any of my business."

"But, ma'am, it ain't right. I'm the one she's promised to. It just ain't right that this city feller should come between us."

Even as Rachel searched for the right words, she couldn't help realizing that, had she come to Brooklyn just one year earlier, this man would have been one of her students just as his sweetheart had been. Nevertheless, there couldn't be more than three years between herself and Ed. She didn't feel the least bit qualified to advise him.

"Ed . . . you know Dorothy's flighty."

"Not really, ma'am. Thoughtless, maybe."

At least he understood that much. "She's just excited because Mr. Sinclair is new in town. In a few days, she won't be so interested. And, I'm afraid, Mr. Sinclair is the kind of man who flirts with every woman he meets. It doesn't mean a thing."

She hoped Ed, if he noticed, put her pink cheeks down to the sun or the wind. Certainly it wouldn't occur to him that Rachel had any personal interest in Mr. Sinclair. To the young man, she probably seemed as old as his own mother.

"Maybe, ma'am. But I tell you what . . . I catch him doing more than talking to her and they'll be finding bits of him clear to the county line."

Rachel wished Ed had laughed after this threat, but he didn't. He tugged the brim of his slouch hat and turned to join the others. Passing Hal, he ran his shoulder accidentally-on-purpose into the other man. Grunting an apology, he walked on.

Hal, rubbing the left quadrant of his chest, looked quizzically after the younger man. "What's riding him?"

"You are."

"Me?"

How could he look so innocent? "Don't you care that every time you flirt with Dorothy you're tormenting Ed?"

"You told me that before. Are you sure it's Ed that's bothered?" His grin quirked under the line of his mustache. Rachel hated the fact that it took all her self-will not to answer that smile. She wished she could say that her palm itched to slap it off his face, but it didn't.

She said determinedly, "I don't really care what you do, but Ed does. And I warn you, Mr. Sinclair, Ed's a good shot."

Hal's eyebrows went up. "Are we back to Mr. Sinclair? You called me Hal on Saturday."

Rachel bit her lip to trap the hasty words that strove to escape, for his grin told her he remembered perfectly the reason she'd sighed his name. She turned on her heel, her shoulders as straight as a soldier's, and marched back to the safety of numbers. The soft warmth of his laughter followed her.

They all went up on the porch to pay their respects to Mrs. Garrett. She sat, as always, in a wheeled chair, a webby crocheted shawl arranged over the puffs of her pure white hair, her gnarled fingers busy with some scrap of knitting. She had round little cheeks exactly like crab apples only they came from the smile that never entirely faded from her lips. Rachel waited her turn to speak to Mrs. Garrett, taking a moment to look beyond the pillars of her homebound world to the fields beyond.

The brightly colored shirts of the menfolk of Brooklyn moved among the sprawling crops of squash and pumpkins. A large wagon stood in the middle of the tangled vines, while young men and boys tossed the vegetables hand over hand to pile in the back in tumbling stacks.

Women and girls sat on blankets spread out between the house and the fields, talking while they stripped the husks from the ears of Indian corn. Rachel could almost hear the squeak as the husks were jerked away from the sweet, nutty kernels underneath.

The small fry tumbled around, shrieking and calling and getting in the way. Rachel looked around for Lyle but he'd vanished for a while. She felt certain she'd see him again in time for lunch. Fried chicken could conjure him from the back of beyond in a twinkling.

"How are you, Mrs. Garrett?" She went up to the wheeled chair as the others went about their business.

"Well enough. It's good to see you again, Miss Pridgeon. I understand school will start in another day or two?"

"Yes, ma'am. I do hope you're planning to give us another talk before winter."

"I'd be pleased," Mrs. Garrett answered, her incessant knitting paused for an instant. "If you don't think they'll be too bored."

"Oh, no. It was the one thing they couldn't keep from talking about, and you heard yourself how they cheered you."

"What's this?" Hal asked, stepping closer to the older woman. "Do you lecture, Mrs. Garrett?"

She looked up at him and a twinkle came into her eyes, so dark against the pure white of her hair. "I do, Mr. Sinclair. I gave a speech on what it was like in the old days, before the town was established. Children today don't understand the hardships of their elders; it makes them disrespectful. I remind 'em of what it was really like."

"You've met?" Rachel asked, surprised by their easy conversation.

"I'm not likely to mistake the only stranger at my party, Miss Pridgeon."

"No, of course not."

"'Specially when he's good-looking. Oh, don't blush!" Mrs. Garrett said, shaking her finger at him. "An old woman is granted privileges and being outrageous is the first among 'em."

"Then I'll just say thank you for the compliment. There's a few people around here who could learn to do that from me." He cast an admonishing glance at Rachel.

Mrs. Garrett let her laughter free. "My, that does my heart good! I'm glad my brother sent such a charmer to Brooklyn!"

"Your brother?" Hal asked, his dark brows twitching together. An intensity came into his face that reminded Rachel of a cat waiting by a mouse hole, a cat with reason to believe the mouse was at home.

"Yes. Before I married Mr. Garrett, I was Lucia Clyde. My father had a taste for grand names. My mother had to talk him out of calling this farm 'Villa Borghese.' So he called it 'Capri.' My husband changed the name and my, I was glad. It got so tiresome explaining my father's whimsy."

"But you and your brother grew up here?"

"Oh, the times we used to have." Mrs. Garrett dropped her knitting in her lap, the first time Rachel had ever seen her put it down entirely except at meals. "Marcellus was a limb, Mr. Sinclair. A genuine limb! That's why I like to have Miss Pridgeon bring Lyle when she visits me. He reminds me of when Marcellus and I were both young. You wouldn't guess it to look at me now but I could kick a bucket off a fence post when I was a girl. Once I remember, I kicked the hat clear off a hired hand's head. He'd tried to get fresh."

"It sounds as though your brother wasn't the only limb, around here."

Mrs. Garrett smiled a young girl's smile. "Can I count on the loan of your arm later, Mr. Sinclair? Takes a couple of strong backs to lift me down these stairs but only one pair of arms to push me along on the grass. If you don't have other fish to fry?"

She tossed her head toward Rachel.

"I can spare him," Rachel said. "Gladly."

Mrs. Garrett laughed again, the happy sound trailing off into a cough that left her patting her chest lightly. "Get me a glass of water, there's a good boy."

Hal hurried to the spindle-legged table just behind Mrs. Garrett's chair and poured out a glass from the pitcher that stood there. He even steadied it for the elderly woman when it seemed her hands were too weak to hold the glass.

"Much better. Seemed to catch me in the chest."

"We'll come back in a little while," Hal said. "Maybe you should rest. There's going to be a lot of excitement today."

Rachel could take a hint. She started to walk down the porch steps when she heard Mrs. Garrett say, "Wait."

She'd grasped Hal by the coat sleeve and said, "I want you to know that I was powerful fond of Mr. Rudolph, who ran the paper before you came. He was a good man."

"I haven't heard anything but praise of him since I arrived," Hal said, putting his warm, strong hand over Mrs. Garrett's. "He sounds like that rarest of birds, a reporter and editor who is fair and honest. I shall have a hard time living up to his legacy."

Rachel came very near to falling in love with Hal at that moment. Especially when Mrs. Garrett began fairly to glow, and not from any outlandish flirtatious talk. Rachel knew, from gossip, that Mrs. Garrett, then the lovely Miss Clyde, had wanted to marry the penniless German teacher who'd been passing through Brooklyn. Though their romance had come to nothing, even after the passing of Mr. Garrett some thirty years later, it was rumored that Mrs. Garrett had always kept a soft corner of her heart for Mr. Rudolph. He'd stayed in town instead of moving on as romances would have it. Yet he'd never seemed happy with his choices. He'd certainly never married.

Hal had divined Mrs. Garrett's desire to hear Mr. Rudolph praised, though he might not know the reason, and every word seemed to breathe his sincerity. It didn't seem a calculated effort to charm the older woman at all; rather his respect for his predecessor seemed to be perfectly natural and easy.

Perhaps something of these feelings shone in Rachel's eyes, for later, when he found her alone by the backyard pump, he said, "I hope you're not going to go on being mad at me."

"I'm not mad at you."

"No?" If she didn't know better, she'd swear he'd been cast down by her coldness and only her reassurance perked him up again. But she knew better.

"No. Why should I be? Here, hold this bucket."

"Maybe I should do that," he said, watching her take a hold of the pump handle.

"It's all right. There's a kind of a special knack to it. Look." She shook the handle as she brought it down. There came a clank and . . .

"Are you sure you know the knack?" Hal asked. He lowered the bucket she'd given him.

"Of course." Somehow nothing worked right when he watched her. She'd never known a day of nerves in her life, but under his sardonic eyes everything seemed to be a little too much for her.

Rachel gave a solid push on the handle and the water gushed out. Some splashed onto his trousers, but he only laughed and swung the bucket down to catch the rest. "Go on," he said. "I need a bath. Though I'd hoped for a warmer one."

"There are towels in the kitchen. You better dry off before you catch your death."

"It's not that cold. But if you'll show me where . . . ?"

She led him through the kitchen, a swarming hive with women preparing cakes and puddings and getting in each other's way. Some eyes turned when Rachel and Hal went through. "We had a little accident with the pump," she said in general explanation as they passed.

Rachel took two flour-sack towels out from the pantry

and took him into the hall to show him where he could be private.

"You seem to be at home here," Hal remarked.

"I come every Monday to read to Mrs. Garrett. She's been very kind to Lyle and me. She's kind to everyone. She hires folks to work here when their own farms don't prosper, and she gives this harvest party every year."

"Oh, so that's what we're doing here. It's a party."

"The biggest party we have."

"You always talk as if you've lived here all your life. But you lived somewhere else before. Even before you lived with the McLeans. Where was that, by the way? California, wasn't it?"

"That's right. You'd better be taking care of that water. Has it already soaked right through?"

"It's not that bad," he said, blotting his trouser leg with one of the towels. "The crease may never be the same, though."

"I'm sorry."

The sunlight couldn't reach into the hall with the over-hanging porch in the way, but the upstairs window sent dazzling beams pouring in from above. They brought up reddish-brown glints in his hair and showed the fine lines at the edges of his eyes. The faint darkness on his strong chin invited her fingers to run over the prickling skin.

"How old are you?" she asked suddenly.

"You obviously haven't been talking to Mrs. Schur. She knows everything about me down to my birthmarks. I thought I knew how to get the facts from an unwilling subject! She should give lessons. And she seems so timid too."

"You didn't answer . . . never mind. It's none of my business."

He caught her hand when she turned to go. "You're the first person I've met so far who meant it when she said it. I'm thirty, Rachel. And you?"

"That's old to be starting over in a new place."

"I'll get back to New York one day. A big story . . . bigger than cows in the graveyard, I mean."

"I liked what you wrote about that. It made it sound like an adventure," she said, smiling reminiscently. "Everyone laughed when they read it."

"You didn't answer my question, Rachel. How old are you?"

"Twenty-two."

"Twenty-two!" He released her hand so suddenly it was as if he'd thrown it from him. "That's awfully young to be teaching."

"Not really. Not when you've got to earn your keep. Some girls start teaching as soon as they're out of school themselves. Eighteen . . . sixteen, even."

"But you're such a little thing. How can you keep order?"

Drawing herself up, Rachel looked him in the eye. No one had ever called her a 'little thing' before, yet when he said it, suddenly she felt fragile and petite. That might sit well with Dorothy Schur but it wouldn't do for Egan Delmon's daughter.

She said, "I've never had any problems yet that was too big for me, Mr. Sinclair. I can make the children mind me, and without using a willow switch either."

He grinned down at her. "You know," he said, as if commenting on the weather. "Every time you call me 'Mr. Sinclair' in that uppity way, I want to kiss you again."

Now she did turn on her heel and walk away. Her steps slowed as she reached the door and she glanced back at him, her forehead rumpled. " 'Uppity'?"

His grin widened. "It's a good word, isn't it? Benson Hunnicut taught it to me. There's a lot of good words out here. Let me see. I'd describe you as 'an ornery chickabiddy in need of a good smooching.' How's that?"

"You never learned all that from the marshal!"

"No, ma'am. That was Mr. McGovern's father-in-law's advice when Mr. McGovern and his bride had a falling out . . . oh, twenty-five years ago. But good advice improves with age, like good wine." He watched her intently, but Rachel was determined not to show any weakness. Then he asked, starting toward her, "By the way, what's a 'limb'?"

"Oh, yes, you should know that," she said, putting her hand on the door behind her. "It means 'limb of Satan' and that describes you to a tee!"

She trotted out, letting the swinging door close in his face. She returned to the pump, hoping none of the busy women in the kitchen noticed her confusion. Either Hal had taken the notion—with reason!—that she would welcome his kissing at any time, or he thought of her as a somewhat foolish child. As she pumped the water, however, she decided that he'd told her exactly what he thought of her. "An ornery chickabiddy," she said to herself, and smiled.

At dinnertime, the separated sexes came together on the grassy field in front of the house. Bright blankets made a patchwork quilt on the grass while opened baskets sent a waft of good smells through the air. Rachel found herself a space and waited for Lyle to appear. She could see Hal, as promised, pushing Mrs. Garrett's chair over the grass. As was usual every year, she would park near the Schurs' and enjoy some of their meal. Dessert, however, would come from her kitchen. If his sister's fried chicken didn't bring Lyle, some molasses cookies or iced pudding ought to do it.

A shadow fell over her and she looked up to find Marshal Hunnicut standing above her, his very shoulders expressing his depression. "Do you mind if I set down?"

"Not in the least," Rachel said, moving her skirt out of his way. She tried to hide her momentary flash of disappointment that it had not been Hal seeking her out. "Chicken?" she asked.

The marshal took a drumstick and chewed meditatively. After he swallowed, his Adam's apple jerking, he asked, "It's not my hair, is it?"

"I beg your pardon?"

"From something Hal said, I thought it might be my hair that Sissie minds."

The marshal's hat hid the worst of the black toupee, the high pompadour front. The length over his ears and down the back of his neck was only mildly odd-looking, as if he'd gone six months without a haircut.

The marshal added morosely, "I can't help it. I started

losing it when I was in my twenties. She's hardly ever seen me *with* hair. You'd figure she'd have gotten used to it by now."

"Marshal," Rachel said firmly. "Believe me. It's not your hair."

"Well, good. This glue itches like blazes."

Rachel feared that he meant to tear the midnight-black hair from his head then and there, which would put her off her food. Funny how Hal's hair was nearly the same color as the marshal's wig, yet it looked right and natural on Hal and like nothing on earth on the marshal.

Marshal Hunnicut said, "I want you to know that it's all right you're not telling me. I don't expect you to break your word to Sissie."

"Thank you."

"'Sides, I guess I can figure where the real trouble lies. I just thought I'd give this toupee thing a try, just in case it did turn out to be that. Since I'm pretty certain it's not another feller . . . I'd have heard if it was that . . . I guess I know what it is."

Rachel wished she were elsewhere, wished that someone would come along and relieve her of this uncomfortable situation, wished that Sissie would just accept the marshal and put everyone out of their misery. Though she glanced about her, hoping to meet some rescuer's eye, she couldn't catch anyone's attention. Were they deliberately avoiding her?

"Yes, ma'am," the marshal repeated. "I reckon I know what the problem is."

Though she'd been busying promising herself she wouldn't encourage him, an interrogative noise was all but forced out of her by his waiting silence.

"It's money. I just don't make enough. I mean, Sissie's been poor all her life. Her daddy was a no-account and her poor mother scrimped every penny. And here I am asking her to live the same hardscrabble way. No wonder she won't have me."

He hurled away the chicken bone and Rachel winced at

the thought of it hitting someone. But no outraged cry arose to distract the marshal's attention.

He said, "I've asked for a raise but times are hard right now, and it's not like I'm keeping the jail full or anything. Why, we haven't had a serious crime here in more'n two years and then it was just a couple of the boys breaking things up. But I swear, I'll find some way of making more. Maybe if I start a little farm on my own. I can work it when I'm not at the jail."

Rachel was torn in two. She had to keep her promise to Sissie, that'd she'd never tell the marshal the real reason for her refusing to marry him. On the other hand, she couldn't stand by and watch the man work himself to death for nothing.

"Marshal," she began, trying to think of a way to hint him toward the truth. But before she could go on, someone called her name. Suddenly, a lot of people were calling her name.

She stood up, some tone of alarm in the voices starting her heart to beat faster. In the distance, she saw four or five boys, running together with a peculiar gait, their arms stiff, and their bodies sideways. They carried something between them, something on a flat board, something that did not move.

"Oh, dear God," she whispered. "That's not Lyle. Please tell me that's not Lyle."

9

$\mathcal{M}$ARSHAL HUNNICUT ROSE too, his misery seeming to drop away at this call to duty. His long legs carried him to the running boys while the other townsfolk were still pointing and commenting. Their voices were like the wind in Rachel's ears as she rushed among the spread blankets. She felt a presence beside her and turned her head to see Hal, matching her step for step.

Then she heard him say, "I'll find the doctor."

She didn't even throw him a word of thanks.

Lyle lay on the board, his arms trailing limply off the sides. Under his tan, his face had a pale, waxy quality, his eyes shadowed by dark rings. At his temple, an ugly gash had already started to purple the surrounding flesh, while a trickle of blood ran off. The hair there was already stiff with the copious blood that had already flowed. Rachel seized one of his hands, calling, "Lyle! Lyle!"

"What happened, boys?" The marshal's deep voice added

a note of calm to the gabble of explanations, broken by the snifflings of frightened children.

One boy said, his face showing lines that should not have appeared for years, "Honest, we never guessed he'd follow us. We was climbing down the ravine at the back of the house like we done every year and he—"

"Oh, never mind that now!" Rachel said in anguish. Their pace had slowed while they talked. "Hurry him onto the porch where the doctor can see him."

Mrs. Garrett waited at the bottom of the steps. "Carry him into my room, Rachel. You know where it is. Keep him warm 'til Doctor Warren gets here."

"Hal went to find him."

"Then he'll find him. Always trust a newspaperman, my girl. They get the job done!"

When Mrs. Garrett's legs had failed her, she'd had her bedroom suite moved down into a second parlor that had rarely been used except on the most formal occasions. She'd kept the dark maroon paper and the dusty flowers under glass that her grandmother had made. The double-lined curtains did more than keep the sun from fading the rugs; they kept out every vestige of light. The first thing Rachel did was jerk them open, their brass rings rattling as if in protest.

The marshal lifted Lyle onto the bed as tenderly as a mother. The Bannerman boys stood around, dumbly, not knowing what to do with their hands. There were six of them, each wilder than the last.

Rachel, wringing out a lace-trimmed cloth in water, heard their explanations without heeding them. One thought played over and over in her mind. *What if I lose him too? What if I lose him too?* She almost couldn't bear to look at Lyle as she laid the cool, damp cloth on his bruised forehead.

"I just heard him call out and then fall, Marshal, sir. None of us was near 'nuff to grab him. He must've fell twenty feet and the bottom's all lined with rocks. Reckon he must've caught his head on one of 'em."

"What's all this crowd?" the doctor demanded crisply

from the hall. "Begone, you boys, begone! Can't have a mischief of boys hanging around. Pride of lions, flock of birds, mischief of boys, don't you know!"

Doctor Warren bustled into the room, his girth belying his fleetness of foot. He measured his waist size by watch-chain links and had been heard to boast every time he had to add another. There had to be at least twenty-two of them from pocket to pocket across his vest.

"Understood that scamp Lyle's been and done an injury upon himself again. Now, don't fret," he said grandly, patting Rachel on the shoulder as she turned anxiously toward him. "I'll soon have him put to rights. Not much damages the young, my dear."

"They said he may have fallen twenty feet. Maybe more. And he's unconscious. He's never been that before."

"Hmmm." The doctor pulled on his lower lip as he raised the damp cloth with the other hand. "Has he moved at all? You, boy, did you see him move after he fell?"

In unison, the boys shook their heads. "All right," the doctor said. "Dismissed. Fall out."

When they were gone, Doctor Warren said, "You get along too, Miss Rachel. There's nothing you can do right now. The marshal and I'll undress him and then I'll check him over—make sure nothing's broken."

"I'd like to stay," she said.

Perhaps something in her eyes or bearing made the doctor believe she meant to stay no matter what. He said, "Very well. But I'm also going to be checking to see if he hurt his spine. It's just as well he's out of his senses right now."

She held Lyle's head steady as the doctor began to unbutton Lyle's worn and now-dirty jacket. Watching as he lay the jacket on a chair, Rachel saw that it needed mending yet again and went cold at the thought that she might never have to set needle to one of Lyle's rips again.

"Now, girl, crying over him won't help matters."

"I'm sorry," Rachel murmured, letting the tears cool on her cheeks.

A gentle rap at the door was quickly followed by Hal

looking around the edge. "Marshal Hunnicut, could you step out here for a moment?"

Hal glanced at the still boy on the bed. He added, "If you can be spared?"

"What's up?"

"This crowd out here. They're not rowdy, just interested, but I think Mrs. Garrett would be glad if you could move them off her flower beds."

"Go on," Doctor Warren said. "You're just a pair of hands to me. You, Sinclair, come in here. You can help me get this boy's clothes off him."

"I'll help you," Rachel said. "You don't need to trouble Mr. Sinclair."

"It's no trouble," Hal said, closing the door behind the marshal. "I've had experience in taking off clothes."

Rachel flashed him an angry look. If he was going to be flippant now . . .

He said to the doctor. "I was an orderly in the War."

"The War?" Doctor Warren asked, slipping off Lyle's shoes. "Which side, sir?"

"I'm a New Yorker, born and bred," Hal answered with a smile that reminded the doctor that the War had ended long ago.

"Conscientious objector, maybe?" Doctor Warren cast a professional glance at Hal's obviously healthy body. "I only ask because being an orderly is dirty work which, saving your presence, Miss Rachel, was left to those not worthy of fighting."

Hal lifted the boy on the bed tenderly as a mother so the doctor could slip off the ragged shirt. His blue eyes flicked to Rachel and he threw her an outrageous wink. Rachel only looked down at Lyle, her heart strangely warmed.

Then Hal moved his hand to cover hers and squeezed lightly. "Don't look like that," he murmured. "It'll be all right. Small boys bounce."

Rachel turned her head away lest a tear fall onto his fingers. She would refuse to think of anything but Lyle. Yet, the touch of his hand had been comforting.

Hal turned again to the doctor. "I might have been worthy

of fighting, but I couldn't lift the carbine they'd given me. I was only fifteen. I'd enlisted, but when my sergeant found out . . ." He grinned. "That's when I learned how to swear! They did their best to send me home and when I didn't go, off to work in the hospital tent! I think they did it to scare me off and it almost did the trick. But I'm sure you remember as well as I."

Hal shook his head as if shaking off clinging memories. Doctor Warren shook his head more ponderously as though burdened by their weight.

During the examination that followed, Hal moved and held the boy as the doctor instructed. Rachel watched their faces, alert for any sign that would offer her hope.

Finally, the doctor stood back and began rolling down his sleeves. "I can't find any serious damage." He held up one large hand to stop Rachel's exclamation. "That doesn't mean there isn't any—just that I can't find it. Now, you keep this boy quiet and warm. Don't let all the weeping women come crowding in. Get what liquid you can down him . . . once he wakes."

Hardly able to form the words, Rachel asked, "Will he wake?"

"Of course, of course!" The doctor's bluster meant, as she knew, that he hadn't any idea whether Lyle would ever open his eyes again or not. "In his own time. I'll stop by tomorrow regardless, but if he should wake, send for me at once."

He put on his coat, which he'd put on top of Lyle's clothes on the chair. "Bless my soul, what's that?"

Bending down, a feat he accomplished only with difficulty, he picked up a rock from the carpet. A few inches square, it looked to Rachel like a piece of dirty ice when he held it up in his fingers. He chuffed between his lips and said, "Boys! They pick up all kinds of truck and stuff their pockets with it. This must have caught his eye for it's very unusual. I wonder if it was to reach this that he fell."

He looked at it for a moment more, weighing it in his cupped palm, turning it in the sunshine. Then he dropped it onto the tail of Lyle's coat. "Ah, me. It was when I was a boy that I first became interested in medicine . . . well, bird-stuffing. The things my dear mammy used to find . . ."

Still reminiscing, he went out, pausing only to say, "I shall call tomorrow."

As soon as he was gone, Hal said, "Now don't look like that, Rachel. The doctor is hopeful."

"He just . . . lies so still."

"That's nature's way of healing. It wouldn't be good for him to thrash around."

"No. But it's alarming. He's usually on the move . . . even in his sleep." Rachel smoothed the lank hair away from her brother's brow. "He's all I have in the world," she said softly.

For once, Hal found himself at a loss for words. He'd seen many men die while he was still a boy and only he knew anymore how it had hardened him. He could recall hearing his mother weep the day he came home at last, knowing that she didn't weep for joy but because the open-hearted boy had gone forever, leaving her a stranger for a son. There were no words then either; no words to tell her that the process had begun long before with the death of his father and her too-speedy remarriage.

Now, hearing Rachel weep softly for her young brother, he realized again that, in the end, words are valueless things. So he acted.

He put his arm around her shoulders, and gently turned her away from the bed. "There now," he said, offering her his chest to weep on.

At first she stiffened as though to move away, but after he made no moves but comforting pats, she relaxed against him. She did not weep again. She only sighed, making Hal understand how sweet it was to lay down this burden, or at least to share it, if only briefly.

"You're a brave woman, Rachel."

"No, not really. I'm scared all the time."

"Scared?"

He felt her nod against his jacket, her face all but buried in his lapel. "Always scared. Lyle and I—we live upon . . ."

"Hmmm?" Hal dropped his head down to bring his ear closer to her lips.

"Nothing." She put her head back to look up into his eyes and was disconcerted to find his face so close. Her hair, loosened and falling, tumbled in half-pinned waves down her back. Hal smoothed his hand over the disordered mass. He smiled and tangled a strand around his finger.

She tried to turn away from him but it tugged and she said, "Ow! Let me go."

A knock at the door brought guilty color into her cheeks. Hal thought she'd never looked so fine. He disentangled his finger and moved away. For lack of anything better to do, he picked up the stone that the doctor had found.

Surprisingly heavy in the hand and with a greasy sheen, it caught the rays of the sun and turned them back, despite the large black crack that seemed to run through the stone. It looked a little like the rose quartz he used to find sometimes when he played in a gravel pit as a boy. Only this was white, clearer and somehow colder than quartz, as ice is colder than frost, its cousin.

The knock came again. "Miss Rachel? Can you come out?"

Hastily Rachel finished tucking up her hair, sticking in the pins haphazardly. "Just a minute, Mrs. Garrett."

She opened the door, casting a look over her shoulder at Hal who returned it blandly. He returned the chunk of stone to Lyle's pocket, hearing other things crunch and jostle as it fell in.

Just then, one moment too late, Hal realized that the hair on the back of his neck prickled while his hands suddenly started to tremble. He knew these sensations well and understood exactly what they meant. He'd felt this way when he'd picked up a bottle outside the window at the scene of the Bolton poisoning, thus proving that the nurse had done it. He'd felt the same sense of excitement when he'd gotten the anonymous letter that led to the destruction of the opium ring. It was as if he held in his hands a globe made of the thinnest glass and inside, waiting for the glass to be broken in just the right way, was the big story.

This feeling never came without cause, and Hal had learned long ago not to question it but to act. He reached into the pocket of Lyle's coat to fish out the strange stone again but failed to bring it up out of all the other junk tumbling around in there. With determined patience, he began to bring things out one at a time, his fingers patting over the knobs and bumps in search of the stone.

A piece of tarred string, wonderfully involved in a hard knot, the broken-off arm of a china statue, a cat's-eye marble that sent Hal's hopes leaping up, a lost tooth . . .

Behind him, Mrs. Garrett asked, "How is the boy?"

"Doctor Warren is hopeful that his back isn't injured, but I don't like the gash on his forehead."

"Did he sew it up?"

"No," Rachel answered. "He hardly looked at it."

"Let me see." The chair rolled on fat little tires to the bedside. Using the bedpost, she pulled herself out of it to stand erect, if not steady, beside the boy's pillow. She leaned down close. "It's a right gash all right. He's lucky he was born to be hanged, Rachel."

"I'm doing all I can to prevent that," Rachel answered with a laugh that sounded more than a little forced to Hal's ears.

"Well," said Mrs. Garrett, straightening up with a grimace of instantly suppressed pain. "If you'll fetch my sewing basket, I'll have that stitched in one minute. Won't be the first one I've done."

"Yes, I'll get it." Rachel hesitated on the threshold and then repeated. "I'll . . . get it."

Hal had dug all the collection out of Lyle's pocket, but the stone had not been among them. Instead, his questing fingers poked through a large hole. He was on the point of dropping the accumulated rubbish in order to snatch up the coat and feel in the lining, when he heard Mrs. Garrett's soft, polite cough.

"Would you mind bringing my chair back? It's rolled."

Hal dumped the strange amalgamation of the boy's interests on the shiny surface of an occasional table and brought Mrs. Garrett's chair closer to the bed.

Mrs. Garrett sighed as she rested herself. "I hate getting old," she said. "I'd take all my sorrows back again if I could do a decent day's work with them. But the doctor does say I'm lucky to be able to stand at all so I shouldn't complain."

"Why not?" Hal asked. "It's a human right. In my book, the right to complain would come second only to the freedom of the press. It should fall before the right to bear arms. You don't need to defend your opinions if you only have sunny ones."

He thought she might be shocked, since so many people of her generation had been brought up to worship the Founding Fathers that anyone questioning their wisdom could be thought of as sacrilegious. However, Mrs. Garrett only looked at him, looked *through* him really, and laughed. Softly, because of the boy on the bed, but thoroughly. "I lay you odds my brother sent you here because he doesn't like you."

"You win."

She nodded, tucking her lips in. Then she said, "Is he still as ornery as ever?"

"I didn't know him long. He owns the paper I worked for in New York. I'm afraid I wrote something he didn't approve of."

"Yes, Marcellus always wanted money and lots of it. More than that, he wanted power over people. When he first bought the paper—I mean the *Herald* here in town—he bought it for the power, I think. Then, when that wasn't enough, he sold it and bought another one in . . . oh, I don't know. Chicago maybe. I often wonder if he lost anything in that fire they had up that way a few years ago."

Hal said, "I remember reading that he lost almost all he owned then."

"Almost all? That's like him too. Now he's started over in New York. Well, he always was ambitious."

"You talk as if you don't hear from him very often."

"I don't. I get letters from a cousin who follows what he does when he gets written up in his own papers. But I didn't even know he'd bought the *Herald* again until you walked up here today. I think Marcellus wants to forget he came from here."

She smiled, a contented, peaceful smile. "You'd never know it to look at us now, but he and I are only a year and a half apart. But I'd guess Marcellus doesn't look near as old as I do. Oh . . . don't bother to think of something pretty to say. I've earned every line and white hair. And not by doing folks out of their money or building empires to glorify my name. I got 'em by working on this land, and sacrificing. I don't think Marcellus and I have much in common but our blood anymore, do you?"

"No, ma'am. But your brother is the one that's the poorer for the lack."

She shook a gnarled finger at him and spoke with mock severity. "You're a smooth-talking devil, Mr. Sinclair. Is my brother still keeping that singing trollop?"

Hal wondered what kind of papers her 'cousin' read. "Umm, is that Rachel coming back?"

"No. Mrs. Schur's in the parlor where my sewing basket is. She'll keep Rachel praying for a while. Answer the question." But she didn't wait to hear what he had to say. Hal felt certain she already knew.

"He would have saved himself a lot of time and trouble if he'd married the girl he wanted in the first place."

"Who was that?"

"She up and died a good . . . let me see . . . forty years ago come spring it must be. My! Could it really be so long? Seems like I can see everything so clearly. I had a dress of mulberry wool and we all went to a Christmas dance out at the Merryweathers' and danced while the dirt shook down from the ceiling. Ruined the dress . . . oh, you don't want to hear all that. But Marcellus should have married that girl. Her father hadn't the best reputation for honesty but, my, she was pretty. Looked a bit like our Rachel, though her hair wasn't all that red."

"Miss Pridgeon's a very pretty girl."

"Yes. A good girl, too, and those things don't often go hand in hand. I had her and Lyle stay here with me when they first came to Brooklyn. And never a week fails but what she's here to read to me or just talk about the old days."

This time, they both heard her quick step on the hall floor. She came in, her eyes snapping, the basket in her hands dangerous with pins stuck in the quilted top. "I told Mrs. Schur three times I had to hurry back but she kept calling on the Lord for one more prayer."

"Bless her heart," the older woman said. "She means well. Though I wish someone would tell her that while she makes cakes lighter than angel's wings, her pie crust is like molded lead."

She went on talking about Mrs. Schur, her husband and their daughter, while picking out her finest needle and silken thread. "What do you say to this brown?" she asked, lying it against Lyle's forearm. "It's about the right shade. Pick the right color and nobody'll notice the stitches. At least, that's what my mama used to tell me. Though come to think on it, she was talking about mending a gown. Oh, well."

This time, when Hal put his arm around her, Rachel sagged against him. "Maybe you should step outside. Get some fresh air," he suggested.

She shook her head slowly, as if she'd been drugged. Then she shook all over as thought taken with a sudden chill. "I felt strange for a moment, sick even, but I'm all right. I'll stay."

Hal studied her, looking at the firm set of her delectable mouth and the strength in her lovely eyes. She stood on her own two feet and met his look squarely. "If you're sure . . . ?"

At her emphatic nod, he turned to Mrs. Garrett, busy threading a needle against the sunlight. "Let me do that for you, ma'am."

"Thread a needle? No man ever . . . Well, for the cat's sake! You're right handy, Mr. Sinclair."

"More than you know. For instance, I can stitch Lyle's forehead as well as you can and probably better than Doctor Warren could." He winked.

"You're right about that! My dog could do a better . . . no, that's uncharitable. Doctor Warren is a good man and he's not killed anybody that wouldn't have died anyway. But sewing up cuts is women's work."

"Well, whichever of us sews it up, the first thing we'll need is to clean that cut."

"There's water on my dresser there, child," Mrs. Garrett said, pointing it out for Rachel.

The boy didn't twitch a muscle as Hal took five tiny stitches to close the wound. Hal felt strangely pleased by the fact that his skills hadn't deserted him. He still recalled the stomach-churning nervousness he'd felt as he stitched up his first patient for a busy physician. The field surgeons had urged him to go into medicine after the war but Hal had witnessed his fill of responsibility by then.

His orderly duties had stood him in good stead in more than one place, when he'd gotten the story while other newspapermen, less hardened, had been overcome with revulsion at the scene of some dispute turned violent. Battlefields were often cleverly disguised as a waterfront bar or an apparently peaceful home.

"There," he said. "Put a clean dressing on it and he'll be able to boast about it all next week. There may be some pain where the stitches went in but it won't last. I doubt there'll be more than a faint scar there."

Rachel said, "I'm impressed. Thank you."

Her words must have sounded offhand. But Hal took no offense. The look of gratitude in her eyes went deeper than words. He winked at her and watched with pleasure as she tried to fight a smile.

Mrs. Garrett said, "I'll invite you to our next quilting bee, Mr. Sinclair. You've got fine, light hands for a man."

"Thank you, ma'am."

Mrs. Garrett dismissed him and his flourishing bow with a hand flip. "Now, don't you worry, Rachel. You leave that boy right where he is—he won't take a mite of harm. You go on out and have some fun. After all, this is your last free day before school starts. Take that handsome feller there and go bob for apples or something."

"Oh, no. I couldn't."

"'Course you can. I'll watch him and there's a dozen

women within call if he should wake." She'd already begun to work her knitting needles, raised from her lap. The soft wool sock seemed almost to grow before their eyes.

"I'd much rather stay and read to you."

Hal saw the older woman looking at him from beneath the hem of her lace head-covering. He decided, under the pressure of that steady gaze, to put in his two cents' worth. He said, "I've never husked corn or picked pumpkins. I need a guide."

But to all he could say, at least at the persuasion he could offer with a third, conscious person in the room, she would only say, "I'd rather stay."

Then, just as Hal drew breath for one more try, aware of Mrs. Garrett's steady, silent and forceful gaze, Lyle moaned. He moved the arm above the covers aimlessly, his movements random and without purpose. He murmured something in his sleep and tried to turn over. At once, Hal stepped forward and put his hands on the boy's warm brown shoulders.

"Try not to move too much, Lyle. You've got a banged-up head and the rest of you doesn't look too good either."

Now the ladies were outraged. Mrs. Garrett's whispered, "Mr. Sinclair!" smacked of a nurse rebuking a child's foolish attempt at independent thought. But the boy quieted down at once, responding to something fatherlike in Hal's voice.

Hal couldn't help flashing a quick look of triumph around at their scandalized faces. At the back of his mind, an opinion formed that he might actually *have* children one day. He didn't know why people made such a fuss about how hard it was.

Mrs. Garrett said, "Rachel, you and Lyle stay overnight. You'll get to rest, Rachel, and it won't do that boy any good to go jouncing over the roads. Tomorrow's soon enough."

As Hal escorted Rachel out, he cast a last, longing glance at the tattered coat still hanging on the ladder-back of the chair. There was a story in that coat, he'd swear to it. Maybe a story big enough to take him back to New York. Strange how he had to think hard before he could see himself back there.

10

*H*AL MANAGED TO snare Ed Greely out of the group of concerned townspeople that met Rachel as she came down the steps. Not that Ed was one of those who asked questions and didn't listen to the answers. Instead, he stood by, keeping watch over Dorothy who stood gabbing with her mother. Hal, forewarned that Ed didn't like him, didn't expect the kind of instant cooperation he got in response to his quick question.

Ed only nodded, scuffed one boot toe into the dirt and said, "Meet me over at the end of the lane."

Reaching for Rachel's arm, Hal steered her away from Mr. Schur, whose need to pray for Lyle was even more intense than his wife's. Many of the women were joining in, while Rachel rolled her eyes and backed like a shying horse.

"Come on," he said. He drew her out onto an open sward of grass at the side of the house. "We'll catch a ride into town with Ed Greely. He's getting the wagon."

"Town?" she said vaguely.

"You'll want to pick up a few things for the night. The boy's going to need clean clothes and you . . . you'll need things."

"Yes." Her voice seemed to come from a long way away while her eyes were fixed on things he couldn't see.

Shock, Hal said to himself.

Catching Sissie Albright's eyes, noting she looked a little dazed herself, he pantomimed drinking. The little milliner brightened, nodded and ran off toward some long tables set up in the yard. Hal noted the girl had a very attractive pair of ankles and didn't wonder that the marshal was love-stricken.

He said to Rachel, "Sissie's getting you something to drink," but it was like talking to a seamstress's dummy. He was surprised to find in himself no shadow of impatience with her. Then he said with a deep inner certainty, "Lyle will be all right, you know."

"Will he?" she demanded, clutching his arm suddenly with a fierce strength he hadn't known she possessed.

"I think so." Her clamp on his arm relaxed.

Sissie crossed the lawn to them, a sweaty glass of cloudy liquid in her hand. Mrs. Garrett must have an operating icehouse, Hal reasoned, as there were definitely jagged icebergs floating in the glass that Sissie pushed into Rachel's hand. They reminded him of the stone in Lyle's pocket.

"Now drink that," Sissie ordered.

Rachel took an automatic sip and instantly shuddered, her eyes watering and her throat muscles working spasmodically. "Mrs. Dale's?" she gasped, then coughed.

"She swears there's sugar in it but she likes it 'tart.'"

Hal took the glass. Warned but undaunted by either the bits of lemon pulp floating there or the alarmed looks of the two girls, he took a sip. "Holy cats!" he exclaimed when able to speak. "What does she make it with? Vitriol?"

Sissie said, "She claims it's an old family recipe belonging to her husband's side of the family but I think she must misread the directions."

"I think she uses vinegar by mistake for water," Rachel

said. Then she looked up at Hal. "Sorry I've been such a fool. It was the shock."

"Don't mention it. We better go. Ed will be waiting."

Sissie walked with them to the wagon. She asked Rachel in a low voice, while Hal pretended not to hear, "You haven't seen Benson anywhere?"

"Not for a while. He went out to talk to some folks. Do you want him?"

"No," Sissie said, shaking her head with a somewhat too careful air of unconcern. "I just hadn't seen him around, that's all."

At the wagon, Sissie gave Rachel a quick hug. "I'll go and sit with Lyle until you get back."

"Mrs. Garrett's there now."

"Oh, good. I wanted to ask her about a knitting stitch I saw in the *Women's Weekly*. I'm so stupid about knitting."

Hal had hardly put himself in the back of the wagon, after helping Rachel in, before Ed snapped the reins over his horses. Consequently, Hal fell lengthwise in the hay. He sat up, spitting out a strand.

He said, "Obviously Ed doesn't mind doing *you* a favor but I think he just let me know his opinion of me."

Reaching out to brush him off, Rachel said, her brilliant smile flashing out, "I did warn you."

"You know, people who say 'I've told you so' always have well-attended funerals."

Her smile did have the effect of making a man believe himself wittier or wiser or more kind than even he thought of himself. A smile like that could get to be a drug, eternally craved, and a man could be made to suffer eternally without it. Dangerous thoughts, for a bachelor.

Hal moved closer to her in the sweet-smelling hay. The wide skirt of her pretty, plain blue dress dimpled over her long legs and gathered in folds to emphasize her narrow waist. He tried not to think about these things as he slid his arm around her, telling himself he was being no more than brotherly toward her.

Rachel sighed and rested her head on his shoulder. "I

don't know what we would have done without you today, Hal."

"I didn't do anything." A few loose strands of her hair tickled his nose and he furtively rubbed it.

"You did a lot. And you hardly know Lyle at all."

"I didn't do anything for *Lyle*," Hal said with emphasis. "He's a nice kid, always interested in what's happening. He'd make a good correspondent, if he ever learns to write good English. Of course," he added, chuckling, "he says he wants to go West and rob trains for a living. But all little boys want to be that at one time or another. Or locomotive engineers. Rob trains or drive them, nothing in between. Now, when I was about Lyle's age—"

"I tell you one thing . . ." Rachel said, sitting up, her voice becoming fierce. "That boy is at the end of my patience. I don't care if he does break out and become wild as a coyote later on; I can't stand this. Never knowing where he is, alive or dead, 'til he comes home, often through the window. . . ."

"Wait a minute," Hal said. He removed her sharp forefinger from his chest, where she'd been pounding home her points with it. "Why do you let him run so wild? I don't know much about raising children, but don't you have any control over him?"

"Not much," she admitted. "I almost don't dare to."

"Why not?"

Her eyes half closed, she turned her head away from his searching gaze. Hal had to resist the temptation to take her chin in his fingers and force her eyes to meet his. "I have my reasons. But from now on, he'll be tied to my apron strings if I have to make 'em into nooses!"

Hal lay down in the hay, putting his arms behind his head. The sleeves of his coat were tight around the upper part of his arms but not as tight as the constriction he felt around his heart. "I wish you would trust me," he said.

"Why? You're practically a stranger to me."

"All right. Which of your friends do you trust?" He looked at her, warmed by her beauty as much as by the sunshine. She didn't answer his question, only turning her head to watch the changing trees go by.

"You don't trust anyone, do you, Rachel? Not Sissie, not Mrs. Garrett, not the marshal. Isn't that lonely?"

"What do you know about it? You know exactly . . ."

"What?" he urged, propping himself up on an elbow.

"Nothing. Just . . . nothing."

Hal collapsed back into the hay with a disgusted sigh. It would have been so much easier if his old feeling would sweep over him, if he'd get goose pimples and a raging inner certainty that Rachel Pridgeon would make a good news story. Then he'd know exactly where he was with her. He'd ask her questions and get out of her life. If only it were that simple. He kept finding himself more and more involved with her in an emotional way that troubled him intensely.

He said after some thought, "I wish you would believe that I am your friend."

Her mood had changed. She looked down at him and her bewitching smile caught at his heart. "I haven't believed a word you've said since you came to Brooklyn. It's safer that way."

Ed stopped in front of her house and Rachel stood up, swaying a little. "Thanks, Ed," she said as she got down.

"I'll wait for you," Ed answered. His habitual glumness seemed as though it might lighten in a smile but then the moment passed.

Hal followed her, brushing hay off his coat as he got down. "Now what's that supposed to mean?" he asked, catching up with her as she opened the gate. "What do you mean you haven't believed anything I've said?"

"Did I insult you? I'm sorry. It's just—well, you're not like other men in town."

"Why would I want to be?"

Her eyes snapped at that. "For one thing, they're honest, hard-working, down-to-earth people. They don't stand around and sneer at other folks."

"I resent the implication that I'm somewhat dishonest. Besides, I do not sneer."

"Yes, you do. You walk around with your head in the air like you don't even want God to know you live here now."

"I happen to flatter myself that I'm fitting in pretty well around here."

She stared at him incredulously. "You do?"

"Of course. I even played checkers yesterday with one of the men at the General Store."

"Did you win?"

"Yes."

"There. You see?" She stepped up onto her porch, but Hal didn't want her to get away yet. The color burned bright in her cheeks. The wan ghost who'd looked down at her unconscious brother with tears trembling on her lashes had gone. There was also the honor of not letting a woman win an argument to be considered.

"What possible difference does it make whether I won or not? I happen to be a very good checker player."

"Mr. Madison *let* you win."

"He did not!"

"Of course he did. You're a stranger—it would be impolite to beat the pants off a stranger. Excuse the expression."

She had her hand on the doorknob when Hal went on the attack. "I suppose you think you're part of this town."

"I certainly am. Everyone treats me just like part of the family. They—"

"Talk about you behind your back," Hal finished glibly. "They wonder about you all the time. And they're never catty. Not to mention the fact that Mrs. Schur always makes sure you or I have the biggest pieces of cake."

"What does that have to do with it?"

"I think that's a very clear indication that to her mind you and I are *both* strangers in town."

"That's ridiculous," Rachel exclaimed. "She's just nice. Everyone's been wonderful to me and Lyle. They don't care where we've come from or who . . . I think it's horrible and mean of you to try to spoil things. Just when I . . . when I . . ."

"Rachel . . ." He put his hand over hers where it rested

on the doorknob. Trying to keep the tenderness out of his voice made it gruff. "I didn't mean to make you cry."

"I'm *not*."

He wiped her cheek and showed her the wetness on his fingertips. Her hand twisted under his, opening the door. "Do you always have to prove me wrong?" she demanded.

Stepping over the threshold, she shut the door in his face. Hal glanced over his shoulder at the wagon. All he could see of Ed were his boots, protruding from the wagon bed, crossed at the ankles. Hal opened the door and followed Rachel inside.

He could hear her upstairs, the mutter of her voice as she found all the clever answers she'd thought of too late, the thump and thud of her feet as she stomped around, stomping *him* in absentia. At least she wasn't weeping or, if she was, they were tears of anger. He hoped that he'd never see her miserable again; it did terrible things to his insides.

Hal went out the door, pulling it quietly closed behind him.

The town was sleepy and still under the benediction of the afternoon sun. A stray piece of paper blew along the boardwalk and, with the perversity of its kind, tangled with his leg.

Reaching down to pluck it off, he saw it was a copy of his own child, the *Brooklyn Herald*. Hal decided to be charitable and assume it had wound up an orphan by accident, not because some evil-minded person had hurled it away from him.

It was while he folded it carefully that he heard his name being called by Marshal Hunnicut. He sat out in front of his jail in a chair. Hal crossed the street to speak to him.

"Where you going?" Hunnicut wanted to know.

"Train station. I'd like to send a telegram."

"Can't. Nobody's there now but Ralph's boy and he can't use the telegraph. Doesn't know the code."

"Damn," Hal said without heat.

"Is it something important?"

"Nothing that can't wait, I suppose. It'll have to."

The marshal unfolded his long legs and stood up. "I can

send your message. Ralph can't stop a law officer from using the telegraph if he needs to."

"I'd appreciate that . . . though it's not official government business."

The marshal only shrugged as if, his heart being broken, he didn't mind bending a few regulations. The two men strode along in silence, broken only by the *chuff-chuff* of Marshal Hunnicut's corduroy trousers.

Then he asked, "How's the boy?"

"Except for the clout on the head and being unconscious, pretty well. He'll live to walk again. He's lucky."

"Lyle's a good boy. He's let run too free, though. Often thought of mentioning it to Miss Pridgeon, but it's none of my business 'til he gets in trouble with the law."

Hal said, "I've heard you've been almost a second father to Lyle."

"You've heard wrong. 'Sides, the boy doesn't seem to have a *first* father. I've never heard the boy so much as mention him. Miss Pridgeon doesn't talk about him either."

"All I know is that he had a mustache," Hal added. He didn't know he was smiling as though at a pleasant memory until he noticed the marshal's sideways glance. Then he switched it off. He had no business treasuring up Rachel's words to smile over them later.

As he'd noted when he'd first arrived in Brooklyn, the train station smelled like dust, paper and, surprisingly, vanilla. Hal sniffed, as perplexed by the unusual fragrance as before. But now he had someone to ask.

"'Bout two years ago, this shipment come in mislabeled. It stood in the corner for a day or two—having come in on Saturday and there not being any more trains 'til Tuesday. Then Ralph had to figure out where to ship it on to and he's not the fastest figurer you ever met. After a bit, folks started to notice that smell. Turns out the shipment was a mess of vanilla extract on its way north. But some of the jugs busted and soaked a big ol' patch of the stuff into the floor. It's never come out yet."

"Could have been worse," Hal said, amused, but not likely to fill newsprint with the story.

"Yep. Week before they were shipping onion juice."

The door to the stationmaster's private room, the inner sanctum from whence he dispensed tickets and gossip, was locked. Hal could see the telegraph setup, key and pad all correct, as though they taunted him through the grill. "I guess I'll have to wait 'til he comes back from Mrs. Garrett's," he said glumly.

"Now wait." The marshal craned his long neck to look out each of the exits from the depot, one to the street, one to the platform. Seeing no one but a couple of sparrows, he reached up to the top of the door and slid out a brass key.

"Don't tell anybody you saw this," he warned as he turned the key in the lock. With the same precautions as before, the marshal returned the key to its hiding place. Hal wondered whether there was a living soul in Brooklyn over the age of three who didn't know where the sationmaster kept his spare key. Somehow he doubted it.

Benson Hunnicut seated himself behind the telegraph station and gave a few preliminary taps on the key. "Just to wake the boys up at the next relay," he explained.

"I'm surprised a town this small has a telegraph," Hal said.

"We were surprised too. Some folks think Mr. Clyde might have had something to say about it. Some think he'll want to know quick if his sister gets bad sudden. Though why he should start taking an interest all at once . . ."

A sudden clicking from the key interrupted him. "Here, do you know what you want to say, Hal?"

"Oh! Yes, wait a second." Taking up a pen from the stand, he leaned over the side of the table to fill in a message form. After giving the address of Evans in New York at his old paper, Hal said, "Request at once all information regarding diamonds, chiefly how to identify. Stop. Bill books to Clyde. Stop. Sinclair."

The rapid clicks and stutters of the telegraph sent his message almost as soon as thought. The marshal's expression didn't change while he keyed the message. The moment he stopped though, he echoed one word. "Diamonds? What in tarnation are you asking somebody about diamonds for?"

"Just an idea I had," Hal explained easily. "Did I happen to mention that I write books as well as work for the newspaper?"

"I remember you saying something about it the night I got so drunk on your whisky. Sorry 'bout that, by the way, I'll buy you a bottle one day when the saloon opens up again."

"Is that day likely to be soon?" Hal asked. "I ask for purely medicinal reasons."

The marshal shook his head. "Not likely at all, I'd say. Not that I mind. Why, since they closed the old Hatch, I hardly have a thing to do. Crime's way down when men stop drinking. It's just sometimes a man's got to be able to drown his sorrows."

"One thing is for certain, Marshal," Hal said, watching him go through the elaborate ritual of the key.

"What's that?"

"Sorrows float."

"That they do. You never said if you have a girl in New York."

"Nobody whose crying couldn't be comforted," Hal said lightly. His landlady's daughter, a widowed armful named Stella, had always been very friendly but he'd never touched her on the principle of keeping the place he lived clean. He'd managed always to avoid the trap of the not-yet-widowed as well as the young and innocent.

He thought about Rachel. Innocent? Undoubtedly. Young? Twenty-two wasn't old but she had a warm maturity about her that belied her years. Maybe it was the responsibilities of her life that had ripened her or perhaps she'd been born with that quiet wisdom. She certainly didn't tattle on about herself, even shying away from direct questions.

The marshal was silent for a while as they walked up the main street together. Hal wondered if the older man's thoughts were centering around Miss Sissie Albright. He wouldn't bet against it.

As they approached the jail, Benson asked, "Are you

intending to drive back out to the Garrett place with Miss Pridgeon?"

"I don't think so. She doesn't need me."

"Then how 'bout a game of checkers?"

Thinking back to Rachel's accusation, Hal said, "Only if you promise not to let me win."

"Don't worry. I won't."

The jail, like all such places, was utilitarian, clean and depressing as the devil. Like a cat looking into every corner of a new home, Hal wandered back to the grille that separated the office from the three cells in the back. "Anybody occupying your accommodations, Marshal?"

Benson looked up from laying the pieces out on the black-and-red board. "Nope. We're empty. Not much business since the spring."

"I know many a New York policeman who'd be willing to have half your complaint. Between the hooligans and the riots, we have had few empty jails."

"Want some coffee?"

"Sure." Hal thumbed through the wanted posters, stacked three deep on the wall behind the marshal's desk. "Strange how villainy looks so much like . . . say, here's a face I haven't seen for a while."

Benson put the battered old coffeepot on top of the stove and said, "Who's that?"

"Nixon Sharp. Wanted in . . . let's see . . . four states for everything from spitting on the sidewalk to shooting a man in the back for twenty-five Golden Eagles."

"I don't recognize the name. Did they catch him?" the marshal asked with professional interest.

"I'll give you a copy of the book I wrote on him. *Sharp's Sins—A Confession of a Misspent Life*. Illustrated copiously and serialized in the *Police Gazette*. Taken from the lips of the condemned man himself." He shook his head, a bit sheepishly. "He was pathetically glad to talk to someone about himself. Most of the criminals I interview for my books are that way."

The marshal put two and two together. "You write those

yeller-backed novels? Say, the saloon used to sell those from behind the bar. Some of 'em were pretty good."

"Mine, no doubt." Hal laughed at himself. "I fell into the work by accident, you might say. I interviewed one of our local killers a few years ago. The crime wasn't very interesting, an argument over a woman that turned ugly. But a Mr. Hohenberg who is the publisher of a whole line of dime-novels thought I'd be a good man for the job. The pay's not bad and I can do it in between my reporting."

"They were pretty good," the marshal allowed. "Not that I have much time for reading. But sometimes the nights get right long when you ain't got company. . . ." He hitched his thumb toward the cells. "But, Land o' Goshen, the lies in 'em were fierce!"

"Lies?"

"I'm not one to brag, but I been in some tight spots in my day, and I'd be crazy as a hoot-owl if I did some of the . . . Going up against a mad grizzly bare-handed? Fighting whole crowds of Indians with nothing but a whip? Busting into a cave of outlaws without nobody to watch my back? If I didn't wind up dead, you could put me into some nice safe asylum when I got back."

Hal laughed at the marshal's sudden animation. "Our readers don't usually have your advantages. My books are especially popular with newsboys, or so they say. And one of the best letters I ever received was from an old lady not far from here in St. Joseph who told me she'd always regretted not taking a wagon train west in her youth but after reading my *The Red Stream* she gave up her regrets, for she was sure she would have been murdered if she had gone."

As the marshal shook his head at the folly of women, the coffeepot had begun to rock vigorously over the heat. The marshal took it off the fire and poured out two cups of thick liquid that looked and tasted like pure explosive.

Benson hadn't seemed to notice anything amiss with it. He sat in his chair, pushing away with his feet and hands until he seemed to be lying nearly horizontally. He said, "If I were you, I'd keep this about your writing under your hat."

"I hadn't intended to tell anyone. People get strange when

they find out you're writing a book. Everyone asks if you're intending to put *them* in the next one, not realizing that most people are too dull to be written about."

"Don't worry. They won't hear about it from me. More coffee?"

11

RACHEL TRIED HARD not to be angry when she returned to Mrs. Garrett's. Yet a spurt of white-hot anger burned her heart for an instant, just as quickly repressed, when she saw how people were enjoying themselves. Some were even dancing, she noted, as the distant music of a fiddler reached her ears.

She acknowledged that it was unreasonable to expect them all to give up a long-awaited pleasure because a boy had fallen while being naughty. To do them justice, if Lyle had been killed they would have gone quietly away.

She took her bundle of clothes into the house. Unpinning her hat, she hung it on the proper hook, just as if she were coming in as usual to read to Mrs. Garrett. She heard a whispered hiss and turned to see Sissie coming out of the sickroom pulling the door closed behind her.

"There you are."

"How is he?" Rachel demanded, hurrying toward her friend.

"Sssh. Mrs. Garrett nodded off in her chair." Taking Rachel's elbow, Sissie guided her into the front parlor and to a wide-skirted armchair. "Now don't get excited, Rachel, but Lyle woke up for a few minutes while you were gone."

The sigh Rachel gave came from her heart, leaving her feeling dry and empty. "Thank God," she said. "Did you send for Doctor Warren?"

"At once." A smile trembled on the dark-haired girl's lips. "His chin was dripping with butter from eating corn and he had kernels clear to his sideburns, but he came quick enough. He says Lyle's going to be just fine."

"Is he sure? I mean—a bang on the head like that . . . ?"

"Oh, Doctor Warren asked a whole lot of questions, silly stuff like what's your name, how old are you, such nonsense. Lyle remembers climbing down the ravine perfectly and can even name the first president of the country, though it passes me why Doctor Warren would even ask."

"I suppose to see if Lyle's in his senses."

"Oh, I didn't think of that. Here, take my handkerchief," Sissie said, pressing the soft white cloth into Rachel's hand.

"I'm gathering a collection of them, it seems." Rachel laughed at herself even as she wiped the tears from her face. "I have one of Mrs. Garrett's and one of Mr. Sinclair's . . . now yours. I shall have to launder them all and make sure everyone gets their own back."

She stood up, stuffing the handkerchief into the pocket of her skirt. "I'll go see him now."

"He's asleep again. But you can peek in. He and Mrs. Garrett look like a couple of babies, sweet as sugar."

But when Rachel peeked around the door, she saw that her brother's eyes were open, looking around in an aimless way. When they fell on her, his blank expression was replaced by a kind of trembling eagerness. He held out his arms to her as he had not done since he was a toddler whose greatest joy had been being swung up in the air by his adored older sister.

Rachel clasped Lyle in her arms and began to rock back and forth, his sleek head pillowed on her breast. "How you've scared me," she said, pressing kisses to his hair. "Swear you'll never do anything so foolish again."

Lyle, like all boys often impatient with female tenderness, submitted to being embraced and berated all at the same time. From the depths of his sister's love he said, "Gosh, I'm hungry as a cougar in spring. Can I have something to eat, Rachel?"

A discreet cough told Rachel that Mrs. Garrett had awakened from her doze. "I think there's some doughnuts in the pantry. Would you mind, Miss Albright?"

"Oh, but the doctor . . ." Sissie said.

"Pshaw! If a boy can eat three of my doughnuts and keep 'em down there's nothing wrong with him."

Realizing that others saw him 'gush,' Lyle squirmed out of Rachel's arms. He lay back on the pillow, looking tired, but once again a tough, self-reliant boy. Only Rachel knew how his hand sought hers among the covers.

"Could I, Rachel? And a glass o' milk?"

"I think so. Sissie?"

"I'll bring some for everyone," Sissie said, smiling. "I love your doughnuts, Mrs. Garrett, best of anyone's in Brooklyn."

"That's right," the older woman said complacently.

Rachel noticed that Lyle was reaching under the bed-clothes with his free hand. She saw the raised impression it made as he moved it under the blankets. "What's wrong?" she asked in sudden alarm. "Does something hurt? Your leg? An arm?"

Lyle shook his head with an impatient jerk. With a glance at Mrs. Garrett, he demanded in a sharp whisper, "Where's my clothes? Somebody done stole 'em."

Knowing him as well as she did, Rachel knew that if he had his pants he'd be gone, bang on the head or not. "We had to take 'em away," she said. "They were all covered with mud."

"Oh." He shifted uncomfortably on the clean, smooth sheets, a savage trapped and destroyed by the luxuries of civilization. "Guess you gotta wash 'em then?"

"That's right. Besides, you're not getting up today," Rachel said with all the firmness she could muster.

"But I'm all right, honest. And I gotta——"

"You 'gotta' stay put! I'm not taking any more chances with you, Lyle. Like it or not, you're going to have to start minding me. No more running around like an Indian boy."

"Aw, but . . ." His protest was a masterpiece, a whine so irritating as to command capitulation.

"No."

Lyle slid his hand free. Rachel had been treasuring the touch of that callused palm, for it showed that Lyle still trusted and needed her. But giving in on this wouldn't keep Lyle by her. On the contrary.

She added, "And you'll be going to school come Wednesday It's high time you learned something besides your letters."

The boy scrunched down under the covers, suddenly looking helpless and pathetic. "I don't feel so well. Maybe I'll have to spend a couple days in bed."

"I suppose if I let you off school, you'd make a mighty quick recovery." She couldn't help smiling, though she guessed it might undermine her authority.

Sissie came in, carrying a tray balanced by a glass of milk and a plate loaded with a pyramid of sweet, browned circles. Rachel, making room on the bed for the tray, caught a glimpse of Lyle's face. The prospect of half a dozen doughnuts seemed to act like a tonic, though when he caught her eye he did his best to look wan again.

From behind her, she heard Mrs. Garrett's low, warm laugh, the laugh of a cheerful young girl. It had nothing to do with her outward appearance, that of an old woman whose only safeguard against being bed-ridden was her indomitable spirit. "Help yourself, Miss Rachel. You look a mite peaked."

Earlier, Rachel would have been willing to swear that a bite of anything would have choked her almost to death. Easier never to eat again in her life than try to swallow past the huge lump in her throat that had formed when she saw Lyle apparently dead upon that improvised stretcher. Now, watching Lyle and the two ladies eating and enjoying doughnuts, she took one and liked it so well she took another.

"Dog my cat, I don't know what we would've done without that nice Mr. Sinclair," Mrs. Garrett confided to Sissie, biting into a soft circle for emphasis.

"Mr. Sinclair? Why—what good could he possibly be?" Rachel pinned her friend with a sharp glance. Sissie had no business speaking in that tone about a man she hardly knew. As Mrs. Garrett explained Hal's part in today's emergency, Rachel found herself dwelling less on his medical skills than on the comforting pressure of his arm. When she thought of how she'd accepted that reassurance and even leaned into the warmth of his encircling arm, trusting that it would not be suddenly withdrawn, she could only marvel.

She'd never relied on any other human creature, she reminded herself sternly. Yet even as the prideful thought crossed her mind, she acknowledged it to be false.

As she looked around at her friends with astonishment in her eyes, it was as if she'd never seen them before. But it was not they who had changed. Mrs. Garrett and Sissie, deep in gossip, had proved themselves worthy of her trust again and again. Was she finally forgetting the lessons learned from earliest childhood? She remembered how often her father had explained to her and her older brother his philosophy. He had trusted no one, not his wife, not his children, not the men who had ridden with him so long and into so many dangers. He'd kept them in safety, or so he believed, but at the price of never letting anyone into his heart. Nor had she; her loneliness was her father's legacy.

She thought again of Hal Sinclair. Of course, she had made it a point of honor not to believe a word he said, but what if she could? A thrill ran over her, like the surface flames on a log before it catches fire. Even if, as she feared, he turned out to be a fly-by-nighter, mightn't a heart that blossomed with affection for one man open again for another? A wide vista seemed to open up before her as she pondered this, a view full of fresh sights and delicious possibilities.

"Are you gonna finish that?" Lyle asked, breaking in upon his sister's reflections to point with undisguised greed at the upraised doughnut in Rachel's hand.

"All yours," Rachel said. She smiled and gave it to him. As he ate it, showing as much enthusiasm for his fifth doughnut as for his first, she said, "But don't think I'm going to spoil you rotten just because you took a little bang on the head. You're going to school and I wish I could say you'll be treated just like the other boys."

"Huh. Knew you'd spoil me."

Rachel wiped the smirk off his face with her next words. "You'll work far harder for the same grades. It's not fair, but I'm not having you raised wild. A boy your age ought to know a great many things and you're as ignorant as a Gila monster."

"Hey!" Lyle protested, obviously eyeing the distance he would have to leap to slide out the window. As if she could read his mind, Rachel saw that he was trying to decide whether taking the time to grab his spare pants would give him a better or worse chance of escape.

She fixed him with a baleful eye, the glare she'd seen so many mothers use with awe-inspiring effectiveness on their young ones. It seemed compounded equally of exasperation, command and a threat to inform father when he came home from the fields.

Its only effect on Lyle was to send him off in whoops of laughter so uncontrolled as to make a brief visit under the bedclothes necessary.

The two other women looked up, their eyes dazed from following up the varied peculiarities of the neighbors. Though Rachel's attention had been very much occupied, she seemed to hear as though in echo a discussion about how many more years Mr. Gladd's yellowing paper with his speech of thanks for his reelection would hold up, wondering if Mrs. Dale's corsets would continue to hold *her* up, and whether Marshal Hunnicut had been so lulled by the law-abidingness of Brooklynites that he would be totally useless in a holdup.

Rachel said, "I think the marshal is equal to anything."

Now it was her turn to receive a dagger-glance. It hurt all the more in that it came from Sissie. But Rachel reasoned that Sissie couldn't stop someone else from speaking well of the marshal. She didn't own him, even she did cry buckets over him. Tears, fortunately, seal no bargains and could hardly qualify as a mark of possession.

Lyle sat up, his laughter lost. "My head hurts," he said.

"I'll get some ice. You've got five stitches in your head."

This news brightened Lyle, as Rachel thought it might. "Wow," he said, twisting and wriggling to make a bear's nest of the sheets and blankets in an effort to see his own temple.

"Here's a mirror," Mrs. Garrett said, rolling back in her chair until she could reach the heavy silver-backed toilette set on her dresser.

Lyle gazed at the red wound as a girl might study her hair, turning his head this way and that to get the full effect. "None of the other boys got nuthin' like it. They'll be so pea-green! Hey, you got a bandage for it?"

"Why?" Rachel asked with concern, as this request was very unlike her brother. She still felt that a blow hard enough to render his stone head out of commission must leave some mark upon his spirits.

"Well," he said, squinting in thought. "If it's right out in public where just anyone could see it, then how'm I supposed to get anything for a peek at it?"

"I don't understand."

Lyle rolled his eyes at her stupidity, a mistake as he suddenly gasped and made a grab for her hand. To judge from his expression, the bed was pitching like a storm-wracked ship. Sissie obviously thought the same for she raced for a basin, lest the five doughnuts make a return appearance.

Shrinking down again into the pillows, Lyle closed his eyes. "I'll be all right," he said fiercely, with none of the fainting airs he'd put on when making a pretense of illness.

Rachel changed her position on the bed, coming to sit beside her brother, her arms around his skinny body. He laid his head against her and sighed. She would treasure this moment forever.

School got off to a late start that year. The adults understood that Miss Pridgeon's scapegrace brother had to come first with her and the children frankly rejoiced. A week between harvest and school, with nothing but their regular chores to do, was a gift from heaven. To do them justice, they gave credit where it was due.

Not a day went by that a child did not appear at the door of Rachel's little house, some treasure clasped in a grubby hand. The live ones—frogs, spiders fat with eggs, a mouse—were refused with thanks. The gift of a visitor, however, was treasure indeed. Rachel, as much as she loved Lyle, recognized in him the failing common to so many males—namely, being a rotten patient.

Doctor Warren had sentenced Lyle to a week in bed, not realizing that this was also a sentence of hard labor for Rachel. Or perhaps he expected no less of a woman. She ran up and down the stairs a dozen times an hour, fetching a pillow that had slid to the floor, or a cool glass of something to soothe a dry throat.

Rachel was wearing only her camisole over her long brown wool skirt when the front door opened and a familiar voice called, "Yoo-hoo."

"In the kitchen, Sissie," Rachel called, and turned to hang up the pantalettes she'd been washing out on the line run in front of the fireplace. She hardly had a minute to do all the tasks of the household and had never liked to hang up unmentionables where the neighbors could see.

"Lands!" Sissie said when she saw her. Rachel looked up to see her friend trying frantically to back up in time to keep the person behind her from coming into the kitchen. But she was too late.

Hal stood stock-still when he saw Rachel. As if time had slowed down and stopped, he had leisure to look at her, every detail impressing itself on his mind. Her long arms, bare to the shoulder and moving with a grace that a ballerina would envy. Her hair, tumbling down as usual when she was busy or moved emotionally, curled in the steam of her washtub. The long point of her camisole, the same soft ivory as her skin, made her figure look even more elegant and slender than it was. And when she turned aside to pick up her blouse, shrugging it on without hurry or alarm, the fluid curve of her back as she bent struck him to the heart.

He heard Sissie say something fast and laughing about compromising positions to Rachel. He couldn't have told what she said exactly for it seemed his wits had gone wanting. Even as he thought it, time resumed its normal course. He realized that he'd happened upon the right phrase. His wits *had* gone wanting and what they wanted was Rachel Pridgeon.

Rachel herself was glad that the steam from the laundry water had already flushed her skin or she would have been scarlet with shame. But she didn't know whether to pass off the embarrassing incident with a light word or to ignore it completely. Thank heaven for Sissie's artless chatter.

"I do wish this telephone thing Mr. Sinclair was telling me about would come to Brooklyn. If only we could call before coming over it would save . . . why, last week I hear Mrs. Dale walked in on Miss Feldster and that good-looking Welch boy kissing in the kitchen. Well, you know her—blind as a bat doesn't even come close—but even she could see what was going on there . . . and she's five years older than he is if she's a day!"

"Mrs. Dale and Arnold Welch?" Rachel asked, for she hadn't been listening with more than half an ear.

"No, Miss Feldster. And what will his mother say, for you know they haven't hardly spoken since that business with the frosting last Christmas."

Rachel noticed that Hal looked lost, as well he might. Certainly that was the safest construct to put on the way he was staring at her. Turning away from his gaze, Rachel ran her fingers over her bodice with an assumption of carelessness. Maybe, in her haste, she'd misaligned the buttons on her blouse. But all was well.

"Anyway, if we had a telephone in town I could have just called you on it and you wouldn't have been taken by surprise."

"It doesn't matter. Heavens, what a fuss over nothing. I think I'm as well-dressed in my camisole as most of the ladies Mr. Sinclair saw in New York."

"Better dressed than many," he said gallantly, though the strange severity with which he regarded her had not lessened.

Sissie added, "But it's gospel truth about Miss Feldster. It passes me, though, how she could be interested in that Welch boy when Mr. Allen himself—over at the Twin Hills; you know, the one with them long fingernails—he asked her to marry him."

"You shouldn't say such things in front of Mr. Sinclair, Sissie," she said. "It's nothing but gossip. After all, Mr. Allen didn't tell *you* he'd asked Miss Feldster."

"No, but it's common knowledge that he used to drive up to her folks' place every couple of days with a little token—a box of chocolates, store-bought if you please, or a bouquet of his mother's roses—and then all of a sudden he stopped dead so everyone just knew she'd refused him."

"Don't worry, Miss Pridgeon. I won't print a word of it. I can't. There are such things as libel laws in this state."

"I like that!" Sissie said in mock surprise. "That's just the same as calling me a liar! I suppose it's libel too to say that Mrs. Dale might very well have seen more than a little kissing going on if she'd happened to be wearing her glasses, which isn't very likely, of course, considering she's too vain to ever perch them on the end of her nose. Everybody knows those Welch boys are hot at hand. Why, wasn't it Maris Randall who said it was all she could do to keep her skirt down when—"

Rachel said suddenly, "Would you care for something to drink, Mr. Sinclair?"

"Thank you, no. I just stopped in to ask you a few questions for the paper."

"And I just came by to bring Lyle a few things. Do you want me to run up and sit with him while you start supper?"

"I'd appreciate that, Sissie. I've eaten scorched food the last two days because no sooner do I start cooking than he needs me for something."

"Never you mind," Sissie said with a feather-light touch on her friend's arm. "I'll keep him occupied. I brought along a couple of new books . . . you know I get my little shipment every few months and these are brand-new. Oh," she added, on the point of going out the door. "There's nothing I should know about *under his pillow*, is there?"

Trying not to look conscious of Sissie's real meaning, Rachel said, "No, I made him give the snake back to Bobby Bannerman."

When they were alone, Hal said, "Let's step outside for a little air. The steam in here's curling my mustache."

Rachel laughed. Aware of how nervous she sounded, she said, "That's fine. Let me wrap up." She took a thick woolen shawl, all shades of green and navy blue, and wrapped it around her head and shoulders.

The narrow back porch now had few trappings of vine or leaf to soften its naked contours. Yet a woman could lean against one of the supports to gaze out toward a lazy moon drifting between wings of cloud and look as beautiful as if she stood in a burgeoning bower. Her face emerged white and noble between the enveloping folds of shawl.

Rachel shied away when he would have come close. She said, "I'm worried about Sissie. Her tongue has always run like a fiddlestick but lately . . ."

"I've noticed it too. She's combining many of the worst traits of the old maid into an obnoxious whole. She's becoming arch, and meddlesome, and gossipy."

"I can only put it down to unhappiness. Oh, I wish she'd marry Benson Hunnicut, even if . . ."

"Even if . . . ?"

She shook her head, warning him that the subject was no longer open for discussion. Turning toward him, she leaned back on the rickety railing, her hands supporting herself behind. "What did you want to ask me?"

"Ask you?"

"For the paper, you said."

"Do you know the Welch boys?" he asked, not the question he'd meant to ask at all.

"They're younger than I am," Rachel answered in surprise. "I'm more Miss Feldster's age."

"But you know them?"

"I've met them. And I must say, Arnold Welch has a line in pretty talking almost as good as yours. If I wasn't naturally hardhearted, I might have given in to him when I first came here. To tell the truth, he made kind of a rush at me."

"Did he really? He must have good taste."

Rachel pretended not to hear. "I'm not surprised that Miss Feldster yielded to him. She's lived all her life under the thumb of a strict mother, or so they say. A few sweet words would go a long way with somebody who's never heard any."

He chuffed with a brief laugh. "To hear Sissie talk you'd swear Miss Feldster was at her last prayers for marriage."

"Twenty-two or three is old in the country. Some girls around here who are my age have four children already."

"Do you wish for that?"

"Not at all. I'm happy doing what I do, being what I am."

"With no hopes for the future?"

Rachel realized her position against the railing was not the best from a tactical point of view. She had nowhere to back up as Hal began to walk slowly toward her. She could only stand her ground, easier to do if the ground were not shifting beneath her.

"I have high hopes for the future," she said in a ringing voice. "I think the local superintendent will be very pleased with our school's progress when he comes next spring. Our classes this year will be bigger than ever before and . . . What are you doing? I thought you came here to ask me questions."

"I did," he said, his fingers under her chin, tilting it up. He ran the ball of his thumb over her lower lip, awakening it to a life of its own. Her grip on the railing tightened. Hal's eyes looked so dark in the lowering light, nearly all pupil now.

Ever so gently, with no pressure, he brushed his mouth over hers. A shuddering gasp broke from her. "Do you like that?" he asked.

"Like it?"

"Ah, ah," he said, smiling at her with his eyes. "I'm asking the questions."

12

FUNNY HOW HAL never seemed big until they stood this close. She had to reach up to grasp his shoulders, and he bent low to taste her mouth. His mustache prickled her lips.

His hands never seemed big either until she felt them on her, tantalizing so much of her skin with a single touch. They glided over her clothes while all she could do was grip the cloth of his coat and hang on.

His voice changed too, becoming deeper and quieter, slower and succinct. No fancy words now, just need pulsing behind every simple one. "Open for me. Oh, yes, sweetheart."

Rachel knew she'd give him anything if he asked like that. She pressed against him, knowing she'd regret it, that she'd be ashamed later of her very shamelessness. She felt the sweet, slick glide of his tongue meeting hers while his hands roamed beneath the folds of her shawl.

His roughened fingertips stroked her throat, dipped into the collar of her blouse, ran along the line of her clavicle. He snatched his hands back as though he'd burned them on her, dragging together the edges of the shawl like a curtain to conceal what lay beneath. Drawing his mouth away from hers, he said, "God, Rachel. I shouldn't . . . it was wrong before. It's wrong now."

She shook her head, longing to deny that he was right. The shawl brushed the sides of her face. "Kiss me again, Hal. Please."

"No. I . . ." He groaned, taking the Lord's name in vain. She could feel his hands tremble as they clamped on her shoulders. Hal dragged her forward a step and caught her against his heart.

They stood like that, not even kissing, silently waiting for their sanity to return. She couldn't even get her arms free to put them around him.

Rachel was not naive. She'd heard much, and seen some things that were only explainable in the light of what she'd heard. Before this moment, she'd always found something more than a little funny in the secrets women whispered, one of those things that it is easier to laugh at than to believe. Standing in Hal's arms, so close to him that there was no space at all between them, she knew perfectly well what the hard eagerness of his body meant. Laughing was the last thing on her mind.

"Hal . . ." She put an inch between them when his arms relaxed. Looking into his face, she said, "It's all right, really. I trust you."

"You shouldn't. Not when I can't trust myself. It was bad enough the first time. . . ."

Being human, and female, she didn't hate herself for asking a natural question. "Why did you kiss me then?"

"I wanted to see what it would be like. I found out . . . my Lord, how I found out!"

Though this opened an even more interesting subject to pursue, Rachel restrained herself and asked, "And this time?"

"I kissed you this time because I kissed you the first time. And I've been dreaming of it ever since."

"Dreaming? Of me?"

What there was in these questions to make him kiss her again, Rachel did not know. If she had known, she never would have stopped asking.

He kissed her over and over again, Rachel trying to give him back a tenth of what he showered on her. Her whole body ached with desire. No longer the least bit cold, she didn't try to keep the shawl from slipping off her shoulders. Realizing what was happening, Hal made a grab for it. His fingertips grazed her breast. Rachel caught her breath on a sob.

Hal looked down into her face. Studying every shade of emotion in his eyes, Rachel reached out and guided his hand to her softness. His fingers spreading over that firm yet yielding flesh, Hal closed his eyes.

Then, as fast as summer lightning, he took his hand away and turned sharply away from her.

Rachel put her hand tentatively on his shoulder and he said, "No!"

As he stumbled away, she saw that he'd crossed his arms, tucking his hands away under his upper arms as though he had to physically restrain them from seeking her. Strangely touched, she said, "Please tell me what's wrong."

He turned back to her, his provocative smile tempered by melancholy. "I'm only going to be in Brooklyn for a short time. That's what I want to talk to you about. I think I've got my big story."

"Then I'm pleased for you. But what does that have to do with . . . you and me?"

"Everything. Do I have to explain it to you?" At her nod, he groaned. "I would have thought you'd understand. What kind of man would I be if I let my attraction to you get away from me? To put it baldly, how can I seduce you if I'm planning on leaving town soon?"

"Oh!" Rachel put her hands to her cheeks, fearing that the heat there might burn down the house. Fumbling to find words, she said, "I hadn't thought that far ahead. I don't believe I was thinking at all."

"I'm not a cad, you know. Or an imbecile. And marriage for a man in my line of work would be foolish. I've seen a lot of reporters get married—and I've seen a lot of unhappy wives."

"Who said anything about marriage?" Rachel asked proudly. He was taking too much for granted—assuming she'd give in to him. Within herself, she admitted honestly that clinging to a man and sobbing with pleasure when he kissed her was not the best way to give the impression of virtue coldly rebuking vice.

"Don't you think someone in this town would force me to marry you if it got around that we'd made love? In case you hadn't noticed, people take an interest in that kind of thing here. For all we know, our names have already been linked."

"That's possible. We are both unmarried and we have spoken in public. That's enough for some folks."

"More than enough. People the world over are in agreement on this . . . that a man and woman cannot be just friends."

"Are they wrong? You do keep kissing me."

"You don't seem to mind very much."

Rachel angled a glance at him. She saw the way the corners of his lips twitched, though he tried to keep on frowning. Tossing back her hair, she let her own smile break through. Then, as their eyes met, laughter bubbled up between them like a spring.

"I promise," she declared with mock solemnity, though giggles still shook her shoulders, "I won't try to seduce you before you leave."

"We'll be friends—good friends."

"That's right. Besides, you're not the only one who isn't interested in marriage. Schoolteachers lose their jobs when they get married and I can't afford it."

"Good!" Hal said with decision.

He closed his eyes to the way the golden afternoon sunlight turned her red hair to bright copper. He made a steadfast effort to forget the sound of her glad cries when their lips met, and ordered his curiosity about how she'd sound in bed to stop at once. He could control the way he always knew where she was in a room, he could even control his leaping pulse when she passed by. The only things he couldn't control were his hands. They insisted on remembering with painful clarity the exquisite weight of her breasts in his palms and the subtle firming of their softness as he brushed over their peaks. But if, as she said, she trusted him, then he owed it to her to forget that along with the rest.

Hal nervously did up the buttons on his coat, all the way to the high-cut lapels. Fortunately the skirt of the coat was long enough to hide what needed to be hidden. He found himself wishing with all his heart that the saloon hadn't closed. At a time like this, a man needed a shot of whisky and some none-too-choosy female companionship—maybe a redhead with skin like dimpled cream and eyes to shame the forest. . . .

"Maybe I should come back later," Hal said, feeling unequal to the struggle.

"It's getting late," Rachel said. "But if it's important . . ."

"Yes, it's important. I want you to brace yourself for a shock." He reached out to take her hand, trying to pat it as if he were her uncle. "I have some news for you, Rachel. Something that I saw after your brother was carried to Mrs. Garrett's house."

"Something you saw? I don't understand." Thank goodness she'd talked Lyle out of having his name tattooed on his arm the way he'd wanted in Santa Fe. A red flag would be considered only mildly interesting to a bull compared with the name of Delmon to a man searching for a big story.

"It would be easier to show you. Have you cleaned out Lyle's pockets since he was hurt?"

"No, I've had more than enough to do without that. Why?"

"There's something in his coat pocket that you should see. Where is it?"

"Hanging up on the back of the kitchen door, as always. What's so important about his coat pocket?"

He opened the door and walked back into the kitchen without so much as a by-your-leave. Rachel, with a rare mix of curiosity, disappointment and irritation, followed.

Hal took down the ragged coat, shook it, and put his hand

in the pocket. With his finger through the hole, he fished for the clear stone.

When he brought it up, Rachel saw triumph on his face. It made him look older and somehow harder. "This is it," he said, holding his opened palm toward her.

"It's just a bitty ol' piece of glass. Lyle picks up things like that all the time. His pockets always bulge like a chipmunk's cheeks."

"No, it isn't glass. Look . . ." With a confidence he was far from feeling, Hal stepped up to stand before one of the little panes of glass in the kitchen window. Raising the stone he wrote R.P.+ . . . then he hesitated. Quickly, before he could think the better of it, he scrawled J.A.G. on the window.

"J.A.G.? Who's that?" She quickly reviewed all the men she knew. Nobody had those initials, unless Hal was going around under an alias the same as she was.

"James Abram Garfield. He's going to be president, I think."

"Oh," Rachel said, trying not to show disappointment. If they were friends, he couldn't very well scribble his own initials next to hers. Only lovers did things like that. And even then, only lovers who were very sure of themselves.

"That's interesting," she said. "I never heard of a stone that could write on glass that way. Oh, wait I remember reading a story about some king—or was it Mary, Queen of Scots?—writing a poem on a window like that. Only she used a diamond ring . . . Oh, mercy me! Are you saying that this ugly lump of worthless rock is . . ."

"Why not?"

"Because . . ." She sorted among all the reasons. "Because diamonds don't come from Missouri."

Hal juggled the stone in his hand. "Why not?" he said again. "Somebody found one in Wisconsin about four years ago. I wasn't sent on the story, but I saw it when Tiffany and Company bought it. The fellow who dug it up didn't know what it was and it was sold the first time for a dollar. Tiffany didn't say what they paid for it, but I bet they made Morgan pay more."

"Morgan?"

"J. Pierpont Morgan. He owns one of the largest collections of diamonds in the world and is always interested in buying more. The more unusual, the better he likes them."

Rachel's head was spinning. She tried to hold on to one fact. "Wisconsin is almost clear to Canada. What goes on up there doesn't have anything to do with down in these parts. Diamonds just aren't found in Missouri."

"Actually, no one's ever found many diamonds in the United States. Funny, since we've got everything else. But that doesn't mean they aren't here to find. Maybe no one's found the right place yet. Maybe Brooklyn is the right place." Hal took a breath. "There hasn't been any mining around here, has there?"

"No. Folks would think a man crazy to start mining here. There's coal to the south but not here."

"Most people find diamonds when they are looking for something else. A lot get thrown away because the miner is looking for gold or silver or something. They've found a few in California and some in Indiana."

"You know a lot."

He passed his fingers over the stone again, tilting it to catch the light. "Look, I had my editor send me some books on diamonds. They arrived on yesterday's train and I spent half the night reading them. Mrs. Jergens is going to charge me a fortune for extra candles." Then he grinned. "Once I get my old job back, I'll send her a check."

"I still don't see . . . what do you mean, get your old job back?" Somehow, he looked and sounded different from all the times he'd said that before. Less as if he were keeping his hopes up, and more as if he knew something for sure.

"Of course. Once this story gets out . . ."

"Gets out?" Rachel felt a cold spot in her chest, as though her heart had suddenly frozen.

Hal rubbed the diamond between his hands as if it were a die. "This is a big story, Rachel. I'll beat every other newspaper with it. The *Regard* will be the only New York paper—hell, the only paper in the world—with a man on the spot. The other editors won't be able to stand it." He chuckled with glee. "Sometimes I'm so lucky I can't stand it."

"Lucky isn't the word for it," Rachel murmured. She gazed at Hal as if she'd never seen him before. His deep blue eyes were alight as if with unholy joy. The idea of 'beating the world' seemed to delight him even more than the fact that he held a possible fortune in his hands.

He said, "I knew the moment I saw you, you beauty, that you'd bring me luck."

Rachel wished that he'd speak to *her* in the same loving tone that he spoke to an inanimate lump of rock. Then she remembered that they'd vowed friendship, and friendship only.

As a friend, she said, "You can't write this story, Hal."

"Hmmm? Sure I can. I'll make it good. Of course, I'll need to interview Lyle. Ask him some questions. For instance, I don't know where he found this. Did he see it winking at him in Mrs. Garrett's ravine? Is that why he went down there, to get it? Let me see . . . Boy Risks Life for . . . Not snappy enough." He smoothed his mustache, thinking hard. "Well, Evans can write the headline."

"I know you *can* write it . . ."

"Thanks."

"But you can't." She put both hands on his arm and tried to shake him out of his journalistic daze. Surprised by her fervor, he dropped the diamond.

"Hey! Where did it go?"

"Never mind that now. You can't send this story to your New York paper."

He glanced at her, his brows drawing down. "What do you mean I can't?"

At last she had his attention. A pity she didn't know where to begin. "I haven't lived all my life in Brooklyn."

"I know it. So what does . . . ?"

"Please, Hal." When she recalled how she'd last put those two words together, her mouth dried up. She had to lick her lips to start again. He didn't make it easier by staring at her mouth, a hungry look in his eyes.

Rachel started over. "I've lived other places and I've seen things . . ."

"Ghosts?"

"Oh, try to listen!"

"I will. But you're not making much sense."

"Listen, have you ever seen a town where they've discovered something precious like this?"

"No, I can't say I have."

"Well, I can say it. We . . . my family and I were living in Colorado for a while . . . before Lyle was born. I was just a baby really but I remember it all so clearly. They found silver, I think, or something that men go crazy over. It was a nice little town until word got out. Then the next thing they knew they had men pouring in from all over, everybody that could swing a pick or work a shovel."

"And that's bad? Don't you think your mayor would be thrilled to have that much business come pouring into town, all of them spending their cash at his store?"

"Not if he has the brains of a flea," Rachel snapped back. "How do you think Marshal Hunnicut's going to react when all of a sudden he's got shooting and drinking and murder over a chance word to deal with? And then in come the saloon-keepers and the snake-oil salesmen and the ladies who aren't exactly ladies."

"Come on, Rachel. You're exaggerating. Brooklyn won't turn into Sodom and Gomorrah because of a little newspaper article published all the way in New York."

She counted to ten before she spoke, willing her anger to die down. By clenching her teeth, she managed not to say what she felt when he patronized her. The moments she'd clung to him seemed far away now.

"That's exactly what I think," she said. "Only Sodom and Gomorrah are going to look mighty tame by comparison. Please, Hal. Please don't send that story in."

"It's too late," he said. "I sent it off by telegraph an hour ago."

Later, Rachel tried to convince herself that she'd seen remorse in his eyes. She wished fervently that she'd had more practice in lying to herself. Hal's eyes had been alight with happiness at the thought of going back to the big city and he didn't care who he hurt in the process.

She wanted to believe that she felt this grinding depression of her spirits because of the disagreement that lay between them. It had been more than a disagreement, though, she knew. They'd raised their voices so that Sissie had come downstairs, claiming that Lyle couldn't hear her reading to him over their shouts. After that, Hal went stomping out of the house, only barely remembering not to slam the door. The cushioned care with which he closed it had somehow seemed more final than a slam would have been.

At least Hal had left without talking to Lyle. She'd gone up to question her brother herself. The diamond in her hand hadn't suffered from rolling under the stove nor from being swatted out with the wrong end of the broom handle. Was it true that diamonds were indestructible?

Lyle sat up in his bed, his nightshirt clean for once, and a lock of his brown hair falling over the mark on his brow. Even as she noted that he needed a haircut to be respectable, Rachel sent up a prayer of thanksgiving that Lyle at least seemed to be indestructible. It was not her first such prayer, nor, she feared, would it be her last.

"Hey," he said when he saw her in the doorway. "Miss Albright's been teaching me gin rummy. It's almost as int'restin' as poker. See, what you do is—"

"Lyle," she interrupted. "I'd like to ask you about this." She held up the diamond, seeing how light from the candle beside his bed broke and sparkled in the heart of the uncut stone.

"Thanks, Rachel," the boy said, holding out his hand. "I thought I'd lost it forever, falling down that way."

Rachel put the stone on his brown palm. "It's an especially nice one, isn't it? Where did you find it?"

Strange beyond words to see suddenly her father's fierce expression stamped on Lyle's childish features. His green eyes sharpened as they searched her. Rachel felt the sting of guilt. She must be failing Lyle if he could look at her like that, almost as if he didn't know her at all.

He said, "I brung home a ton o' trash like that. You never asked me where I found any of it before."

"No. It's just that this one is so exceptionally pretty."

"It's a diamond," Lyle said complacently, folding his fingers over the stone. They barely closed around it.

"I beg your pardon?" Had Hal snuck up here to question Lyle without her knowledge? She wondered if he had any morals at all, where a story or a woman were concerned.

"It's a diamond . . . or a ruby. I forget . . . which one of 'em is the red 'un?"

The schoolteacher in her answered at once. "Rubies are red. Diamonds are white."

"Like I said, it's a diamond."

"What makes you think so?"

He flashed her a glance that told her outright that she was a fool. "It was that book you read me—the one I liked."

Rachel couldn't recall reading him a book in which a diamond figured at all and said so.

"Maybe it weren't you, then. It might have been the marshal, but I know there was something about a diamond in it and this is one of 'em."

Rachel nodded absently, then reached out to take Lyle's hand. Holding on to him was the best way to keep his attention. "Lyle, now, I want you to listen to me carefully. Where did you find that stone?"

"Why?" His eyes, his tone, were still suspicious.

"Because if, as you say, it's a diamond, it could be valuable. Lots of people might try to take it away from you."

"You mean steal it? Wow!" He seemed to find the very idea breathlessly exciting. "I never had nothing worth stealing before."

"You never had *anything* worth . . . never mind that now. Do you understand that owning something like this is a responsibility?" She shouldn't have said that word, she realized. Nothing made Lyle lose interest faster than a reminder of responsibility.

"I don't know where I found it. I'm always picking up

stuff. You oughta know that, considerin' how many times I been yelled at for it."

"I don't yell at you, do I?"

Suddenly he gave his most endearing grin. "No. I'll tell you who sure can yell, though, and that's Mr. Sinclair. He was practicing war-whoops t'other day and he liked to have yelled my ear off."

Realizing what a compliment this was in a boy's eyes, Rachel said, "I didn't know you and he were such good friends."

Lyle shrugged, giving away more than he suspected. "He's all right. Gave me a jawbreaker one afternoon and had one himself. Plus, he tol' me how they saw a man's leg off."

"I'll have some words with Mr. Sinclair," Rachel vowed.

"Oh, leave him be. It's not like I'm meaning to do it myself; it's just int'restin'. None of the other boys know how to do it."

Rachel shook her head at her brother. "Mind you don't practice what you preach," she said.

"I won't." He leaned back against his pillows. "When can I get up?"

"Tomorrow." He brightened, then Rachel added, "Just in time for church."

As she stood up, she thought of all the things she should say. Warnings, advice, requests, all jumbled together in her thoughts. "Lyle . . ." she began.

He'd crossed his arms behind his head. She couldn't see the stone now, she didn't know if he'd palmed it or hidden it in the bedclothes. "I wonder what Dad would do," he said, apparently asking his bedroom's sloping ceiling.

"Dad?"

"Sure. Seems to me, he never found anything like this. Mind how he robbed the gold shipment in '74? But he didn't get to keep much of that. Mama said it was all gone by the time I was born. And didn't you say he did a bit o' mining in the gold country when you and Slade were little?"

"He made a living off the miners," Rachel said. "I don't know how but I could make a guess."

Still meditating, Lyle said, "I don't think I'll make my

living like Dad did. Seems to me there's no real money to be made thieving."

"I think you're right," Rachel said softly, hope leaping up in her heart. If only Lyle could keep his feet on the straight and narrow way, one day she'd know for certain that she did the right thing in wresting him away from their family's free and easy approach to the law. Slade never could have taught him that, no matter if he could have taught Lyle to be the fastest shot, the most charming outlaw, the toughest *hombre*. Better Lyle should learn to be a good citizen, a husband and a father.

Rachel bent low over her brother and brushed his forehead with her lips. She murmured, "I love you," though it had been a long time indeed since she'd heard him say it in return. But she didn't have to hear the words to know they were being said.

"You take a nap now," she said as she closed the door. "I'll wake you for supper and then you can get up for a little while afterward."

Lyle nodded and then said, "'Course, there's not a whole lot to be said for bein' honest, neither. Seems to me a feller works mournful hard to be honest and don't get much pay."

Sissie was still in the kitchen when Rachel came downstairs. She'd picked up some mending and sat under the lamp, pulling fine stitches through a pair of Lyle's out-at-knee jeans. Naturally, Rachel protested.

"Tush," Sissie answered. "I enjoy a mite of plain sewing now and then. Dealing with frills and feathers gets wearing after a while."

"The least I can do is invite you to stay to supper. It's not fancy. . . ."

"And are you thinking I need a pheasant under glass?"

"A what?"

Sissie laughed and bit the thread with her strong white teeth. "I read about it in some magazine. Let me see. The young governess was being plied with liquor by some feller—I seem to remember it being a marquis—and the waiter brought in a pheasant under glass. Sounds elegant anyway."

"I wonder if you could serve cornbread under glass. Doesn't have the same sound to it, somehow."

"Oh, I suppose those serial stories are awful silly when you think about 'em, but my, I do enjoy them."

"So do I," Rachel admitted without a blush. "When I was a girl, we only had but one magazine. A *Harper's Bazaar* with the cover torn off. My stepmother and I would read it by the hour. 'Least, I'd read it to her and how she'd wish we had the next issue so we could find out what happened to Lady Ermintrude and the Alpine Guide."

"Was that your only book? We were poor but we had some great books. I think . . . I think my father liked to read."

"Mine didn't. My *madrastra* and I used to hide the magazine under our . . . well, we had the encyclopedia too. That's where I learned to read and most of what I knew before I went to the McLean's Indian School."

"*Indian* School?" Sissie asked, cocking her head to one side like an inquisitive cat.

Rachel said defensively, "It's a very good school in California. Most of the students are Indians who could work you or me into the ground. I wasn't the smartest girl in school, not by a long shot." She realized Sissie was laughing at her and her words sputtered away.

"I wasn't meaning anything, Rachel. I was just surprised. I always figured you went to some fancy school back East. You talk so proper and you know so much."

Not displeased by the compliments, Rachel said, "The school board knows where I came from."

"Well, they haven't said a word, which is something of a record if you think of it. Mercy! How does a boy rip his shirt *there* of all places?" Sissie shook out the shirt Lyle had been wearing when he tumbled down Mrs. Garrett's ravine. Rachel held her breath, expecting a rajah's fortune to come out the seams. When nothing happened, she turned to the stove and began to prepare the evening meal.

By common consent, the two girls talked about everything under the sun with a single exception. They did not discuss the men in their lives. Rachel was left wondering how much Sissie knew or guessed about Hal. If the milliner had known that he and Rachel had kissed, there would have been questions flying around like migrating birds.

Nonetheless, the evening was one of the most pleasant Rachel had spent in a long time. Lyle woke up, ate, and went right back to sleep, recruiting his strength for the next day's services no doubt. Sissie and Rachel got through the whole basket of mending. Though she always kept up with Lyle's tears or he'd have gone bare, her own things were usually shunted aside. Tonight, however, Rachel could exclaim, "Gracious! I can see the bottom of the basket. I can't thank you enough for giving up your evening, Sissie."

"I would have just been sitting home alone. I tell you, that apartment gets downright spooky this time of year. There's an old tree in the backyard and two of the branches rub together when there's a wind! I always think of all the ghost stories I've read 'til I'm certain some *thing* is creeping up the stairs to gobble me up in my bed!"

"Don't!" Rachel said in mock horror. "I won't shut my eyes all night now."

"Once it's midnight, it'll be Sunday and nothing bad can walk then."

As though in answer, Rachel's unreliable clock struck ten and the two young ladies looked at each other in surprise. "It can't be as late as all that," Rachel said.

Sissie fumbled to see the time on the watch that hung from her blouse. "My goodness, but it is. I better be getting along home."

"If you're scared to sleep there . . ."

"I was only kidding, Rachel. Besides, Benson's waiting for me."

"Benson? Have you . . . ?" Her eyes expressed questions she could not put into words.

Sissie's lip quivered and she shook her head. "No. I'll never feel toward another man the way I feel toward Benson Hunnicut. But I can't marry him." She blinked hard to keep the tears from forming. "All the same, he waits to see me safe home if I'm out late. He used to walk behind me, bless his heart, but that scared me so that I insisted he take my arm. He's always a perfect gentleman, though." It didn't take much intuition for Rachel to understand that this last was cause for regret.

"Oh, don't you hate it when they're like that!" she exclaimed impulsively.

"Hal?"

Rachel cast up her eyes and nodded. "He thinks it's wrong for us to be more than friends if he's leaving town soon."

"Just like a man to go all honorable and deny a girl the fun of doing it herself!" Sissie put on her hat, a charming dish of frou-frou and furbelows. "If he were staying around town, would you marry him?"

"No. But I'd like to see more of him."

Sissie giggled deliciously. "If I wasn't a respectable girl, I'm not saying I wouldn't like to 'see more' of Benson. But I am." She sighed for her respectability.

"So am I," Rachel said, echoing her.

The two respectable creatures embraced. Rachel said, "I'm glad you stopped in tonight. I needed a peaceable evening after the last week."

"My pleasure. May I come again soon? The next time you have mending?"

They laughed and Sissie started down the porch steps. Rachel, standing in the doorway, saw plainly the tall, lanky shadow that stepped out from beside the fence.

"May I see you home, Miss Albright?" the marshal asked in his deepest tone.

Sissie didn't dissemble with a start or a shriek. She simply said, "I wish you would," and took the marshal's arm. Rachel heaved a sigh that was not for herself and closed the door.

She wished that she could look forward to many more quiet evenings with her friend, but she knew it would not be long before the marshal's misery, if not his affection, won Sissie over. The milliner wouldn't be able to stand his doglike devotion without giving something back. Rachel didn't think for a moment that the marshal would accept Sissie's favors without insisting on a proper marriage.

As she sat before her small mirror, pulling the last gallant pins from her hair—all those that had maintained their position in the face of pressure—she knew she should be grateful that Hal would be leaving soon. Otherwise, her own respectability would go right out the window.

Rachel sighed again, for the lost opportunity.

13

*W*AKING UP IN an extraordinarily good mood, Rachel couldn't be downhearted even at the prospect of bullying and harassing Lyle into getting ready for church. In fact, she almost could look forward to it. Her shock was all the greater when she came downstairs to find him washed and dressed. Not only that, but he'd refilled the old woodbox by the stove without being asked a hundred times, as was usual. Rachel beamed at him but said nothing to indicate that she saw anything unusual.

Grateful to her because she didn't kick up a fuss or make some sly comment about still being asleep and dreaming, Lyle stayed in the house until it was time to go to church. If he didn't march along with a light heart, at least he didn't scuff his shoes on the gravel as they walked together. It would have been a different story if Rachel had taken her brother's arm, so she refrained. She knew his dislike of affection, especially in public.

In honor of her good mood, Rachel had put on her

jauntiest straw hat, new last spring, refurbished for autumn by Miss Sissie Albright with a charming whimsy of golden-brown daisies. Tilted over Rachel's right eye, the hat seemed almost too dashing for church. But Rachel wore it with pride, daring anyone to say a word against it.

As she passed the gate, she paused to speak to Mrs. Schur who stood there in a dither. Mrs. Schur touched two fingers to Rachel's hand when she held the gate open for her brother. With a twitch of her head, Mrs. Schur indicated that the boy should run ahead so she and Miss Pridgeon could exchange a few words in private.

"I think you should known," she said in a whispered confidence. "Mr. Schur is planning to say a few words about Lyle's fall into the ravine. He feels—that is, Mr. Schur feels—that it was God alone who kept Lyle from being more seriously injured."

"Oh, dear," Rachel said, following Lyle with her eyes. "Lyle won't sit still for that."

"I'm so sorry. I did try my best to talk him out of it, but I'm afraid I only put Mr. Schur's back up."

"I appreciate your mentioning it." Rachael sighed resolutely. "I suppose I'll have to tie Lyle to the bench. Otherwise, he'll bolt."

"If I can help you . . ."

Rachel smiled at the kind, tired-eyed pastor's wife. "If you see Marshal Hunnicut or Hal . . . I mean, Mr. Sinclair, would you ask him to sit with me and Lyle? I know how much Lyle respects them and maybe he'd mind one of them."

She knew it was too much to hope that Mrs. Schur had missed Rachel's easy use of Hal's Christian name. She could only hope that his services to her half brother would explain that familiarity. No one could say the people of Brooklyn adhered to any rules of etiquette, though their community was by no means as free and easy as the West. All the same, a girl using a man's given name without an engagement announced was asking to be the chief topic at the next gathering.

Entering the church after collaring Lyle, Rachel reflected

on the differences between her life now and her former one. Though the barriers between one person and the next had deteriorated in the lax border towns, so that the town ne'er-do-well could call the mayor by his first name, her father had never allowed that kind of casual mingling. He'd enforced a strict discipline backed up by his swift draw. Anyone caught using a familiarity to one of Egan Delmon's family might wind up on the wrong side of his famous Colt.

Not for the first time, Rachel wondered what her father's background had been. He'd never seemed to care much for reading and writing, though she'd received most of her instinctive grasp of grammar and usage from him. He had not spoken like an uneducated man, for all his wild ways. Her *madrastra* had even sworn that he'd recited poetry to her during their brief courtship.

Rachel wished vainly that she'd thought to ask her father questions while he was alive. Not that he would have been forthcoming—she knew that—but she grieved for a chance that would never come again.

"Sit down, Lyle. You can talk to the Bannerman boys later."

She nodded toward Mrs. Bannerman, seemingly borne into the church on a tidal wave of her offspring. The Bannerman children were hellions to a man, from the oldest at fourteen to the youngest still at the toting stage. Mrs. Bannerman claimed that the baby was her long-awaited girl, a declaration greeted with silent skepticism, for the infant had the same face of tough pugnacity as all the others.

Yet there were good in those children, a good Rachel had not suspected when she'd had them in her class. Every day of Lyle's sojourn in bed had brought at least one Bannerman to her door. The other children in town had called as well, but the Bannermans seemed to think that Lyle—struck down while following them on an exploit—had become their property, almost part of the family. It had been they who had brought most of the livestock as gifts.

Mr. Bannerman rarely made an appearance in church or anywhere else. Common gossip had it that he never left their bedroom, worn out by Mrs. Bannerman's insatiable desire for a girl that had led them through all six of their boys.

As Rachel waited for the service to begin, she noticed that there were fewer men than usual in the church. Lyle noticed it too.

"Hey, how come all the menfolk get out of going to church, but I gotta be here?"

"Because life's not fair, Lyle. Sit down."

"Oughta be fair," the boy grumbled under his breath. Rachel thought about rumpling his hair, but restrained herself, knowing how much he'd hate it.

"I'm sorry. You've got to take the rough with the smooth. Stop kicking that pew; you'll scuff the toes off your shoes and that's the last pair you're getting this winter."

A few more women, some out of breath, some distracted by children, came late into the church. More than half of the seats were empty, yet it was already time for the service to start.

Looking around, Rachel didn't even see Mr. McGovern, though his wife was there. He hadn't missed church one Sunday since Rachel and Lyle had come to Brooklyn. Once, he'd boasted in her hearing that he hadn't missed church once in his whole life, except for the time he'd been kept home with the measles as a small boy. Rachel heard some quiet sniffling that might have come from Mrs. McGovern. She made a mental note to find her after service and ask if anything was the matter.

"Sit up straight, Lyle, please. Try not to fidget."

"But this suit itches!" he complained, wiggling like a tadpole. Surreptitiously, Rachel scratched his back through his coat. Lyle sighed with enjoyment.

Mr. Schur walked out to the pulpit. As always, he wore his best blue serge suit, shiny now with wear. He bowed his head for a moment before beginning to speak. When he lifted it, she plainly saw the consternation in his expression when he noticed the shrunken size of the congregation.

Then the big door at the end of the aisle swung open with its individual creak and the pastor's expression lightened with pleasurable anticipation. But it was only Hal, who, though he must have been surprised to see Mr. Schur staring at him, walked sedately up the aisle to Rachel's pew.

"Mrs. Schur sent me," he said in an undertone.

She moved over to give him room and again gave respectful attention to the pastor. Mr. Schur moved his lips as though in silent prayer. "Counting the house," Hal murmured.

Rachel hissed at him, a warning to be silent. She bowed her head, giving Lyle a nudge with her elbow so that he'd follow suit. Then, wisely, she pointed a similar nudge into Hal's ribs. He grinned, but bowed as well.

Under the cover of singing the day's first hymn, Rachel explained to Hal why she'd wanted a man to sit with them. Hal nodded, in time to the music, and added, "I'll sit on him if you'd like me to. I think I'd do anything . . . ," but the song came to an end before he could finish.

As the congregation sat down again, Rachel scooted down the bench a little, for it seemed that Hal had moved closer to her. Her thoughts would follow their own path, no matter how she tried to keep them on a tight rein. She almost always found her thoughts wandering in church, whether to the question of how to make the older boys mind her or to the important issue of how much longer Lyle's shirts could be expected to last. Ashamed to admit it even to herself, Rachel knew she looked forward to church for the very reason that made her feel guilty. So often she literally hadn't a moment to herself, to reflect, to plan or even to daydream.

Lulled by the sound of Mr. Schur's voice, Rachel fell into a daydream now. Instead of autumn on the cusp of winter, spring bloomed. Instead of a shabby dress and a defiantly refurbished hat, she wore damask silk and pink roses in her hair, the one flower above all others she could *not* wear in her red hair. A handsome man kneeled at her feet, offering hand, heart and a diamond ring. . . .

Quickly, she changed the sparkle of the ring to a radiant purple glimmer. Diamonds were all very well for fancy people, but a ring set with a Brazilian pebble had the merit of being smart and inexpensive. After all, she didn't want the moon. Just a nice, sensible husband with enough to keep the wolf from the door.

After having surfaced for a moment, in the manner of a trout to catch a fly, Rachel relaxed again into her innocuous dream. Mr. Schur hadn't said anything about Lyle yet, going on about something St. Paul had said.

The nice, sensible man kneeling by the hem of her damask gown looked up suddenly with a flirtatious wink. He had a small, neat mustache, eyes of twilight blue and a smile to charm the heart out of a woman. "Say the word," he said, "and I won't go back to New York."

Rachel stiffened the easy posture she'd fallen into. As if she were brushing off crumbs, she gave her skirt a shake. Diamonds were bad enough, but if a girl started dreaming about completely unsuitable men . . .

With the sixth sense that reveals when one is being looked at, Rachel felt Hal's eyes on her. She didn't meet his eyes. Even that, though, couldn't stop the rich color from flooding her face. He had made it very clear that, though he was attracted, he could see no future for them. Rachel knew she should honor him for his honesty. Outrageous to think that if he had lied to her, she wouldn't have held it against him. Her good mood of the morning dimmed ever so slightly.

Hal wanted to know very badly what made Rachel blush like that. She couldn't have appeared more guilty if he'd caught her with her hand in the collection plate.

He recognized the signs of guilt in her because he felt so guilty himself. He knew why more than half the men of Brooklyn were not in church this morning, and knew also that Rachel would have cause to blame him when she found out. Hal shifted uncomfortably, only in part because the hard wooden seat beneath him had been designed and built by a carpenter with a higher purpose than comfort.

Glancing down at the backsweep of her bright hair, Hal tried to remember that they'd sworn friendship yesterday. He'd spent half his time since telling himself what a good idea it was to have everything spelled out in plain English. They'd be friends, an example to the world that a man and a woman could have a warm relationship without crossing the border into love. The problem was that he'd convince himself that this was the right direction for them to take, only to find the arguments running through his mind again an hour later. It seemed almost as though he were having trouble convincing himself of the quality of their solution.

He could stand it better if he didn't remember how she'd felt in his arms. With that, it was less like remembering and more like reliving. She'd clung to him so sweetly, with a womanly innocence that stoked fires a more practiced approach would not have awakened. He was neither a virgin nor a fool; he could tell when a woman hadn't much to do with men. He could flatter himself that he was Miss Rachel Pridgeon's first beau, let alone first potential lover.

Hal clenched his fists so hard he left half moons in his palms. He suffered the pain gladly for only this way could he keep from reaching for her right this instant. With an effort, he called up all the reasons he couldn't have Rachel. Sitting next to her, surrounded by her soft fragrance, those reasons seemed the babblings of a pair of superficially intelligent children. So might two overeducated men discuss farming, child-rearing or any other subject that required one to face certain unsavory facts. Though their discourse had sounded like common sense last night, he realized now that they'd left out several important facts.

Hal came back to a sense of his surroundings when a word penetrated his consciousness. Like all good reporters, he'd been listening with half an ear even while he'd apparently been a million miles away. The word that woke him was "pit."

"Surely it was the hand of our Lord God Himself who kept our young brother from dangerous injury when he tumbled into the pit . . ."

Hal stretched out a long arm and neatly snagged the back of Lyle's coat. With a firm pressure, he dragged the boy down when he would have taken flight. Lyle looked around to see what had caught him. When he saw, he opened his mouth as if to exclaim bitterly. But, catching sight of two sets of adult eyes fixed on him in a threatening manner, he subsided, his lower lip mutinous, his eyes black as the pit he'd been saved from—for a while.

From one point of view, Hal supposed this was satisfactory. He had kept Lyle from escaping as Rachel had asked. So long as he had hold of the boy, the service could continue in peace and Rachel wouldn't be embarrassed by her brother bolting from the church, through an open window if necessary.

On the other hand, things couldn't be worse. Hal and Lyle sat on either side of Rachel. As long as Hal maintained his grip on the boy, his arm would lie across Rachel's breasts. She'd already realized this, he knew, because she'd caught her breath. He wondered how long she could go, squeezing as far back as possible against the unforgiving bench, her stomach sucked in almost to her backbone and her breath permanently abated.

"You're turning blue," he murmured.

"I don't suppose . . ."

"He'll be gone if I do."

"Very well. You look uncomfortable."

"At least I'm breathing."

After that, she breathed in shallow pants which did nothing at all to tame Hal's imagination. His ear was close to her lips and she panted in a rhythm as troubling as jungle drums. He considered and discarded various ways to tell her what she was doing to him.

Every now and then, Lyle would give a convulsive wriggle, testing Hal's control. Especially when Mr. Schur began to mention him by name or by the dreaded insult "this little boy." Giving the pastor a dirty look, Hal was tempted to release his hold. Only the thought of Rachel's disappointment kept his hand clenched in the material of coat and shirt. The boy would have to strip half naked to get away. Listening to Mr. Schur but watching Lyle, Hal knew he was thinking it might be worthwhile.

Rachel whispered, "Can't last much longer."

Then Mr. Schur said, "If I can ask the little boy to come up to the front of the church while we sing our hymn of thanks for his deliverance."

Feeling delivered himself, Hal stood up, dragging Lyle to his feet. He hauled Lyle out into the aisle. He glanced down at Rachel. "We'll be back."

Fortunately, most of the women in the congregation were too busy wiping their eyes to notice Lyle's sullen expression. The children were either too young or too busy thanking Heaven that it was not they standing up there looking foolish. Considering that yesterday the children had all been bitterly jealous of Lyle's luck in falling down the ravine, Hal had a moment to reflect on the transitory nature of all glory. After that, he was busy holding on to Lyle, who wriggled like a gaffed fish all during the hymn.

Hal delivered his charge to Rachel the moment the hymn, and the service, was finished. "I'd ask you to have dinner with us," she said. "But we always eat on Sunday with the Schurs."

Then she and Lyle were mobbed by crying women. Hal could only step back to get out of the way, the wisest thing any man could do under the circumstances.

Hal went off to make himself nice to Mrs. Schur, just coming down from the harmonium. "You play so well, ma'am."

"Oh! Do I? I try but it's difficult. The pumps don't work properly and little Bobby Bannerman *will* whistle while I'm trying to work the keys."

"I'd find myself playing what he was whistling. You should tell him to stop."

"I would, but he does it when he breathes. Something's wrong with his nose, I think, so he whistles. Mr. Sinclair," she said with a gasp so that Hal wasn't sure if she had appended his name to her sentence or was starting a new subject. Hal just waited.

She said, "I saw the whole thing."

Hal swallowed, afraid his sins had found him out. What exactly had she seen and when? "You did?"

"I was so impressed."

"Were you?" He considered saying that she wasn't the first woman to say so but decided to hold his tongue until she made herself clearer.

"Oh, yes," she said, blinking her faded eyes. "It's not every man who can manage a wild thing like that. That's how I think of them, you know."

Hal wondered if the natives became easier to understand after one lived in Brooklyn for a while. Though certain Mrs. Schur wasn't talking about what she might very well have been talking about, he felt a headache starting from the pressure of her conversation.

"It's a funny thing," Mrs. Schur went on. "You can't help liking them, and somehow you like the ones that are ruffians even more than the ones that aren't. Take Lyle, for instance."

Hal sighed in relief.

Mrs. Schur misunderstood. "Oh, he's a handful but a *good* boy at heart. All he needs is a man's steadying hand . . . nothing against Miss Pridgeon, you understand. She's been like a mother to that boy, but a boy needs a man in his life."

"I like Lyle. He has no more moral sense than a Wild Man from Borneo, but I like him."

"Now there, you see *good* in the boy too. I know the marshal does, but a boy needs more than a part-time father."

Strange to realize how he bristled at the thought of anyone being a father to Lyle. "Being friends with Lyle isn't the same as taking on fatherhood. Even part-time."

"That's what I mean."

Hal wanted to shake his head in the hopes of clearing it but it would be rude. He said, "A lonely bachelor like me, eating my meals at Mrs. Jergens's . . . I like Lyle's company even when he's troublesome."

"Won't you come have dinner with us? Nothing fancy, just a ham that's been in the smokehouse since spring, a bitty dish of green beans I put up myself and a morsel of cake."

"For your cake, Mrs. Schur, I'd swim Lake Michigan."

He cast a glance toward Rachel, who was trying to save Lyle from being smothered in a weeping woman's ample bosom. At the same time, she was nodding at something Mrs. McGovern was saying.

Their eyes met across the room. Hal, taken aback by the sudden look of cool dislike she threw at him, felt a resurgence of guilt and suddenly wished he could get out of the invitation he'd wrangled. But that was silly. After all, no one with a sense of justice could blame him for the fact that the male population of Brooklyn had left town that morning to go out to Mrs. Garrett's place to begin digging for diamonds.

14

RACHEL WAS NOT given to swearing, for she'd heard too much of it in her youth. Yet, standing before her desk in the schoolroom, she said bluntly, "This town is going to hell."

The ladies gathered there muttered agreement. Some had babies, some had young children clinging to their knees like jungle vines. The older children were out in the yard. Sometimes a gust of wind brought their voices into the schoolroom, not shrieking in play, but in serious discourse like their mothers. Everyone was worried.

"We've got to do something," Mrs. Schur said. "But what?"

"It's no good talking to 'em," Mrs. McGovern said from the third row. "I've tried."

"They come home too tired to talk." Mrs. Gladd shook her head, though she looked more angry than sympathetic.

"If they come home at all," Mrs. Bannerman added. For once, she had only the baby with her. The rest of her brood and her husband too were all out at the Garrett place. Ordinarily a woman who shone with contentment, she had tense lines between her brows and she rocked her whimpering baby at a faster tempo than the slow, gentle swaying of a happy mother.

"It's downright shameful," Mrs. Schur said. "You'd think they'd all lost their minds."

"It's the diamond fever," said Mrs. Dale. When she'd first come into the meeting, no one had recognized her. Wearing her glasses publicly for the first time in months, she'd laughingly explained that with no men in town, there was no point in vanity. "My grandfather took gold fever, they say, and went out to Sutter's Mill and spent five years out there. Left three children and a wife behind, promising to get rich. The only reason he came back was that he got sick. He'd only found about forty dollars worth of gold in all that time."

"For shame!" some women called from the back.

"It's the same thing!" Mrs. Jergens said. "My husband . . . well, you all know about him . . . he took off chasing some dream of silver and I got one letter eight years ago. Never another word."

Mrs. Schur said, "Call it what you like. It's greed, that's all. Just pure greed."

"That's right," Rachel said. But she wasn't thinking of a man's lust for what he could rape from the earth. She thought of Hal's need to get back to the life he'd once known, never caring who he hurt in the process. She'd hardly seen him since Sunday dinner at the Schurs' almost two weeks ago. The one time he did come to her house, she'd refused to speak to him.

She said, "The one I feel sorry for in all this is Mrs. Garrett. Sissie, you saw her yesterday. How is she holding up?"

Sissie rose from her seat up front. Her cheeks were drawn and hollow. Black marks like bruises circled her eyes. Rachel thought she looked like a specter who had wandered in from the graveyard.

Sissie said, "She's holding on somehow. Her hired

man—you all know Mr. Sheppard?—is staying on. He told me he wouldn't pick up a diamond if he saw it lying at his feet. But even he can't keep folks off her property. Even . . ." Her voice broke but she caught her breath on a shaky sigh and went on. "Even Marshal Hunnicut told him to his face that he didn't have the right to force people off that ravine."

"Did you see the marshal?" Mrs. Schur asked sympathetically.

Sissie glanced around at her neighbors, then up at Rachel. Rachel saw only compassion and understanding in the faces of the women, friendship freely offered. No one whispered, no one looked angry for scandal. She nodded to Sissie.

"I saw him for a minute," she said. "He . . . he looked at me like he didn't even know who I was! Then he told me to go home and . . . and stop bothering . . ." She broke down, falling onto the shoulder of Mrs. Dale, who sat beside her. The widow rubbed and patted Sissie's back until her sobs died away.

After lying awake half the night mentally preparing for what she'd say now, Rachel declared, "I don't think that there's anything we can do to bring the men back to their senses."

Holding up her hand to quiet the resulting uproar, she said, "I know! I know, they're good men and they'll come to their senses sooner or later. I just don't see how . . . I mean, you've all tried to talk some sense into them, right?"

"It's like Miss Albright said," one of the women at the back said, standing up. She was a farm wife, whose children were too young for school. "I went up there to see my husband—to try to make him come home. And he looked right through me as if I was a ghost, which I ain't."

She turned sideways and they could all see her rounded waist under her calico dress. "All I can say is it's a good thing that young 'un didn't find that there rock before the crops were in or we'd all be in a way now. I can manage the livestock, for a mite longer anyhow, but if the crops weren't in, I reckon my young 'uns and me would starve for all the menfolk seem to care." She shook her bonneted head and sat down.

"Exactly!" Rachel said. "The problem isn't so much that the men are out digging up Mrs. Garrett's potato patch . . ."

The laughter at what was after all a feeble joke seemed to take some of the pent-up anger out of the schoolroom. Rachel breathed a sigh of relief. They were going to listen.

She said, "The problem is that they're not doing what we need them to be doing. All right then. *We'll* do their jobs."

Instead of hearing the cries of outrage and helplessness that she expected, she saw nods of agreement and whispers of approval. Then Mrs. Hudson stood up, beautifully dressed in a corded plisse dress, her shoes, hat and gloves all to match. In her clear, ladylike voice, she announced, "I can run the bank as well as my husband can. When we were first married, I did all the books myself. I've always had a head for figures."

"And I spend more time at the store than my husband does, since he went and got himself elected mayor," Mrs. Gladd said, popping up in her turn.

The schoolroom erupted with clapping and cheering from the women. Several babies woke up and started to cry. Mrs. Warren stood up, as did the dentist's wife. But they were all silenced instantly, when the handsomest woman present, a blond Juno dressed in black from head to foot, rose to her feet as elegantly as a queen addressing her subjects. "I am more than willing to help anyone who needs it—though it's to be hoped no one will."

Rachel glanced at Mrs. Schur. "The undertaker's wife," she whispered hoarsely. "You wouldn't know her; she's been away."

A moment later, Mrs. Schur was on her feet as well, speaking into the silence. "I can't do my husband's work, not being ordained, but I can do my part. For instance, I may not be able to preach from a pulpit, but I can certainly give Mrs. Hollis a hand with milking her cows and Dorothy can watch over her young ones while she takes some sleep."

The pregnant woman who'd spoken before stood up

again. "I'd be right glad of the help, ma'am. It gets awful wearisome waiting for a baby."

Everyone began to talk rapidly to her neighbor, offering help where help was needed and support when it was required. Overall, they united in condemning the greed of their men.

Then Sissie rose, still wiping her eyes. "Wait! We're forgetting a thing or two."

"Like . . . ?" Rachel prompted. She vigorously shushed a couple of women in the back row.

"Like running the town. We need a committee. I'd like to nominate Mrs. Schur and Mrs. McGovern, as the oldest of us. We'd better have someone who understands money too . . . Mrs. Hudson?"

The new town banker said, "I regretfully refuse. If I'm going to be running the bank and taking care of the twins . . . But in my place I nominate Miss Albright!"

It took quite a while for Rachel to quiet the ladies this time. The new town committee was elected by acclamation without one dissenting voice, not that they would have been able to hear it. When they'd settled down, Sissie was still on her feet.

"I would like to recommend that the committee's first act will be to appoint someone to uphold the law in Brooklyn, as our marshal isn't married . . . and won't be if I have anything to say about it. Treat *me* like I'm nothing, will he?"

Amid general laughter, the committee of three agreed to consider who would be best suited to handle law enforcement for the now-all-but-manless town. Rachel had an unpleasant hunted sensation in her midsection. When Sissie addressed the group one more time, Rachel knew her time had come.

"I'd like to put forward a name as a suggestion. This woman is used to controlling headstrong people, and she does it very well. She is also essentially peaceable, which is an important thing to consider. We don't want some hothead in charge of the law. She'd only get overpowered by the first ruffian to cross her path. Also, this woman is one of the finest shots around as she proved to me one afternoon not

long ago when she drilled twelve out of twelve cans set up
on a split-rail fence twenty-five yards away. I might as well
tell you that I couldn't hit even one!"

"Who is it?"

"Yes, tell us."

"It's Dorothy Schur!" someone said with a laugh.

"Sissie," Rachel said, fixing her dearest friend with a look
that would defeat a gorgon. "Sissie, I'll get you for this if it's
the last thing I do on this earth."

Sissie only smiled broadly and said, "The perfect marshal
for our town is Miss Rachel Pridgeon!"

"Let's be sensible about this!" Rachel said, trying to be
heard over their cheers. "There's someone else . . . much
better . . . please listen . . ." As her first speech as the
new arm of the law, it was a lamentable failure.

Women were coming up to her to wring her hand and to
promise a world of support. She tried to protest. No one
could hear a word she said, or they'd gone willfully deaf. As
if everything had been accomplished, the women began to
leave the schoolhouse to collect their scattered children. In
a few minutes, with the exception of a few stragglers talking
at the back of the room, only the new town committee and
Rachel were left.

"Sissie," Rachel began threateningly.

The milliner held up her needle-pricked fingers, a look of
mock contrition on her face. "Now, Rachel, don't get hot
under the collar. It's only temporary, and you are the best
shot in Brooklyn, at least right now."

Mrs. Schur turned at that. "Is that true, Rachel? Are you
a good shot?"

"Passable. My . . . my father taught me how to use a
gun when I was a girl. He thought a woman needed to
defend herself."

"He was right," Mrs. McGovern said. Her eyes were red
and dimmed by tears. "Only there's some things a gun can't
help you with. After all, we can't shoot our husbands just
because they're acting crazier than a bee-stung mule."

"It's awful tempting though," Sissie said, her lips tightening. "If women served on juries, every one of us would get off scot-free for it too."

Rachel said, "It's bad enough you all made *me* marshal. Let's not go after the whole system of justice."

Mrs. Schur glanced at Rachel, her kindly eyes concerned. "Are you sure you can do this job? After all, it's a difficult one—probably the most difficult one."

A moment ago Rachel had been ready to consign this whole idea to the devil. Now, though, responding to Mrs. Schur's kindly meant concern, Rachel said, "Of course I can. There's nothing to it. Besides, the residents of Brooklyn are largely peace-loving, wouldn't you say?"

"Oh, yes. Love thy neighbor is more than just a phrase here." Her tone indicated a complete loss of hope for those unfortunate enough to live in any other part of the world.

"Then with any luck at all I won't need to demonstrate how good I am with a gun. I don't think . . . no, I don't think I could kill anyone."

"Lands! No, no, no," Mrs. Schur exclaimed.

"Certainly not!" Mrs. McGovern crossed her arms in front of her bosom. "If we thought it meant killing, we never would have put you in charge."

Rachel said, "I was going to nominate Hal Sinclair for marshal, if anyone had let me squeeze a word in edgewise."

"Hal? Why?" Sissie asked.

"Because he's a man, that's why." Rachel confessed inside that she didn't much care for Sissie's using his name so freely. "If trouble comes, I don't mind supporting a man but I don't want to be right out in the middle of trouble any more than anyone else does. If that makes me a coward . . . all right, I'm a coward."

"Makes you a sensible woman to my way of thinking," Mrs. McGovern said. "But it didn't seem to me that the mood of the meeting was going to go for a man doing anything. I don't think it would have changed anybody's mind about you if you had stood up and mentioned Mr. Sinclair."

"Wouldn't have changed mine," Sissie said. "So far as I'm concerned a man is good for just two things. Digging a garden's one and . . . well, I'm not supposed to know about the other one."

Both married ladies tried to look shocked at this free speaking, but their knowing smiles betrayed them. Rachel flattered herself that she managed an expression of blank incomprehension. Sissie winked at her.

Rachel said, "I suppose I'll have to head out to Mrs. Garrett's to get the keys from Marshal Hunnicut."

"The keys to what?" Sissie asked.

"The jail. I may need to lock somebody up."

"Oh, those keys are hanging on a nail just outside the lock-up. And he never locks the office at all."

"Never?"

"Hasn't ever been a reason to, that I can recall. Mrs. McGovern, do you remember the last criminal we had?"

The older woman shook her head and glanced at Mrs. Schur. "I remember," the pastor's wife answered. "It was that nice man from Bella Ridge. You remember. The men were fixing to tar and feather him, so Mr. Hunnicut put him in jail for protection. Of course, I don't know exactly if you could call him a criminal."

"Oh, Lucy!" Mrs. McGovern said. "Only you . . . he was nothing but a snake-oil salesman. That stuff he was peddling killed the Spenglers' pig, you know it did."

"Now, that might have been an accident. That pig didn't look well long before Professor Hightower came through here."

"How on earth can you tell if a pig looks sick or not?"

"Something about their eyes, Mercy. Anybody can tell you when their eyes get all sunken-like . . . and that pig looked just like my grandfather McLean before he died."

The two older women left the schoolroom, thrashing out the question of who had looked worse, the grandfather or the pig. Rachel and Sissie laughed together. "Do you supposed we'll be just like them when we're that age?" Rachel asked.

"Oh, it's likely. Only I'll be the old maid . . . I'm not sure if I should be a cranky one or one who keeps the heart of a girl within her withered bosom."

"What's that? Sounds like Alcott."

Sissie chuckled and shook her head. "I think you'll make a lovely comfortable wife for some lucky man."

"I think the last time we talked about this, you'd decided I should marry a widower. Have you decided on one yet?" More seriously, Rachel asked, "Then you're still determined not to marry the marshal?"

"I confess, Rachel, I was weakening. He looked so miserable and such a fool in that toupee that I was downright on the point of taking him just so he'd pull himself together. But now . . . he's run out on his responsibilities and his pride and me too."

There came the rattling whine of the schoolroom door opening. Both young ladies looked in that direction, their eyes big and startled at being interrupted. Hal stood there, his hat in his hand. He gave them both his most charming smile. Rachel heard Sissie sigh and knew her friend was studying her face.

Hal said, "I hear there was a meeting held here today. Any chance you can tell me what it was about? For the next edition?"

"Our new town committee member will be happy to talk to you, Mr. Sinclair," Rachel said coldly. "Go on, Sissie."

"No, I can't," Sissie said with an apologetic glance. "I have to fit Mrs. Herby for a new hat."

"Mrs. Herby? I don't think I know . . ."

"Sure, you wouldn't. She's been away."

"You mean . . . the undertaker's wife? Mrs. Schur said she'd been away. Where has she been?"

Sissie fluttered a glance at Hal. "You know . . . away-away. She doesn't care to be asked about it." Rachel knew she must look as quizzical as she felt. "Anyway," Sissie went on. "She wants a new hat and I want to sell her one. So I'll fly. Good-bye, Rachel. Since you're going to be you-know-what, you'll need to come to the committee meeting. We're having it at the Schurs' house tonight—she's going to bake something and Mrs. McGovern's going to bring supper so don't bother to bring anything or eat early."

"But Lyle?"

"Oh, bring him. Mrs. McGovern always overdoes it. She says too much is better than too little. Bye!" Her heel-taps on the floor couldn't have been more rapid if the big globe had leaped from its cradle and come rolling after her.

Rachel turned away from Hal and went to sit behind her desk. She felt safe there, secure in the position from which she was accustomed to dispense authority. "I'll be happy to tell you what happened here. Won't you sit down?"

Then she had no choice but to look at him. She kept her eyes politely cool. His dark hair had been cut since she'd seen him last, negating the smooth wave that had so impressed the women of Brooklyn. Mrs. Jergens had taken good care of his clothes but his face had thinned down. Rachel wondered, almost against her will, if he was eating right.

"What would you like to know, Mr. Sinclair?"

"Whether you're ever going to talk to me again."

She blinked. "I beg your pardon?"

"Look, the cold-shoulder treatment has worked. I'm willing to grovel, if that's what it takes."

"Grovel? I don't understand."

"Sure you do." He hadn't seated himself at one of the desks. He stepped up onto the dais, coming around the edge of the desk. Then he perched on the corner. The definition of his thigh muscles was plainly outlined under the fabric of his smooth, dark trousers. He put a flat package wrapped in brown paper down and kept one finger resting on it lightly.

"Look, Rachel," he said in a low voice. "I'm sorry. I didn't think for a minute that the men here would go crazy over diamonds. They seemed like such solid citizens." His lips turned up, though his eyes stayed grave. "Funny how I'm about the only adult male in town that hasn't gone diamond wild."

"You're too sensible?"

"No. I'm not particularly sensible. I just don't believe that anyone ever got rich quick who didn't wind up regretting it one way or another. I have enough things to regret." He put his head to one side and regarded her with one eye closed. "I wish I could paint. You're the prettiest—"

"I don't respond well to flattery," she said.

"That's because you think if something's pleasant, it's got to be sneakily pernicious. Well, here's something I hope you'll think is pleasant." Still with one finger, he pushed the flat package closer to Rachel.

"What's that?" she asked, not picking it up.

"A peace offering. Go on; it won't bite."

"You don't have to give me anything." Mercy knew what he thought an appropriate gift might be. Rachel thought she'd seen boxes of about that shape and size in Sissie's store, holding the collection of silk stockings that made her so proud. It would be just like Hal to give her a pair of those. Remembering how cool and smooth they'd felt when Sissie had insisted she try on a pair, Rachel felt the telltale sweep of heat in her face.

"How do you do that?" Hal asked.

"I hate it," Rachel confessed in a low, passionate voice. "I can't help it."

"Good." He leaned closer, his forearm dangling negligently off his bended knee. "Rachel, there's something I've been meaning to tell you. . . . The time's never been right. But now I feel I must . . . I don't exactly know where to begin. I'm not often at a loss for words."

Good heavens, Rachel thought, wondering what could make him look so grave. It had almost sounded as though he were on the verge of making some declaration. Rachel felt it was wrong not to stop him at once, before he could make her an offer. How to turn him down without hurting or humiliating him? She sternly ignored the voice that demanded to know why she couldn't just grab what he offered. What was a little misery, the voice asked, compared with the bliss of being in Hal's arms again?

"What is it, Hal?" she asked, taking care to keep her voice low and calm.

"There's no point in beating around the bush. Rachel . . ." He looked deeply into her eyes. "Rachel, I want you to know that no matter what, you'll always have my deepest respect and admiration. I know it can't always have been easy for you: taking on Lyle, becoming a teacher and making a place for the two of you in the daily life of Brooklyn. If I haven't said anything before, it's because I wanted to get to know you first, and have you get to know me. I want your trust, Rachel."

"My trust?"

He laughed shortly and raised his hands halfway as if acknowledging himself as a loss. "Listen to me, making speeches like a Tammany Hall politician. Rachel, it's like this . . ."

"Hey, Rachel! When can we go home?" Lyle whined from the front of the schoolhouse. The line on his forehead had faded to pink, though the brown stitches still showed like the ties on a railroad track. "Oh, hey, Mr. Sinclair. I'll be in tomorrow bright and early to help with next week's edition. I been working on spelling stuff upside down and backward like you told me. Listen." Standing on one leg, his favorite position for deep mental concentration, Lyle began to spell. "E-L-Y-L. That's my first name. N-O-M-L—"

"Lyle!" Rachel interrupted him sharply, hearing the high note of panic in her voice. She couldn't possibly let her half brother spell their true last name to a man who'd shown he couldn't be trusted with a big story.

To avert Hal's suspicion, she plastered a big smile on her face and said perkily, "Lyle. Mr. Sinclair. I have a big announcement and I hope you'll both be very pleased. By general election of my peers, I've been named new town marshal. I start from today."

Lyle looked not only unimpressed but sulky that she'd interrupted him just as he was trying to impress Hal. "Aw, heck. I know that. Everybody was gabbing about it when they left."

"Don't say 'heck,'" Rachel said automatically.

"Listen to your sister, kid," Hal counseled. "Besides, there's a lot more forceful expressions . . ." His voice died away under Rachel's eyes. He at least had the common decency to look appalled, Rachel thought, reluctantly awarding him one grade point for fairness' sake.

Then he said, holding out his hand, "Congratulations on your appointment. I hope . . . I hope it goes well for you."

Rachel slipped her hand into his and they shook. She had to tug to get it back. "I hope so too. I wanted to nominate you."

"Me? Why on earth?"

"A man gets further in life than a woman when it comes to respect. I'm just wondering what I'll do if I ask someone to do something and they laugh at me."

"I can't imagine anyone laughing at you. Women like you—schoolteachers, I mean—are lucky that way." He winked at her, leaving her puzzled.

Lyle clicked his tongue against the roof of his mouth. "At least you can shoot, which is more than he can. Right, Hal?"

"That's right. Good thing the paper is mightier than the pistol, huh?"

Rachel said, "We'd better go, Lyle. We're going to the Schurs' house for supper tonight."

"All right. Guess I better get washed up."

Reeling with shock at hearing her brother *volunteer* to come into contact with water, Rachel said, "Good-bye, Hal. I'm not really mad at you anymore, though I think you could have been more careful."

"Next time," he promised.

She started to follow Lyle. Remembering Hal's gift, she went back for it. But when she picked it up, the raffia twist came undone and the paper opened. A book tumbled to the floor, landing open, facedown. Rachel bent her knees gracefully to pick it up.

Hal took it out of her hand before she could right it and read the title. "On second thought . . ."

"Let me see," she asked, smiling, indulging in a moment's tug of war.

"No, it's nothing."

With a lucky twist of her wrist, she obtained the book and flipped open to the frontispiece. A charcoal sketch, smudgy in details, was revealed. A girl on horseback, her hair streaming out in a tangled mane from beneath a cowboy's hat, her mouth open as though she shouted defiance to the mounted group of men dimly glimpsed behind her, lost in the dust she raised with the fury of her ride. Underneath, the caption:

Rakehell Rachel Rides Again!

15

$\mathcal{R}$ACHEL *FELT THE* choking tide of panic well up in her throat. If was as it he had struck her. In shock, she awaited a second blow.

Lyle said, "Hey, is that one of the books you write? I heard you done a lot of 'em."

"A few," Hal admitted. He didn't take his gaze from Rachel. She thought he would have shown more consideration to a beetle he'd accidentally crushed on the boardwalk. The least he could do was avert his eyes while her world came down around her.

"I ain't much of a reader," Lyle said proudly. "But it's a mighty fine thing to write, I guess."

Hal said, "Lyle, would you mind waiting outside for your sister? I have something I want to say to her."

"Sure," Lyle said with one of his quick shrugs. "You gonna get married?"

That shocked Rachel into straightening up. "Lyle! Get."

"Yes, ma'am!" he said smartly, and ran out, the black

soles of his dirty bare feet flashing. The sound of his laughter floated back to the two adults, an echo from a carefree world.

"Rachel . . ." Hal began, putting out his hand toward her.

"What do you want?" She clutched the book to her chest, a futile gesture since he already knew what was in it.

"I want you to know, I didn't write this to hurt you. I wrote it long before I came to Brooklyn—more than a year ago. I've written one about your brother too, and there's another one on your father that will be out next year."

"I don't know what you mean," Rachel said, trying for a bluff. "My father's dead, and Lyle hasn't done anything to make him worth writing about . . . not yet."

"I mean your other brother. Slade Delmon."

"Who?" Wiping the book off with a soft cloth she'd taken from her desk, Rachel said, "Lyle's right. It's a fine thing to have written a book. Who's this girl supposed to be?"

Hal walked around her and slipped the book from her hands. He tossed it onto her desk where it landed with a flat whack. "Rachel, you can't put me off the scent. I know it's you."

"You're crazy," she said.

"Yes. I know. And I know why."

He wanted to kiss her, she could see it in his eyes. Her heart thumped so hard it almost hurt. His kisses were delicious and she longed to taste them again. But it was impossible to trust him, now more than ever. Was he planning to write about this moment too? Would she live to read his report of what it was like to kiss "Rakehell Rachel"?

She tore her wrists free and slipped behind the desk. "I don't know what you're talking about, Hal. There's no reason for you to write books about me, or about my family. We haven't done anything interesting enough to be written about."

"No? What about the Fort Lawson raid? Twelve thousand dollars in gold stolen in a daring daylight robbery. Then add a handful of train robberies, a few border raids, a smidgen of cattle rustling . . . Your father was a genius, of a sort. He's probably the smartest criminal I've ever researched. Of course, I've written about a few others—the James boys, the Hershey Gang—but they were nowhere near your father's caliber. Just dumb cowhands mostly, with itchy trigger fingers."

"I can't imagine why you think I'm interested in a lot of outlaws. I'm respectable." She'd cling to that respectability tooth and nail.

"Writing these books has been a sideline of mine for about five years now. You see—"

"I'm not really interested."

"You should be. A woman should know how a man makes a living. As I was saying, I have this friend in New York who's a publisher. He inherited his father's business in fact, though when Nathan took over they were mostly publishing sermons."

"Pity you didn't read any," she snarled.

"Sure, I read some. My favorite verse is 'Love Thy Neighbor.'" He smiled at her and went on. "Trouble is, there's not a whole lot of money to be had boring people senseless, so he decided to publish something exciting, something that a lot of shop clerks, apprentices and school-boys would want to read. I needed some extra money myself just then and started writing for him at night or whenever I wasn't working on the paper. Now my first few books were mostly made up. I admit that freely."

"Why?"

"Why admit it freely? I'm not ashamed to say that. I didn't have any extra money to waste on a lot of research so I couldn't interview the actual criminals. But nobody seemed to mind much. The books started selling well. So I started coming West once or twice a year to interview the men I was going to write about. Sometimes they'd get hanged or shot before I got to them, but I could usually find some relative or a widow to tell me all I needed to know."

"No," Rachel said, after trying to break in on his

confession once or twice. "Why do I need to know where you make your money?"

"I just thought you'd like to know. I thought you might be worried about it."

"I never gave it a thought. Now, about this book . . ."

"I'd like you to read it. Not many of my subjects have been around long enough to read what I've written about them. Of course, you may not agree with every word. I had to make your life full of excitement and danger. For instance, Dasher McGuire—how long were you in love with him?"

"Dasher McGuire!" she exclaimed in outrage, remembering the grizzled, unwashed ex-trail cook who'd picked up with the gang for a few months when she was all of ten. Then she recovered her wits. "I don't know anyone by that name."

"No, he's dead now, isn't he? Well, there's the California Kid . . . he dropped out of sight a few years ago. Any comment on him? He was said to be quite a handsome man, if you like cold-blooded killers."

"Really, Hal," Rachel said, trying to find a smile. "Why won't you believe me? I'm not Rachel Delmon. It's just a coincidence that I have the same first name. It's a very common first name. It's even in the Bible!"

Looking at him, standing there grinning all over his handsome face, made Rachel want to pick up the nearest object and fling it at his head. Couldn't he tell she was scared out of her wits that he'd expose her? Why couldn't he say something kind instead of baiting her this way?

"I have to go," she said, turning. "Lyle's waiting and it's starting to get cold."

His voice changed, the teasing note vanishing. "Wait, Rachel, please."

He stepped down from the dais to follow her and she became aware as if for the first time that his body was smooth and hard beneath his clothes. She had no choice but to fight the attraction she felt, to starve it until it died. There was no safety should his arms close tight around her for she was already so near to weakening beyond the level of a few hasty kisses. His shoulders looked broad enough to take the weight of her truth, if she could only trust him.

"I can't wait," she said and rushed away.

If her friends found her distracted during the evening meal, they were kind enough not to mention it. Rachel went over and over her conversation with Hal. Had he believed her denials? Why had he been so open with her? What had he meant by those mysterious words "A woman should know where a man's money comes from."? Would the replacing "her man's" for "a man's" make things any clearer? Could they be read as a proposal?

Rachel's thoughts shrank from following that road. He'd made it plain from their first kiss that he had no intention of marrying anyone, let alone her. He couldn't have been more blunt, as she recalled. To fantasize even for a moment about becoming Hal's wife would only lead to heartbreak.

She became aware someone was asking her something. "Yes, please," she said brightly, and found herself staring at a piece of steak slathered with horseradish, a condiment she loathed.

And that was the whole problem with thinking about Hal. He made her dizzy, put her off her balance. She wasn't the kind of girl who spent her days mooning over some man, dreaming of herself married and getting sentimental about doing housework for him. Rachel admitted to herself with a blush that she'd been thinking about doing more with his sheets than washing them. How often in the last few weeks had her fingers traced the outline of her lips, remembering his kisses.

Men had always been a mystery to her—she'd lived among the roughest and rudest of them and a mystery was all she wanted them to be. Yet she found herself thinking of Hal in a different way, a way that both frightened and excited her. She wondered if this was the "desire" her *madrastra* had warned her against.

As if it had been but yesterday, she heard again her stepmother's husky voice. "I tell you now, querida. *If you ever meet a man whose eyes look at you so steadily, whose words make you feel as if you would run mad if he wished it, run away. Steal a horse, stop a train at gunpoint, fly from the cliffs if you must, but run."*

But where could she run to now? This town was her refuge, these people her only friends. The thought of starting over yet again was so wearisome that she felt aged twenty years by the very notion. Even if she did go, there were no guarantees of safety. She'd believed herself to be safe from the long arm of coincidence here in Brooklyn only to find out she was wrong. The same thing might happen again anywhere.

"The only thing to do is to stay and fight," she said to herself, sitting in Mrs. Schur's rocking chair.

"I agree," Mrs. Schur said, with Mrs. McGovern murmuring an echo of agreement.

"Absolutely," Sissie said. "We'll show them what we're made of. Who needs men, anyway?"

"I hope someone here needs me." Mr. Schur spoke plaintively, poking his head around the entrance to the parlor.

Mrs. Schur brightened at once. "Of course, I do, Joshua. But I don't blame anyone for being fed up with men right now."

Mr. Schur came in, his pants streaked with mud, his hair plastered to his forehead by the misty rain that had begun to fall with the twilight. "I've been talking to those men until I'm hoarse and they're not listening to a word. I tell them their wives and children need them. They answer with a promise of good times with all the money they'll have when they find diamonds. I tell them they're neglecting their businesses and they talk about a fortune to be dug out of the ground. I'm about fed up with men myself."

His wife had gone to his side and now she patted his arm. "Come on in the kitchen and I'll heat up something for you. Go on without me, girls, I'll be back."

Sissie sniffed. "If I could have a marriage like that . . ."

Mrs. McGovern said, "Seems to me it's a gift you're given on your wedding day. My mama always told me a good marriage needs working on, like everything on a farm.

Well, I been working on mine for lo these many years and see what I got? I thought I knew that man of mine inside and out. . . ." She shook her head.

Rachel wondered which viewpoint was right. Was a happy marriage a gift or a craft? Which kind would she have, provided she ever found the right man?

Then she heard Hal's voice, inside her head. Had he been talking about her past when he'd said those words about how much he admired her? Or was it possible that he'd been talking of her future, a future he could share?

Rachel remembered that he had no intention of staying in Brooklyn. She remembered how he had kissed her, only to offer friendship. She remembered the way he looked at her sometimes, with such warmth and understanding that her heart turned over. She tried to tell herself that friendship would be enough. She knew she lied.

She was already in love with him.

When it had begun or how, she couldn't say. She wanted to smile when she thought of him, and cry too. If he'd walked in the parlor right then, she wouldn't have had a word to say to him, yet she felt an inner certainty that he'd know how she felt the moment he saw her again. That idea sent a shiver through her.

His name caught at Rachel's ear and she looked up with an inquiring glance at Mrs. McGovern. "I hope you don't mind?" the older lady said.

"Mind? Mind what?"

"Oh, I'm sorry. You did look like you were about a million miles from here. I said that I invited Mr. Sinclair to stop by. Mrs. Schur and I thought the best thing would be to have the facts published in the paper. What did he call it? A special?"

"That's a good idea," Sissie said. "If we don't try to keep things a secret, they can't say we didn't warn them."

"Who?"

"Why, the menfolk, my dear." Mrs. McGovern and Sissie exchanged a glance that was very nearly a mutual shrug. "We're going to let them know in print that they've all been replaced. If that won't sting their pride, then I wash my hands of them."

Mrs. Schur came back and seated herself. She took up the knitting that kept her hands from idleness and forced the devil to look around for another victim. "My, how that boy can put away three big slices of cake on top of that dinner passes me. I swear you could see his belly bulge clean through his clothes."

"Your husband?" Sissie asked wickedly.

"No, Lyle."

"Oh, don't let him impose on you," Rachel said swiftly.

"Tush! Everybody knows a boy of that age has got two hollow legs instead of just one. And I don't begrudge any living creature a bite of cake."

"Where is he now? I hope . . ."

"Oh, him and Joshua are going to take a walk down to the railroad and back. I imagine Joshua will quote a bit of the Bible at him, but he don't have to listen if he don't want to. Now, before Mr. Sinclair gets here, I think we ought to talk about this budget the men worked out. . . ."

Rachel shook off her thoughts of Hal and tried to focus on the paperwork the women had brought to this meeting. But she couldn't help a quickening of excitement inside that bubbled up like fresh water from a stagnant spring. He was coming here!

"Aren't they spending money they haven't got yet?" Rachel asked, looking at the figures that marched down one edge of the book.

"Yes, but they make it up with the taxes in the new year," Mrs. McGovern said, running her finger down the page. "But I don't see where that comes in."

"Right here, under your elbow. Only that's . . . yes, here it is," Sissie said. She sighed. "My own books are bad enough but this is really complicated. If I didn't know better, I'd swear Mayor Gladd's been dipping into the till."

"Oh, don't say that, even in jest, Sissie. You know how things like that get around." Mrs. Schur counted on her fingers. "That looks right, only where'd that extra comma come from?"

"Maybe we should look at the record for '79 to show us what they did last year."

Nodding at Rachel's suggestion, Mrs. Schur turned back a page in the big red-leather ledger. That told the whole story. The ladies looked at each other, aghast, appalled or amused according to their temperaments. "The old bustard," Sissie said.

"What is it?" Rachel asked. Though she was ashamed to admit it in front of even her best friend, Rachel had only just squeaked by the mathematics portion of her teacher's training. She could add, multiply, divide and subtract, but long columns of numbers confused her as they seemed to stretch ever taller above her. The only way she could manage was to divide the column into groups of not more than four and add them up, then adding the answers. Following a set of books from month to month seemed so pointless with all the other things that were going on.

Sissie explained what they'd found in the ledger. "Mr. Gladd takes a little here and there. The most has been a thousand dollars, the least five."

"But that's stealing!"

"He always puts it back in a week or so. I'd like to see his store's records. I bet they show deposits of exactly the same amounts as are missing from the town's books. He's using the town funds as a private bank."

"Was that Mr. Sinclair I heard just now?" Mrs. Schur got up and went to peek out the window, her ball of yarn bouncing to the floor and rolling after her as faithfully as a dog. "Quick, put up that book before he sees it. It's bad enough to catch a member of the congregation succumbing to temptation. We don't want to splash it all over the *Herald*."

Sissie closed the ledger and looked swiftly around for someplace inconspicuous to hide it. With great presence of mind, she stood up and ditched the book under her seat. Then she drifted into her chair again, as languidly graceful as a leaf spinning down from a sycamore.

Mrs. Schur said, "No, it wasn't him."

They all breathed a sigh of relief, especially Rachel. She

had a few more moments to compose herself, to block the memory of his kisses from her mind. It was unexpectedly difficult. The more she told herself to stop letting him dominate her thoughts, the more effortlessly he possessed them.

The other ladies, all unaware of her turmoil, were still discussing the breach of public trust revealed in the town ledger. "It just can't go on," Sissie declared. "Even if he has been paying it back, it's still wrong. Don't any of the other committee members ever look at these books?"

"No," Mrs. McGovern said. "Mayor Gladd is both mayor and town treasurer. It was put to a special vote a few years ago and nobody else wanted the job."

"Leaving the road clear for the mayor to 'borrow' whenever he wished. I wish I had a private bank myself; the railroad would never have to take back another shipment of straw hats because I can't pay the freight."

"Does that happen often?" Rachel asked.

"Often enough to be inconvenient! Maybe *I'll* offer to be treasurer of the old committee as well as of this one!"

"If the men ever come back," Mrs. Schur said wistfully.

"They'll be back," Mrs. McGovern said with a decided, wise nod. "Wait 'til they get hungry . . . good and hungry."

"Most of them are coming home to eat and sleep, and only that," Mrs. Schur told her.

"I didn't mean that kind of hungry, Lucy. Sooner or later, they're going to start missing their wives and then we'll see 'em come trooping home with their tails tucked! And if the womenfolk have half the wits I think they do, they'll stop supplies until their husbands come to heel."

Mrs. Schur said, "Maybe we should spread the word around. No connubial sweetness until they come home. For good."

"You can't do that," Sissie protested. "A man and a wife . . . I mean . . . it's sacred, isn't it?" She floundered as her ideas were overturned, her cheeks all but crisping with the heat of her blush.

"Oh, my, no!" Mrs. McGovern said. "It's special, but it's not sacred."

"Except to some Indians," Mrs. Schur added. "Indians from India, I mean." She looked around at their faces, each registering some degree of surprise. "We used to have a stereograph with pictures of the temples," she explained.

Rachel finally caught up with the conversation. "Are you suggesting that wives 'refuse' their husbands until they come to their senses?"

Mrs. McGovern said, "I know it sounds harsh, but we must fight this 'diamond fever' with whatever weapons we possess."

"I suppose it *might* work, for the married ladies. But what about those men who aren't part of a family?"

Sissie piped up. "Make them wish they were."

"That's the spirit," Mrs. McGovern said.

Rachel marveled at the changes that had already taken place in the tiny committee. Mrs. McGovern, who always seemed a pleasant enough woman, wrapped up in her home, her garden and her husband, had revealed a startling side of her nature. A natural-born leader, she took command of the committee and moved it in the way she wanted it to go.

Mrs. Schur, always so timid and scattered, was showing a real flair for amplifying and improving her leader's commands. Though perhaps not cut out for leadership, she had every quality needed in a good lieutenant. Sissie also seemed more sure of herself, as though the cloud she labored under had begun to lift. Rachel wondered if her friend was still as adamantly opposed to marriage as she'd once been. She certainly seemed to be taking a lively interest in the committee's plans to bring men, including Marshal Hunnicut, back into town.

Rachel examined herself . . . surely she'd changed the least of all. Yesterday, she'd been angry at Hal and afraid. Tonight, she knew she loved him but she was still afraid.

It was the fear in her eyes that Hal saw first when he came into Mrs. Schur's comfortable parlor. The fancy touches of bobble and swag no longer oppressed him. They'd become but a background to the people that he now found so interesting.

Hal shook hands with the two older women and Sissie. Then he sat down as close as possible to Rachel. "I'm sorry about this afternoon," he said softly.

Aware that the ears of the other women must be pricking up, he added more loudly, "You left the book I lent you behind at the school. I dropped it at your house on the way here. I hope you'll read it."

"Is it one of your books?" Mrs. McGovern asked. "I've never met a real, live author before."

"We're the same as anyone else, ma'am. Sometimes a little denser than most." His eyes couldn't stay away from Rachel for long. He noted each feature of her face with concern. Little lines had come between her brows and at the edges of her eyes, lines he hoped would soon fade. He didn't want to see lines there yet; lines that shouldn't come for years and then only from laughter. Suddenly and with all his heart, Hal wanted to see Rachel laugh again. Outlaw's daughter or meek schoolmistress, she should never look so sad.

"So," he said, leaning forward. "You ladies have started a revolution here in Brooklyn. All males are to be overtaken from their positions and a new legion of women are to take over. From mayor to . . . marshal?" His gaze challenged her. If he couldn't see her laugh, he could see her spark.

"It's not like that," she said. "We haven't 'overthrown' anyone. They abdicated."

"And you all rushed to fill the void? Very public-spirited. Tell me, Marshal Pridgeon, when the real marshal comes back, will you step down?"

But Sissie interrupted before Rachel and he could start sparring. "Of course not. I don't think Benson Hunnicut deserves to keep his job. Nor does Mr. Gladd, Mr. Hudson or even Mr. Herby!"

"Now, Sissie," Mrs. Schur said admonishingly. "We don't mean to go so far, now do we, Mercy?"

"Lands, no! This is just a temporary kind of thing. Just 'til this silly diamond thing dies down. And that's why we asked you here, Mr. Sinclair." Mrs. McGovern took easy control of the group. "We think you'll be fair and see our point of view. Now if it hadn't been for you running away with this diamond find of Lyle's we wouldn't be in this mess now."

"I don't admit that," Hal said. "The way people talk in this town everyone would have found out about it anyway."

"But you published it as fact," Rachel protested. "No one knows for sure that what Lyle found *is* a diamond. You don't even have the stone."

"No, if I had, I would have sent it to New York for analysis. But you don't know that it *isn't* a diamond. Not to mention that if you'd read my story, you'd see that I never said that's what it was. I only suggested it."

"But . . ."

Once again, someone interrupted before Hal was entirely satisfied with the way Rachel looked. She did have more color, but she didn't quite have all the sparkle in her eyes that he wished to see. Plus, her hair had not yet tumbled down, though a few wisps escaped the pins. He wished that they could be alone. A few moments in his arms and her eyes would be glowing, her red hair down, his hands plunging into the cool strands . . .

Hal shifted in his seat and tried to remember what they were all talking about.

Mrs. McGovern was saying, "So if you'll just write *another* story saying the first one wasn't right, then all this will die down and everything'll get back to normal."

"I can't do that," Hal said apologetically just as Rachel said, "He can't do that."

They looked at each other, his eyes alight with amusement, her eyes stern and yet wincing ever so slightly. He bowed for her to go first.

"Hal can't do that. That would ruin his chances of ever going back to New York City. And that's all he cares about, isn't it?"

With a violent push that left the rocking chair jerking as if taken with a spasm, Rachel jumped out and went to stand by the window, her hand tight on the curtains. Hal faced the gazes of the three ladies, their eyebrows all but crawling into their hairlines. He said, "I can't take the story back because I stand by what I wrote. What you're asking me to do is against every ethic of a newspaperman. I just can't."

Mrs. McGovern sniffed. Sissie said, "Ethics! I didn't know you had any!"

Ever the peacemaker, Mrs. Schur said, "Now, now. I'm sure we all admire Mr. Sinclair for his attitude, though we wish he wouldn't be so . . ." She tightened her lips as though keeping in by force all the things she'd like to call him. "Mercy, I'd appreciate your help in the kitchen," she said, telegraphing by the twitch of her head that she had something important to say.

The two older ladies left. Sissie remained, her narrowed eyes fixed on Hal as though she'd compel him to change his mind by mental telepathy. Hal himself turned his head to watch Rachel. If she were crying . . .

All at once, Sissie stood up and said, "I'll go see if I can help too."

She paused dramatically on the threshold. "Behave yourselves while I'm gone."

To Hal's amazement, she threw him a sudden wink and an upthrust thumb which she then jerked toward Rachel. When he stared blankly at her, she stamped her foot silently. Then a sappy expression distorted her features and she pressed her hands to her heart, closing her eyes as if in ecstasy. Then with her fists on her hips, she stared at him, obviously hoping some part of her message got through.

Hal touched one finger to his brow in a salute. Sissie left, whistling.

"Really," Rachel said, her back still toward him. "What came over Sissie? You'd think she was having a fit!"

Realizing she'd seen the milliner's performance in the black mirror the window had become, Hal rose to his feet and crossed to her. "Just giving me some sage advice."

He put his hands on her shoulders and turned her. She came easily enough, which got his hopes up. "Rachel," he said, looking down into her eyes. They'd haunted him, all their moods going through his mind in the dark of the night and the light of the day. He loved their laughter, their somberness, their anger. The only thing he couldn't bear about them were their tears.

"What now?" she asked, only her voice was soft as a lover's.

"I don't have anything to say but your name. I told you how I felt at the school. I respect you no matter what you've done."

"Thank you."

His thumb skimmed over her cheek, tracing the smooth contour of cheekbones and hollow. Her eyes fell, half closing. "Rachel . . ."

"What?"

"Just . . ." He tilted her chin, his kiss featherlight against the fullness of her lips. He deepened the kiss slightly, then drew back, watching her raise up to follow, reaching out for more. He chuckled, "I've never kissed a lawman before."

Her hands had crept up to his chest, light as leaves blown by the wind. Her fragrance surrounded him, wild and sweet, making him dizzy. His arms tightened around her in response. She murmured, "Just shut up, Hal. For once in your life, quit with the smart-mouthing."

"You don't know how smart my mouth can be, love."

Before he'd finished speaking, her arms were around his neck, bringing him down. Rachel rose up on tiptoe, pressing against him with her warmth. Hal groaned in his throat as she kissed him with all her ardor. His whole body awoke under her onslaught, but what really moved his heart was that he could taste in her kiss a hint of desperation.

They heard Lyle shouting in the distance. Hal reluctantly lifted his head. "I may have to do something about that boy."

Rachel rested her head on his shoulder. He could feel the swift pace of her breathing in the rise and fall of her chest. "He's incurable. Hal . . ." She broke off. "Is he calling me?"

"Of course he is. I think he knows whenever I want to kiss you and comes around on purpose."

"He's too late, then."

Nevertheless, she moved away from him. Hal wondered at his longing to snatch her back again. Even five feet seemed too far away. He crossed his arms, deeply troubled by his feelings.

Then running feet came to a stop at the parlor entrance. Rachel said, turning, "Lyle, don't run in the house . . . oh, Mr. Schur! I'm sorry, I thought—"

"Miss Pridgeon, you'd better come quickly."

The pastor was out of breath, his face red. "What's wrong?" Hal asked, feeling the prickle of a story.

"The last train just pulled into the station, loaded to the brim with folks."

"Folks?" Rachel asked. "What kind of folks?"

"All kinds. Mostly men. They're all asking the same question. 'Where are the diamonds? Where are the diamonds?'"

16

*L*ITERALLY OVERNIGHT THE whole character of Brooklyn changed and not, as the women decided in a
second meeting, for the better. A tent-town had sprung up on the
outskirts of town, halfway to the Garrett farm. The field
where the newcomers camped, once a grassy meadow, had
overnight become a slough of mud. The weather hadn't
helped. The misty drizzle of the evening had become a
downpour by midnight.

The next wave of people started arriving the next afternoon, some by wagon, others on horseback. They came to
find every spot taken, every pick, shovel or crowbar sold,
every tent occupied. "I'm afraid it's going to get ugly," Hal
said to Sissie as they parted inside the church, he to sit with
the others, her to take her proper place with the committee.

He'd accompanied Sissie to the meeting at her request,
calling for her at her shop. She'd sent him a note by Lyle,
confiding that she was afraid to walk down the main street
alone; there were so many strange men in town. Hal

couldn't refuse to help her. He understood the reason for her nerves. More than one hard face had turned in her direction, even while she walked arm-in-arm with him.

Tonight, the women met in the church. They were fewer than last time and not so militant. When Mrs. McGovern asked where the rest were, Mrs. Dale stood up and said, "Home. Staying up all night with their husbands' shotguns in their arms, if they have any sense. Someone stole a pie, right off my windowsill this morning! What is the world coming to!"

"That's nothing." A woman who had tucked all her hair inside a bonnet, making her round face appear even rounder stood up. She looked so angry that Hal was afraid she'd cry. "They stole two chickens and a shirt right off the line. If this keeps up, I won't be able to feed my children!"

There came a roar of agreement that made Hal jump. He hadn't realized women could sound so fierce. Mrs. McGovern had to rap on the table where the committee sat before the audience settled down.

Complacently, Mrs. Jergens said, "I haven't had any trouble. I been taking food out to them and they pay good, cash on the spot! I've made forty dollars already which is more than I usually see in a month. I say there's money to be made off these strangers and we should take advantage of it."

What made Hal turn around to look at the door at that moment he preferred not to know. There stood Rachel, a man's duster thrown over her shoulders, dark with rain. A man's low-crowned hat sat atop her beautiful hair. She took it off and shook away the water. Hal noticed Lyle, wrapped in a rubberized coat, at her heels.

Then Rachel took off her coat, laying it in a housewifely way over the end of a pew to dry. She said something to her brother and he also took off his coat, but Hal had no eyes for him then.

Her dress was in two pieces, a mannish jacket over a skirt, made of some dull gray fabric. A pewter star was pinned to her breast. But the accessory that caught the eye and strangled the breath was her heavy brown belt, studded with brass-tipped bullets. The wide leather made her waist look tiny, especially in comparison with the big Colt she wore in the holster on her right hip. She started up the aisle, Lyle dogging along behind her.

"Rachel!" Sissie yelled.

"Yes?" She stood there in the middle of the aisle, her posture easy, the heel of her hand resting on the butt of her pistol.

Hal cleared his throat. "I think Miss Albright objects to a weapon in church."

"You know, I forgot I had it on. I was just putting someone in jail, which is why I'm late."

"You arrested someone?" Hal demanded. "Are you crazy?"

Heedless of the women's fascinated eyes, Hal popped up out of his pew. "That gun doesn't make you a man, Rachel. Don't you know you could be seriously hurt playing marshal?"

To his surprise, she didn't get riled. She just smiled at him as though he were no older than Lyle. "I'm not playing," she said, as she continued up the aisle.

The boy stopped and looked at Hal as if he were asking for something. Hal waved him forward, and the kid came and sat beside him. Considering all that had happened, Lyle looked to be in disgustingly good health. Even the line on his forehead was fading. "Gee, thanks, Hal. I ain't been outta Rachel's sight all day and she's startin' to itch me."

"I know how you feel," Hal answered from the heart. Frustrated, he glared around at the assembled women. Many of them had put aside their private worries to stare at him, their interest caught by him making a spectacle of himself. When he found himself wondering how he'd describe his behavior in a column, Hal sat down. All his protective instincts had been aroused. If Rachel wouldn't let him exercise them on her behalf, he'd bottle them up until she did need him. Sooner or later, she was bound to get into more trouble than she could handle.

Somehow, though, Rachel's appearance at the meeting calmed the women's fears. Though Mrs. McGovern did her best to control the agenda, no one wanted to hear from anyone but Rachel, longing with one mind to know what kind of dangerous criminal she'd caught.

"Was it the rascal who stole my pie?" Mrs. Dale demanded.

"Somebody stole a pie from you? Come down to the jail and make a report. No, the man I arrested had been drinking, not eating. I figure someone must have brought whisky from home, a lot of it. He's the second one tonight."

"That reminds me," Mrs. McGovern said. "I want to know who bought the saloon when we closed it down. Did the town buy it?" Blank looks were all she got in answer. "Well, come on. Someone must know if their husband bought the Hatch or not."

"Ask Mrs. Gladd; she'll know what happened to it," Mrs. Schur said shyly.

"I'll do that," Rachel offered. "I see what you mean, Mrs. McGovern. With all these strangers in town, someone might decide to wring money from them by selling them liquor. Seems none of them know the value of a dollar. Why, I was offered two hundred dollars . . ." Suddenly she blushed and all but visibly bit her tongue. Hal determined that he'd get the full story from her and then some stranger was due to be knocked down and stepped on.

"Anyway," Rachel continued, "it'll be a disaster in the making if somebody opens up the saloon again. I know I can count on you ladies to be sensible, but someone might decide a few dollars are more important than this town's peace of mind."

An uncomfortable silence fell, broken by a few stagy coughs. Rachel looked puzzled. Hal realized she hadn't been there when Mrs. Jergens had urged the town to exploit the newcomers. Judging by Mrs. Jergens's fulminating expression, she thought Rachel was twitting her for her greed. Hal hoped that it didn't turn out that the danger he would save Rachel from would be Mrs. Jergens and a cat fight.

The rest of the meeting was brief. Mrs. McGovern explained what their committee had accomplished so far:

coming to an understanding of how the town functioned, acquiring use of town funds during the emergency and confirming Rachel Pridgeon's appointment as marshal. None but the last item seemed to interest the women. Only when Rachel's name was mentioned was there applause.

She rose to her feet and held up her hands for silence. "I do have a favor I need to ask. First of all, if I'm going to be putting people in jail I'm going to need a deputy. I'd like to ask Mr. Sinclair, that is, if he wouldn't mind serving under a woman."

Hal hesitated. He thought about his bound duty not to become a part of any government so that his reporting would remain uncorrupted. However, he also thought about protecting Rachel. When it came to a choice between his professional ethics and Rachel, he was afraid that ethics would only be the first thing to go. "I accept with pleasure. I shall enjoy serving under you, Miss Pridgeon."

He purposefully gave his voice extra warmth to convey more than a polite sentiment. Rachel's hand crept up to push in her hairpins more securely. Hal bit the insides of his cheeks to keep from laughing. Teasing her was a two-edged sword. It delighted him that the desire between them was mutual; it tortured him to know that it would be utterly wrong to seek any satisfaction.

She had to give herself a shake before she could continue with what she wanted to say. "I . . . I also need you all to help me with one other matter, and to have those here ask everyone else—your children and those who are absent tonight—to help me as well. I'm concerned about Lyle."

Now Hal could feel the attention to the meeting catch and hold. Perhaps no other kind of worry could have drawn them from their private concerns and fears. But the needs of a child came first with all of them.

The child, however, groaned and cast his eyes up at Hal. "I can take care of myself," he said, loudly enough to be heard by his sister.

Rachel ignored him. "Thanks to a certain newspaper story in New York, everyone knows that the diamond was found by a boy. I'm very glad to be able to say that the story didn't mention Lyle by name, for which I am more than grateful." Her eyes fell on Hal for a moment, making him acutely embarrassed, especially when a light volley of applause broke out.

"Yet all these people are asking to talk to him, or rather demanding the boy who found the diamond. I don't want anyone talking to him, or telling the newcomers where he can be found. Not that they'd hurt him——"

"Anyone who'd steal chickens and a shirt from a poor widow will do anything!" the plump, angry woman said. "You can count on me. I don't have a word to say to anyone who wasn't born and raised right here in Brooklyn! Uh, present company not included, of course." She turned beet-red and sat down more quickly than she'd stood up.

"I appreciate that, Mrs. Fulton," Rachel said.

Mrs. Schur said, "Why don't you send him to our house? Dorothy can look after him—it'll do her good. Get her mind off Ed Greely."

This time only Hal heard Lyle sigh. "Not Dorothy Schur!" he moaned.

"Hush, son. Sometimes it's best just to let the women do what they want."

"Yeah. But I sure hate bein' blubbered over."

"Don't tell me Ed's gone diamond-crazy too!" Mrs. McGovern exclaimed.

A tear glistened in Mrs. Schur's eye and she sniffed. "I'm afraid so."

"Oh, it's ridiculous!" Sissie said and hit the table with her fist. "I wish that stupid rock had never been found."

"Me, too," Rachel said. "But we can't blame Lyle for finding it or for losing it."

"He lost it?" more than one voice called out.

Rachel nodded, her mouth turned down. "When I asked him to give it to me so we could send it away to be tested, he told me that he lost it. He doesn't know where."

"Ain't that a boy for you!" someone from the back said loudly.

"Hey!" Lyle protested. "Can I help it if I got a hole in my pocket?"

On that depressing note, the meeting broke up.

Keeping his hand on Lyle's thin shoulder, Hal waited for Sissie, who'd begun to talk to Rachel in an undertone almost before Mrs. McGovern closed the meeting. The young milliner had her hand on Rachel's forearm as she leaned forward, talking rapidly. Rachel nodded and only once in a while dropped a word.

Hal started moving forward with Lyle against the press of ladies eager to get home to count their chickens. Mrs. Fulton and the very pregnant Mrs. Hollis stopped him, together with some of their friends. They were all weary-looking women, with the dry skin and lusterless hair that spoke of a life filled with responsibilities and short on luxuries. Despite that, their eyes were clear, their hands more honorable than their pampered sisters' by virtue of hard work.

"Mr. Sinclair," Mrs. Fulton said, all the power of her uncompromising personality focused on him. "I want to say that we're all right glad you're staying to fight it out with us. We wish our husbands had your backbone."

Hal was afraid she was going to pat him heavily on the back. Years of avoiding glad-handing politicians had made him adept at sidestepping any such displays. He caught her hand as it swung down and pumped it hardily. "Nice of you to say that, Mrs. . . . Mrs. . . . ."

"Fulton. Ezekiel Fulton's my husband. We've got a farm out at Peach Rock Hollow. It's a good farm but it won't make it if he keeps up this diamond nonsense."

Mrs. Hollis said, easing her back, "It's a cryin' shame, that's what it is. And what they done to Mrs. Garrett's farm is a shame and a disgrace too!"

"Now I went out there today," Mrs. Fulton said, "and I looked that man of mine dead in the eye. I told him that he'd better come home or I'd know what to do about it."

"What did you do?" Hal asked, fascinated despite himself. Testing the grown-up's attention, Lyle gave a wriggle, boneless as a worm, but Hal managed to hang on to the boy.

"He told me some fiddle-faddle about getting rich as Sneezus and showering me with diamonds and rubies. I told him all I wanted to be showered with was corn and potatoes, then I gave him a shove and he went headfirst into a mud puddle."

"Serves him right!" Mrs. Hollis said.

"No, it don't. But I figure it might remind him of our wedding night." Without any further explanation, and leaving Hal with his mouth open, Mrs. Fulton looked past him, said, "Joe and Mary Ray Fulton, you stop that!" and took off to care for her children.

Hal excused himself from the others. Sissie was still talking intently to Rachel, though the schoolteacher/marshal had disengaged her arm. Now, as Hal and Lyle came up, she said, "Sissie, I said I'll do my best. But if he wouldn't talk to you, is he likely to listen to me?"

"You're talking about Benson?" Hal asked.

"Sissie feels that if we could just get one of our own men to come back . . ."

"Then maybe the others would see the light too," Sissie finished. "We can't go on like this. It wasn't so bad before; maybe we could have limped along. But with all these strangers . . . I don't like the looks of some of them. They look like the people you read about in those penny dreadfuls."

"You read a lot of them?" Hal asked.

"Oh, no. I never read that kind of trash. But you hear things. . . ."

Lyle asked, "What kind of trash do you read?" saving Hal from asking.

Rachel leaned down and gave her brother an earnest look. "You're going to Mrs. Schur's tonight, Lyle. Don't you dare give her or Dorothy any trouble or I'll know what to do about it."

"Aw, I'll be good. But it's a darn shame that a feller can't even find a rock without stirring up trouble."

"Isn't it?" Rachel said dryly. She looked up, her lovely face flushed from stooping. "Would you mind walking Lyle and Mrs. Schur home? Sissie and I will wait here for you."

"As long as I don't have to watch him," Hal said, giving

the kid a wink. "I'm happy just to be a deputy. I don't want to risk my life chasing after him. Er . . . shouldn't I be sworn in or something?"

"Why? I wasn't." Rachel looked at Sissie. "You should go home and lie down, Sissie. You look all in."

"I'm all right. Besides, I think you need two deputies."

"Two?" Hal asked, crossing his arms. "I'm not enough?"

"It's not that," Sissie said. "It's just . . . if Rachel's at the dig, and you're on the streets, who's going to watch the prisoners? When we got more than drunks, that is."

Hal unfolded his arms. "She's got a point."

"Are you up to the job?" Rachel asked her.

"The way I see it," Sissie said, "it's either me or Lyle."

"I can do it!" Lyle announced. "It's not a girl's job. I'd druther face a posse than Dorothy Schur."

Rachel took two gun belts out of the marshal's safe in the storeroom. Hal asked, "Where did you get the combination? Hunnicut didn't give it to you."

"I'm not even sure Marshal Hunnicut knows he's been replaced," Rachel told him. "I just hunted around until I found what I was looking for. He'd written it on the back of the safe itself. I've erased it now."

Hal sighed heavily and Rachel shot him a brief glance. Was it possible he was beginning to realize what a change his simple story had brought to Brooklyn? She wanted, very badly, to take him in her arms and tell him it was all right, that they'd needed shaking up, anything to make him feel better. She wondered if all women felt like this about the men they loved—one minute maternal, the next furious, passionate the moment after.

"I must say," Hal said, "that belt does something for you."

"This?" She looked down at the wide leather, the brass buckle shiny-new. She'd had to punch an extra ragged hole in the leather to make it small enough to fit without sliding off. "I think it's ugly. Every man I've ever . . ."

She turned away from him with a jerk to slam the safe

door. He always had that effect on her. He made her so easy and comfortable that it just seemed natural to talk about her past. She'd never spoken about her father before Hal had come to town nor let the memory of her days on the mesa interfere with her work, but he hadn't been in Brooklyn a day before she'd started revealing parts of herself to him like a slave girl in a veil dance.

Hal said, "I meant it, you know. When I told you I respect you now more than ever."

"But you don't like me being marshal."

"Because it's a dangerous and I . . . don't want to see you get hurt. That's not a story I'd enjoy covering."

He reached out and brushed the backs of his fingers down her cheek, a gesture that seemed to have become a habit with him. Her reaction was not tempered by repetition. His touch had the power to make her breath come short and to dry her mouth to a desert. If anything, her reactions got stronger the more he touched her.

"You . . . you just don't think it's a job for a woman," she said, striving to keep her tone light.

"Not for my . . . not for you. God, Rachel, don't you know what it would do to me if anything happened to you? Especially since I wrote the story in the first place?"

"Nothing's going to happen to me," she said, sounding more confident than she felt.

"I wish I could be so sure."

She shook her head, several locks of her hair tumbling. She sighed, shifting the heavy gun belts to her left hand. "I hate this," she said, poking at the strands. "If only my hair would just stay put!"

"Be awkward if it tumbled down in a gunfight."

"Let's hope it won't come to that," she said. "If I had a pair of scissors . . ."

Sissie looked up from the pile of wanted posters she'd been thumbing through as Rachel and Hal came into the main office. "What's he done now?" she asked.

"Nothing. Nothing more than usual, anyway." Rachel dumped the belts on the desk. "Here, Sissie. You and Hal should both wear one of these."

"I couldn't," Sissie said. "It won't go with what I have on." She indicated her pretty dress of red scotch plaid.

"You can design a hat for it later," Rachel said. "Just imagine the challenge *that* will be."

"Hmmm." Sissie half closed her eyes, smoothing the air before her with her hands as if spreading out a piece of paper. "Not straw . . . felt. Heavy felt with . . ."

"Not now," Rachel said, laughing. "Get that gun on and I'll introduce you to the two desperadoes in the lockup."

"Gee," Sissie said, sighing in admiration. "You might have been a lawman all your life, Rachel."

Try as she might, Rachel couldn't keep her gaze from flying to Hal. He leaned against the wall, his gun belt already buckled, the holster tie already around his leg. With his black mustache and cool eyes, he *looked* like every criminal's worst nightmare. He said with his wickedest grin, "Her family has had more than one member take part in the workings of justice."

Rachel's attempt to look stern was a lamentable failure. Only Hal would describe her family's unfortunate tendency toward dishonesty that way. But he was right. Surely the justice system would fail to operate if there were no criminals like Egan Delmon.

"Really?" Sissie looked curiously from one friend to the other. "You never told *me* that, Rachel."

"It never came up. Let me help you with that."

Sissie needed two holes picked in the leather belt before it stopped sliding down over her hips. "It feels funny," she complained.

"It's really just for show." Rachel stood back to admire her handiwork, the awl still in her hand. "Is that snug enough?"

"Yes, I think so."

"Can you draw?"

"Art lessons?" Hal asked dryly.

"That's right. You're next," Rachel said.

With the jerky hesitation of a machine, Sissie laid her hand on the protruding butt of the gun. Then she hitched her elbow up high, bringing the weapon up and out of the holster. She turned her head to look at the oil gleaming on the barrel as though the sight of the gun in her hand was utterly unexpected Then she dropped her elbow, bringing the barrel of the pistol in line with a wanted poster on the wall.

"Like that?" she asked with pride.

Rachel smiled, trying to conceal her concern. Sissie was so slow that anyone could have pumped her full of holes before she'd even brought the gun out. "I'm sure you'll never have to use it. Just remember what I showed you before. Take the safety off, hold it in both hands and squeeze the trigger firmly but slowly."

Noticing how Sissie's small hand trembled with the weight, Rachel added, "You can put it back now."

She turned to Hal.

"Never mind me," he said. "I've never learned how to shoot a gun yet."

"But . . ."

He grinned, a light of unholy confidence in his blue eyes. "I don't need to be able to shoot, Rachel. I have the power of the press."

"That won't help you when somebody starts firing at you."

"You'd be surprised. A lot of newspaper editors get shot every year and go on to tell the tale. I'm not saying I'm looking forward to joining their company, but you and I both know it's damned hard actually to kill someone by shooting them. Bullets go astray. Even if you do get shot, more often than not the bullet misses everything important. As long as I can write, I'm safe."

"You really believe that?" At his nod, she said, "I'll try to believe it too. Will you come with me to Mrs. Garrett's and help me?"

"I'll help you with anything under heaven. What did you have in mind, particularly?"

"I want you to help me knock some sense into Benson Hunnicut. Sissie hasn't had any luck doing things her way so we'll have to try something different." She kept her head up as she admitted her weaknesses. "I know darn well that I can't keep 'playing marshal' as you put it. I'm not cut out for the job and that's all there is to it. But neither is anyone else around here except for Benson. So we're going to go get him if we have to bring him back with the muzzle of my gun stuck in his liver."

"You won't hurt him?" Sissie squeaked.

"Do you care?"

"No." Sissie tossed her head. "Yes."

Hal clapped his hat on his head and said, "I'll go see if I can find us some horses, Rachel. I don't know about you, but I don't feel like walking all the way to Mrs. Garrett's in this rain."

Sissie hardly waited for the iron-barred door to close behind Hal before she all but leaped on Rachel. "Are you in love with that man?"

Rachel didn't trouble to deny it. "I'm afraid so."

"Rachel . . . !" Sissie stopped, her arms outstretched to embrace her friend. "Why afraid?"

"Because he is the most irritating, arrogant, troublesome male in the universe! With one or two exceptions," she added, thinking of her two brothers.

"He couldn't be that," Sissie said, her fists on her hips. "Benson Hunnicut is that to his fingertips. Not that it has stopped me from falling in love with him. When I found out he'd gone on this darned dig, I was so mad I wanted to kill him. Then when he looked right through me, I was so hurt I wanted to kill myself. Now . . ."

"Now?"

"Now if I don't see him soon, I'm just going to bust!"

Rachel laughed. Sissie joined her, showing all her white teeth. "But what about you? When did . . . ? Has he asked you. . . . Come on, tell me!" Sissie's eyes were as intense as a hound dog's on the scent.

"I can't tell you when I fell for him. I didn't know it until just the other day, but I've been neck deep for a long time, or at least that's how it feels. Like it's always been this way and like it's brand-new. As for what happens next, I don't know. He wants to go back to New York and I couldn't ever live like that. So I guess that's it." She shrugged, adopting Lyle's bad habit because it was so expressive of a fated heartache.

Sissie said, "At least you haven't done anything you need be ashamed of . . . have you?"

Taken aback by the eager curiosity in her friend's eyes and tone, Rachel said, "No, at least there's that."

"Darn."

"What? Why 'darn'?"

"Well . . . " Sissie's cheeks grew pink and her confusion was evident in the way she hung her head. She mumbled her next words so that Rachel had to ask her to repeat them. Somewhat loudly, Sissie said, "I was hoping for some pointers and I can't very well ask Mrs. Schur!"

"Why, Sissie Albright! You don't mean to say that you're going to . . . to . . ."

"Listen, I'm sick to death of Benson Hunnicut being the only one around here who's allowed to be a fool! He needs someone to keep an eye on him and make him content. Well, if he and I . . . if we . . . you know! Well, then he's bound to marry me and I'll have to marry him. It's as good a way as any to get my courage up."

"But what about the drinking? I know that worries you."

Sissie nodded somberly. "It does. But if I haven't taken to the bottle with all this going on, I don't believe I'm going to. I'll tell Benson all about it and then it can be our problem to guard against. If I can put up with his toupee and this damned diamond fever, the very least he can do is share my troubles."

"The very least," Rachel agreed. "I'll take over duties here as soon as Hal and I get back with Benson. Then you can do whatever you feel is right."

Sissie took a deep breath and crossed her fingers, her arms crossed on her chest like an Egyptian queen. "I'll wish and pray you can bring him back."

"If I knew where a Bible was, I'd swear on it," Rachel said, raising her right hand. "Since I don't, I swear by

Heaven that I'll bring your man back if I have to hog-tie him."

But when Rachel and Hal arrived at the dig, Rachel was so appalled by what she saw that it was a long time before she started to look for the marshal.

17

"HAVE WE COME to the right place?" Rachel asked. "This can't be Mrs. Garrett's."

They drew rein at the end of the drive. The once glorious trees had lost all their bright leaves, their branches black and gleaming with wet. The house itself looked tired, the curling vine all gone away to brown sticks like the skeleton of a snake still gripping its prey in death. Such things might look normal—for the nodding quiet of autumn was giving way to the healing sleep of winter—were it not for the land behind the house. There the gently rolling hills seemed to crawl with men while the air was shaken and shattered by a ceaseless bustling energy. All the peace, all the silence of this place, dedicated to the slow growth of life, was overrun and destroyed by the stirred-up anthill of human greed.

"I've seen battlefields that look like this," Hal said in a whisper as though he spoke to himself. "Destruction for the sake of destruction."

"At least war has some purpose," Rachel said. "But this . . ."

"These men would claim a high purpose. But I can't think of anything that is worth all this."

Neither could Rachel. She had struggled to establish some kind of peace in her life if only for Lyle's sake. Seeing the peace of Mrs. Garrett's life destroyed hurt as if it were her own that had been lost. "I want to go see if she's all right."

As they approached the house, a thickset figure rose from a rocking chair on the porch. He cradled an old over-and-under shotgun in his arms. "Stop right there," he bellowed. "Or I'll blow you off'n your horses."

"It's me, Mr. Sheppard. Rachel Pridgeon."

"Miss Pridgeon?" Rachel could see him peer at her through the misty air,. "I didn't recognize you. Have you come to see the missus?"

Hal dismounted first and came to help her. Rachel let him lift her down. Her mind, however, wasn't on the touch of his hands, though the memory came back later to warm her. She would have hated him if he'd taken this moment to remind her of the attraction between them. He didn't hold her too long or squeeze her waist, which made her love him all the more.

Rachel looked up at him, knowing the sunlight that broke through the lowering clouds must have clearly illuminated all she felt. His half smile faded. "What is it?"

"Nothing. Ask me later."

He followed her and the sound of his footsteps on the wooden planks of the porch made her happy. Could she be content with only this much happiness, she wondered? Or would she eat her heart out for him after he went home?

The hired man said, "She's awful low, Miss Rachel. I've never seen her this low, even when Mr. Garrett died."

Rachel reached out to the gray-haired black man, patting his forearm where he held the shotgun. "I know, Mr. Sheppard, and I'm sorry. Oh, I forgot. Mr. Sheppard, this is Hal Sinclair. Mr. Sheppard is Mrs. Garrett's right hand."

His eyes narrowed. "This that newspaperman? Get off our property," he said, and the shotgun swung to cover him.

Hal's hands went up at once. He said, "Let's not be hasty, Mr. Sheppard."

"Put it down," Rachel said sharply. "He's here to help me."

"No, ma'am. He's not the helping kind. I can see it in his eyes. If it weren't for him, none of this would ever have happened. He's just waiting to write more lies. Diamonds! Phooey!"

"Phooey?" Hal asked, lifting a wry eyebrow. It went down when the man poked the shotgun into his stomach.

Rachel said quickly, "Now, Mr. Sheppard, it's all right. Hal's sorry now that he wrote what he did and he's here to make amends. Right, Hal? *Right, Hal?*"

"Absolutely." He stepped back from the muzzle in his breadbasket. "I'll print a retraction in the next edition."

"You'd better. Diamonds, my . . ." Mr. Sheppard turned his whisky-colored eyes toward Rachel. "There's never been a sign of diamonds here that I've seen and I've walked this land as man and boy. If there'd been anything worth the finding don't you think somebody would have found it by now?"

"Have there been any more stones found?" Hal asked. Rachel could see by the light in his eyes that he'd forgotten all about the shells aimed at his backbone from the wrong side. He was thinking about his story.

"They keep on saying somebody's found another one here and there. Nobody ever shows 'em around though. Last time, they all went rushing to the creek bottom to take a look, but it turned out to be a bit of an old broken bottle. I recognized it—it was an old liniment bottle."

"Throat liniment?" Hal asked, to Rachel's confusion.

"Four-year-old 'throat liniment,' son."

"Got any more? My throat's powerfully sore."

"Why, sure. Come on 'round back." Mr. Sheppard winked at Hal and lowered his shotgun. Hal absently rubbed the spot above his navel where the metal had dug in. Rachel wondered at the strange ways of men.

"Don't you want to see Mrs. Garrett too?" she asked. "I think she took a liking to you when you were here before."

"Yes, I should. Maybe a rain check, Mr. Sheppard?"

"You better make it a sunshine check, son. It's going to be raining from now 'til Christmas by the looks of it."

They all looked at the sky. The tiny gray clouds were stained like glass toward the west, the sun hidden but still an important presence like a leading actor about to go onto stage. "We'd better hurry if we're going to find Benson. But we'll see Mrs. Garrett first."

"It'll cheer her up, ma'am. Especially if you show her that star." He flicked his fingers toward her left shoulder. "The missus always did think women ought to get into more professions. She encouraged my girl Sandra . . . you never met her, did you, Miss Rachel?" Rachel shook her head regretfully. "Mrs. Garrett talked her into going to college. She'll be done next year. Smart as a whip, they say."

He opened the door for them. Rachel asked, "Is she alone?"

"No, Mrs. Dale's in there. Reading the Bible to her."

But when Rachel and Hal went into the room where Lyle had once lain, it was to find Mrs. Garrett alone. She lay on the bed, the hand-knitted coverlet drawn up to her breast. Her hands rested on the top, her arms clad in the sleeves of a heavy flannel nightgown. Her eyes were closed and Rachel's heart all but stopped.

"Mrs. Garrett?" she whispered, feeling a cold chill on her back. She had never seen her friend in anything but her wheeled chair, her clothing as neat and up-to-date as any woman's in Brooklyn. Never had those veined and wrinkled hands been idle, not even when pain tormented her. To see her lying so still with her hair in two thin plaits either side of her face was like looking on her in death.

From behind her, Hal said huskily, "Mrs. Garrett?"

The translucent eyelids lifted. "Mr. Sinclair? I was hoping you'd come by."

He came to the bed and took one of her hands in both of his. His voice was just as usual but Rachel saw the anguish in his eyes and the glistening of tears. He had to swallow hard before he spoke. "I'm sorry. I never intended . . ."

"You don't have to say," she said. "I know. You're just like my Mr. Rudolph. He would have done the same thing. Who's that with you?"

"It's me, Rachel."

"Oh." The old woman smiled, her eyes fluttering closed. "I hear they gave you a star. I'll get mine soon."

Rachel met Hal's worried gaze and lifted her shoulders, shaking her head. She didn't know what Mrs. Garrett meant. "You'll do fine," she said lamely.

Even here, in this peaceful sanctum, the confused noises of the diggers penetrated. Small wonder Mrs. Garrett looked like a shadow on snow. If this went on morning, noon and night, with never a moment's silence, a healthy young person would soon get to feeling low, let alone a woman who had lived treasuring her peace and quiet for years.

"Don't worry," Rachel said. "I'm here to put a stop to this."

"You can't stop it," Mrs. Garrett said, her voice weak. "Only Lyle can stop it. He's got to tell where he found that stone."

Hal asked softly, "And if it was here he found it?"

"Then I shall die."

A clatter from the doorway made Rachel turn. "Now you don't mean that," Mrs. Dale said, pushing in, her arms loaded down with a tea tray. "Here's Miss Pridgeon come to see you and you talking like that!"

She thanked Rachel for taking the tray. Then she saw Hal and, with the smooth speed of long practice, snatched the silver-framed spectacles from her nose and stuffed them into her apron pocket. She blinked blindly, her pansy eyes widening in a fruitless attempt to see. "Mr. Sinclair, is that you? Oh, I'm sure I'm a sight."

"A sight for sore eyes," he said gallantly. Rachel noticed that he was folding up his handkerchief with his left hand, sooner than let go of Mrs. Garrett's hand. He helped her sit up, despite her saying fretfully that she didn't want anything to eat. "Food chokes me."

"She's not eating," Mrs. Dale said in a loud whisper as she fumbled with the teapot and cups.

"Of course, I'm not eating," Mrs. Garrett answered with some of her old vinegar. "How can I eat when I'm choked?"

"Come on, Hal," Rachel said, feeling that Mrs. Garrett was more likely to get wholesome food if Mrs. Dale would put her spectacles back on. Otherwise, operating blind, she'd probably put salt in the tea and spread jam on the napkins.

But Hal remained by the bedside. "I want you to know . . . I want you to know that I never would have done it if I could have foreseen what would happen. I never expected everyone to lose their minds so completely over this."

"Seems to me that nobody'd do anything if they could see all the ends. Life's like a skein of yarn tangled in a coil; you just got to follow your thread all the way through. 'Course, some knots aren't meant to be broken." Mrs. Garrett looked right at Rachel, then sighed but not unhappily. "I hope I can be spared for one more wedding. Well, come on, Georgia. Where's my tea?"

Rachel left Hal on the porch and went back to the bedroom. She peered around the door just long enough to be sure Mrs. Dale had put on her spectacles again. Relieved that all would be well inside the house, Rachel went back to Hal.

"Just checking something," she said in answer to his glance.

"Rachel . . ." A tender note in his voice stopped her. She looked at him out of the corner of her eye. His mouth was turned down sternly, his forehead was creased. "Rachel . . ."

"What is it?"

"I want you to know that I meant what I said to Mrs. Garrett just now."

"I figured you did, or you wouldn't have said it. I know

you're honest, Hal. That's one of the things I like best about you. You're honest."

"I try. What else do you like?"

Rachel couldn't contain the smile that trembled on her lips. She lowered her lashes, a ridiculous feminine trick she hadn't even known she knew. It was the kind of thing Dorothy Schur would have done, only better. "Lots of things."

"Will you tell me what they are?" He stood very close beside her now, beside her and slightly behind her. A quivering impatience grew in her heart as she waited for him to put his hands on her. "Or is now not a good time?" he asked.

Rachel's conscience spoke up, even as her knees turned to water. "We did come here for a reason."

A moment later, she wished she'd left her conscience at home. "That's right," he said, and she could tell he'd moved away emotionally if not physically. Digging his hands into his pockets, he asked, "How are we going to find Benson? There must be two hundred men on that land."

Her own hands hungered for the feel of his warm skin. She plunged them into the pockets of her skirt, trying to keep them from roaming over his face and shoulders. She wondered if Hal had felt the same need. She declared, "The easiest thing would be to get him to come to us."

"Yes, that would be easiest. But how?"

Ten minutes later, Hal stepped back from the fence railing. The last can wobbled and looked as though it were about to fall. "Straighten that out, will you, Hal?" Rachel called from twenty yards away.

They'd already begun to collect an audience. Mud-daubed, mud-streaked, mud-coated men stood around, apparently impervious to the freshening breeze. Some still carried picks and shovels, others sat on the ground, their heads hanging, their exhaustion catching up with them the moment they laid down their tools.

Hal straightened out the can, weighted in the bottom with stones picked up around the farmyard. At first, Hal had been afraid he'd started another diamond rush when tired diggers had jumped to the conclusion that he'd made a strike. It had been all he could do to keep them from attacking the chicken house. Rachel's nod of approval at his fast talk still warmed him.

"Okay," she said. "You'd better move out of the way."

"I thought you said you were a good shot."

"I am. Darn good."

"Then I'll just stand here."

Someone called out, "You're a fool, man! Never trust a woman with a gun!"

"Aye, unless you want a hat with a hole in it and a head to match!"

There was some laughter and rude jests thrown with the carelessness of schoolboys who cared only for the laughter of their peers and not for the consequences. For some reason known only to the male kind, they all began to sing, "The Man on the Flying Trapeze."

Rachel looked around at them. If they'd really been schoolboys, she would have known what to do. Though she herself had yet to use physical punishment, it was allowed by the school board and some—who might be here now without her knowing it—had actually reminded her of the biblical injunction "spare the rod and spoil the child."

Then she looked at Hal, his elbows resting on the topmost fence rail behind him, his feet crossed at the ankles. He looked as though a strong wind would blow him away. He also appeared to be calm, trustworthy and completely grown-up in a nice contrast to the men around here. She smiled at him and he touched two careless fingers to the brim of his hat.

Rachel remembered her father teaching her to shoot, telling her to find the calm center of herself and fire from there. Seeing Hal smile, feeling his confidence in her, made finding that center the easiest it had ever been. The distractions of the crowd faded out. There was only the gun and the target. And Hal, waiting for her behind it all.

The back of Hal's neck began to tingle. He wanted to shift

restlessly from foot to foot, but was afraid that he'd distract Rachel. Her stance was so familiar to him, her feet slightly farther apart than her hips, her hands hanging easy at her side without so much as a twitch of her thumb to betray nervousness. Her heavy coat was tucked behind her, lest it entangle her drawing hand. He'd described her position a hundred times, only it had always been one gunslinger facing another under a blazing sun, not a woman facing a row of tin cans.

Hal recognized a great story. Outlaw's daughter, finest female shot in the West, turns marshal. It would sell a million papers to those shop clerks and apprentices back home. The upstairs maids in the house of the rich and mighty would dream of being Rakehell Rachel while their young mistresses fantasized that they too could impress their friends by shooting like Rachel Delmon.

He could foresee Rachel Delmon cigars, Rachel Delmon hand-engraved derringers for the ladies, Rachel Delmon face soap. The novelty of a young and beautiful girl who could shoot the eye out of a fly at a hundred paces . . .

Had had been watching her with half-closed eyes while he planned a glittering future for her. When she went for her gun, he'd hardly had time to register that she was drawing before she began firing. It was like watching a flash of lightning dart down out of the sky. With never a pause or hesitation, she'd snatched the gun from the holster and started shooting. She slapped the hammer of the gun with the edge of her left hand while aiming and pulling the trigger with her right.

The firing came as a crackle, so quickly did each explosion follow on the other. Next to Hal, cans jumped up and did back-flips. They did everything except jump back onto the fence for a second turn. All told, start to finish, drilling the six cans took considerably less than six seconds. Her revolver was back in the holster before Hal had a chance to look around to watch her do it.

There were no jests now from the crowd. Just awed silence as they stared at the downed cans through the pale-blue smoke of gunpowder. Hal glanced at them. He hadn't seen so many mouths open and gasping for breath since his last fishing trip.

"Set 'em up again, Rachel?" he called.

"No, thanks."

No sooner had he stepped away from the fence than the witnesses were scrambling in the wet grass to find the cans. He heard some of them speculate that the whole demonstration had been a trick of some kind. But when someone found the first can, sliced through with a bullet, all the scars brand-new, a whistle of incredulous approval went up.

As Hal approached her, he knew without a doubt that he was in love with her. With her background and abilities, she should have found herself the subject of a story with his byline before she knew her left from her right. Rachel had enough news value to keep him writing for weeks. Yet the very thought of writing about her in any exploitative way made him feel physically ill. He couldn't betray her like that.

Instead of the supreme confidence of a professional at work, Hal approached her, his knees apparently made out of jelly-filled sponge cake. "Good shooting," he said inanely.

She smiled at him warmly, biting her lower lip. The sight of her white teeth against the rose-pink of her lip made Hal understand the torment of a starving man. He didn't dare touch her now, not even with a brush of his fingertips against her satin-smooth cheek.

"It's not working," she whispered, as she reloaded her cooling pistol. Hal noticed that she handled the gun automatically, breaking it open and slipping in the brass bullets like one born and raised around guns. She had good-sized hands too, big enough to handle the Colt but with tapering fingers that negated any possible remarks about her accomplishments making her less feminine. Hands so lovely shouldn't handle weapons, perhaps, but Hal couldn't complain, not while he still remembered them brushing like flower petals over his face.

"He's not here," Rachel said bitterly.

"He must be busy. Have them set up again. Maybe six shots weren't enough to bring him."

Rachel nodded. "Hey, gentlemen? Set 'em up again, please."

Hal was amazed to see how smartly the ragtag diggers could jump to, given an order by someone they respected. Many mud-ringed, dirt-rimmed hands worked to find the cans and replaced the weights in their bottoms with something equally good, worthless rocks from their own pockets.

"What surprises me most," Hal said as they waited, "is that you don't seem to have to think before you shoot."

"What good would thinking about it do? It's either something you do right or you miss. I don't like to miss."

"Who taught you to do it?"

"My father. He believed in guns and what they can do."

Hal remembered that Egan Delmon had died in a literal hail of bullets fired by cavalry soldiers when he refused to surrender. "Rachel, I'm sorry. Were you close to him?"

She shook her head, her eyes on the targets. "Nobody was close to him. I'm sorry he's dead because he was my father, but I think he always knew what was going to happen to him. He had that verse from Matthew engraved inside his watch."

"Yes, I remember hearing about that. 'All they that take the sword shall perish with the sword.'"

"That's right. I forgot you know as much about me as I do. Did you say you wrote a book about Slade? Did you see him?"

"I saw him briefly in New Mexico two years ago. That's when I decided I should write books about your family. My publisher—"

There were shouts from the crowd, a demand that Rachel shoot again. She turned and gave them a wave. "I'll want to talk to you about Slade," she said to Hal. "I want to know if he's still looking for us."

"Us?"

"Lyle and me."

Hal nodded and stepped away from her right side. Rachel

took a moment to rearrange her coat, which had fallen in front of her holster. He saw her lips move, but she didn't speak aloud. Her eyes narrowed as she took a deep breath, staring down the field at the cans.

"Just what in the Sam Hill is going on here?" a deep voice, scratchy with disuse but still redolent of authority said.

A tall man, the top of whose head gleamed when he took off his hat, stepped out from the crowd. "Rachel Pridgeon, is that you?"

"Sure is, Marshal Hunnicut. Glad to see you."

Hal said, "Okay, folks. Show's over for today."

A groan of disappointment went up, accented with individual voices. "Ain't she gonna shoot no more today?"

"Dang, never seen a woman shoot like that before."

"Boys won't hardly believe it when I tell 'em."

A glare from Benson Hunnicut, badgeless but still a force to be reckoned with, dispersed the stragglers, sending them back to their fruitless searches among the rocks and stones. Benson shambled up the rise to Rachel and Hal. With every step, dirt sifted off him except where he was muddy. It caked on his shirt, and had rubbed into the creases of his neck. His eyes were red with it, and his fingers black. The top of his head was the only clean part of him.

Hal heard Rachel draw breath, undoubtedly for a diatribe that would not only knock the dirt off him, but skin him alive as well. He rushed in with, "Hunnicut, I'm ashamed to have shared a bottle with you. Are you out of your mind?"

"Huh?" The other man blinked at him. "What burr's gotten under your saddle?"

Rachel tried to jump in, but once again Hal forestalled her. "At least I'm doing my duty as I see it," he said. "I've gotten out every issue of the paper without fail. Whereas you're up here trying to find a chunk of worthless rock."

"Worthless? When all I need is one . . ."

"One? One diamond won't buy you happiness, man. Nor will a bushel of them. What will make you happy is a good wife, a worthwhile job and the respect of this town. So far, you don't have any of that."

A red tinge had come up under the mud-splashed cheeks. "What do you mean? I may not have a wife . . . it isn't for want of asking. But on the other things . . ."

Rachel didn't say a word. She just flipped up the collar of her raincoat to show the star gleaming on the fabric. Benson's eyes bulged in surprise. Then Hal added, "And if it weren't for the fact that all the other men in Brooklyn are up here, you probably would lose their respect too. It's pretty shaky among the women right now, as I've heard." In a few words, Hal told the marshal what had been happening in town, the influx of strangers, the women's determination to carry on. Benson didn't seem to be taking it in.

Then Rachel stepped forward, her eyes shining. Hal felt a sharp hunger in his soul looking at her. She said softly, "You can marry Sissie if you stop acting like a fool. She needs you, Benson. We all need you."

"She needs *me*? But . . . but . . ." Hal thought that one of Columbus's sailors must have made a face like that when he saw land for the first time, when all his superstitions had told him that "here be dragons." Benson Hunnicut put his hand on his chest as though to reassure himself that his heart was still beating.

"Well?" Hal said. "Go on. She's waiting for you at the jail."

"The jail," Benson repeated.

Rachel added, "There's two men in the lockup. Drunk and disorderly. I suggest you let 'em go, and . . . um . . . take a bath."

For a moment, Benson's face lit up with the idea that all his dreams for a life with Sissie were not only possible but within his grasp. Then he shook his head, and dug a toe into the wet ground. "No, I promised myself I'd only go back to her if I was rich. She deserves all the good things that I can't give her on my salary."

"Of all the . . ." Rachel caught back the hasty words. "You give me no choice. You're under arrest."

"What charge?" Benson demanded, his voice going up in hurt anger.

"I don't know!" she said, as if impatient with his expectation that she should know anything about *his* job.

Hal chuckled. "There's always dereliction of duty."

"That's it. Dereliction of duty. Not to mention trifling with the affections of a lady."

"That's not a crime," Benson protested.

"Well, it ought to be."

"You can't arrest me," Benson said in disgust and turned as though to walk away.

"Wait there," Rachel demanded.

"I would if I were you," Hal added.

"Why?" The once-marshal looked back.

Hal had seen Rachel draw once. Benson never had. He was completely unprepared for the speed with which her pistol seemed to leap into her hand. He slapped at his hip, to find that he was not only unarmed, but slow as cooling taffy.

Hal, impervious to his fellow male's pleading look, stepped back. He'd done his best. Now he'd let Rachel handle it. He only hoped she wasn't going to be impulsive. A hole in her lover would be a difficult thing to explain to Sissie.

She said, "I guess we'll call that resisting arrest, Mr. Hunnicut. Now, my deputy here will . . . get along, Hal! He'll walk with you back to where your gear is so you can collect it. But then you're going to the jail if I have to perforate you to get you there. I'll meet you by the horses, Hal."

"Where are you going?" he asked.

"I want to say good-bye to Mrs. Garrett."

A few hours later, a very tired Rachel, minus her badge, walked up Main Street to her house. It was cold enough to see her breath, a white ghost before her, and there was a dank chill that lay like a shroud on her skin. She was very glad to be able to lean on Hal's arm. "It's a good thing that's over," she said. "Being marshal wasn't so bad, but when it comes to arresting your friends . . ."

"I can see how that would be a little hard on a woman."

She smiled up at him, a darker shadow in the fast-falling twilight. "You're very understanding, Hal."

"About some things, I am." His voice sounded amused.

She drew a little away from him, realizing how much she was liking the support of his arm. She couldn't help wondering if he was planning to write about today. The suspicion was hateful but she couldn't entirely dismiss it.

"This used to be such a quiet town," she said, introducing this new topic to distract his thoughts from her.

"It's not now."

The quiet October night was full of noises. Shouts from the far ends of town, a near-professional-sounding quartet singing, and sounds of hammering and sawing from the saloon. Rachel and Hal stopped on the other side of the street from the no-longer-empty building. "I wish I knew who was opening The Hatch again," she said. "I'd get a group of public-minded women over to his house first thing in the morning and put a stop to it."

"You can't blame someone for opening up a legitimate business."

"This town is dry, Mr. . . ."

"Don't start 'Mr. Sinclair-ing' me again, Rachel. I . . . I don't think I could stand it."

Rachel subsided. She said with just a little sparkle, "I'm too tired to fight tonight anyway."

"Good. You give me hope." He brought his bent elbow and her hand a little closer to his side. Rachel could feel the solid muscle there beneath his coat. She didn't know if the feel of his body made her weaker or stronger, only that a new buoyancy came into her walk.

He walked with her up the street and down the path to her door. They hadn't said a word for half their walk. Now she drew her hand out from beneath his elbow and offered it to him to shake, saying meekly, "Good night, Hal."

He looked down at her hand. Though she couldn't distinguish the features of his face, she knew he smiled wryly. With the extra sense of self-protection that comes to a woman when a man is chasing her, Rachel realized she had about half a second to get inside before he kissed her.

She delayed. "I certainly appreciate. . . ."

Though his hands were hard and hungry as he dragged

her to him, his lips were gentle as they brushed lightly over hers. It was a sweet kiss, the kind a boy gives a girl. Rachel enjoyed it, and waited for more, for the onslaught that would drive her past her own barriers.

It didn't come. Hal let her go, though she could feel the reluctance in every cell of his fingers. "I'll see you tomorrow," he said. "I'm proud of you, Rachel."

"Wait!" She grabbed his arm. Realizing how forward she must seem, she instantly took her hand away. "Don't you want to come in?"

"Yes. Very much. Which is why I'm not going to."

"I don't understand."

"Think about it." He started down the porch steps and she ran the few yards between them. A glimmer of moonlight touched his face as he looked up at her. He said, "Rachel, I want you. I want you badly. It's not getting better with time; it's getting worse. I don't know if I can trust myself alone with you."

All the practiced compliments that dropped so easily from his mouth had never had the power to move her. The sight and sound of his need for her stole her soul away. "Everything's upside down," she said. "Please, I want you to be here."

Then she was in his arms and he was devouring her with kisses, a thousand in the first minute, a million in the next. She felt as though she'd been swept up in a tidal wave and all she could do was hang on and try to catch her breath. Her hat fell unnoticed to the floor.

She laced her fingers through his hair, cool against her heated skin, as she tried to slow him down. She wanted more. He said her name, thick and low, and took her mouth in a long, moist kiss that seemed to have no ending. Though they tried new angles, said half words, sighed and breathed, still it was all one kiss, on and on until she was more than drunk, more than crazy with it and from the heat that built with every second.

She could feel him trembling. "You're cold?" she whispered incredulously.

"No." He unwrapped one of his arms from around her,

bent to the side and picked her up in his arms. She gasped as she lost contact with the ground. He carried her across the porch.

"Let me," she said, reaching behind her to turn the knob. The door swung wide. Hal carried her into the rich darkness and kicked the door closed behind him. "You better put me down so I can find a candle. And it's cold. We'll need a fire."

He put her down, letting her slide down his hard body. She stumbled when she touched the floor, but not because she had lost her balance. She reached up to him and the kiss began again.

Rachel knew what he wanted. She'd expected a man to ask it of her one day. She'd never thought for an instant, however, that she would want it as badly as he did. When he ran his hands with a smooth pressure down her back to lift and flex her hips against him, she responded with an instinctive eagerness that made him gasp.

"Rachel . . . My God, are you sure?"

She laughed in answer, an intimate, womanly sound that startled her as much as him. Wanting to show him that she was more than ready, she reached under his coat and pulled out his shirttail. At the glide of her hands on his bare waist, he sucked in his breath and shuddered. "Your hands are frozen, woman! No. Don't stop."

"I'll start a fire . . ."

"Too late."

He put his hands on her shoulders, his thumbs massaging her collarbone. Rachel's head fell back as if unable to sustain its own weight. Watching her face, Hal rested the heels of his hands just above the smooth roundness of her breasts. Then he slid them down, slowly, slowly, over her front to her waist and back again. Her eyelids quivered as she bit her full lower lip. He put his fingers to the first button of her man-tailored jacket and she sighed. "Yes."

But he stopped before he'd done more than glimpse the rickrack that decorated her chemise, dark against the white cotton. He was so ready for her that he didn't think he could take much more without a moment or two to collect his self-control. Resisting the lure of her satin-soft cleavage, he said, "Maybe you'd better go find that candle. I . . ." He turned his need into a small joke. "I don't want to stub my toe on the way upstairs."

She smiled, her eyes dark. "That would be a pity. Wait here."

Hal crossed his arms, trying to think of other things. He remembered the look on Benson's face when he'd walked into the jail and found Sissie there, her feet up on his desk. He remembered how she'd thrown aside the *Police Gazette* and literally jumped into the astonished marshal's arms. She hadn't cared that he reeked of sweat or that he was filthy. Hal smiled as he remembered that Benson hadn't been astonished long. Amazing how quickly some folks took to kissing . . . Realizing that he'd come back to the things he was trying not to think about, Hal tried again.

Rachel was worried about the saloon opening again. He decided that tomorrow, bright and early, he'd look into the question of its ownership. Then he corrected himself. Not too bright and early, for he fully expected to be one exhausted, if satisfied, man by then. He wondered at what point it would be best to tell Rachel that he loved her. Maybe as soon as she came back from the kitchen, candle in hand.

That would be his moment, he decided. Not in the dark, but in the light, when he wouldn't be cheated out of seeing her face. He'd tell her that nothing mattered, not her family, not her past, only that they should be together. She would love New York with all it had to offer. Thinking about their future, reaching for a vision of their life together, Hal knew he could give her all the love tonight that she deserved. He waited with impatience for the glimmer of light that meant Rachel was coming back.

Then someone struck a light in the living room. The sputtering sulfur glare of a lucifer match swiped into life against the sole of a boot. The little flame came up to illuminate a bearded face, the beard darker than the light hair. The flames reflected in his eyes were aimed right at Hal as the man lit his cigar. So was the black mouth of the gun pointed at Hal's heart.

The match went out.

18

$\mathcal{R}$ACHEL KNEW SHE should take these few minutes away from Hal's heady presence to ask herself some hard questions. She'd always been so levelheaded, so sensible. She'd been focused on her goals, whether it was getting free of her past or becoming a qualified teacher in one year instead of two. She'd been determined to set a good example for Lyle and to stay far away from trouble.

Hal was trouble. He was a side road leading away from the straight and narrow way and into a mysterious forest. A sensible woman ignored such paths. A sensible woman would thank Hal for his interest and send him on his way. The satisfaction of having done the right thing should be sufficient for any woman.

Staring at the spear of light atop her candle, Rachel asked herself those hard questions. Was she ready to face disgrace, ignominy and shame? Could she bear to hear her name hissed while people she respected looked at her askance? What about Lyle? What would he think of his sister then?

She couldn't just throw away everything on a gamble with desire.

After all, she reasoned, what did she know about love? Hal might only be interested in her because there were so few single women in his orbit. Certainly the way he'd behaved with Dorothy Schur, toying with her affections, turning her head with his compliments, could lead one to the conclusion that he was nothing but a trifling man.

Rachel suspected that it wasn't any special quality in *her* that drew Hal. Any girl would do, especially if she'd shown herself so eager. Rachel knew a blush for her behavior. He must be thinking her shameless.

Then she thought of his kisses and her knees went weak, along with her principles. She felt a deep ache, bone-deep, soul-deep, born of his touch. She guessed that it could be cured the same way it had been created. The memory of his hands on her body was stronger than a mere memory and the candle flame flickered as she sighed. She'd been away from him too long.

Carrying the candlestick carefully, she started toward the kitchen door. She'd talk her feelings over with Hal. She trusted him enough to know that he wouldn't try to sway her for selfish reasons, though she felt her aching need deepen as she remembered the way he wanted her. That couldn't be counterfeited, not the way he breathed, the way his kisses seemed almost devouring, the heavy heat of his body pressing against hers.

Rachel accidentally blew out the candle and had to go back to light it again at the stove.

Her light was met by light and an acrid smell, something like a cloth soaked in skunk-odor and set alight. "Hal?" she called, her own candle dimming in the lamplight. "Did you find a lamp? I think you need to trim the wick."

"In the parlor," he said. His voice sounded strained.

He stood, hands shoulder-high, in the middle of the floor. She walked to him, frowning in confusion. "What on earth . . . ?"

"Hello, sis."

Rachel squeaked as she spun around in surprise, dropping

the candlestick. It fell on the rag rug. Hal stepped forward to stomp the tiny flame out. As if in answer to a command to stop, he said angrily, "You want to burn down her house?"

Rachel had eyes only for the bearded man. He sat in her best chair, his muddy boots crossed, his whole pose relaxed and at ease while he nursed a lit cigar. But the wicked eye on his pistol never varied an inch from its fixed aim on Hal's heart.

She swallowed the first, instinctive words that sprang to her lips just as she'd controlled her instinctive urge to draw on him. Instead she said, with a calm that she admired in her voice, all the more so since she knew how she really felt, "Is that you, Slade? I don't quite know you with the beard."

Her brother raised his free hand to slide it over the dark strands that covered his face south of his upper lip. He spoke around his cigar. "Not a bad beaver, huh? Didn't take me long to grow it once I decided on it. Our own mother wouldn't recognize me, I fancy."

"Hiding out?"

As always, his laughter was dauntingly silent. Only long ripples shook his stocky body while he breathed out the soft huffs of laughter and smoke. Though his eyes squinted when he laughed, the steadiness of his right hand remained unimpaired. A simple squeeze of the trigger and Hal would fall, bleeding his life away on her floor.

Her brother said, "I've missed you, Rachel. It ain't been the same since you up and left."

"Can he put his hands down now?" Rachel asked, flicking her eyes at Hal.

"Sure. Stick 'em in your pockets, son, and no sudden moves lest you care to be deader 'n Homer."

"Not a problem." Hal put his hands, as ordered, into his pockets. She was relieved to see he didn't look scared. He stood there, his eyes alight with interest, though his face remained expressionless. Judging solely by his attitude, he might have been observing interesting native customs or sketching the flight of swallows, rather than watching the family reunion of siblings outside the law.

Slade Delmon said, "I'm right disappointed in you,

Rachel. Here you haven't seen me for 'most two years and you don't even got a word of welcome for me."

"What do you want I should do? Kill a fatted calf? Sorry, I don't have one."

He laughed again but she didn't think he was really amused. "You've changed, Rachel. My, how you've changed. I remember when you dasn't say 'boo' to a goose."

Slade always did have the cold eyes of a Gila monster. She remembered how she'd adored him once. Five years older than she, he had seemed like a young god, able to do anything from jumping his horse over a river to dancing an improvised fandango with their *madrastra*. Rachel didn't know when her feelings for him had begun to change to dread and fear. Maybe the first time she noticed his cold, cold eyes.

"What do you want, Slade?"

"What should I want but to see my pretty little sister again. And my brother. Where's Lyle, anyway?"

"He's not here. He's gone away to school."

"Don't lie!" His voice slashed at her. Then, more evenly, he said, "I been all through this house. There's a room upstairs with all his stuff in it. You're doing all right for yourself, ain't you?"

Automatically, as if his coming had turned back the hands of time, Rachel said, "Don't say 'ain't,' Slade. Daddy'd whip you for that if he was here."

"He *ain't* here and I'll talk how I like. And how I like is comfortable talk." He cut his eyes to Hal. "He talks mighty fancy from what I heard sitting here in the dark waiting for my little sister to come home. Yeah, your face had oughta turn red, Rachel. Kissin' and huggin' and carryin' on. I ain't the only one Daddy'd whip if he was here."

Slade dropped out of his lazy pose, putting his feet flat on the floor and leaning forward, his hand coming down to reinforce his grip on the pistol. "Seems to me, my little sister ain't got sense enough to stand up for her honor. So I reckon I'll have to do it. You . . . sidewinder . . . what's your moniker?"

"I'm Hal Sinclair, Mr. Delmon. You might remember me."

"Remember you? What in tarnation would I want to remember a little pissant . . . Good God Almighty! You're that newspaper feller, the one as is writin' a book about me!"

"That's right."

"Well, well. Ain't it a funny world, though! I want to say so! What are you doing here, a-canoodling with my sister?" Though his tone was jovial, he didn't drop his gun. "Rachel, you know this feller's business? He writes about out-laws . . . 'course I'm just an ordinary rancher myself." He snickered cynically. "Never nothing's ever been *proved* to the contrary. But if he's a-using you for some low reason, you let me know and I'll scatter his guts from here to Yuma!"

"It's a little late to play protective big brother, Slade. Besides, he wrote the book on me last year. He's got no reason to be using me." She turned and looked at Hal, the power of what she told her brother reaching her more readily than it did him.

"That's right," Hal said. "No reason at all."

Rachel wanted so much to believe him. It would be easier to do so if there wasn't a chance that he spoke merely from the compulsion of the gun. "Put that away," she demanded of Slade. "You don't need that here."

"'Cause we're just one big ol' happy family," Slade said with a sneer. "Not 'til I see Lyle we're not."

"I don't want you to see him." She had her eyes fixed on the glowing end of his cigar as he moved it out of his mouth, the ashes clinging to the end. "Hold it! Don't you dare flick those ashes on my nice clean floor!"

No man raised by a woman ever disobeyed that tone. Slade, as big and bad as he was, held his hand. "You stay right there and don't say a word," she told him, though her eyes took in Hal as well. "I'll be right back."

She hustled into the kitchen to fetch a plate. The men eyed each other, united by their obedience. Hal half lifted his hands out of his pockets to shrug. Instantly, the other man's posture stiffened. "Keep 'em where they are," Slade growled.

"This is preposterous. I'm not armed."

"Heard you was carrying a piece earlier in the day."

"Yes, I was. Good God, man, I can't hit the broad side of a barn. Unlike your sister. Has she always been good with a gun?"

"Hell, yes. Our dad used to say it was a pity she was a girl 'cause she could have made a name from one end of the West to the other."

Rachel came back in time to hear this tribute. "And I could have killed ten men by the time I was eighteen like that simple-minded Billy Bonney."

"Hey, I saw him a couple of months ago. He's fighting in that range war out in Lincoln County. I didn't want no piece of it. 'Sides, I've kind of lost interest in New Mexico and Arizona. I'm looking for greener pastures."

Rachel handed him the plate. "Knock your ashes on this, then get rid of them when you're gone. I shouldn't allow you to smoke in my house anyway, but since I haven't seen you for a while I'll stretch the point."

"Now you make me feel more welcome, Rachel. I was starting to think you weren't glad to see me at all."

Defiantly, Rachel went to sit down on the threadbare settee in the corner. She looked up at Hal as she passed. "Come sit with me," she said. "He can shoot you just as well if you're sitting down."

"Thanks," Hal said dryly. "That makes me feel much better."

"I practice half an hour every day," Slade said, modestly running his fingers along the barrel of his pistol as an ingenue toys with a fan. "I make one of the boys yank a can along the ground. I can hit it five times running."

"Is that all?" Rachel asked. Strange how she could be more aware of Hal now than ever. She supposed she should be grateful to Slade for coming here when he did, saving her from making love with Hal. Instead, she felt resentful.

Her brother said, "Remember how you used to do 'most

all the hunting for the gang, soon as you got big enough not to get knocked on your rear by the recoil?"

"Dad taught me how to shoot," Rachel said. "But you taught me how to draw."

"You still as fast as you used to be?"

"I'm out of practice." She shrugged.

"That's not what I hear. That little show you put on today up at the digging . . . they're all talking about it."

"Were you there?"

"Nope. I got my own business to attend to."

"You?"

"That's right. I've gone respectable." He chuckled at the disbelieving look in her eye. "You know, I gotta hand it to you, sis. Nice little setup around here. Quiet little town, nice folks, easy life."

"That's all you know about it," Rachel said, thinking of the last week. "There's more going on here than you might realize."

"Oh, I know. This diamond business. Anything in it?"

Hal answered, "I thought there was."

"Lots of folks seem to think it's worthwhile coming out here. That's where I come in. This nice little nest here's just right for picking up golden eggs in. With your help, Rachel, we'll be owning the whole burg inside of a year. Then we'll be living high on the hog. How does 'Mayor Delmon' sound to you?"

"Like you've lost your mind. What are you talking about?"

"Oh, it'll be easy enough. I brung some of the boys along, and you know how handy they are." He chuckled again and lowered his gun to his knee.

"The boys?" Rachel asked.

"Sure, didn't think I'd come all this way alone, did you? You know how lonesome I get. So when I heard about this business going begging, naturally I called some of 'em in on it. You'll be glad to see one of 'em at least. Ramon Rosario . . . eh?"

"Uncle Ramon . . . here? Who else?"

"Couple of fellers. You remember Digger Cosgrove and Lemon Malloy, don't you?"

"Yes. I remember Digger." The memory made her shiver involuntarily. Casually, Hal's hand clasped over hers, warm, strong and above all steady. He didn't seem frightened at all. Maybe he didn't realize how quickly Slade could lift that casual hand and shoot to kill.

"They're good boys. Trustworthy, within reason. I ain't like the old man, Rachel. Sometimes I trust people, providing I keep an eye on 'em. It's funny, you know. You make something worth a feller's time and he won't sell you out nearly as fast."

Afraid of the answer, Rachel asked, "And what's 'worth your time' here in Brooklyn, Slade?"

"*Our* time, little sister, *our* time. I want you to come in with me on this deal. It's a dandy. I could use somebody like you; smart, quick-fingered, pretty—did I tell you how pretty you've gotten? Hardly recognized you when you came in here just now. You ain't so scrawny as you was."

"Thanks. You're looking well too." She felt a cold hand squeeze her insides. What could draw Slade here but a chance to make quick, dirty money? He wasn't the kind to get his hands dirty digging in the earth, making his money by the sweat of his brow. Not when he could rook people out of their hard-earned money safe behind his gun. She prayed he didn't mean what he said about staying put in Brooklyn. He'd be on his way soon, she hoped.

Then she took a good look at him. Something struck her about him. He actually looked semi-civilized, as though he'd taken some pains with his appearance. She didn't for a moment think he'd neatened up just for this reunion.

Despite his heavy beard, muddy boots and dusty coat, there was something of the beau about him. His light brown hair was clean, his nails pared and his collar had to have been new this morning. She remembered how much he'd hated the red dust of Arizona, getting in his teeth and dirtying his clothes.

Suspicion darkening her voice, Rachel asked, "What deal are you talking about?"

Slade smiled, and for a moment they looked very much alike around the eyes. "I knew you'd go for it! They can't be paying you much to teach their brats. You come run the tables for me and I'll give you a twenty-five percent cut of whatever we rake in. What the hell! I'll be generous and give you five percent of the drinks too. After all, you've got Lyle to raise. Oh, don't worry! I won't be putting my oar in there, unless I think you're running off the rails with him."

"Thanks again. My, you turn my head with all these compliments."

"You always did have a smart mouth. If I'd said half the things to Dad that you did, I'd've been wearing my head back to frontwise."

"He wanted you to be tough," she said regretfully.

"Never mind that. What do you say? Do you want to work with me or not?"

Hal cleared his throat. "I take it that you're opening up the Hatch?"

"Yep. But we're not calling it that. Has a low sound, don't you think, like a shanghai dive in 'Frisco. I thought maybe Rachel here could come up with some fancy new name. Something with class."

Rachel made a face. "I'm not going to have anything to do with a saloon, Slade. And put that gun away, will you? You don't need it."

"Might yet," he said. "This feller might need a little prodding with it to get him to say the right words in front of the preacher."

"Preacher?" Hal's hand tightened on hers.

"Sure. Only thing to do after what I saw here tonight. 'Sides, can't have you working for me unmarried. That's a good way of asking for trouble, having a pretty woman working in a saloon without a ring on her finger. The flats break too many chairs and mirrors fighting over her and that just about kills your chance of making a decent profit."

Rachel rubbed her forehead, feeling the twisting pain of a headache starting behind her eyes. The last time she'd seen her brother he'd been saddling his horse for a raid on the railroad. He'd had no thoughts in his head beyond the next day, the next passel of trouble. Now he sat across the room from her, making plans for his future—questionable though they might be—talking like a born businessman and showing concern for her honor. She couldn't quite take it all in.

"You're going far too fast for me," Rachel complained. "You're going to have to make things clearer. And put that gun away. When Hal gets married, he won't need to be prodded in the back by one of Colonel Colt's children."

"Nice, ain't it?" Slade said, turning the pistol this way and that so the lamplight glittered on the steel set into the white bone gun butt. "Took it off a feller in Albuquerque. Tried to bluff with a pair of twos. That's when I figured on changing my profession. Uncommon lot of idiots you meet 'round one of them green baize tables."

He shifted his weight in the chair to push his weapon back in the holster. "So when I heard about this little diamond rush you all were having here, I rounded up some of the boys and came through for a look-see. Didn't take me more'n a minute to see where there's gonna be money to be made. Asked around and the next thing you know . . . I'm a businessman."

"Who sold you the Hatch?" Hal asked.

"Lady at the boardinghouse told me a feller named Clyde owned it. I wrote him a telegram to New York and he sold it to me outright. Didn't charge much . . . took my first price."

"Marcellus Clyde?" Hal shook his head. "I'm surprised he didn't give it to you. I had wondered if Mrs. Garrett knew he was the owner."

Rachel could feel Hal's yearning to leave there and get to his press. She felt certain that the story of the change in ownership of the Hatch was going to be the headline in the next edition. Though she didn't want to lose his support, she said, "It's late. You better be getting along, Hal. Don't forget to stop by the Schurs' to tell 'em I won't be over there tonight. I hope she can keep that cake overnight."

She turned a steady gaze on him, trying to communicate by pure mental telepathy. Above all, she did not want Lyle walking in while Slade was still there. Lyle always did think his big brother hung the moon. She had to get to him first, to make one last try to persuade Lyle that Slade was no good.

As Hal stood up, he promised, "I'll stop there first thing." He looked at Slade and smiled. "Mr. Schur is the local pastor, by the way. If you want a marriage, you'll have to talk to him first."

"I'll do that. You might as well get used to the notion that you're going to marry her. I know you city types—love 'em and walk away. Wasn't there a gal weeping over you when we met before? A sweet little thing as I recall."

"Must have been someone else. As *I* recall, you were in jail when we last met. Robbery with violence, wasn't it?"

Her brother smiled, his eyes narrowing. "Sure. But the sheriff had the wrong man. Couple of guys testified I'd been playing cards with 'em all the time. He had to let me out with an apology and a handshake."

"Digger Cosgrove and Lemon Malloy, by any chance?"

"Funny thing about that . . ." Slade's smile widened to a grin. "They're the kind of friends you can count on."

Rachel had enough of this male one-upmanship. The air seemed thick with their voices and the way they leaned toward each other, too busy being tough and macho to give brains a chance. She said sharply, "I'm not going to marry Mr. Sinclair, Slade. And I'm not going to be working for you. If you want to open that saloon again, it's your business. But me and every other woman in this town will stand against you."

"You?" Slade said, looking her over. His derisive grin faded when he met her eyes. "You'd set yourself up against your own brother?"

"Quicker than a flash of lightning," she said.

Hal asked, his tone as hurt as Slade's but much more believably, "You're not going to marry me?"

"Of course not! You're not the marrying kind, remember?"

"He will be, if I got anything to say about it!"

"You don't, Slade. Not one word. I've been getting along

just fine without you and I mean to go on doing fine. Now why don't both of you get out of here and go about your business."

They both said, in the same breath, "But I want to talk. . . ."

The men broke off to glare at each other. Rachel said, opening the front door, "I don't want to talk now. I'm tired. I've had a long day."

A whisper of cold air blew over her ankles. "You better dress up warm," she said. "Have you got a coat, Slade?"

"Didn't think I'd need one. I forgot what real cold weather's like. I ain't been on the trail much lately. Kee-rist! Is that snow?"

Rachel looked out. Fat white snow flashed in the lamplight like flakes of silver drifting out of the sky. "Wait a minute," she said. She fetched the coat she'd found hanging on a hook at the marshal's office. Giving it and the hat to her brother, she said, "Buy a new one tomorrow at the General Store and take these back to Marshal Hunnicut. Tell him I borrowed them and you borrowed them from me."

Slade's eyebrows rose up so far they all but crawled down the back of his neck. "You want me to go into the marshal's office? Of my own free will?"

"Why not? You're a businessman now, remember? You should make friends with the marshal. You might need him to break up those fights you were talking about."

Slade didn't look happy at the prospect, but Rachel felt she'd done all that could be expected of her. She stood on tiptoe to press a kiss against his bristling cheek. "I *am* glad to see you, Slade. But I'm warning you flat out. I won't have you making trouble for me here."

"I don't want to make trouble for you," he mumbled. "I've missed you and the kid. Family's important, you know?"

"Yes, I know."

Hal said. "Wait a minute!" He reached over and closed the door. "You can't let on he's your brother! Everyone knows the name 'Delmon' and what it stands for; it'd be a dead giveaway for you, Rachel."

"Damn!" Slade said with an exasperated sigh. "You don't think I'm going by my real handle, do you? Nope, so far as anybody 'round here knows, my name's Flanders. Slade Flanders."

"That's going to complicate things even more," Hal said. "Couldn't you clear out, for Rachel's sake?"

"So you got a clear chance to ruin her? Not on your nelly!"

"Will you get it through your thick head that what was going on here tonight was just a brief madness? I'd already made up my mind not to go any further."

"Oh you had, had you?" Rachel put her hands on her hips and advanced on him. "I don't suppose it mattered to you that I was perfectly willing to do what you wanted. You decided to be a little gentleman about it without even asking me what I wanted."

"Now, Rachel, it wasn't like that. . . ."

"Men!" She threw her hands in the air, an anger bright as a campfire flaring in her veins. "Get out, the both of you. I've had quite enough of your company for one night."

Slade, no fool, had jerked open the door and was already halfway down the steps before she finished speaking. There he stopped, however, to wait for Hal, obviously not trusting him.

Rachel respected Hal's bravery even though she was mad at him. Not every man would stay around while a redheaded woman got angry. Let alone remain behind while her overprotective brother waited outside armed for bear. He even reached out to shake her hand and hold it for a moment. "I'll still go by the Schurs' and ask them about that 'cake.'"

"You can send Lyle home now. We need to have a talk. And thank you."

"For what?"

"For being here. For . . . being you."

"Rachel . . ." He brushed his fingers down her cheek in that soft, caressing gesture that seemed to have become a habit with him. Rachel wanted nothing more than to melt into his arms. If only he wasn't such a . . . a man.

She jerked herself upright, snapping open her eyes. "Get going," she said. "I'm too mad and too tired to talk anymore."

"I just wanted to say that your brother has the world's worst timing, even worse than Lyle's."

She couldn't repress a chuckle. "It's a family trait." Then despairingly, she said, "Oh, what am I going to do? I can't believe that Slade has just shown up here through coincidence. I can't believe that any more than I believe he doesn't mean to try to take Lyle away from me. You didn't hear what he said. . . ."

"What? Did he threaten you?"

Rachel closed her eyes. "He's got a strong family feeling, Hal. He loves me, in his way. But Lyle's a boy and a Delmon. And there's the family business to consider. If only he hadn't found us . . ."

Hal coughed and dug his hands into his pockets. "Rachel, there's something I've been meaning to tell you."

"What?" She knew she must look as suspicious as Slade himself. Certainly, her trigger finger had begun to itch.

"I mentioned your name in a story I sent to New York . . . not Delmon . . . no, I promised I wouldn't. But I wrote that a pretty schoolteacher, Rachel Pridgeon, had been named the new marshal of Brooklyn. Slade might have seen the story . . . it's probably been copied on inserts all across the country by now. News travels fast these days."

"Especially with you so willing to help it on." Rachel had never before given full rein of her temper. She had one, a fiercely raging inferno of passion that she'd kept under control since she was three and given to tantrums. All of a sudden, it slipped its leash.

"Get out," she whispered. "Get out or so help me, Hal, I may not wait for *Slade* to shoot you!"

19

WHEN LYLE CAME home, the first thing Rachel did was look at his feet. Bare as always if she wasn't around to hound him into shoes, pale with cold, they were not wet. She asked, "How did you get home without getting your feet wet?"

"Hal carried me," Lyle said, shrugging. "I wasn't gonna let him but he tossed me over his shoulder like I was a bag of grain. For a man what works with words, he sure is strong."

"Yes, isn't he?" More loudly, she said, "I'm glad you like Hal. You know, I'm fond of him myself."

"Betting is you're gonna marry him. Hey, what's that funny smell? Something burning?"

"No, that's . . . who's betting?"

"All of 'em. The kids especially. But they won't let me get a bet down," he said in the tone of one nursing a long-standing grievance. "They figure I know too much 'bout what's going on. It's like . . . I don't know . . . it's like they think we talk about mushy stuff like that."

"Well, we are talking about it."

"Oh." His head dropped between his shoulders as though he'd draw it in, turtlelike. "Yeah."

"Not that it matters. I don't want you betting on anything. It's just a waste of money."

"Heck, we don't none of us bet *money*. None of us got any. The Bannerman boys bet that they won't beat nobody up for a week. Lucy Hudson bets kisses but nobody wants *them* but Bart Bannerman and she don't like him. Her sister bets sugar cookies and everybody takes her up on that! I once won five of 'em 'cause she didn't have sense enough to quit. Broke her for two weeks that time!" He sighed as if looking back on some golden age that would never come again.

This was a new vision of her students, as a sort of Wall Street Exchange in miniature. Rachel guessed, however, that it would be fatal to ask what the bet had been that let Lyle get five cookies ahead of Sarah Hudson. She'd learned long ago never to ask Lyle a question unless she intended doing something about the answer. "Never mind that," she said. "There's something else I want to talk to you about. Go upstairs and get ready for bed. I'll come up in a few minutes with your milk."

"Okay. Boy, it's pretty neat that it's snowing! Mr. Schur told me they ain't had snow on Halloween since he was a kid himself."

"Halloween?"

"Sure, that's tonight. Only us kids decided not to do anything about it this year, everything being so topsy-turvey right now."

"That's good of you. I don't think I could stand soaped windows or finding my door all tangled with strings in the morning." Those had been but two of the pranks played on her last year. Apparently the schoolteacher was a tempting target for every child in town.

"Oh, we figure we'll make up for it at Christmas, if there is one."

"You better scoot, Lyle." She put her hand over her mouth to stifle her smile at his mixture of cunning and naivete. If only she didn't have to tell him tonight that Slade had come into their lives again. If only she never had to tell him . . .

Lyle called form the top of the stairs. "I forgot to tell you, Rachel. Hal says if you want him to come in for a little while, you should put a candle in the kitchen window. He'll wait 'til midnight."

"Lyle Delmon!"

"Hey, you didn't call me Pridgeon!"

"I'll call you something else in a minute!"

She hurried into the kitchen and lit a new candle. Of course, Hal would probably think . . . she wouldn't let him inside. She'd open the back door just a crack and talk to him through it.

But when he appeared in answer to her summons, snow had powdered his hair and melted, dampening the shoulders of his coat. "You better come inside before you catch your death," she said.

"Is it safe?"

"Safe? I'm not going to skin you alive, if that's what you're worried about." A fleeting expression of comical relief crossed his features. "At least not with Lyle upstairs."

Rachel wished she could forget how much she loved him just long enough to tell him that she hated him. But she couldn't help giggling a little at his mock-apprehensive expression.

He lightened even further. "I thought you'd never laugh with me again. Rachel, I swear all I wanted to write was a human story about this debacle I've caused and you've been on my mind so much that I wrote about you."

"I thought you said you just 'mentioned' me." He looked sheepish. "Never mind that now. But listen! Do I have your solemn vow . . . solemn, mind you . . . that you will never again write another word about me or my family without my permission?"

"Have you got a stack of Bibles say . . . forty feet high?"

"No jokes now, Hal. I'm serious. Do you swear?"

He raised his right hand, his face completely composed. She looked into those eyes that had all but mesmerized her from the hour they'd met. No sparkle, no twinkling gleam, just a straight, serious honesty. "I swear it, Rachel. So far as I'm concerned there's never been a Delmon family."

"All right."

"Just one question? Can I keep the money I've already made? All of it together would just about buy a nice . . ."

"Rachel!" Lyle called. "I'm ready."

Hal sighed gustily and whacked the kitchen table with the flat of his hand. "Do you *have* to have brothers? I hear sisters are more tactful."

"It's too late for me to change them. As much as I'd like to. I'm scared of Slade, Hal. He's ruthless."

"I got that impression myself. You said he has considerable family feeling, however."

"Oh, yes. He gets that from my father. He'd kill a man as soon as look at him, but not family. His brother . . . did you ever hear of Wayne Delmon?"

Hal shook his head.

Rachel poured milk into a glass from the pitcher in the pantry. "Uncle Wayne was long gone before I was born. He and Dad used to ride together until Uncle Wayne stole Dad's share. Dad said he tracked his brother down like a grizzly bear tracking fresh ham through the woods."

"Where is Uncle Wayne buried?" Hal asked dryly .

"That's just it. Dad tracked him, found him, scared him but didn't lay a finger on him. Just told him he was very disappointed and Uncle Wayne shouldn't ever come back. At least, that's the way Dad told it."

"The way things are going for you, Rachel, I expect to discover that *I'm* Uncle Wayne."

"Rachel!" Lyle called again.

"I better go. Will you wait for me?"

"I'd much rather stay here where it's warm than go back to the boardinghouse. Mrs. Jergens has been so scattered lately cooking for the newcomers that she hasn't given me a hot-water bottle the last two nights. My room is freezing!"

Rachel smiled at him as she filled one of the square iron

bottles that had been heating before the stove. Between the heat of the warm iron and the hot water inside, Lyle should be warm as a puppy all night long.

"What's so funny?" he demanded, his tone hurt. "You think the idea of my freezing my . . . um . . . my toes off is funny?"

"No, it's the way you said 'newcomers.' Like you've lived here all your life."

"To tell you the truth, I've lived more in one crowded hour in Brooklyn than in all my life in New York."

"We're glad you like us," Rachel said as she went out. She was still smiling as she went up the stairs. But it all faded away as she went into Lyle's small room.

It too was cold. Lyle was already tucked into bed, his gray blankets and pieced quilt drawn up to his nose. "Would you mind putting that bottle by my feet? They're powerful cold."

"You've got to start wearing your boots and socks, Lyle. You run around in weather like this barefoot and you'll wind up missing some toes."

"Cats and dogs don't seem to mind it."

"You are neither a cat nor a dog." She lifted the blankets at the end of the bed and put the iron bottle close enough to his feet to warm them but not so close as to cook them. "How's that?"

"Grand. Just leave the milk. I'll drink it when I'm thirsty. Good night." He closed his eyes. "I—I can't think when I been sleepier. Must be the snow."

His breathing instantly became deep and regular. Rachel knew there was no way her active little brother had fallen that rapidly into a doze. However, she was glad of a momentary pause to catch her breath and organize her thoughts. Going to the window, she opened the mulberry red curtains and looked out. Though she could see almost nothing, she could hear the slow heavy plot of the snow on the slide roof. "It won't stick," she said philosophically. "The ground's too wet."

"'Sides, ol' man McGovern says snow never stays 'til

after November. Too bad. The Bannerman boys were gonna go sliding down Dead Man's Hill."

"I thought you were asleep."

"Who can sleep with you thumping around?"

She sat down on the edge of his bed. He clutched the blankets closer from underneath. "Lyle," she began. "How much do you remember of your life before we went to California?"

"You mean . . . the mesa? I remember everything." His eyes opened to slits, the pale green moving behind the dark lashes. "Why? You never want to talk about it. I remember when we got to that stupid mission you told me that I never lived there; that I dreamed the whole thing."

His voice told of his resentment. "I'm sorry," she said. "That was wrong of me. Mr. McLean suggested I tell you that. We thought you were too young to understand what had happened."

"I remember Mama dying. I stuffed my fingers in my ears, but I still remember."

Rachel blinked back the tears that had leaped up suddenly to sting her eyes. "I remember that too. Believe me, Lyle, that was the worst night of my life. But your mother was concerned most of all that you be safe . . ."

"Safe from what?"

"You're not a fool, Lyle. Even as a little boy, you knew what our father did for a living. He robbed people and sometimes he killed them. He made it sound like some great adventure and made us love him because he seemed so grand and wonderful. But it wasn't like that. It was mean and petty and wicked."

"Don't you talk that way about him!" He lay very straight and still under the covers but his eyes were fully open now and blazing. "It wasn't like that!"

Rachel said, "That's the only thing your mother asked of me. That I keep you away from that life. From the life our father led 'til it killed him. From the life Slade leads now. Do you remember him . . . Slade?"

"Sure. A feller doesn't forget his only brother. He was the

most wonderful brother . . . I mean, sure I remember him." A shrug, muffled by the blankets.

Rachel knew then that she'd bungled. She'd let her emotions run away with her and now Lyle wouldn't listen. He would lie there, his mind as adamant as the diamond he'd lost. Nothing she could say would work. Come tomorrow, he'd be down at the saloon as he'd once spent his days at the marshal's office and the newspaper.

She said simply, "Slade's here, in Brooklyn."

"He is? Where?"

"He's opening the Hatch. He's . . . he's thinking about going on the straight and narrow."

"The Hatch? That's great! I can't wait . . . do you think he remembers me? I was just a little kid . . ."

"He remembers you. He'll be glad to see you again." She stood up. "Are you comfortable? Warm enough now?"

"Sure. Thanks."

"Okay if I take the candle?"

"Would you mind leaving it a piece? I . . . uh . . . got this book I want to read."

"A book?" A horrible suspicion grew in an instant from a mere insinuation to a full-grown certainty. "Not *Rakehell Rachel*?"

"Heck no. That's a sissy book. No, this is something I got from Mr. Schur. It's about knights and crusades and stuff like that." From beneath the blanket, clasped to his thin chest, came a book bound in red leather. The covering was cracked and dry with age. One of his fingers, slightly grimy, was inserted between the thin leaves, only a few pages into the story of *The Talisman*.

"I'll leave you to it," she said.

"You mean it? I can read it now?"

"As late as you like . . . or at least until the candle burns down."

"Thanks," Lyle said, real gratitude shining in his eyes. "Some of the words are awful hard going but I'm kinda getting into the swim of it."

She knew he'd resent a kiss so she merely blew him one from the doorway. His dark head was already bent over the page and he did not see her do it. Yet she hoped that some part of that tough-minded, pugnacious young spirit felt her love. In the end, it was all she had to offer him.

She could not protect him from the disappointments that awaited him, the disillusionment that was inevitable. Lyle had never had the kind of childhood that encouraged a belief in Saint Nicholas or fairies. She almost wished he believed in those things, for they could be outgrown with hardly a pang for their passing. But the inevitable moment would come when he would learn that his adult idols had feet of clay.

Holding on to his doorknob for strength, Rachel prayed hard that the moment when he learned that she too was no more than mortal would be long delayed. She couldn't bear to see him look at her with the beginnings of adult pain in his eyes.

When she went into the kitchen, she didn't speak to Hal even though he stood up when she came in. Rachel sat on her hardest chair, her arms wrapped around herself as if for warmth. But the coldness in her heart couldn't be eliminated that way.

Hal thought she looked like a woman who'd lost everything in a fire or other catastrophe. He put his hand on her shoulder and she flinched. "Rachel?" he asked, trying hard to keep the reproach from his tone.

"I'm sorry. I think you'd better go."

"You afraid Slade will come back and find us together?"

"It wouldn't be good if he did."

"His ideas have some foundation, Rachel. If you hadn't gone in search of a light, we might have been interrupted even more embarrassingly than we were."

"I know. Though I was already having second thoughts."

"*You* were?"

"Were you?"

Rachel flicked her eyes up at him and then away. "It's just as well then that we didn't go any further."

"I'd agree with you wholeheartedly except for one thing."

"What's that?" she asked after a long moment.

"I'm in love with you."

She sat there and stared at him, believing that her mind had finally broken down under the strain of the last week. Her expression must have been amusing for he laughed. "Did you hear what I said? I'm in love with you, Rachel."

"I . . . I heard you."

"And?"

"I don't know. It's . . ." She passed her hand over her forehead, surprised to find her fingers were trembling.

He nodded as if she'd said something profound. "It's been a long day for you, hasn't it? So many things have happened I'm sure you don't know if you're on your head or your heels."

"That's for certain." She looked up at him, confused. "You did say . . ."

"I love you, yes. I said that."

"And you meant it?"

"You know I do." He made a sudden movement, as though he wanted to go to her, but checked himself. "I shouldn't have told you now. Why don't you go to bed? Relax. Get some sleep. Put a cool cloth on your forehead or some *eau de cologne*."

"I would, if I had any. But you're right, Hal. I need a chance to collect myself. I haven't even told you . . ."

He stepped forward then and laid his forefinger on her lips. "Don't say anything now. I was selfish to have spoken as I did. We'll talk tomorrow."

Rachel almost couldn't bear Sissie's happiness. The milliner positively danced around her shop, flicking around an ostrich feather duster here, pirouetting with a silken scarf weaving about her body there, singing all the while in a tuneless contralto.

"Oh, Rachel!" she cried, fluttering over when the bell over the door tinkled. "I never knew how wonderful life was until last night! Thanks to you and that wonderful Mr. Sinclair!"

"I thought you were calling him 'Hal' yesterday." Rachel had plastered on her biggest smile before entering, but it was a hard thing to support in the face of so much genuine happiness.

"Oh, Benson doesn't think it's right I should call any man but him by his Christian name. And if I can please him in little ways like that, the least I can do is do as he asks. I'm going to study and *work*, really hard, to be the best wife in town. Or the state or world for that matter. Ah, me!"

Rachel wanted to sit down. Watching Sissie flitter about the shop was more dizzying than watching butterfly flights in the spring. A box of dyed guinea hen feathers fell from a middle-height shelf as she brushed gaily by. The box fell end over end. As the feathers spilled out, they floated away as lightly as Sissie herself.

Remembering how the young milliner had cursed like a sailor when such a box had broken open before, Rachel watched in amazement as Sissie danced through the feathers as lightly as a fairy waking the dawn. She scooped up handfuls of the floating things, making a general pass in the direction of the box where they lived. However, it didn't seem to matter to her whether the feathers went back into the box, or swirled away on the slight drafts created by her hands.

Rachel knelt automatically to try to help pick up the feathers. "So I guess things worked out all right between you and Marshal Hunnicut?"

"All right? Oh, you could say that I suppose." Sissie blushed and giggled. "Of course, you'll be my bridesmaid, won't you, Rachel?"

"You know I will! I'm so happy for you, Sissie. This is right, I can *feel* it."

Sissie leaned forward to throw her arms around Rachel. Rachel couldn't tell if her friend was laughing or crying. Maybe a little of both, for that was how Rachel herself felt. She patted Sissie's back and asked the one question guaranteed to catch her attention.

"Have you started to think about what you'll wear?"

"Oh my, yes. The wedding's to be at Christmas and I've seen the most beautiful wedding dress in *Harper's Bazaar*. I can't afford it, but it looks easy enough to make . . .

especially as I've ordered a new sewing machine. It's got white fur around the neck. . . ."

"The sewing machine?"

Sissie giggled again and gave her a push. "Oh, you! No, the dress! White satin, very long and full . . . sweeping I guess you'd say. Wait a minute; I'll find the magazine." She started to get up.

"What about these feathers?"

Sissie glanced around at the drifts of gaily colored bird fluff decorating the floor. It was hard to believe so many had been stuffed into one little box. Sissie said, "I suppose I ought to pick them up. Let me just show you this picture first."

She stood up, a mass of feathers adhering to her skirt. She didn't even trouble to brush them off, so they fell, one at a time, as she walked away into the back room. Rachel thought that it was a good thing Sissie was leaving a trail. Overnight, she'd become so flighty that she probably wouldn't be able to find her way back into the store without a clue to follow.

Love, it seemed, made people very strange.

Take herself. She hadn't had the sense last night to throw herself into Hal's arms when he confessed he loved her. The thrill that ran through her very marrow at that thought had lost none of its power overnight. She'd awakened several times in the night and each time that thrill had awaited her. Hal loved her. For now, that was enough, though she knew that soon she'd begin to ask herself those hard questions again.

Then there'd been the bottle of *eau de cologne* that Lyle had found on the front porch first thing in the morning. Rachel recognized the cherry-stripe-on-cream ribbon around the bottle's neck as being the gift-wrapping ribbon at the Gladds' General Store. She wondered whether Hal had taken Mrs. Gladd away from her supper to open up the store, or if he'd been waiting on the steps when she and her son had taken down the shutters. Either way, the gift warmed her heart even as she realized Mrs. Gladd wouldn't waste a minute before finding someone to confide in about Hal's strange actions.

Rachel was wearing the fragrance now, a subtle scent of honeysuckle and lily that seemed to whisper of spring, despite the generally poor weather. The snow had not stayed, melting into the wet ground to make a nasty, gluelike mud, one more burden for the women of Brooklyn. Thick clouds, like vast sky-borne mountains, drifted overhead, casting cold shadows. A sharp tang followed the wind that pushed the clouds along, promising more snow before long.

"Here it is," Sissie cried, flourishing the heavily illustrated magazine. "Isn't it grand?"

The creature modeling the dress was only vaguely human with her tiny head, large bust and india rubber arms and legs. There was no denying, however, that the dress was heavenly. Even Rachel, with so much on her mind, took a second glance. Shown with a cloak blowing back from a 'womanly figure,' the wedding dress had a charming ruff of fur, echoed around each wrist.

Sissie read the description. "Italian silk with dropped waist and white fox fur. Pearl buttons with glass centers." Then her voice dropped to a whisper. "Seventy-five fifty."

"It's lovely but that price is a scandal! Are you sure you can duplicate it? You're a good seamstress—the best in Brooklyn—but this is something special."

"Well, I think I can. It's got right simple lines, you know. I probably won't use silk—too expensive. But there's some awfully nice figured damask that I can order. It's really for tablecloths and napkins but I think it will do. And, of course, fox fur is impossibly expensive. But I saw some white rabbit fur in a catalogue for next to nothing! And I already *have* pearl buttons, any number of them in all sizes."

She reached out impulsively to show Rachel and another box tumbled off a high shelf. Pearl buttons rained down like hailstones. Rachel could see that being Sissie's bridesmaid would be yet another challenge in a life that already overflowed with them.

When both feathers and buttons were collected and

restored to their respective boxes—the lid of the feather box wouldn't quite close again so they tied it shut with ribbon—Rachel sat Sissie down and fixed her a soothing cup of tea. With the door to the rear room left open so that the heat from the small stove back there could warm the whole store, it became as cozy as a home.

With more hope than confidence, Rachel thought that if Sissie could just sit still for a little while she'd regain her common sense. Several times Rachel tried to bring up her own affairs, needing an ear to confide in, but Sissie was deaf to any subject that didn't deal with the innumerable perfections of Benson Hunnicut. When she reached the point of saying that it would be wonderful to be married to a bald man because she'd never have to clean his hairs out of the washstand, Rachel gave up.

When the bell above the door jingled, Rachel saw Hal standing there smiling at her. She couldn't entirely meet his gaze, though she felt her smile must be as wide as his. Sissie, the quickest person alive to scent romance, got out of her chair and all but danced toward Hal.

"I owe it all to you," she practically sang. "If it weren't for the two of you . . . Would you like a cup of tea, Hal . . . I mean, Mr. Sinclair? I think I have another cup. . . ." She floated away into the back room, without feathers this time. Rachel wondered if they'd ever see her again.

"I'm glad to see you," she said in a hurried whisper.

"Are you?" He brushed his hand over her arm, a gesture that looked noncommittal but felt entirely possessive. Rachel knew she should be bridling, but somehow she didn't mind a bit.

"Yes, you have no idea!" Knowing she was getting his hopes up, she added wickedly, "Finally someone who doesn't want to talk about Benson Hunnicut!"

"Actually I do want to talk to you about him."

"Oh, no!" she said in simulated horror.

Hal glanced toward the rear of the store. "Isn't she taking a long time to get a cup of tea?" he asked.

"She's probably lost," Rachel muttered. Louder, she

added, "Lost in thought, I mean. Getting engaged does strange things to people."

"Does it? Are we speaking from personal experience, Rachel?"

Strange indeed how this morning she didn't mind his teasing, knowing that he loved her. "So," she said, looking at him from under her lashes. "Why do you want to talk about Marshal Hunnicut? Don't tell me *you* dote on the shape of his head?"

"Does she?"

Rachel nodded, treasuring his laugh. "At length," she added. "It's wonderful."

"Maybe I should talk to him for you. I've had lots of practice in keeping a straight face. You'd take one look at him, remember what Sissie said about his head, and break out laughing in his face."

"Talk to him? About what?"

"About the fact that there's a dangerous criminal in town running the saloon."

Rachel put her head to one side, her forehead wrinkling in confusion. "You mean Slade? You want me to turn him in? I can't do that."

20

To ADD TO Rachel's frustration, the marshal himself showed up not five minutes later. Like Sissie, he looked almost indecently pleased with himself. He had his thumbs tucked into his braces and if he didn't exactly crow with triumph like a lucky rooster, he gave off the glow of a satisfied man.

Judging by Hal's face, he thought it was a little much when Benson and Sissie stopped dead as they caught sight of each other. Then, completely disregarding their audience, the two flew into each other's arms as though parted not for a few hours but for long and lonely years. Which, as Rachel thought with her mania for fairness, was in some sense true.

"Come on," she said to Hal, tugging on his coat sleeve. "Let's get along. They don't know if we're here or not."

The lovers separated as though about to make some answer, but it was only to change position. As Hal went out, he turned the sign hanging in the glass panel of the door from OPEN to CLOSED. "I hope they have sense enough to draw the blinds."

"Hal! You're not suggesting . . . ! But they're not married!"

"You sound shocked. What do you think they did last night after we left them?"

"I am shocked! And I don't want to think about it."

"Considering how close you and I have come on more than one occasion, your shock surprises me." He turned up his collar against the cold breeze. Facing her, he did the same with her collar. "Button up, dear. I don't want you catching cold."

When he did thoughtful things her knees turned to melted butter. But it was the note in his voice, both caressing and possessive, that undid her every time. No one had ever troubled to take such tender care of her before; such things fell to her as part of her self-imposed yet inescapable duty to others. No doubt if Slade were here now, she'd be buttoning up *his* coat.

She looked down the street at the two-story building in the middle of the block. Already someone was up on a ladder tacking down the shingles on the roof of the overhang. Almost every man who walked down the main street paused outside to look in. More than one of them edged in through the half-open side of the double doors. "Are they open for business already?"

"I can't imagine that your brother lets much grass grow under his feet. The sooner he opens, the sooner he'll start making money."

"That would appeal to him." She looked up at Hal, hoping she wasn't going to ruin his affection for her. "I can't tell Benson about Slade. I'm hoping that he means what he says and aims to go straight. If I tell Benson who he really is, I could ruin that chance for him. I can't do it."

He shook his head at her, but still with a warmth in his eyes as though he loved her. "I think you're getting your hopes up too high. Slade didn't sound to me as though he were looking for a chance to change his life. He sounded like he was looking for a chance to be a criminal in a string tie instead of a bandana mask."

"Maybe you're right. But I have to give him the benefit of the doubt . . . though I'll probably regret it. One thing's for certain, however. I won't be working *for* him. And if any of my students sticks his nose inside that place, I'll be down on him like a ton of bricks!"

"I still think—"

"Yoo-hoo! Rachel!"

They turned at the sound and saw Mrs. Gladd running down the boardwalk toward them, her skirt lifted to the tops of her button-shoes. Mr. and Mrs. Schur came along behind her, less precipitously. A droopy and depressed Dorothy Schur brought up the rear.

"Good morning, good morning," Mrs. Gladd said breathlessly. "Isn't it dreadful! Right here in the very heart of town."

"The saloon?" Hal asked. "Miss Pridgeon and I were just discussing it."

"The saloon? Why, yes, that's dreadful too. But there's even worse news. Haven't you heard?" She lowered her voice impressively. "Diamonds. Behind the blacksmith's. They'll be swarming there in an hour."

"No, I hadn't heard," Rachel said. "Are you sure it's not just another rumor? There were all sorts of rumors running wild at Mrs. Garrett's, but no one seemed to know if they were true."

"I heard about it from Mr. Schur who talked to Mr. Larrimore's oldest girl. Isn't that right?"

The pastor and his wife caught up to them. Mr. Schur looked his most imposing, his chin all but buried in his collar. "No, ma'am. I heard about it from my daughter, who'd spoken to the blacksmith's girl. She said her young brother found the stones."

"Let's see . . . that would be Bill Larrimore," Hal asked. Rachel was amazed that he could pinpoint the right child that quickly, considering that so far as she knew he'd never met the family. "I'll have a talk with him."

Mrs. Schur blinked her pale eyes rapidly. "And here I was

hoping that all this nonsense would end soon. I mean, when nobody's found *anything* in a week, you figure they'd up and go back where they came from. But if there are *more* diamonds, I suppose they'll just stay around forever."

"Wickedness!" Mr. Schur said suddenly in his most resonant voice. "Wickedness and more wickedness. Greed, seductions of the flesh and riotousness all in the town I believed to be a station on the way to Heaven. It's a black time, a black time."

"There now, Joshua," Mrs. Schur said, patting his arm.

"I have asked the Lord why we should be so afflicted, when we have been innocent. All our peace shattered and for what reason?" He spread his hands helplessly and shook his head. "I can't understand it."

Rachel, feeling this was all somehow her fault, said, "I'm sorry Lyle ever . . ."

Mr. Schur's head came up. Rachel was surprised to find no sign of censure in his deep gaze. "I wasn't blaming you, Rachel. Or your brother. It's God's will that ordains the instrument of our chastisement. Maybe it was our pride . . . I don't know."

Mrs. Gladd said, "And now the saloon's opened up again and I suppose we'll have nothing but noise from now on. You weren't here when it was open before, Miss Pridgeon, Mr. Sinclair. It was dreadful. A decent woman could hardly go out after dark and it wasn't so very safe in the daytime either."

Rachel noticed that Dorothy had been gazing at the saloon for some time. The girl must have felt her eyes on her for she said suddenly, "Ed's in there. I saw him go in."

Her mother put an arm around the girl's waist and squeezed. "Never mind. He'll come to his senses soon."

"Oh, who wants him to? Not me." Dorothy broke free of her mother's tender clasp and stalked off. When Mrs. Schur acted as though she'd follow, her husband stopped her.

"Give the child a few moments alone to pray."

Rachel thought the young girl needed time to cry but perhaps it would be accounted a prayer wherever the angels kept track of such things. This wicked time might have some good come of it, if it served to show Dorothy her own heart. Tucking her cold hand in the bend of Hal's elbow, she knew she never would have come to love him so quickly if the current of life in Brooklyn hadn't been so disturbed.

Mrs. Gladd, still looking at the saloon, suddenly frowned. "That's not . . . that's not Clarence going in there, is it?"

Rachel looked up too late to see more than the back of the latest patron. "Clarence? Your Clarence?"

Clarence Gladd was only sixteen but already out of school. He'd whipped through everything the previous teacher had been able to show him and had been studying college texts prior to going off to an Eastern school next year. Rachel hadn't been able to help him much, knowing nothing about Latin and but little mathematics beyond algebra.

Mrs. Gladd shook her head. "No, it couldn't be. I left him home, studying philosophy or philology or some such truck. Besides, Clarence would never . . . No, it couldn't be."

Someone coughed behind them in a meaningful way and the four citizens turned around as one. A woman none of them recognized stood there, her posture dragged down on one side by the baby she toted and her skirt pulled tight on the other side by the three- or four-year-old boy keeping a death grip on the material. The woman's cheeks were pale with the cold, her nose pink. She had only a shawl over her shoulders against the wind and half of that was wrapped around the baby. The baby's lips were blue beneath its running nose. The other child's teeth chattered, elbows and knees showing through his shirt and pants.

In a surprisingly cultured voice, the woman said, "Can you tell me where I can find some milk?"

"Milk?" Mrs. Gladd repeated.

"Yes, ma'am. There's none up at the tents and the children had nothing but crackers all yesterday."

Rachel saw the Schurs exchange a long, speaking look. Then Mrs. Schur stepped forward. "Come with me, my dear. All my children are grown and the cow doesn't seem to realize it somehow. My, what a lovely baby. Is it a boy, too?"

The woman watched Mrs. Schur take the baby, as if mesmerized. "No, she's a girl. Delia."

"Delia? Isn't that pretty?"

Meanwhile, Mr. Schur had knelt on the boards, rummaging in the pocket of his woolen coat. "Now I know I have lemon drops somewhere in my . . . Here!" He brought out a twisted screw of paper. "Would you like one?"

The boy glanced up at his mother. Then he shook his head with the vehemence of the very young. He tried to hide himself behind his mother's skirt. Mr. Schur chuckled as he rose to his feet. "Not much for candy? Well, I'll tell you. My wife bakes cakes like an angel. Why don't you and your mother come on up to the house? Mrs. Schur baked a Spanish cake yesterday and my, it's good."

"Yes, indeed," Mrs. Schur said. "And I have half a turkey left over from Sunday dinner."

"We don't take charity," the woman said, but with puzzlement in her tone, as if she wasn't sure that they were offering that pity, as cold and drear as the day, which any right-thinking person must refuse.

Mr. Schur put his hand on her shoulder. "My good woman, I would give you faith, for I have faith; I would give you hope, for I have hope. But the greatest good you can do me is to accept my charity."

Mrs. Schur added, "I should mention that my husband is the pastor of this town."

The woman still looked puzzled but a faint smile had appeared in her thin cheek. "All the same . . ." she began.

Rachel said, not ungently, "You might as well get your children where it's warm while you make up your mind."

Mrs. Schur led the way, babbling at the baby. Mr. Schur had taken the woman's arm to help her over the gaps in the boardwalk while the little boy tagged along behind, giving wondering glances up at the tall man.

Hal said, "I wonder . . . I wonder if Mr. Schur has found the answer to his question."

"What question?" Mrs. Gladd asked.

But Rachel knew what he meant. "I expect they'll have a houseful by sundown. Actually, I expect we'll *all* have a house full of guests by sundown. Have you ever noticed how hard it is to say no to really good people?"

Mrs. Gladd said, "I hope I'm 'really good people,' Rachel, because I'm going to ask you a favor. Do you think you could be marshal again just for a few minutes?"

"Me? But the real marshal's right inside Sissie's store."

"Is he?"

Mrs. Gladd crossed the few steps to rattle the doorknob. "It's locked and the blind is down."

"Is it?" Rachel asked, afraid to look at Hal. Sissie might get married, she reflected, somewhat before Christmas at this rate. She might have to.

To take Mrs. Gladd's mind—and her own!—off that drawn blind, Rachel asked, "Why do you need a marshal?"

"I'm going in . . . over there." Mrs. Gladd pointed one gloved finger toward the saloon. "I *know* it isn't Clarence I saw going in there, but I'm determined to make sure."

Hal said, "I'll go with you, Mrs. Gladd. There's no need to take Miss Pridgeon into a place like that."

"That's very good of you, Mr. Sinclair, but I need a woman's support. I've never been in a place like that either, and I could bear it better knowing I had a decent woman by my side."

Rachel's feet had been cosy inside her boots, but the thought of going into her brother's place made her feel as though she were barefoot in the snow. "But, Mrs. Gladd, if it does turn out to be Clarence, won't you embarrass him by confronting him in there?"

"Miss Pridgeon, when you have children of your own you'll learn that sometimes the best thing you can do for them is to embarrass them, the more outright the better. Come on!"

With a militant air, Mrs. Gladd set out to cross the street. Rachel threw a helpless glance toward Hal and followed her. She racked her brain for a way to get out of going in there. If only she could trip and sprain an ankle.

Then Hal was beside her and she suddenly knew she could face whatever life threw at her, so long as he stood beside her. For the first time, Rachel began to hope he meant marriage. She hated to hope for anything, since without hope there could be no disappointment. However, hope insisted on growing in her heart.

No sooner did she realize this than she began to discourage it. Better not to get her hopes up, she thought sternly. If he'd meant marriage surely he would have mentioned it by now. With his sudden drawing back last night, when she'd been on the brink of telling him his feelings were reciprocated, he took on the appearance of a man afraid he'd committed an imprudent act and who hoped to evade the worst of the consequences.

She peered at his face. He didn't seem to be scared of the future. On the contrary, he smiled at her so warmly that some of the frozen feeling left her feet. Rachel began to hope again.

Hal said to Mrs. Gladd, "Let me look in and see if Clarence is there. We might be chasing a shadow."

He rose up on his toes to look over the frosted part of the glass where the protective boards had been taken away. At the top of the window was a pattern of clear and etched glass interwoven in a lattice. Rachel would have thought it a pretty effect on any other building.

While Hal slowly scanned the interior, Mrs. Gladd said, "It was the most expensive building in town when it was put up. I think it bankrupted the feller who built it."

Hal came back down onto the balls of his feet. "I couldn't see all of the place. Why don't you ladies wait here? I'll go in and look for Clarence."

"Have you ever seen my boy?"

"No, ma'am. I don't know how I missed him; I've spent days trying to get to know everyone."

Mrs. Gladd flicked her gaze toward Rachel. "Must be interesting work. Clarence spends most of his time with his nose in a book; you probably wouldn't have seen him around."

She extended her hands toward the door handle. Hal intercepted them and gave each one a pat. "I'll go in. What does Clarence look like?"

"He's not so tall . . . medium I guess. And his hair's

brown. Some folks would say he's a good-looking boy; he takes after *my* side of the family."

"Then I'll be sure to recognize him," Hal said. Rachel heard some of the city-folk glibness come into his speech and she knew he was at his most persuasive.

It almost looked as though he'd won Mrs. Gladd around to his point of view. But then she said, "I thank you, Mr. Sinclair, but I'm going in. Come along, Miss Pridgeon."

Catching Rachel's eye, Hal said quickly, "I didn't see the owner anywhere."

"The owner?" Mrs. Gladd frowned. "Have you met the cad already? I hope *you're* not a drinking man, Mr. Sinclair."

"On occasion, ma'am. But I met Mr. Flanders under other circumstances than over a bottle."

"Glad to hear it." Mrs. Gladd marched up to the door, twitched her coat into a better position on her shoulders, and gave a yank to the doorknob. Rachel felt she had no choice but to follow the other woman. Besides, she'd sworn to give pepper to any student of hers that went into the saloon. Just because Clarence Gladd wasn't *officially* a student didn't mean she could renounce her responsibility.

Hal watched her shoulders go back and her head come up. He saw her body stiffen into a calm, proud carriage as she transformed herself once again into the consummate schoolteacher. He murmured into her ear, "I'll back you against any outlaw in America."

Her eyes flashed as she bowed her head graciously. Hal made a mental note to propose as soon as they left.

He stepped between the ladies and took an elbow in each hand. "This way, please. Watch your step; it looks like they've been repairing the floors."

The air in the saloon was stale and cold, thick with dust. Most of the furniture was still covered in dingy cloths. Especially well protected were the sheeted shapes of the wheel-of-fortune and the billiard table. Neither the incomplete amenities nor the dirt seemed to bother the patrons that had already found the place. They sat, farmers, miners and loafers, around the few tables that had been cleaned up. One of these was Ed Greely, nursing a glass of nearly clear alcohol. A couple more men stood at the bar. It, at least, was gleaming.

The greasy-haired bartender paused in the act of wiping out some glasses. He stared at the unaccustomed sight of a gentleman escorting two women who were undoubtedly ladies. Then he gave a start of unfeigned surprise. "Rachel! Well, tie me to a bronc and call me Dizzy."

He put down the glass and with both hands on the bar swung himself over as lightly as an acrobat. "Hey, Digger. Lookit!"

Under a black hat, a man looked up from the lines of solitaire he had dealt. A virulent scar ran from the middle of his left cheek down to his throat. When he smiled, it puckered all along its length, adding immeasurably to his devil's look. He smiled when he saw Rachel. "Didn't think we'd ever see you again, sweet thang," he said, his soft voice accented with the South.

Hal saw Rachel's hand twitch as though she sought a gun that was no longer hanging on her hip. She said, sounding calm enough except to someone who knew her well, "Hello, Digger. How are you, Lemon?"

Wondering what lay between her and these men, Hal wanted to protect Rachel, to get between her and the eyes that stared at her with such speculation. Not the bulging blue eyes of the little man nor the black-eyed gaze of the other, but Mrs. Gladd's eyes, whose gaze had the most power to hurt her.

Lemon Malloy came frisking up to her like a puppy. One whiff of the heavy hair oil that plastered down his yellow hair and Hal knew why they called him Lemon. "It sure is grand to see you again, Rachel. Goodness, I remember when you was just a little sprite of a thing in your daddy's arms! You reckon it means I'm gettin' old?"

"Not you, Lemon," Rachel said. "Just me."

Hal noticed that she didn't look at Mrs. Gladd and that her proud carriage didn't alter in the slightest though she had to know what speculations must be running in the other woman's mind.

Digger stood up from behind the card table. He had slow movements, as though each were thought out in advance. "Who are your friends, Rachel?"

"This is Mrs. Gladd, acting mayor of the town. She's looking for her son."

"I want my boy," Mrs. Gladd said, her voice squeaking with nervousness.

"Feel free, ma'am." He swung his arm wide, as though inviting her to look under the tablecloths if she so wished.

"Come with me, Mr. Sinclair," Mrs. Gladd said.

But Digger put his hand in the middle of Hal's chest. "Not so fast. I haven't been introduced to this gentleman."

Hal swiped at Digger's wrist, knocking his hand down. "No offense, old man, but you have no idea how tough it is to get a shirt washed right around here."

The scar puckered. "Tough guy," Digger sneered.

"That's enough," Rachel said coolly. "This is Mr. Sinclair, Digger. Slade knows him. Go on, Hal. Give Mrs. Gladd a hand."

Hal looked into these green eyes that had bewitched him from the day they'd met. He'd never felt so possessive of a woman before or so reluctant to leave one. He wanted to kiss her, to show these men she belonged to him now. It might protect her.

Mrs. Gladd seemed only too happy to get away from Digger's black eyes. "What's going on?" she whispered. "How does Miss Pridgeon know all these . . . these dreadful men?"

"It's a long story. Let's look for Clarence, shall we?"

"I don't think he's here. I must have been wrong . . . I wonder if there are more rooms upstairs?"

Digger's voice, still soft but carrying, said, "Yes, lady, but they're not in use. We have no ladies to occupy them yet."

Mrs. Gladd gasped and turned pink. Some of the strangers at the tables laughed at her discomfiture. Ed Greely looked up from the depths of his glass. "No way to talk to a lady," he said, and hiccoughed.

"Yeah," Digger sneered. "Get up and tell me to quit it."

Ed Greely staggered to his feet and stood there, swaying

like a tree in a high wind. Digger crouched, his hand flirting with his gun.

"That's enough!" Rachel's voice snapped like a whip. "You still need to learn to control your tongue, Digger. I remember my father beating you up for your impertinence."

"Me, I also remember." The man who now appeared in the doorway to the saloon made Digger Cosgrove look like the cheap punk he was.

As he came in, Hal detected no trace of swagger or egotism. If this man were to shoot, it would be for a good reason and not merely to prove he was the better, faster draw. His black hair curled slightly back from his high forehead, a few silver threads catching the light. Lines of age, of long days in the sun, crisped the corners of his eyes. He could have been any respectable man were it not for the air of danger anticipated that came in with him. This was not a man to turn his back and hope for the best.

He came up to Rachel. "How have you been, *querida*? I have missed you, and the little squirrel."

"Hello, Uncle Ramon," Rachel said, and accepted his kiss on her cheek like a dutiful niece.

"Uncle!" Mrs. Gladd said and pressed her hand to her heart. "Mr. Sinclair, your arm please. I—I have to get out of here!"

Uncle Ramon said to Rachel, "Maybe we should not let her leave? Slade has told me that you are a teacher here?"

"That's right. I went to California first where I met a Mr. McLean and his wife. They helped me get my teacher's certificate, then, as the pastor's wife here in town is related to them, they gave me some references and sent me here to teach."

"And now we have come to spoil it all," Ramon said, with pity in his cinnamon-brown eyes.

Rachel shook her head, denying what he said, though the tear that slipped down her cheek gave her true feelings away. "It's not your fault. I knew it was too good to last."

"If you are happy here, then I am happy too. We will keep this woman here until she agrees not to speak," Ramon said.

Mrs. Gladd gave a shriek, digging her fingers into Hal's arm. He disengaged it with a grimace.

Hal decided it was time to make his intentions toward Rachel known publicly. He would have preferred not to speak in a saloon watched by the eyes of killers but at least this way, Mrs. Gladd would have something else to talk about. Knowing Brooklyn, the news that he and Rachel were planning to marry would outweigh the revelation that she knew some unsavory people.

He said, "Mr. Rosario, I'm Hal Sinclair. I write books."

"Yes, I remember Slade telling me about you. What are you doing here with my niece?"

"I'm also the town's newspaper editor, among other things. And I intend to marry Rachel."

"Oh, Hal," Rachel said, but his quick ear caught more sorrow than joy in her tone.

He went to her, and put his hands on her shoulders. "You're going to marry me, Rachel. I don't care if you have every wanted man in the country as cousins."

She brushed her cheek over his hand, letting a sparkling drop fall on his fingers. It burned down to the soul. In a whisper, she said, "As much as I want to say yes, I must say no."

Uncle Ramon asked, "Rachel, you want to marry this *hombre*?"

"No, Uncle Ramon."

"Maybe I should say, 'Rachel, you *got* to marry this man?'"

Hal answered without hesitation. "Yes, she's got to marry me. For all the low reasons you think."

"Hal!" she protested.

Hal did not expect there to be general rejoicing among Rachel's friends and relations at the idea of his having carried off Rachel's virginity. He should perhaps have expected every single one of them to draw a gun on him.

The sight of all these unsheathed weapons was too much for the acting mayor. Mrs. Gladd made a break for it, running toward the door, shrieking like the noon express. Uncle Ramon caught her about the waist and she fainted, folding over his arm like a rag doll. He bore her weight with remarkable ease, hefting her slightly. "Nice woman," he said.

"She's married, Uncle Ramon," Rachel said. "Now, every one of you put those things away."

Ramon bent at the knees and swept Mrs. Gladd up in his arms. He carried her, tenderly, to the bar and laid her out on it, smoothing her skirts around her ankles for modesty's sake. Standing over her like an artist admiring his creation, he said, "Too bad she's married. I have always liked little blondes. And a woman of maturity . . ." He kissed her lax hand regretfully and laid it down at her side.

His long pistol, of the kind known as a 'hogleg,' appeared again in his hand, pointed none too negligently at Hal's heart. Hal was beginning to get used to it. "Now, as the oldest member of her family still living, I got to ask some questions. You say, *Señor* Sinclair, that my niece has to marry you because you have trifled with her honor. *Sí* or no?"

"I'm getting the boss," Lemon said again. He holstered his gun and set off at a trot for the back room.

A moment later, Slade came rushing out, an apron around his waist. He took in the situation with a glance and snatched off the spotted white cloth, the strings breaking. "Damnation! A man can't even cook around here without all hell breaking loose! Do you know I've got a bunch of idiots out there digging up my backyard looking for diamonds?"

"Never mind that," Ramon said. "This man claims to have soiled our dove."

"Gimme a gun," Slade snarled to Lemon. "I suspected this much last night! Should have seen to it then!"

"No," Rachel said. Hal almost could have laughed to see her still trying to maintain her calm in the face of all this. "No, he hasn't done anything wrong."

"Forgive me for saying so, *querida*, but a woman often lies to protect her lover. I have seen this happen many times. No matter how bad a man is, some woman somewhere will love him."

Slade said, his hand shaking a little, "It's a good thing

I've come here, Rachel. I'll see to it he marries you, if I have to pump him full of lead to do it!"

Hal slid his arm around her waist. "I'm afraid we don't have any choice, Rachel. You'll have to marry me or they'll shoot me."

No tears in those emerald green eyes now. They burned like green fire as she shook free of his grasp. "All right, then!" she said furiously. "Shoot him!" Then she walked out.

21

$\mathcal{T}$HOUGH SHE VOWED that she'd never reveal it to a living soul, Rachel waited outside the saloon until she was satisfied there'd be no shooting. She couldn't hear what the men said but at least she didn't hear gunshots. Then she stalked away, trusting Hal to see Mrs. Gladd safely home.

She spent an hour running Lyle to earth. He was at the Bannermans' house, halfway between the boardinghouse and the church. That house, where Rachel had dined on one memorable occasion soon after coming to teach, always looked as though a tornado had recently torn through it. Though there was no stick of furniture unbroken and none of the 'civilized' knickknacks to be found, say, at the Schurs' home, the walls rang to the sound of happy laughter and the meaningless quarrels of children, which is in itself a joyous sound.

When she knocked, the door was snatched open at once, "Ssh," Mrs. Bannerman said, her finger pressed to her lips. "He's home and asleep."

"Your husband?"

Mrs. Bannerman nodded. "Wandered in here at four o'clock this morning, covered with mud and shivering like a toad eatin' lightning. Wanted vittles and me. He got the vittles."

"I'm sure you're wise. Is Lyle here?"

"He's in the back with the boys. Funny, since he took that fall, they seem to like havin' him around. I think they think he's lucky."

"Luckier than he knows."

"He's the kind that falls on his feet—I got one like that. Stanley, my second. Doesn't seem to matter what happens around him, he always comes up smellin' sweet."

"That's Lyle. No," she said, when Mrs. Bannerman opened the door wider to let her pass inside. "I'll go around. I would hate to disturb your husband."

"I appreciate that. You sure you don't mind? It's powerful cold. I reckon we'll have some heavy snow tonight."

"Oh, dear," Rachel said, trying to peer at the sky from underneath the small porch roof. "Do you really think so?"

"I've lived around here since the day I was born, and I've never seen a sky like that without it having snow in it. See how it's dirty gray and all kind of ripply looking underneath? Those are sure signs."

Rachel thanked Mrs. Bannerman and stepped off the porch. As she went around to the rear of the house, she shot some anxious glances at the heavy gray clouds that now blocked out all of the weak sunshine. The last train out of town left at eight twenty-five in the evening starting the first of November. It would be dark by then. If she and Lyle cut behind the fences on their side of town, they could be safely away with no one the wiser.

Rachel thought of a flaw. If they went that way, they'd pass right behind the Hatch. That was too risky. So they'd cross the street and cut along behind the houses. Though they would have to pass the newspaper office on the way to the depot, she'd rather take her chances with Hal rather than with Slade. Hal was less likely to shoot first and ask questions later. He might break her heart, but it was already breaking at the thought of leaving him forever.

"Lyle," she called over the gate. A tangled pile of boys separated itself into its component parts, one of which proved to be her half brother. "Lyle, come on. It's time for dinner."

He came with dragging feet. At least he had his shoes on, scuffed and marred from roughhousing with the five Bannerman boys. Now that they'd all stood up, she saw that they'd been vying for possession of a somewhat ragged rubber ball.

"Isn't that yours?"

"They can have it. If I take it away, they'll have to stop playing." He picked it up and tossed it to Bobby Bannerman and turned to leave with Rachel.

"That's very good of you, Lyle," Rachel said, surprised by this care for his friends.

He shrugged. "We're gettin' out of town anyway, aren't we?"

"How did you know?"

Another lissome shrug. "Figures. Slade's in town."

"It's not really Slade so much, Lyle. It's what he represents. I wish you'd try to understand."

"I understand. It's 'cause he's brought Digger along."

"What do you know about Digger?"

"Ev'rything, I reckon. I know he tried to kiss you once and my mother hit him with a fryin' pan."

"You were too young to remember that!" Lyle shook his head, leaving Rachel at a loss. Digger had tried to do more than kiss her. If it hadn't been for her stepmother, six months pregnant, coming up behind the gunslinger, Rachel would have been raped.

The first thing Rachel did when she got inside her own house was fetch the gun from beneath her pillow. It had been folly to go out this morning without it, but she'd felt safe enough in the daytime. Besides, Digger was too big a coward to try anything when someone was there.

Lyle watched her from the doorway as she dragged her

bag from under the bed. "I wish we could stay. I like it here."

Rachel glanced at him. She could hardly believe her ears. *Lyle* admitting he liked something? The end of the world would be coming next. "I wish we could stay too," she said. "But it's not possible."

"'Cause of Digger? Slade'd kill him if you asked him to."

"I'm not going to ask him. Go to your room, Lyle, and start setting out what you want to take along."

Rachel didn't ask herself if she might be overreacting. But the force of instinct in her mind was too strong to be overcome. She sat down on the bed beside her open bag and thought.

All her instincts were telling her to take Lyle and run as far as she could go. Find a place so out of the way that the past will never find them again.

She asked herself, not unreasonably, what place was more remote than Brooklyn? But so long as the town held Hal Sinclair, it was no refuge. She had to think of what was best for Lyle. Her love for Hal had to become unimportant.

Rachel made her decision, inviolably. They'd make that eight twenty-five train if she got cracking!

It was amazing how much stuff she'd collected in the not-quite two years she'd been settled in Brooklyn. Most of her things were castoffs, it was true, all given in an offhand spirit that had made them impossible to refuse. Here was the brocade skirt Mrs. Garrett had given her the material for, and the chiffon collar Sissie had made for her last Christmas. A warm muff from Mrs. Schur—"From my courting days! They're not fashionable now, so Dorothy won't look at it. But if you'd like it, Miss Pridgeon, it keeps your hands warmer than gloves." Each thing brought back the memory of a myriad kindnesses.

Rachel snapped shut her carpetbag, hoping to trap those regrets inside. Now to help Lyle pack.

His treasures made a poignantly small pile in the middle of his bed. A spent casing from the marshal's gun, a slug of lead from Hal's office, a dress weight from Sissie's store, together with a small cairn of stones, and a blunt-tipped knife given to him by the Bannerman boys in commemoration of his fall. It looked like so much broken junk. Perhaps some adults would have scorned to take such stuff along, but Rachel recognized the significance of each piece. It made her smile to notice that Lyle hadn't taken out any of his small stock of clothing. Obviously, he could leave every stitch behind sooner than abandon these riches.

As she packed for him, she said brightly, "It'll be fun, starting over. Maybe I won't teach anymore. There's not much money in it, and you're so tied down to a schedule. I'm sure I can find some kind of work that will make us more money so we can live a little better."

"I like this house," Lyle said.

Two positive opinions in an hour! Rachel felt her heart constrict but she refused to reconsider the path she was taking. She'd be tossed back and forth like a ship on a stormy ocean if she didn't hold fast to her decision.

"I like it too," she said. "But you remember how cold it was last winter?" Lyle shook his head. "Sure you do. Remember how your window rattled every time the wind turned easterly? And the cold nipping at your feet from the hole in the floorboards?"

"That's fixed."

"Yes, Mayor Gladd fixed it all right—in the spring! No. I'll make more money and we'll have a nice house, with fireplaces in all the bedrooms."

"I can quit school," Lyle said. "Hal promised me a job as soon as I was done with it. I can be his printer's devil! He says I was born for it. If I work for him, we'd have plenty of money for everything!"

"You're not quitting . . . !" She remembered it didn't matter now. "That was nice of Hal, but you're too young to work yet."

"The kids on the farms . . ."

"No, Lyle."

He took to swinging his feet again over the edge of the bed. "If I hadn't've lost that diamond . . ." he muttered.

"It's just as well," Rachel said, and couldn't repress a sigh. What misery the search for riches had brought her! She could have played "if only" games by the hour if she hadn't better things to do.

Chances were that she'd forget all about Hal in a few dozen years. Surely the memory of the way his mustache tickled, the way his eyes could laugh even while he tried to look stern, the hard beating of his heart against her breast, would all fade with the passage of time. One day she might be able to read a newspaper again without thinking of him. Rachel realized that she didn't want to forget. She'd treasure every moment, fixing every instant in her mind forever. If she ever forgot, then she'd want to die.

But she looked at Lyle's bowed head and her will grew strong again. Their leaving meant a future for him that would not end with a gun or a rope. Maybe one day he'd understand.

She devoted the next half hour to writing Hal a letter. It would have been considerably easier to wring blood from a stone. The first page she spoiled with tears. The second read like a legal letter to someone she didn't like very well. The third sounded as if she'd never written a letter before.

The fourth endeavor didn't please her either for it contained a large lie. Realizing the folly of trying to explain all her conflicting emotions, she simply stated that she was taking Lyle away for his own good. She promised to write to Hal as soon as she got settled, leaving an implicit hint that she'd want Hal to join them then. Rachel told herself it was less a lie than wishful thinking. She'd give anything to make it true, anything but Lyle's chance at a decent life.

She only knew that it had begun to get dark when she could no longer read what she'd written. After she'd sealed the letter with a blob of wax, Rachel looked at the clock, hoping to see that time was short. To her surprise, she saw it was only a little before four o'clock.

Taking her gun off the blotter, she crossed her room to look out the window. The clouds seemed to skim the top of the church spire, threatening to catch on the cross. When she touched the glass, the cold seemed to burn right through her hand. Rachel looked anxiously for snowflakes but the clouds held back, hoarding winter like misers.

Four more hours!

She went upstairs to tell Lyle to take a nap. The train ride would be long and uncomfortable. Though he might be able to lie down with his head on her lap, if the train were crowded with passengers from other stations, there might not be room. In that case, they'd have to sit up all night, bouncing and bumping over the rails.

Knocking lightly on his door, she peered in. He was already asleep, looking deceptively mild, his head thrown back, his mouth slightly open. Rachel drew the covers up over his shoulders and slipped out.

She herself curled up on the settee, her gun tucked underneath the sausage-shaped bolster, a knitted afghan over her knees. Silence lay heavy in every room, not a friendly silence but a secretive one, as if she were already a stranger here. The shaded candle she'd lit only served to make the shadows blacker. The house was so still that she could hear the splutter of the wax where it met the flame.

Rachel slipped into a light, uneasy doze. She woke up every few minutes to glance blearily at the clock. Once she came broad awake, her heart thumping painfully, though she could not tell what had awakened her. If she could only sleep . . .

She dreamed that Hal and Slade were having a tug-of-war, Slade pulling on her hands, Hal tugging on her feet. She knew she wanted Hal to win, but didn't know how to help him. Her bones began to ache.

Forcing herself to wake up, Rachel wrapped the afghan around her shoulders to stay warm as she stood up. The deep cold had seeped in through the windows. Rachel wondered if Lyle was all right. It had been cold last year, but she couldn't remember ever actually being able to see her breath in the parlor. Maybe she should wake him or at least carry him down to the kitchen after making up a warm nest for him.

Someone knocked at the front door. Instantly, Rachel bent to get her gun. Hiding in the folds of the bright afghan, she walked into the hall. "Who's there?"

The voice was muffled yet male.

"Who?"

Had her father taught her to stand with the door between her and an enemy when she opened it? Or was it bred in her bones?

"Damn, it's cold!"

Slade came in, shaking the snow off his shoulders. Flakes clung to his beard and frosted his hair underneath the brim of his slouch hat. Rachel took a deep breath and let it out in a sigh. "What are you doing here?"

"I came to see Lyle."

"He's sleeping."

"I'll wait." He unbuttoned his coat, a long duster that looked as if it had spent some time on the trail. As he started to take it off, he paused. "I'm not sure it's not colder in here than it is out there. What's the matter? Ain't you got wood for the fire?"

"I was asleep too," Rachel said defensively. She shut the door, pausing for a moment to watch in wonder as the fat white flakes came floating down. Though the grass had just begun to change color, the porch railing and the stepping stones were already crusted with white. The sharp air prickled Rachel's cheeks as though with tiny needles of ice. It reminded her of kissing Hal. She shut the door on the storm, and on her memories.

"Come into the kitchen," she said. "It's warmest back there."

She shoved some wood into the firebox and left the door open. Slade extended his hands toward the leaping flames. "That's better," he said with satisfaction. "Ol' Man Winter seems to be getting an early start."

"They had two feet of snow here by Christmas last year. It was pretty."

"Pretty inconvenient. I was up in the mountains 'round Flagstaff last Christmas. I thought I'd die before spring came."

"Is that when you decided cattle rustling wasn't the life for you?"

"Money's good," Slade said, shoving his feet out toward the fire. "And it's less dangerous than robbing banks . . .

least for a while it used to be. Lately, though, they'll shoot you for a sick, one-eyed calf as if you'd stolen a whole herd of prime steer. Sad." He shook his head as if in regret for the wickedness of the world in keeping a man from making a dishonest living.

"Find another town, Slade. That's all I'm asking."

"Now, Rachel, that ain't right. You and the boy are all the family I got left in the whole world. Daddy's dead, *Madrastra*'s dead, and her baby too. 'Course, there's Uncle Ramon but he ain't blood. You and me, we're the same blood, and Lyle's half. You can't turn me away from my own family. That's why I come all this way, soon as I saw your name."

"Hal said he only used my first name and Pridgeon."

"Sure, but how many Rachels are there that shoot like you? It was worth a chance, and it's not like we had much else to be doing. We can't go back to New Mexico and Arizona's gotten too hot to hold us."

There was no point in arguing with him. The important thing was to get him out of the house by eight o'clock so that she and Lyle would have time to get down to the station. It might take a long time to walk in this snow, especially after hours of it falling so thickly.

"What did you do in New Mexico?" she asked.

"Oh, it was Digger. That boy's temper's gonna be the death of him one day, if he don't take us all with him."

"And Arizona? Same story?"

"Nope. There it was Uncle Ramon." He scratched the depths of his beard. "With him, it's this itch he takes for women. Show him a pretty blonde and he's takin' off like a firecracker. That, plus Lemon's so damn dumb he practically tells the sheriff of Mongahela Ridge that we're there to knock off the bank."

"Did you knock it off?"

"After that? What do you think I am? Stupid?"

"But you brought them all along here. Why?"

He made a face of disgust. "Why do you think? They're counting on me to see 'em through. Good times ahead for them . . . 'specially Uncle Ramon. He's getting tired . . .

can't draw like he used to, though I still wouldn't care to go up against him." Slade coughed. "Might offer your brother a drop of something. Just to keep the cold out."

"I don't have any alcohol here, Slade. You'll have to go back to your own place."

"After I see Lyle."

"Stubborn . . ." She put the kettle on, sliding the gun under the pot holder. "You'll have to settle for coffee."

"Good. Could just use a cup." Slade shoved his hands deeper into the pockets of his jeans and tilted his chair back, keeping it balanced on the back legs and the heels of his boots. He started to rock. "Yep, this is what I like. A nice family house. 'Course, I'll be living over the bar, but it's gonna be real nice having this house to come to for a peaceable Sunday dinner. By the way, I like that young feller of yours, Rachel."

"Young? He's older than you are! A lot older than you'll ever be at the rate you're going."

"I was just funning. But I do like him. He's got grit. Stood right there and told me to my face I was no good. Which may not have been very smart, seeing how I was holding a gun to his belly at the time, but it sure was braver than I'd expect from some feller like that."

"Like what?"

"You know. Citified. I never had a chance to test him when we met while I was clapped up. He just come and look at me like I was in a zoo and asked some damn-fool questions. Hear he's written one about you. Any good?"

"I haven't had a chance to read it yet. I've been busy."

"Can't be very good if a feller can't even get his sweetheart to read his book and it about her."

"I'm *not* . . . And it's very good. It's better than the one he wrote about *you*!"

"Couldn't be! The one about me's a rip-snorter! I keep a copy on me . . . see?" He dug in the pocket of his capacious coat and dragged up a dirty, binding-cracked, edge-worn book which was very similar in size and binding to the one Rachel had about herself. Patting the cover, Slade said with pride, "It makes me famous. Folks all over the country can read about me and they'll know my name for ever after."

Rachel held out her hand for the book. She noticed her brother's strange hesitation about handing it over. He almost snatched it back as if changing his mind the moment it was in her hands. Opening it to the frontispiece, she saw a picture as lurid as the one in her book. She bent over the fire to see the words more clearly and was rewarded by a golden coin falling to the ground. When it hit the floor it rang, clear as a crystal bell.

"Slade?" she asked. Bending her knees, she dipped down to pick up the coin. Another fell, bouncing on the floor, ringing another note in the chime.

"Just a couple of dollars hidden away for my old age. Though if things go as I'm planning, this town will put a lot more than a couple of dollars in my jeans."

"There's not much money in Brooklyn. . . ."

"What there is, I'll get. And if they can't pay with money, well, there's always the family farm, or the earrings a wife got for her last birthday. Oh, I'm a reasonable feller, Rachel. I only want what I want."

"We have that much in common."

He was too far lost in his dream to hear anything negative. "Just think . . . with all that money, what couldn't we do? You want something, you take it, and the money smooths everything over. 'Course, we need more. That's where you come in. I offered you a job last night. The pay's good, the work's not hard. . . ."

"Just trade everything I believe in, everything I've worked for." She could feel her temper starting to rise like a hot-air balloon. Soon it would carry her away.

"Worked for?" he said, as if repeating words in a foreign language whose meaning he couldn't be expected to know. "Slaving away in a classroom for thirty bucks a year and this house? Give me six months, Rachel, and we'll build a palace. Seen just the place for it too. We'll buy the Garrett farm and put a big house on that hill across the way. It'll be great. Plenty of room for the boy and my little sister to run the place. From there, anything could happen. By God, if I'm not governor . . ."

"Oh, now it's governor?" she said, mocking him. "Yesterday it was mayor. What tomorrow, Slade? President?"

"Why not?" he shouted back. "Give me enough money and I'll be *God* if I want!"

Suddenly a streak of sobbing boy shot across the kitchen, to bury his head in his sister's lap. "Lyle?" Rachel said in surprise.

"I'm sorry . . . I'm awful sorry," he said, his voice thick and unintelligible.

"For what?" Rachel asked. "You haven't done anything."

"Hey, there, kid," Slade said. His feet had hit the floor when the boy burst in. "Remember me? I'm your old brother, Slade. Say, you've grown a foot!"

Lyle raised his tear-streaked face from his sister's lap and shot a look of pure hatred at his brother. Even Slade's *laissez-faire* attitude toward life withered under that concentration of animosity. "Hey," he said again, less heartily.

Lyle said fiercely, "I'm gonna take care of her, you'll see. You just leave her alone!"

Rachel wiped his tears away with her thumb. "Of course, you take good care of me, Lyle. Everyone in town knows it."

"Sure, kid," Slade said, his eyes worried.

But Lyle was only interested in his sister. "I been thinking and thinking, Rachel. I swear I'll find it again, if I have to look for a hundred years."

"Find what? Your diamond? Oh, Lyle, it doesn't matter."

"No," he moaned, before she'd finished speaking. "I found *that*. I'd thrown it away. . . ."

"What? The kid's out of his mind."

"Ssh! What do you mean, you threw it away?"

Lyle shook his head. "You wouldn't understand. . . ."

Hal, entering the kitchen, knocked on the wall to alert them that he was there. Rachel, seeing him so unexpectedly, was afraid her face gave all her feelings away. She would have run to his arms then and there, were it not for Lyle in her lap. Hal said, "You've had your fifteen minutes, and more, Delmon. Did you convince her?"

"We're still talking it over," Slade said. "This crazy brother of mine says he *threw* the first diamond away. You ever heard of something so nuts?"

"Sure, I have," Hal said. "When I was a boy, if you lost something, you got something just the same . . . or near enough . . . and threw it away about where you figured you lost the first thing. Let's see, there was kind of a jingle that went with it . . ."

"That's right," Lyle said excitedly. "Brother, brother, go find your brother."

"Yes. Boy, it's been a long time since I lost a marble."

Rachel said bitterly, "The last thing I need is more brothers. . . . Come on, Lyle. Are you hungry?" The boy shook his head. "Do you want to go back to sleep?"

Lyle nodded and brushed his hand over his forehead and the line of his scar. "You don't have to come with me. I ain't a sissy." In the doorway, he paused. "I will find it," he said. "Not just the one I lost, but a whole mess of 'em. One of these days, I'll remember where it was, then I'll have a million of 'em. And they'll all be yours, Rachel. Every one of 'em."

After a moment, Rachel went to the bottom of the stairs, just to be sure Lyle was all right. She could hear him sniffling, and now and then he'd talk to himself, airing either a grievance or renewing his vow.

She came back to find the two men wrangling over fifteen minutes alone with her. "Go on and wait in the parlor, Slade," Rachel said.

"I'll freeze!"

"Smoke a cigar to keep warm. I want to talk to Hal."

But when her brother had gone, she didn't say a word. Just stepped into his waiting arms. With his strength around her like a warm cloak, she knew she could do what she felt was best.

Hal sought her mouth and she gave it to him, kissing him

with her whole heart. He must have felt the difference at once. "Why, Rachel, Rachel. Do you love me too?"

"Yes," she whispered.

"And you'll marry me? Please, I really can't live without you."

She drew back enough to look up into his face. "What do you mean by that?"

"Simple. Your brother's gang has promised to kill me if I don't marry you. It seems they believe the seducer, rather than the object of the seduction when it comes to how complete the seduction was."

"Is that the only reason you want to marry me?"

"Well," he said, his grin breaking out. "I can think of one or two more reasons."

Then his eyes became compellingly serious. "I love you, Rachel. I love the way you get mad. I love the way your hair is always falling down . . . you might want to shove a few more pins in now as a matter of fact. Or take them all out, I don't care. I love that you shoot like Wild Bill Hickock and teach children and play the piano and . . . I guess I just love you."

"I can't say it the way you can, Hal. But if it's any consolation, I think I'll love you until I die."

Rachel reached up, twining her arms around his neck. Her afghan tumbled unregarded to the floor. They were locked in a deep, tender embrace when Slade came stumping back into the warm kitchen. "I sure hope this means what it looks like it means," he said.

"I don't know," Hal answered, lifting his head. "She hasn't answered me yet."

"Well, hurry it up," Slade said. "Rachel, you must have a window or something open upstairs. There's a wind blowing down through your hall fit to freeze the . . . ears off a brass monkey."

"A wind?" Curious, she led the way, with the two men following her. "That's strange. It wasn't this cold before. Lyle must have . . . Lyle? Lyle, are you trying to catch your death? Close that window!"

There was no answer and the frigid air continued to move

down the stairs. Frowning now, Rachel started up the stairs, calling Lyle's name. She dashed into his bedroom, to find the window over the cat-slide roof standing open. A small drift of snow had floated in, piling against the carpetbag on the floor.

22

*T*HE WHOLE TOWN turned out. Benson rode to Mrs. Garrett's and awoke the camp. Even the newcomers at the tents dragged themselves off their makeshift cots and quilts to join the search when Mr. Schur rode into their "town." Slade kicked his pals awake and sent them out into the storm.

Hal wiped his face for the third time in as many minutes. Bundled to the eyebrows, he still felt the bone-freezing cold. His mustache had become stone while he'd long ago given up any hope of ever feeling his toes again. He held his lantern high to keep from being dazzled by the endlessly shifting patterns of the snow, all of which seemed to be driving right at him. It muffled sounds, so that even Slade, shouting his brother's name with all his might, was heard only as a faint echo.

"Lyle!" Hal called, using lungs trained in New York street riots. "Come on, boy!"

He'd been missing for almost two hours, out in the worst

snowstorm in Missouri history with no more than a thin coat between him and the weather. Unless he'd found a protected hiding place, he was probably already dead, or so close to it that he might not be able to answer. That thought made Hal want to sink down into the snow himself. He'd come to enjoy Lyle's company and his youthful, if jaundiced, view of life made him take the most optimistic view in self-defense. Hal began to hope that if Lyle was dead, someone else would find him.

But it was thoughts of Rachel waiting at home that kept him searching. He couldn't bear the thought of anyone else telling her the dire news. No one else should see her at that moment, only he who loved her so.

Slade came up to him and had to shake his arm to get his attention. "We're going about this all wrong," he shouted.

His beard had icicles hanging from it and his black coat was sheeted with snow, making him look like the very spirit of winter personified. His bleak eyes were in keeping with the rest of his appearance.

"How so?"

"We gotta think like Lyle! If you was seven, where would you be?"

"Home in bed," Hal muttered. Every time he inhaled it was as if knives slashed his chest. Raising his voice again, he said, "Where do you think?"

"We gotta start looking for hiding places. I wonder if Rachel knows where he usually hides from trouble."

"She didn't say."

Hal saw Slade's lips move in answer but the wind snatched the words away. The two men huddled together until the blast had blown by. Looking around, Hal saw that the trees had the look of harlequins, shaded white and black. White where the snow collected; black where the wind had driven it all away.

"What?"

"When I was a kid . . . old man . . . run away 'til he slept it off . . ."

Hal shook his head to indicate that he couldn't hear, but Slade only turned and trudged off into the woods. Hoping that his soon-to-be brother-in-law knew where he was going, Hal followed him. Slade's footprints in the snow were half-filled before Hal could put his feet into them. Whatever sign the bearded man followed was a mystery to Hal.

Rachel thanked God for the newcomers' children. They were the only reason she held on to her sanity. So long as there were noses to wipe, crying babies to comfort and stories to tell, she could keep her mind off Lyle.

Mrs. Schur had come by as soon as she'd heard Lyle had run away. She'd brought with her, as if knowing their power, the two children she'd taken home earlier and all the others she'd somehow collected in the meantime. The Bannerman boys were there, more helpful than Rachel would have believed possible, judging by their behavior with younger children at school.

Sissie helped too, bringing boxes of feathers and glittery sequins for the older children to make pictures on large sheets of paper borrowed from the *Herald*'s office. The smell of warm glue added a pungent note to the overheated air of the kitchen.

Mrs. Dale, cooking for the searchers despite the children underfoot, said with a laugh, "If Lyle does come back here, we'll probably miss him in the crowd. What's one more child?"

Rachel glanced up from the tub where she bathed a wriggling baby. At that moment, she couldn't have told whether it was a Brooklyn baby or a newcomer's baby. It was sweet, with big blue eyes and a fascination for its pink toes. Rachel had found herself smiling involuntarily more than once before her worries overwhelmed her again.

She said miserably, "I wish he would come back. It's such a black night."

Mrs. Dale brushed the hair off her forehead with the back of her hand. She was flushed with the heat and her eyes were marked by tears from the big onion she'd peeled for the stew. Her glasses kept steaming up in the same humidity that turned her smooth coiffure into a mess of tangled ringlets. She looked about seventeen. "Boys are like animals, my dear. They're much closer to nature than we grown-ups are. If there's a snug burrow somewhere out there, he's bound to have found it by now."

"The little one speaks sense." Uncle Ramon stood in the hall, sniffing the air. He picked his way across the room, nimbly avoiding Sissie's art class and the piles of napping children under Dorothy Schur's supervision. Taking the lid off the big pot of stew, he breathed in the steam. "Exquisite! A wise woman who can cook. Why are you not married, *chiquita*?"

To Rachel's surprise, Mrs. Dale neither simpered nor snatched her glasses off. She rapped Uncle Ramon on the back of his hand with a spoon and said sharply, "Keep your nose out of my cooking! If you want to be a help, take this pot over to the schoolhouse. That's where all you searchers are supposed to go, not coming tramping in here."

"Uncle Ramon," Rachel said. "Is there any news?"

"Not yet, *querida*. You must be patient. And don't let the little one eat the soap, eh?"

Rachel picked the baby up out of the water to dry it with one of the towels warming by the stove. His eyes were closing, dreamy with sleep. She dressed him in his shirt and twisted a diaper around his chubby hips, then carried him over to Dorothy.

"I hope Ma comes back with some more quilts," she sighed. "We're running out of 'em."

"They're used to doubling up," said a woman who Rachel didn't know who'd come in to help Dorothy. "Most of 'em don't have more'n one bed to their names anyway."

"I suppose not," Dorothy said. "At least sharing a bed is warmer than sleeping alone."

Rachel wondered if the preacher's daughter was thinking of Ed Greely. She herself was certainly thinking of Hal. If only he could be with her, his arm strong about her, when they told her about Lyle. No fool, she had known from the first that there was really no hope, no hope at all.

She left the kitchen, wandering down the hall to look out the window. Even the grass was covered now. Even the stalks of her summer bulbs were nothing but ghosts. Looking out toward the street, she could see the yellow glow of a lantern as some searchers hurried along.

Sissie slipped an arm about her waist. "It'll be all right," she said lamely. "Really. Benson's found lost people before. He's a natural-born tracker."

"It's this snow," Rachel said, leaning a little on her friend. "It looks so innocent, so mild. Yet all the time, it's covering everything up. Can even a good tracker find someone if there are no tracks left? Lyle could be lying out there and the snow would cover him up too. . . . That's what I keep seeing all the time. Just a mound of snow and everyone walking right past him because they don't know he's even there!"

Rachel dug the heels of her hands into her eyes. Not all the hot tears she could shed would melt one iota of all this snow, so what was the point in crying? "I wish Hal were here," she said hopelessly.

"Send that nice Mr. Rosario out to find him. You know Hal will come here if you need him."

Rachel wanted that badly. But she shook her head. "No. Everyone who can search, should. What's Uncle Ramon doing here, anyway?"

"Is he really your uncle?"

"Sort of . . . it's a long story."

"And that Slade Flanders is your brother?"

"Yes. That is right."

"And I thought *I* had a family that was troubled! Just goes to show . . . Well, don't accuse me of jumping to conclusions, Rachel, but I sure hope you like Mrs. Dale."

Grateful to be talking about something besides Lyle for a moment, Rachel asked, "Why?"

"'Cause she might wind up your aunt. Bless me if I've ever seen a man take to a woman so fast."

"Oh, Uncle Ramon is a flirt, almost as bad as Hal . . . not that Hal flirts anymore."

"No, Hal doesn't flirt anymore. Though I think every woman in town is going to miss it. It sure was nice to have someone make you feel like the effort you put into yourself isn't overlooked."

"Is that what Hal does?"

"Haven't you noticed?"

"He makes me feel . . ." Rachel paused and said more slowly, "When I'm with him, I feel more awake, more alive. Like . . . like everything is fresh and new. Things I see every day become different when Hal's with me."

Sissie shook her head in wonder. "You've got a bad case, Rachel. Let's hope it's incurable. As incurable as mine."

Rachel's attention had been caught by something strange outside the window. A square of the yellow lights bobbed along, each corner out of synchronization with the others, following one light in the front.

Sissie stared too. "Looks like they're carrying something."

"Is it . . . ?" Rachel gasped, the hope she thought she did not treasure surging up to choke her.

Sissie ran to open the door but Rachel passed her. Heedless of the snow that powdered her hair and shoulders, she ran down the steps, disregarding her slipping footsteps. Peering past the dancing flakes, she cried out, "Who is it?"

Doctor Warren, portly as a snowman, paused beside her gate. In a hushed tone, he said, "It's a tragedy, my dear. Greater love hath no man, et cetera."

They carried him on a gate, his arms falling limply off the edges. Rachel saw at once that he was too big to be Lyle and her heart bounded with joy, only to be constricted with fear that it might be Hal.

The doctor's voice was in her ear. "Maybe you know his name, Miss Pridgeon? I believe he works with your brother."

Rachel brushed at the snow on his cold face. "His name is Cosgrove. They call him Digger. I don't know his real name. Is he . . . ?"

"Just a matter of time, I'm afraid. He must have struck his head when he fell in the snow. We're taking him to my office. Cosgrove . . . I shall write it down. Mr. Herby likes to know their names."

Sissie had come out and now she wrapped a shawl around Rachel's shoulders. "Come in the house. You'll catch pneumonia out here and that won't do Lyle any good."

The moments passed with crawling slowness. Rachel would swear an hour had gone by only to be told by the clock that it had been hardly ten minutes. It seemed as though time had lost all meaning. All but a very few of the children were sleeping now and most of the women nodded.

Rachel could not sit back in her chair and rest. She sat on the edge, every sense at its highest pitch. Her hands caught and pulled at one another ceaselessly. It was only when she felt the sting of a cut that she realized she'd been worrying a hangnail until it tore and bled. The pain seemed to slice through the cloud of worry insulating her against the reality of the situation. Quite quietly, she began to cry.

Then, with the bang of a door and a rush of wind, there was no more time for tears.

Hal and Slade rushed in, carrying Lyle slung between them in Hal's coat. The boy's naturally brown face was tinged with white, the tip of his nose and his ears pale with frostbite. Hal demanded warm water and Rachel pointed out the still-full tub with a shaking hand.

They plunged Lyle in, clothing and all. Rachel ordered Sissie to go for the doctor and didn't realize that her fingers bit the other girl to the bone until Sissie yelped. She went.

The babies who awakened were crying and the other children huddled in the corners, their eyes enormous. Dorothy Schur clapped her hands and ordered, "All you big 'uns grab a little 'un. Get your clothes on and march to the front door. We'll go over to the schoolhouse and have a picnic. Come on. Come on."

The women worked efficiently and quickly. In five minutes, not a child was to be seen except Lyle. Rachel sank onto her knees beside the tub, ignoring or not noticing the spilled water that seeped into her skirts.

Hal and Slade were getting his clothes off, plunging their arms to the elbows into the water, throwing the sopping clothes to the floor. The boy's head lolled on the edge of the tub, his eyes seen only as white orbs through slitted lids.

Rachel held his hand submerged but with the hope that, even unconscious, he could still feel her love warming him.

Slade pulled a flask from his pocket. "What do you think, Sinclair? A little more?"

"He still can't swallow it," Hal said.

"I can." Slade unscrewed the top and took a long swallow. Hal slapped it out of his hand. Rachel hardly noticed as the two men, sopping wet and half-frozen, glared at each other over her head. Then Slade dropped his gaze and stepped back. "Don't waste good whisky, man."

Doctor Warren came hustling in with Sissie, white-faced and panting, on his heels. "Mrs. Schur will be right here," she announced before the doctor could get a word in.

As the doctor looked over Lyle's thin body, he shook his majestic head. "Looks bad . . ."

Rachel felt the room slip sideways, suddenly too hot, too loud, too crowded. She made a grab for Lyle's hand as she fell over. She didn't lose consciousness; it was more as if everything that had held her up for the last two hours let go all at once.

Hal picked her up. She murmured, "Don't let him go to Herby's. Please . . ."

Slade snapped, "Take her out, Hal. I'll be here for the boy."

Doctor Warren was pronouncing, his thumbs stuck in the airholes of his coat. "I can do nothing for him here. We shall carry him to my office."

Remembering that the doctor's office was just above the undertaker's, Hal said, "No. The boy stays here."

Sissie added, "Wait for Mrs. Schur. There's nothing she doesn't know about frostbite."

"My dear young lady, are you saying that *I*, a greatly educated physician, do not?"

Slade looked at their faces, his cold eyes fierce. "I reckon we wait for the lady, and if you don't like it, you blowhard, git!"

"Good man," Hal said. He carried Rachel up to her room. The temperature was frigid but the bed looked warm. When he put his hands to the buttons on her dress, she shuddered and tried to sit up. "Hush now," he soothed. "You're all wet. Don't want you to get sick too."

"Oh, Hal," she said, lying back, one arm flung over her head. "What's happening?"

"Mrs. Schur's coming to help out. Don't worry now. Just let go."

Coming back to her senses, Rachel touched his sleeve where it was dark. "You're all wet too. And Lyle . . . that was *your* coat. You must be frozen solid!"

"Pretty nearly," Hal admitted. "But Slade's was covered with mud . . . didn't you notice? Well, I guess you were thinking of other things. Slade had to slide along on his back to reach Lyle."

"Where was he?"

"Hiding inside a hollow tree. It was a narrow squeeze. I thought your brother would be stuck for good. But he got Lyle out and himself too."

"Inside a hollow tree? How did you ever think to look there?"

"I didn't. It was all Slade. It seems that when he was a boy, he'd hide from your father in a fallen cactus. Saguaro?"

"Yes. I remember hearing about that."

"Rachel?" Hal asked, as he tenderly laid a blanket over her. "Did you father beat you too?"

Rachel shook her head. "Never. I was a girl, you see. That's one reason why I took Lyle away. It had already started with him. Our father thought that beating a boy for every mistake made him tough and manly. My stepmother hated it and when she knew she was dying, begged me to take Lyle away. I didn't even wait until she was cold to do it."

"Oh, Rachel." He put out his arms to comfort her but the touch of his icy sleeves made her recoil involuntarily.

In just her chemise top with her hair tumbling down like red silk around her shoulders, she was a sight to make a man dream for life. Yet Hal wanted only to hold her, so that her tears would have a better place to fall than on her pillow. When she scooted over on the bed to make room for him, he knew it was what she wanted too.

He took off his heavy shirt and the thin cotton one underneath. The bottoms of his trouser legs were soaked as well. Wearing only his underwear, he slipped into the bed with her. Instantly, she shivered nearer, entwining her legs with his. The winter night had no power against the two of them, together.

"Try to get some sleep," he said. "They'll call us when they know anything about Lyle."

The night was long. Hal got up several times, always to find Lyle's condition unchanged. They'd dried him off and dressed him in warm clothes borrowed from half the children in town and tucked him between a dozen quilts. His color seemed better—not so pale.

Mrs. Schur asked after Rachel and, hearing that she was in bed, nodded with satisfaction. "Best thing for her. There's not much to be done now but wait and see. His fingers and toes are the hardest hit. I don't know but what he might lose one or two. That doctor thinks he'll lose 'em all and maybe he would if it were left up to him."

Grasping the sleeve of the shirt Hal had left unbuttoned, Mrs. Schur said, "That feller over there. Is that Rachel's brother?"

"Yes. Slade De . . . Flanders."

"French?"

"I don't know."

"Well, I wish Mr. Schur could have been here. I've never heard such powerful praying in all my life. 'Course, I'm not saying it's right to threaten the Almighty, but he's got the stuff to be a terrible powerful preacher if he takes a mind."

When Hal went back to Rachel, it was to find her awake, propped up on one elbow. "I missed you," she said sleepily. "Is everything . . . ? Lyle?"

"Mrs. Schur says she won't know 'til morning."

"What time is it now?"

"You want me to go see?"

"No. Come here."

When the light of day shone around the window blind, Rachel awoke to find herself alone again. She stretched and then relaxed against the pillow, a healing languor in all her limbs. Considering that she'd never slept with a man before, she had found it surprisingly comfortable to do so. Hal's body, though firm, had been a satisfying pillow. When she thought with what abandon she'd sprawled over him in sleep, she could almost blush.

Then she sat up, broad awake. "Lyle," she said aloud.

Throwing off the covers, she put her feet resolutely on the floor. How could she be so unfeeling as to abandon her brother when he had needed her so desperately? Snatching at her robe, she thrust her arms into it and dashed out into the upper hall without bothering to tie the sash.

"Whoa!" Hal exclaimed, clutching the tray he carried. "You'll have it over!"

"Hal! Where's Lyle?"

"Next door, of course. Eating like a sailor rescued from shipwreck and regaling some of the Bannerman tribe with his adventures. It seems nearly freezing to death gives a boy an appetite. At least, I hope it's that. Because if Lyle eats like this all the time, I don't know how I'll support all three of us on my salary."

All the while he was talking, he was backing Rachel into her room, maneuvering her with the tray. She sat down on the bed, having nowhere else he would allow her to go. "Feet too," he said. "You're having breakfast in bed."

"Breakfast in bed? I've never heard of such a thing!"

"All the wealthy ladies of leisure breakfast in bed, according to Sissie. I wouldn't know. According to Mrs. Schur, however, bed is the only place you're going to be for a few days."

"No, I have to . . ."

"Whatever it is, Mrs. Schur says it can wait. Now, don't look at me that way. I'm just putty in Mrs. Schur's hands. What she says goes so far as I'm concerned. After the way she kicked Doctor Warren out of here last night—"

"Quiet little Mrs. Schur?"

"A tigress in disguise," Hal assured her. He didn't mention that the reason for the forcible removal of the doctor had been his talk of fetching his small saws to remove Lyle's toes from his left foot. Doctor Warren might have tried to overawe Slade Delmon but he met his match in the pastor's wife.

He waited until she'd drunk half her coffee and eaten enough bacon and eggs to put the bloom back into her cheeks. Then he said, "Rachel, this has gone far enough."

"What? Breakfast?"

"No, you know perfectly well what I mean." He fixed her with a reproachful glance, though he was afraid the muscle twitching beside his mouth gave his true feelings away. "You have to marry me now. You have to make an honest man out of me."

"What?"

"I talked it all over with Sissie this morning. Since I have no relatives living here to protect my good name, she has agreed to act on my behalf and hold a gun on you at the altar."

"Hal, have you lost your mind?"

"Absolutely. But if you think you can trifle with my affections in the most blatant manner . . ." He batted his eyes like a sorrowful maiden whose good name had been besmirched but she only laughed at him. Then he laughed too for the sheer pleasure of watching her.

Rachel lay back against her propped-up pillow. "It was awfully nice sleeping with you last night."

"Thank you, ma'am."

"Kind of comfortable and easy, like we'd been doing it for years."

"Would you really say 'comfortable' and 'easy'? Because that's not how I felt at all."

"No? Maybe it was all the strain of yesterday catching up with me at last, but I can't remember when I last slept so soundly. For one thing, you're the *warmest* person! If I'd known how nice sleeping with a man was, I would have started doing it years ago."

"Rachel," he said, moving the tray to the floor, "shall I show you how *I* felt when I woke up this morning?"

The last thing she saw before she closed her eyes was the desire that burned in his. He kissed her and she could taste a mingling of love, longing and a desire that scorched her to her soul. They slid down on the bed together, her arms around his back, restlessly reaching for something just beyond her grasp. He didn't have to work at all hard to coax her own passion into being, though he seemed to relish every instant. His hands wove magic spells over her skin, while whenever he could speak, he breathed such wild, half-mad adoration that she would have surrendered to his lightest demands.

Rachel knew he had too much honor to do more than this. Even now, he was muffling her cries with his mouth, sheltering the others in the house from the embarrassment of knowing what was happening. Rachel learned with a laugh how fragile her own self-control was. In a few moments, she was gasping, naked to the waist.

"You're right," she said, shivering. "I've got to marry you. Or we'll shock the whole world."

"Not so comfortable and easy now?"

She cradled his face in her hands, meeting his eyes. "The funny thing is . . . that it's both. Right now, I feel like a runaway train, but at the same time, because it's you, I know I'm safe. Isn't that funny?"

He had to blink away the moisture in his eyes before he could say, "Sounds like heaven to me."

Epilogue

SISSIE, ELEGANT IN a red velvet dress cut to conceal her tummy, pushed the last hairpin into Rachel's high-piled hair. "There!" she said with a pardonable note of triumph. "That'll hold in a hailstorm! I swear it."

"Maybe just a few more?"

"You're already prickling like a porcupine. Besides, there aren't any more." She laid the pure white veil over Rachel's carefully arranged hair. She sighed, utterly content. "That's the prettiest dress I reckon I'll ever make, no matter how many orders I get. And with all the newcomers staying put instead of heading out, I reckon I'm going to get so many I may have to start hiring."

Rachel had no attention to spare from the vision she saw in the mirror. She couldn't believe her eyes. The elegant hairstyle and the transparency of the veil worked some kind of magic to make her more beautiful than Helen of Troy. "You're a genius, Sissie. I'm just sorry that you didn't get to wear it first."

"Oh, pish! I'd rather have a husband without a wedding dress than a baby without a husband. Besides, I decided a while ago that I'm really too short to wear a plain skirt like that. It might have been dreamed up just for you, though."

Sissie patted down a stray curl that insisted on springing free from Rachel's brow. "Hal will just about split a gusset when he sees you." Then Sissie's eyes softened. "You're not scared, are you, Rachel?"

"Marriage is a big step. Naturally, I'm a little nervous." Rachel hoped her true feelings didn't show in her voice.

"Well, yes, but that's not what I'm talking about. Later on tonight, when you're all alone with him . . . I mean, I've been there already so if you have questions . . ."

"No, I can't think of anything to ask." Rachel couldn't meet Sissie's concerned gaze. She fussed with her veil instead. "I do hope my hair won't come down. Hal has this strange effect on my hair. Why, last night . . ."

A gentle rap on the door behind them presaged Mrs. McGovern. "Oh!" She sighed. "Aren't you the loveliest thing!"

When Mr. Gladd's irregularities with the town books had been discovered, a quick election had been arranged. Though Mrs. McGovern couldn't vote, there was no law that said she couldn't run. Though Mr. Gladd took enough votes to keep his defeat from being embarrassing, Mrs. McGovern, her worth shown plainly by the emergency change of government, won handily. Yet even a mayor could get misty-eyed at a wedding.

"Is it time to go?" Rachel asked.

"Yes, honey, but let me talk to Sissie a minute first."

Rachel tweaked the petals on the red roses she was to carry. They'd come yesterday, all the way from New York on a block of ice. A night in warm water had perked them right up. Hal had sent them. Called back to New York City by virtue of what he knew about Marcellus Clyde, he'd intended to turn down whatever job he was offered as bribery. All he wanted was the *Herald* for his own. He'd take care of a few loose ends in the city and come home to claim his wife. She smiled, a tender, secretive smile, at the glowing bride in the mirror and returned to stroking the rose petals.

Even while she sniffed their fragrance, her ears were on the catch for any stray word from around the inadequately closed door. Had someone pieced together the mystery of a man sneaking in her back door last night and the candle in her window that had burned half the night? Had the secret she vowed to take to the grave been exposed? No one knew better than she how hard it was to keep a secret in Brooklyn.

"I'll tell her," Sissie said.

Her face was somber and pale above the white lace tucker at her throat, a sharp contrast to the red stain burning Rachel's cheeks at the memory of the night before her wedding. "Rachel, the train just pulled in and . . . oh, Rachel! Hal's not on it!"

"Isn't he? Oh. I'm sure he'll be along soon. We'd better go to the church. It's time." She stood up, her full skirt sweeping around her. Smoothing the white fur of her collar and cuffs, she tried to catch a glimpse of her complete self in the mirror. Not quite managing it, she asked, "Is everything straight, Sissie?"

"Didn't you hear me? Hal's not here. He wasn't on the train."

"Yes, I heard you. It will be all right." She picked up her flowers. "Wasn't it sweet of him to send me these? I wouldn't have thought such a thing was possible, but he's always telling me transportation is the key to the future."

"Maybe . . . maybe you better stay here a minute. I'll ask Mrs. McGovern . . ." Sissie slipped out of the room and went heavily down the stairs.

In a moment, the lady mayor was at the door. "Now, Rachel," she said in a reasoning tone. "I'm sure it's not that he doesn't *want* to marry you . . . or anything silly like that. He probably just missed the train."

Rachel didn't want to lie but neither did she want to speak of last night, both because she was afraid of what might be said and because the memory was too precious to share.

Hal's eyes had grown deep and dark as he pressed hot kisses to her throat and shoulders. The heat between them was enough to make her feel faint. As he slipped the lace dressing gown from her body, he'd told her again and again that she was the most beautiful woman alive, that thoughts of her had tortured him while he was far away. He swore that if she wanted to wait until tomorrow when their lovemaking would be sanctioned, he would. But her own longing had grown to be a monster while he was gone, a monster that he alone could slay.

Mrs. McGovern said, "No doubt you'll get a telegram telling you when to expect him."

Rachel brought her mind back to the present with an effort. "Mrs. McGovern, it's all right. Hal will be there."

"It's all very well to have faith, Rachel, but you can't beat a timetable. There's not another train . . ."

She'd have to say something. Everyone was so worried. "I know it's all right because . . ." She sought for words.

"That's right, dear. Have faith." Mrs. McGovern shook her head as though giving up. "Now, there was something else I wanted to say, Rachel. I've been a married woman for years and there's nothing I can't tell you about men. Tonight may be a little nerve-wracking at first, but you soon get used to it. Just remember, he's only a man and they can't help it."

He'd begun by kissing her until the room had spun around her. His body had been a rock that she'd clung to while waves of pleasure lifted her higher and higher.

Rachel said, "Thank you, Mrs. McGovern. I'll keep that in mind."

Fifteen minutes later, Mrs. Schur was saying, "That's it. He probably had to change trains in St. Louis . . . they always make you change trains in St. Louis nowadays and if one train is late, then he probably missed it."

"I always said it was foolhardy to have the wedding the same day he was supposed to come back," Sissie said. "Stands to reason something would go wrong."

Rachel just smiled, her cheeks pink. "You're very sweet," she said. "But it's all right. And it's time to go to the church. Hal . . . I know Hall will be there."

Mrs. Schur hung back a moment to whisper, "Now, Rachel, just put yourself in the hands of the Lord tonight and don't be afraid. It only hurts for a moment and then you'll feel fine."

Shivers of delight had taken hold of her body and Rachel had become aware only slowly that Hal lay over her, his body tense with longing. It had been she who had precipitated the last act of their love story.

" 'Course a man isn't like a woman. A woman likes to talk things over, but a man is happy just to say 'thank you' and fall asleep with a smile on his face. The way I look at it, that smile's the best gift a woman can give her husband."

Hal's tears had slipped from his cheeks to hers as he whispered of his joy. The words he said were a treasure to be kept in her heart forever, a memory that would never tarnish or fade. Then there had been laughter, shared again and again as they explored their newfound land of happiness in the long hours of the night.

The New Year's snow looked like a glittering crystal carpet when Rachel stepped onto the special walkway the town had built from her door to the church. Her gown of white damask didn't get a mark on it while the fur collar and cuffs kept her warm.

Sissie preceded her but threw so many reassuring smiles over her shoulder that Rachel saw more of her face than her back. "How nice that the sun is shining," Sissie said for about the fifteenth time that day.

Halfway to the church, Rachel saw the one man, besides her groom, that she most wanted to see. Slade dismounted from his horse and picked his way among the sludgy puddles toward her. "Are you happy?" he asked, taking off his hat as an afterthought.

"Terribly happy."

Slade nodded toward his horse and Lemon, who held the reins. "We're clearing out. You were right. There's no money to be made from gambling and drinking in this town. And the whoring is downright depressing. 'Specially without any whores."

Rachel had to laugh. He didn't look disappointed, just rueful. "But the cooking was wonderful, Slade. Maybe . . ."

He shrugged and for a moment, seemed no older than

Lyle. "I figured we'd haul our carcasses out of here before you married, but you know Lemon . . . I'm right glad to have seen you in your wedding togs, Rachel. I . . . I . . ." His tanned face turned red.

Rachel brushed a kiss on her brother's cheek. "Don't disappear altogether, Slade. Write to me?"

"Sure . . . sure. When I get settled. I'm thinking of Montana, Rachel. Get a little ranch of my own 'stead of rustling cattle from other folks. Maybe . . . if it works out for me, you could let me see the boy sometime? He's a right handful but you could trust me to look out for him—so long as he don't go picking up any more diamonds."

"I think I could trust you even if he did."

"He ever find that thing?"

"You know Lyle. After all the craziness, if he found a whole mine of diamonds he'd probably never mention it to a soul. Not even to me."

"Probably not. Well, it don't matter now, does it? I mean, look at this town. When I got here it would be ashamed to brag by calling itself one-horse and now . . ."

Rachel followed his gaze as he glanced around the bustling street. Many of those who'd come to search for diamonds had felt so warmed by the town's welcome that dark November night that they'd decided to settle here. Brooklyn now had four streets where once there'd been only one. New farms were being tilled and some who had left professions behind in the search for sudden wealth had found them again. Every day a new building was begun or a new business founded. The *Herald* need never fear another empty page.

Slade gave his hat a little toss and caught it. "Say so long to Uncle Ramon for me. Ever since he married that widow, he's turned too respectable to talk to!"

Without another word, and certainly no word of blessing, Slade trotted back to his horse and his waiting friend. Rachel watched him go, and didn't expect the backward glance she didn't get. Yet somehow, she felt blessed.

Sissie was waiting by the church door. "Everything all right?"

"Yes. Slade's moving on."

"Is he?" Sissie paid no attention, her eyes narrowing as she gave a professional twitch and pat to Rachel's skirts.

Rachel said warmly, "Thank you for being my friend. I honestly don't know what I would have done these last weeks without you."

"I want you to know . . . oh, just be happy!" She threw her arms around Rachel, veil and all, and hugged her.

"Sissie, I . . . about Hal . . ."

"Oh, men are never on time for anything!"

"Hal's usually a little . . . early. He even 'jumps the gun' sometimes. Like last . . . " Words failed her. She gave her friend a quivering smile. "We'd better go in, don't you think?"

The moment Sissie entered the church she stopped dead. Rachel, whose mind was on other things, ran right into her. "Heavens!" Sissie breathed, hardly noticing. "He's here! How'd he do that?"

Rachel just smiled and turned to Lyle, who was waiting to take her down the isle. The cut-down cane that he flourished with such pride was hooked over his arm. When she came to take his elbow to walk down the aisle, he turned and handed it to the oldest Bannerman boy. Grinning as though the whole wedding were his doing, Lyle walked his sister toward the man who waited for her.

Hal turned and smiled. Rachel felt the slow slide of her falling hair as his eyes claimed her again. "Don't worry," Lyle whispered. He nodded toward Hal. "I won't say a word 'bout him turning up last night. 'Sides, he gave me five dollars to keep my mouth shut."

Then Hal turned toward her and Rachel forgot to think about anything, not the town, not her brothers, not the secret she and Hal shared. She had just enough good sense to hand her bouquet of roses to Mrs. Garrett, sitting in her chair just behind Hal. Rachel didn't even know if she made the responses in the right places. All she knew was that in what seemed only a few seconds, she had a shiny new ring on her finger and Hal's lips on her.

As their first kiss as husband and wife ended, she felt her

hair tumble down under the transparent veil. With a laugh, she reached underneath to pull out the hairpins and hand them to her husband.

Hal pressed the brass wires to his lips, then, with an exultant shout, he tossed them in the air over his shoulder. They rained down on their friends. Laughing, Hal glanced up into Mr. Schur's surprised face. "A new tradition," Hal said lightly and turned to escort his bride from the church, accepting the cheers of their hometown.

FREE
Romance

(a $4.50 value)

Send in the Coupon Below

To get your FREE historical romance and start saving, fill out the coupon below and mail it today.. As soon as we receive it we'll send you your FREE Book along with your first month's selections.
